To Lyndsay,

THE SECRET OF GHOSTS

By

Andrew Detheridge

Hope you enjoy the tragic story of Wolfie and Rachel!

from A...

Copyright © 2016 Andrew Detheridge

All rights reserved, including the right to reproduce this book, or portions thereof in any form. No part of this text may be reproduced, transmitted, downloaded, decompiled, reverse engineered, or stored, in any form or introduced into any information storage and retrieval system, in any form or by any means, whether electronic or mechanical without the express written permission of the author.

ISBN: 978-1-326-74544-8

PublishNation
www.publishnation.co.uk

For Alex, Grace and Daisy

And the staff and students at

Hagley Catholic High School,

Who offered so much encouragement and enthusiasm

to read more of the things running around my head,

it inspired me to work harder and write faster!

CONTENTS PAGE:

Chapter One: End of the World — 1

Chapter Two: Crying Wolf — 4

Chapter Three: The Start of a Beautiful Friendship — 13

Chapter Four: The Russian for Optimism — 27

Chapter Five: Lessons Learnt Behind the Boiler Room — 35

Chapter Six: Maggie's Advice when Dealing with the Mob — 41

Chapter Seven: The Kindness of Strangers — 48

Chapter Eight: Cry of the Hunters — 55

Chapter Nine: The Night of Broken Glass — 61

Chapter Ten: Der Giftpilz (The Poisonous Mushroom) — 74

Chapter Eleven: The Straw that Broke the Bully's Back — 80

Chapter Twelve: Sad Violins in the Bandstand — 84

Chapter Thirteen: One Step Forward, Two Steps Back 90

Chapter Fourteen: Tanzmann at the Captain's Table 94

Chapter Fifteen: A Glow-Worm of Hope 99

Chapter Sixteen: Kill or be Killed 104

Chapter Seventeen: Unorthdox but Effective! 118

Chapter Eighteen: The Final Solution 126

Chapter Nineteen: The Search for Rachel 135

Chapter Twenty: A Small Square of Stars 142

Chapter Twenty One: Too Cool for School 148

Chapter Twenty Two: A Cry in the Dark 153

Chapter Twenty Three: Keeping the Candle Alight 156

Chapter Twenty Four: Visit to Camp Belzec 165

Chapter Twenty Five: Making the Most of the Time Given 176

Chapter Twenty Six: The Blameless and the Wicked   182

Chapter Twenty Seven: Date Night   189

Chapter Twenty Eight: Letting Rachel Go   195

Chapter Twenty Nine: The Stuff of Nightmares   199

Chapter Thirty: Resistance is Far From Futile   202

Chapter Thirty One: New Beginnings   212

Chapter Thirty Two: Misery Moves Faster Than Joy   217

Chapter Thirty Three: God Created Tomorrow so we can move on from Yesterday   220

Chapter Thirty Four: Someone to Walk Away With   225

Chapter Thirty Five: In Stasis   229

Chapter Thirty Six: High Above the Clouds   237

Chapter Thirty Seven: The Truth Will Out   241

Chapter Thirty Eight: Hunting for Wolfie — 247

Chapter Thirty Nine: Time to Say Goodbye — 252

Chapter Forty: Staring Down the Barrel of a Gun — 257

Chapter Forty One: The Good Samaritan — 265

Chapter Forty Two: The Secrets of Ghosts — 272

Chapter Forty Three: The Flower Garden — 280

Chapter Forty Four: Moving Between Dreams — 289

Chapter Forty Five: The Lord Looks at the Heart — 294

Chapter Forty Six: Double Date — 299

Chapter Forty Seven: An Awfully Big Adventure — 307

Chapter Forty Eight: Speaking with the Dead — 314

Chapter Forty Nine: Don't Cry Because it's Over — 319

CHAPTER ONE:

END OF THE WORLD

'There are only two ways to live your life.
One is as though nothing is a miracle.
The other is as though everything is a miracle.'

Albert Einstein

January 1st 2000,
Early morning of the New Millennium.

Harry sat slumped against the side of the bed with his face lost in the palms of his hot hands. His cheeks were flushed and stung as the steady trickle of tears spilled over them and meandered on down, thoughtlessly staining the black and white logo of his 'Oasis' t-shirt. Blinking them away angrily, he sniffed defiantly and stared out at the new millennium peering in nervously through the undrawn curtains. It was still early: owlish night had barely finished her nocturnal hunt and the sky was little more than a pale wash of colour; an unwashed-van-white upon which someone should have scrawled 'clean me' across the grimy clouds.

   Harry girded himself with sudden new-found resolve as words flooded his brain: *'For Christ's sake, come on son! Time to pull yourself together! What the hell is this moping about going to get you?'* That's what William would have said. He smiled sadly at hearing his voice so clearly inside his head, as clearly as if he were speaking to him right now on the telephone (or was he, in fact, communicating from the other side?) and, hauling himself to his feet, he turned to face his mentor again.

   He had never seen a dead body before that morning but Uncle Keith (who was a Funeral Director and, therefore, dealt with death on a morbidly daily basis) said relatives would come and view a body and frequently comment on how their deceased loved one looked better dead than alive. Something to do with the pain and stress draining from their faces once the agony of illness and dying was over apparently; the facial muscles relaxing after the merciful solace of death.

   Forcing himself to look more closely, he doubted now whether that were true. Certainly not in William's case anyway. Admittedly, he didn't look *particularly* dead... more caught in a waxy suspended animation; like astronauts placed into stasis on long journeys through the cosmos in sci-fi films or like a cryogenically frozen Walt Disney; if the rumours were true. His features were as weather-beaten as ever, yes, and full of the easy bruising of frail old age and he looked, thankfully, peaceful... but his complexion was already too ashen while, as the first fingertip smudge of lapis lazuli stained the bed sheets, it was obvious it would take more than dawn's healing hands to wake him from this night's slumber.

Biting down hard on his lower lip to stop the tears from starting again, Harry wondered what to do now. This was supposed to have been a surprise *'welcome to the new century!'*

William was always bemoaning his 'gift' of being able to sleep half the day away, given half a chance; it looked as if the joke was on him now. He considered the options: phone the Police? Or Maggie? Mom? Walking over to the bedside table, he proceeded to press the buttons for his home number, but it wasn't his mother who answered. Harry registered brief surprise as he heard his own voice speak in muted reply, but it sounded like someone else, speaking lines in a movie, and so very, very far away. He thought he could see himself, as though he were floating on the ceiling and looking down on his hunched body and shaking hand, holding this impersonal phone to his ear, speaking these surreal and incomprehensible words. None of this felt even vaguely real to him.

"It's me, Harry."

On the other end of the line the voice immediately knew his whole world had changed in those three simple words.

Harry felt his voice waver and he blurted out the rest before he lost it altogether.

"You need to come home... now."

CHAPTER TWO:

CRYING WOLF

'I am a doormat in a world of boots'

Jean Rhys

'Of all the friends I've ever had, you're the first'

Bender, Futurama

August 1938.
Saturday afternoon, a park in Berlin.

"Why are you crying?"

Wolfgang looked up, flushed and furious, to find a boy and a girl standing over him silhouetted against the sun. He shielded his eyes and could see their faces more clearly. They were looking down on him with the same mild curiosity and pity they might have had upon discovering a chick that had fallen from the safety of its nest. Wolfgang had his chin tucked tightly under his knees and his cheeks were wet with tears. Unsurprisingly, he didn't feel much like talking.

Sullenly, he shrugged by way of response.

Despite it barely warranting being worthy of being called a response (and certainly not one his father would have accepted), the two children in front of him seemed satisfied enough and happily introduced themselves.

"I'm Rachel Braverman," announced a brazenly confident girl of around fourteen, with glossy black hair that danced on her shoulders and saucers of brown eyes that captured the light mischievously as she smiled, extending an outstretched hand in his direction. Wolfgang stared at her, mouth agape, deciding there and then she was, undoubtedly, the most beautiful girl in the entire world and he would endeavour to spend every moment he possibly could in the presence of her undeniable beauty.

Unsure whether the extended hand was meant to shake his own or pull him to his feet, he managed to combine the two, attempting a smile as he reached eye level.

"I'm Ariel Koplowitz," said the boy, "and I'm *nearly* fourteen."

Wolfgang smiled more easily now and shook his hand in the exaggerated way children often do when imitating observed adult behaviour. Blinking back the embarrassment of tears from his eyes, he examined the boy more closely: his hair was dark, brushed forward on top and shaved skin-short on the sides. He wore little round glasses that accentuated the size of his pupils, making him appear permanently pleasantly surprised. Wolfgang realised the boy hadn't stopped smiling at him the whole time he had been eyeing him up and now attempted to smile back himself; albeit pretty self-consciously.

With remarkable ease, they began walking through the park, enjoying each other's company and the lazy bees droning and the cheerful twittering of birds and the distant cries of street hawkers somewhere beyond the spiked extremities of the park. The girl walked on the fringes of the perfectly trimmed lawns, pretending to balance like a tightrope walker, almost over-balancing before flapping her arms wildly and laughing with the thin boy at the hilarity of her performance. Wolfgang's argument with his father was already forgotten and suddenly seemed as foolish as the squabbling jackdaws he noticed only now, brawling and cawing angrily in a nearby flowerbed.

He closed his eyes and made a conscious decision: to let it all go... all the anger and the frustration and the resentment... let it fly up past the treetops, drifting through the cumulonimbus and the cirrus and on, into the beauty of infinity. He opened his eyes and, instantly, felt a colossal weight lifted from those tenterhooks stretched so tautly across the width of his shoulder blades.

Immediately, he started to notice the astonishing beauty all around him, starting with the sun above; a perfect orange in the sky, shedding golden pips over the neatly trimmed shrubs and the curving pathways. Not to mention the strange new company he found himself in. Wolfgang found himself revelling in the easy silence in which they now walked; noting how it suggested the familiarity of old friends, rather than the virtual strangers they actually were. He began to feel the first twinges of hope that everything would be all right after all; as the heat of the sun burnt the last salty streak of a childish tear from his cheek.

Life in Berlin had certainly not started too auspiciously for Wolfgang, that much was undeniable. The Wirth family had only moved to the bustling capital a matter of weeks ago and, up to this unexpected interchange, Wolfgang had hated virtually every solitary minute of it. Before his father had secured his top secret and, apparently, very prestigious promotion, they had lived in Munich... and it had been an oasis of happiness in comparison. They had moved into their new home at the start of the summer term, when the summer holidays should have been stretching ahead of him like a yellow brick road all the way to a glorious emerald horizon of fishing, football, sun-splashed lakes to swim in and countless other activities to fill the long laughter-filled hours. Instead, he knew no-one, had no new school friends to share secrets with until September and, consequently, had barely left the house; choosing rather to sulk in his room and read his adventure stories, rather than seek out real adventures.

As a matter of fact, that had been the source of his argument that day: father had knocked politely at his door and Wolfgang had reluctantly invited him in. He had perched stiffly on the end of his bed, back straight as a coffin lid, and asked him how he was settling in. Wolfgang hadn't been very forthcoming in response. Father had suggested going outside into the garden to 'get some exercise and play games', but Wolfgang had argued you couldn't play games on your *own*... you needed *friends* like the ones he had left back in Munich. (Which wasn't strictly true, he had often played by himself in Munich and used to enjoy his own company, but he was making a valid point, he considered.)

Father's face had clouded over then, like it seemed to do a lot nowadays. Before, he had smiled so much more and laughed and taken him to see Bayern Munich play football, standing together on the terraces and joining in the chants of the home fans with their scarves held triumphantly above their heads. He had told Wolfgang he would take him to see Bayern when they played Hertha Berlin or any of the other plethora of teams that were based in Berlin, but Wolfgang knew that Bayern didn't play in the Gauliga Berlin-Brandenburg league that the Nazi Sports office had introduced; so it wasn't going to happen. He had also told Wolfgang Berlin had a wonderful zoo that he would take him to as well; he hadn't done that either. Consequently, Wolfgang felt neglected and betrayed; overlooked and trodden underfoot. All for a stupid promotion. He had wanted to tell father all of this, to scream it in his face, furiously and petulantly, but instead he shrugged and miserably refused to speak. So, father lost his patience and shouted and raised his hand threateningly, leaving it hovering there ominously, until Wolfgang raced down the stairs and out of the house; suddenly afraid of his father for the first time he could ever remember.

Without giving it a second thought, he had ended up at the park: the single place he had discovered on his infrequent scouting missions that reminded him of home. Munich. *How he missed it!* In his imagination, he was already idealising it as a lost paradise: a city of wide avenues and friendly over-reaching trees; of laughing street vendors and the smell of roasting horse chestnuts; of school friends to roam the parks with, pulling sticks along railings just to delight in the delicious clatter of it.

Then, of course, there had been the *Oktoberfest*!

Every September, the biggest park in the city had filled to bursting with beer tents and bustle and rides and excitement; a ludicrous, marvellous spectrum of glorious colour and vibrant humanity. The men in their chequered shirts and lederhosen, the girls in their dirndl: the tight bodices and blouses, the full, flowing skirts and the aprons; traditional costume of the Alpine peasant dating all the way back to the foolishly extravagant days of King Ludwig I. Late in August, seemingly out of nowhere, the beer tents would magically begin to take shape; vast linen citadels, their sides and entrances proudly emblazoned with the names of the six big Munich breweries: *Paulaner, Augustiner, Hacher-Pschorr, Hofbrau, Lowenbrau, Spaten*. Wolfgang and his friends-Matej, Gerhard and Heinrich- would sneak up to an obscure corner of one of these marvellous contraptions and tentatively lift the corner of a flap... to reveal a delirious world of revelry and happy drunkenness within! The oompah-bands would be in full throat, waitresses, laden with frothing steins, would be steering a protracted course between the long trestle tables packed like sardines with swaying, singing, rosy-faced patrons, while the roast chickens and ducks turned invitingly on their rotisseries. The whole spectacular scene seemed to leave reality far behind and none of them ever wanted it to end.

Outside was just as much fun, if not, more so: the carousel... the helter-skelter... and Wolfgang's absolute favourite...*the Devil's Wheel!*

The Devil's Wheel was a circular platform that looked innocuous enough to the uninitiated. Indeed, to begin with, it was. But it was a trick; a con; a charade to tempt in the unsuspecting visitor as stealthily as a Venus fly-trap! Inevitably, already teetering and light-headed with beer before even stepping foot on the ride, the poor victims were innocently invited by a jovial ringmaster to take their places on this deceptive-looking giant tiddlywink. Those who knew what was coming sat down, linked arms, braced themselves... winking at each other conspiratorially. They had been here before. They knew better. But the novices stood their ground, naively unprepared for what would happen next, laughingly full of bravado for the baying and beery crowd.

Slowly, at first, the wheel would began to inch round...to the nervous glances of the participants, the knowing cheers of the onlookers. Then the pace quickened... gaining speed at a frightening rate; the spinning sending the room into a drunken blur.

The novices were, of course, the first to go, centrifugal force sending them careering unceremoniously off the twirling disc and crashing, full pelt, into the bales of hay encircling the ride!

Others found themselves slowly, slowly, pulled ever closer to the edge, invisible fingers seeming to grasp at their ankles, yanking them further from the communal safety of the middle ground. Shrieks of laughter and panic ensued; gales of hysteria rose from the slobbering, spit-flecked mouths of the crowd, howling at their newly-chosen favourites to hang on more tightly; to be the last man standing.

Others fly free; their resolve at an end, until only the hardiest remained. *Surely it is almost over*, they think, their mouths set grimly, the scent of victory in their flared nostrils. In their minds, they are already imagining the glory of victory and the moment they can receive their hard-earned plaudits. But they have been hoodwinked. It is not over yet. Not by a long shot. Only now, now, when aching muscles are stretched to their tendon-ripping limits, does the ringmaster smile his devious smile, reveal his true nature, play his trump card and, with a flamboyant wave of a hand... call for *the wrecking ball!*

Expectant gasps and *Oohs!* fill the rafters. The crowd are delirious; wide-eyed stares of disbelief and regret from the hangers-on as the giant foam-filled ball dives and swoops overhead, spinning and swooning, dive-bombing and crashing into them, finally dislodging their best of intentions. Until only the single exhausted victor remains. The wheel slows. Now, only now can he receive the adulation worthy of a gladiator in ancient Rome; nay, of a God. The thumbs of the crowd are raised…*upwards!* Grinning, he lives to fight on another day.

***

"Where do you live?" asked Rachel, in between chasing birds pecking idly on the pavements for no apparent reason other than it looked like fun.

They had left the park some way behind them now and were strolling through Alexanderplatz. The Ufa-Palast, (the largest and most famous movie theatre in all of Berlin) was directly ahead of them and, behind it, the spire of the Kaiser Wilhelm Memorial church pointed instructively to the heavens. The Alexanderhaus and the Wertheim department store dominated the rest of the square, while trams scurried here and there, criss-crossing the busy city centre like columns of ants, each knowing their job and clear where they should be at any given moment. In answer to her question, Wolfgang recited his address to her as though in a dream for, indeed, the words meant little to him yet, held no emotional attachment; unlike the address in Munich with all its happy connotations glued symbolically to each luscious syllable. Rachel and Ariel exchanged meaningful glances.

"So, you're *rich* then?" Ariel announced; more a statement than a question.

Wolfgang raised an eyebrow in surprise. He had never thought of himself as rich; or anything else for that matter. He paused to consider the question. To his surprise, he considered his cosy existence of maids; cooks; gardeners; chauffeurs…and had to suppose it meant it was a reasonable assumption. He bit his lip and felt oddly uneasy about the whole thing.

"Where do you two live?" he replied, ignoring the question.

"Over there," Ariel pointed, "in the Scheuenviertel near Alexanderplatz."

They walked towards where he had pointed before he added, unprompted, "it's where nearly all the Jews live now. We used to live in the Wilmersdorf district, but we had to move." He didn't elaborate on why and Wolfgang didn't think to ask.

They walked on a little further in contented solitude.

"This is me," Ariel announced, pausing at the entrance to a courtyard and a cluster of dark apartments just visible beyond. Trails of dingy washing could be partly seen, hanging gloomily through the archway. He broke into another big grin and, rather formally, reached out his hand, took Wolfgang's in his own and shook it firmly. Rachel burst out laughing and both boys felt themselves blush uncontrollably.

"What?" insisted Ariel tetchily, "this is how gentlemen bid farewell."

That only made Rachel laugh all the more, "Well, when I see some, I'll be sure to let them know! You act as though we'll never see each other again."

Ariel and Wolfgang paused, still mid-handshake to consider this.

"Well, we might not... mightn't we?" mumbled Ariel.

"What school are you going to?" asked Rachel, turning to Wolfgang with an expectant look.

Time seemed to stop as Wolfgang searched his memory for the name and finally, remembering it, gave it voice.

Gleefully, Rachel clapped her hands together and exclaimed, "Well, there you are then! No need for all the dramatic *gentlemanly farewells*... we'll see you at school in exactly one weeks' time!"

***

From the moment Ariel waved from his doorway and disappeared inside, Wolfgang could remember almost nothing of the remainder of their journey; other than that he must have floated all the way to Rachel's apartment, such was his hopeless delirium. Not only had he found two new friends that he suspected would be greater friends than even Matej, Gerhard and Heinrich had ever been, but he would be able to see Rachel every day and, over time, find a way to tell her how oddly she made him feel in the very pit of his stomach. In a good way, of course. Some day he would tell her this... and phrase it in a way that sounded a lot more... romantic, he decided.

He finally started to come to his senses as they passed the Lindenbad, a Russian bathhouse quite near his family's house, as he became aware that Rachel had suddenly slowed her pace.

Turning towards him she smiled and shyly clasped her hands together in front of her expectantly.

"I live just here," she explained, indicating a door and stairs going up, (presumably to Heaven as she was, undoubtedly, an angel, he considered) over her right shoulder.

"I'll... see you in a week," Wolfgang stammered.

Rachel laughed and reaching forward, took his hand in her own and shook it, mimicking his earlier awkward moment with Ariel.

"In a week," she nodded and bounded up the stairs.

Wolfgang continued to stare up at the clouds before, eventually, she disappeared into the sky and he proceeded to float the rest of the way home.

CHAPTER THREE:

THE START OF A BEAUTIFUL FRIENDSHIP

'What is character but the determination of incident? What is incident but the illustration of character?'

Henry James

June 1999,
Monday afternoon, on the way home from school…

Harry stood in the doorway as the automatic doors slid open with an efficient swish, suddenly acutely aware that this was a pivotal moment; a point of no return; a moment that would shape everything else that was to come. He glanced back and they were all still there, grinning and leering like baboons: Paul Harris, Adam and Rob Kellerman, aka *'The Evil Twins'*, Kurt Smalley, Ian Pardoe, Steven Wharton and, of course, Tania Tonks; hanging around with the lads, as usual, like a bad smell on the bottom of your shoe. They pulled faces as he stared, a street away but still clearly visible, and gesticulated rudely at him; Harry wasn't sure if he was meant to take this as a strange attempt at encouragement or whether they were simply mocking him. He supposed, either way, it didn't really matter. Swallowing thickly, he turned and went inside the corner shop before the door slid shut silently behind him…

****

Of course, with Dad having been in the army for so many years, he had grown accustomed to having no friends. When he was younger, every time Dad had been stationed somewhere new, he had tried to make friends and had, generally, succeeded. But that only made it more torturous when they were uprooted again at a moment's notice, and moved hundreds of miles away, maybe even a different country away, where he would never see or hear from his new-found friends again. Eventually, after the fifth or sixth move, he concluded, it was better to keep yourself to yourself, keep your head down and keep out of trouble… and that was exactly what he had been trying to do when he started at St. Joseph's just after Easter.

On his first day, he had gone exploring as he always did and fortuitously discovered exactly what he was looking for: a small alcove, a personal sanctuary, situated off the quad but hidden from the idling throng looking for cruel entertainment; somewhere he could squat at lunchtimes and be pretty much left alone in self-imposed seclusion.

That had been until last week.

Two Year 11's had stumbled across him purely by chance; the bigger of the two literally doing so, falling over his outstretched legs as he had been chewing meditatively on a sandwich.

"Gis a quid," he had demanded, as soon as he had got over his initial surprise and regained his composure. No introductions, just *Gis a quid* as if it was the most reasonable request in the world.

The response came out of Harry's mouth before common sense could censure it.

"Piss off."

The boys looked at each other in a mixture of mild surprise and uncontained delight. From their expressions, Harry deduced they were far happier for a fight to be the ultimate outcome of this confrontation than an easily won pound. He was, unfortunately, absolutely correct. Without warning, the bigger of the two aimed a kick directly at his face. Instinctively, he managed to get his hands up to protect himself as the steel toe of his aggressor's shoe smashed into his unprotected fingers, forcing the backs of his hands into the soft flesh of his nose. He felt the double surge of pain as the blood vessels popped like balloons within his nostrils and the bones in his fingers cracked like dry twigs.

Harry struggled to his feet in a desperate attempt to defend himself better, but the smaller of the two was already behind him before the blurry mist of pain reluctantly began to clear. Gradually, he became aware that his arms were being held captive behind his back and that the bigger of the two was closing in on him with a dizzying look of hatred and revenge etched on his face that was surely indicative of a far wider-reaching mental issue than the mere refusal to give him a sodding pound...

The blows landed repeatedly and without the chance to reply. First to his stomach, sucking the breath from his lungs like a bellows so that he felt a horrible sensation of drowning; then to his face, in a barrage of punches that landed and exploded like bombs on his cheeks, nose, mouth, ears....

Eventually, the smaller of the two began to sense the scent of danger on the wind: stealing off loners and geeks was one thing, getting done for GBH and being permanently excluded from school was another. He loosened his grip and let Harry slump to the ground as the other boy withdrew his fist for yet another blow.

"Bloody hell, Jase, he's had enough; you don't wanna kill 'im!"

Jason looked at him, unseeing for a few moments, before the red mist cleared and a summer's day came back into his vision again. His fist relaxed and, blinking, he looked around this obscure corner of the quad as if seeing it for the first time; a stunned bear newly emerged from a long hibernation.

"Whatever," he mumbled and, bending down, rifled through Harry's pockets, retrieving a handful of change. He leaned in close to the boy's bloody face and whispered in his still-singing ears, as he held something small and round before his blurry vision, "should have given me the quid when I asked you nicely, dickhead."

****

Harry cautiously made his way down the first aisle: Newspapers, magazines and a chilled freezer full of sandwiches and canned drinks.

What to steal?

That was the first decision he had to make…

His first thoughts turned to alcohol. That would impress them: take something that he wouldn't be permitted to buy legally. But then, it was also taking more of a risk. An *unnecessary* risk, it seemed to him. He might be watched more closely in the drinks aisle, hovering around the gleaming cans of lager and bottles of dark brown bitters with strange names like *'Bishop's Finger'*; which didn't seem a particularly desirable ingredient when he stopped to think about it. What else was in it, for God's sake, *Head Brewer's toenail? Barman's dandruff?* He decided to stick to cheap cider in big two litre plastic bottles that he drank alone in the deserted market place on Friday nights.

Anyway, they hadn't specified *what* he had to steal, just that he had to steal *something*. So why make life harder than it needed to be? No, he would slip something small and inconspicuous into his pocket and then go to the counter and buy a chocolate bar, so he didn't have to attempt to leave the shop without buying anything; which might look suspicious and give reasonable cause for a search. Yes, it was a good start, the beginning of a plan… of sorts.

****

Harry had been torturously cleaning himself up in the toilets when they had appeared out of nowhere; spirits summoned by whispering some chant into a mirror three times, it seemed. He started to wonder what he had done to deserve a day like this.

"You look like shit," announced Paul Harris with relish, stating the absolute bleeding obvious.

He looked at himself in the mirror, tearfully appalled, and didn't bother to deny it: his left eye had closed up, his lower lip had swollen to what seemed the size of an over-ripe tomato and the toilet paper he had shoved up his nose was spectacularly failing to stem the flow of blood escaping in fat gobs into the bloody basin in front of him.

The gang behind him tittered appreciatively. He didn't know their names, but he had seen enough of them around school to know, instinctively, to avoid them. Some of them were in some of his option classes, but they tended to be the kids who sat at the back of the class and stared gormlessly out the window, mouths open catching flies; so he hadn't spoken to any of them before this moment. Harry held his breath and waited, overwhelmed with a terrible sense of hopelessness; he really didn't think he could take another beating.

"Look," Paul continued, heaving himself up on to the sink unit, so he could face Harry, while allowing his legs to dangle and sway absent-mindedly; *big kid still playing on a swing*, thought Harry to himself. "We saw what happened and we were impressed, in a way, weren't we?" he glanced over at his motley crew who mumbled their assent. "Not you getting the shit kicked out of you, obviously..." he added, smirking at his idiotic entourage, "but for having the bollocks to actually stand up to Jason and Gary; not a lot of people would have done that."

Harry continued to wait. He had no idea where this was leading and it was simply too painful to speak anyway.

"So," Paul smiled, leaning back against the glass, so his reflection looked like a Siamese twin, conjoined at the head, "we were thinking you should join *our* gang; that way we can offer you protection and this little... unfortunate incident won't ever need to happen again. Wadda you think?"

Harry didn't know what to think. He was mulling it over when Adam Kellerman cut in.

"Or you can carry on the way you are and decide whether you're gonna give your money to that pair of nobs... *or to us?"*

Harry pursed his lips and whispered through the pain of cold air breaking over his bleeding gums, "why me?"

Paul lifted a finger triumphantly.

"Good question! See? This guy's gonna be an asset to our... organisation; he *thinks* and he's not afraid to ask the difficult questions!"

Again, the others murmured a reluctant agreement. Paul linked his fingers together and stretched them out until they made an unpleasantly loud crack. "You see, the thing is, *we're* the muscle in the school and we can't have the likes of Jason Upson and Gary Bennett thinking they can go around terrorising just anyone they please. So, *you're* going to join us and *we'll* teach them a little lesson about who's the boss around here. OK?"

Harry hesitated a moment, then nodded. He didn't seem to have a fat lot of choices. Having your money taken off you by two thugs was tough enough to deal with, the hopes of outwitting or outfighting a gang of about ten Neanderthals was pretty much zero. Plus, the way he felt right now, the prospect of teaching Jason and Gary 'a little lesson' was starting to sound pretty appealing.

"What I suggest you do now," Paul continued, "is leg it over the fence before the bell for afternoon registration. You can't go into class looking like that; it's too bad to go with *'I just fell over'* and we don't grass... *ever*. So, Michael here is in your form, he'll tell Murdoch he saw you chucking up in the canteen and he'll presume you're in the Medical Room. Got it?"

Harry nodded and changed the bloody wad of toilet paper in his nose for a fresh, less gloopy supply.

"Good," Paul smiled, "and not a word to Mommy and Daddy- you got beaten up for your phone by some kids off the estate on the way home- got it?"

Harry sighed and nodded, carefully pulling his rucksack over his shoulder. He winced and wondered what state his bruised body would be in when he got home, peeled off his ripped and bloody clothes and dared to look at himself more fully in the mirror. Although he vaguely remembered the punches to his face, almost everywhere seemed to ache or throb. It was like he had been through several days' worth of medieval torture; if so, he thought, *pass me the confession, I'll sign whatever you want.*

Weaving carefully through the crowd of thugs, he was stopped by Paul's greasy voice as he reached the toilet exit.

"Oh, there is one more tiny thing..." he announced, "you will have to do a little *something* to prove you're *worthy* of being one of us."

***

Mom and Nan had, amazingly, fallen for the *thugs-on-the-way-home* story, but it was all he could do to stop them calling the police. He'd argued there was no point as they hadn't got away with anything more than a handful of coins because he'd forgotten to take his phone to school with him anyway; that was why they had been so vicious and taken it out on him so cruelly- because they were frustrated at having got away with so little. How he had got away with the *'forgot my phone'* line was more unbelievable; like he *ever* left home without it? Still, swallow it they did and the remainder of the week involved a good deal of pampering at home from Nan while the bruises blackened, purpled and finally started to heal.

Luckily, despite the fact he looked like Frankenstein's monster minus the neck bolts, the doctor had revealed, miraculously, nothing was actually broken. As the swelling went down, he slowly started to look more like his old self. By the following Monday, the bruises were nicely yellowing around the edges to the colour of old parchment so that he resembled a rather battered wasp, but he was deemed well enough by both the doctor and his mother to return to lessons. And, more ominously, to the fateful completion of his 'initiation'.

He'd had a week to try and guess what they were going to ask him to do by way of an initiation task and, if he was being honest, when he eventually found out what they demanded, it was on the lower end of the scale of his fears. He was still uncertain about it though. He didn't believe he was some kind of saint by any stretch of the imagination, but the truth was he'd never stolen anything in his life. In fact, when attending one of his many primary schools, he'd once found a ten pound note on the way to school and, in a state of high emergency, had taken it straight to the Head's office as soon as he'd entered the building. He simply couldn't imagine just putting it in his pocket and keeping it. After a week or so, they'd had an assembly and the Head had called him up on stage and praised him in front of the whole school for his scrupulous honesty and presented him with the ten pound note as no-one had claimed it. It was one of the proudest days of his life. Nevertheless, he was in a difficult situation and, while it went against the grain, stealing something from a shop sounded more like one of those victimless crimes he'd read about; or at least something he could potentially live with- unlike robbing an old granny or playing chicken across railway lines when a train was hurtling towards him, or any of the other myriad of challenges he had lain awake at night fretting over for the past week, thinking they were going to demand of him...

***

His heart had seemingly relocated itself and was pounding away mercilessly in his head. The prospect of actually doing this suddenly didn't seem so easy now that he was stood in the shop itself. Turning to face the chilled cabinet to get his breathing back to some sort of normality, he found the cold air briefly soothing. Harry stared straight ahead and found his eyes settle on an object...

Cheese.

A big block of *cheese*.

He shrugged.

Why the hell not?

He had thought of stealing something small, like a packet of tic-tacs or something, as they would be easier to conceal, but then he thought they might question whether he'd had those in his pocket all along. They certainly wouldn't be able to accuse him of carrying a block of cheese around with him all day at school!

He glanced around surreptitiously. There seemed to be only one employee in the shop: a thoroughly bored-looking teenage girl. Her hair was sticking straight up over her acne-ridden features, before it spilled out in a fountain of bleached pink. She was slouching on the counter, chewing gum in an exaggerated way; in a cow chewing the cud kind of way, while staring blankly at her fingernails. *She shouldn't be too much of a problem,* he thought, relieved at her apparent complete disinterest in her job or in his nefarious activities.

What about *cameras* though?

The thought suddenly struck him and he did a quick visual reconnaissance of the shop: two wall-mounted ones were hanging from the walls at the front of the shop pointing their black sightless eyes down the next two aisles. None were focused on his part of the shop. In fact, the only obstacle to the successful completion of his cheese heist seemed to be one of those convex mirrors; like the ones on the sharp corners of country roads. He blew his cheeks out and prepared himself. OK. This was it. He was going in…

One last thing struck him-

Customers?

The last thing he needed was some do-gooder grassing him up to Gormless Girl on the till. Pretending to be trying to figure out what aisle a random item was in, he moved to the centre of the shop and took in the whole span of the shop…

Apart from a white-haired old man looking at tins of something or other in the next aisle, the coast seemed to be advantageously clear.

Right, no more prevaricating he told himself, the quicker you do this, the quicker you can get the hell out of here…

Harry reached for the nearest block of fully matured cheddar and, keeping his eyes firmly on Still Bored Girl the whole time, slipped it inside his jacket pocket. It felt cold: an ice cold block of guilt and shame. He blocked out all thoughts that would distract him from his goal, especially the pounding of his heart that was now galloping along as though he were in the final furlong...

Right, that was part one complete. All he had to do now was get to the till, buy something innocuous and beat a hasty retreat. He began walking slowly to the counter, desperately trying to effect a relaxed shuffle and failing miserably, until he arrived at the counter. The rows of bright sweet wrappers swept upwards away from him in a gaudy avalanche of calories as he peered over at Apathetic Girl. Dragging her eyes away from her apparently mesmerising nails, she glanced up at him; the sight of which clearly failing in any attempt to make her any less thoroughly demoralised by her life up to this point. Even so, it was enough to make Harry's heart boom even louder in his head, like speakers throbbing at a rock concert, while a horrible sinking feeling in his gut told him the truth he had tried so hard to block out: he was doing something fundamentally *wrong*.

As he reached his moment of destiny, he steadied his nerves and tried to ignore the burning in his cheeks. Couldn't-Care-Less Girl went back to examining the finer points of her choice of nail varnish.

"A Mars bar please," he mumbled, scanning the rows of chocolates to avoid any possibility of unwanted eye contact.

Sullenly, World-Weary Girl reached across, picked up the offending chocolate bar between thumb and forefinger and placed it by the till for him to retrieve.

"Anything else?" she asked, in a sing-song voice that reeked of insincerity.

Harry was about to answer when he felt the firmness of a hand on his shoulder and a voice speaking close by but which was not his own.

"What about what's in your pocket, sonny boy?"

Harry spun around in a panic and found himself looking into the angry face of Mr. Sandhu glaring down at him.

Where the hell had he come from?

In his mind, he quickly retraced his steps and pictured the layout of the shop again. He allowed his memory to rove over the city skyline display of birthday cards… to circumnavigate the rolls of digestive biscuits shaped like dozens of pencil cases… then his mind finally alighted on the dirty plastic curtain that led through to the back of the shop… *That was it!* Mr. Sandhu could have been sorting stock in the back and been bringing something through just as he was slipping the cheese surreptitiously into his pocket and looking the other way….

Just my luck, he cursed to himself.

"*Well?*" the voice sounded angry, vengeful, like he wasn't going to let this drop lightly… he was going to make this young man pay for all the lost stock pilfered over the last six months; all those profits gone in a magician's sleight of hand.

The words refused to come; there *was* no defence. Harry reached in and guiltily took the cheese from his pocket, placing it next to the chocolate bar while he waited for whatever purgatory was to come next.

What *did* come next, however, caught him completely by surprise.

"Got my cheese there, son?"

Harry blinked in stunned disbelief as the white-haired old man from the tins aisle appeared beside him smiling benignly as though nothing untoward at all had just happened.

"Everything all right, Mr Sandhu?"

"No, it is *not* all right," the shopkeeper snapped, "this petty little criminal was trying to steal from me!"

The smile never strayed from the mouth of the old man as he drew level with Harry and rested a hand complacently on his shoulder.

"I think you've got the wrong end of the stick there, Mr Sandhu. This is my nephew, David. I asked him to take the cheese to the counter for me and wait for me there. Can't go more than a day without a round or two of Welsh rarebit! I can assure you he had no intention of stealing it."

"I saw him-" Mr Sandhu began.

"No, you didn't," said the man with a surprising degree of resolve and self-belief in his voice that belied his age and apparent frailty.

"I should call the police…"

The man raised his hand to stop him mid-sentence.

"You *could*," he continued, smiling but with a steel in his voice that made Harry shiver beneath the hand that still rested on his shoulder, "but it would be your word against ours, wouldn't it? Unless, of course, you have some *actual evidence,* like security footage?"

Mr Sandhu scowled and glared at him angrily, Harry realising with a wave of relief that the cheese aisle was out of the scope of the cameras; if they worked at all. He turned to Glum Girl and hissed "Take his money and get them out of here!" before storming off down the aisle and disappearing into the back of the store.

The old man took out his wallet, calmly sifting through to sort out the exact change for the offending block of cheese and the chocolate bar, along with a loaf of bread that he had placed next to them and thanked Bored Girl (who was suddenly looking considerably less bored). Then he blithely smiled at Harry and they exited the shop in a silence fizzing with unresolved explanations. Once outside, Harry turned to the man to thank him and saw the gang over his saviour's shoulder looking at him quizzically. Paul Harris tried to beckon him over, but Harry pretended not to notice and turned his attention back to the old man. Harry noticed suddenly how bright-eyed he was despite his obvious age. There was something unfathomable behind those eyes and Harry wasn't sure if it was hiding something good or something frighteningly bad.

"They with you?" the old man asked, taking in the gang with a single glance.

Harry gave the smallest of nods and tried not to give away the shame in his face.

"Well, they can wait, can't they?" he smiled. "Going this way?"

Harry smiled and nodded, turning his back on the bemused gang and leaving them behind.

***

They were virtually at Harry's estate before either of them spoke again. Harry had been overwhelmed by a strange concoction of emotions as they walked: relief that he'd gotten away with it, surprise at the old man's intervention and a hint of self-loathing that he'd been prepared to steal to ingratiate himself with a gang of idiots. Eventually, the old man broke into his thoughts.

"William."

"What?"

"I'm William, by the way. And you are?"

"Harry."

"Why were you stealing from Mr. Sandhu?" he asked, still staring straight ahead as they strolled in the afternoon sunshine. "You don't strike me as being a thief."

"Why'd you help me?"

William flashed him a smile.

"That's fine, you don't need to tell me. We all have our secrets kept padlocked away in the dungeons of our souls. You don't know me well enough yet to give me the key; but I suspect and hope you will one day. And, to answer *your* question, I believe everybody deserves a second chance; this was yours. I suggest you don't waste it; they don't come along too often."

Harry glanced at him in surprise at the strangeness of his speech but chose to say nothing.

"Sorry," William grinned, his eyes sparkling, "I have a tendency to let my thoughts loose on the world without proofreading them first; just ask Gabriel."

"Who?"

"My oldest friend in the entire world. We live together."

Harry considered how enigmatic this stranger was as they came to a halt at the end of his road; he was certainly not your typical pensioner moaning about their dwindling pension and the behaviour of teenagers that much was certain.

"I live down here," he pointed.

"Walk me to my house," William replied, "I only live in the next street."

"Really?" said Harry, surprised by the coincidence of how close they lived to each other; even though he was sure he had never set eyes on him before. "All right," he shrugged.

They came to a stop outside a neatly maintained Victorian semi-detached house. The front garden had a small island of lawn surrounded by a bright sea of blues and reds and violets and yellows, as everything seemed to have fortuitously bloomed simultaneously.

"This is me."

Harry stood awkwardly, staring at the pavement. He felt he needed to thank William; to do something for him, but didn't know how to broach the subject.

William held out his hand.

"Thanks," Harry said, as he took his outstretched hand and shook it, "for everything."

"Anytime."

Harry paused and bit his lip. "I had no choice about the ... stealing, you know; they forced me to. If I hadn't agreed to do it, they'd have made my life a misery. They probably will now anyway," he added as an afterthought.

William nodded solemnly.

"We always have a choice," he said, grim-faced, "it is whether we take the easy choice or the difficult one."

"You don't understand," Harry sighed, "there's one of me and, like, ten of them- what can I do?"

William nodded. "You say you're too small, too insignificant to make a difference? I say try taking a tarantula to a children's birthday party, then tell me the impact something small can have."

Harry grinned.

"Well, yeah, put like that… Look, is there anything I could do for you… to thank you for helping me?" he added.

William smiled and nodded.

"Come and see me; meet Gabriel- he would be delighted to have someone different to talk to. The greatest thing you could offer me is your time."

Harry shrugged.

"OK," he said, "I'll call around soon; meet this Gabriel."

William nodded curtly. "Then it's a deal."

Putting the key in the lock, he opened the door and let himself in. A dimly-lit corridor with a tiled floor and a large plant in the hallway came obliquely into view. Then the door was closed and he was gone. Harry smiled to himself and turned for home.

CHAPTER FOUR

THE RUSSIAN FOR OPTIMISM

'I see a soldier's service is forgot
In times of peace the world regards us not.'

Peter Woodhouse

June 1999,
Friday night, Harry's bedroom.

Harry lay flat on his back with his hands behind his head, staring at the ceiling and contemplating the strange turn of events that had formed the basis of a most unexpected day. He could hear Mom and Nan busying themselves in the kitchen directly underneath his room making their tea: drawers and cupboards were opened and hurriedly slammed; cutlery was rattled together like sabres as they were snatched up in a big metallic bunch; dishes clattered and crashed together like tiny tectonic plates. All was normal. All was well in the world.

Except it wasn't.

It wasn't because Dad was missing from this picture perfect family unit. Dad... and the dog. Until the last couple of years, they'd had a dog, a Shetland sheep dog with an expression that permanently hovered somewhere between ecstatically happy and incredibly surprised. They'd bought her when Harry had only been three or four years old, so he couldn't remember life without her being there.

***

His favourite part of having a dog had been coming home from school. Whenever he walked up the drive to the front door, the dog would start barking and jumping up the lounge window, desperate for him to enter and shower her with fuss; which he did most happily. For years, he'd always presumed she'd patiently waited in that exact spot for hours eagerly anticipating his return home, but she was way smarter than that. A little while after she died, Mom told him she'd be fast asleep by the fire, whimpering and moaning as she dreamed of chasing imaginary cats when, abruptly, no more than five minutes before he was due home, she would miraculously wake, spring up, make her way over to the window and press her nose against the glass expectantly. Her internal body clock was seemingly infallible.

The only day she got caught out was on a Tuesday.

Tuesday was Chemistry last lesson of the day and, each week, Mr King gave the class a test. Anyone scoring less than 50%, had to stay behind and retake the test: Harry had to stay late a lot on Tuesdays and the dog would stare forlornly down the street, unable to figure out the reason for her miscalculation.

Memory is an unreliable acquaintance at the best of times, but Harry could remember every stage of the unravelling drama of Shellie's last days. He could remember Dad sitting on the bed, unable to look him in the eye as he told him there was nothing more they could do for her now. He could remember blinking back the tears as he stared up at the squadrons of Spitfires and Messerschmitts, Concordes and Boeings, suspended in meticulously-painted detail above his bed, as Dad told him the vet said the kindest thing would be to put her out of her misery.

They'd all said goodbye in their own ways; even Mom, who had never been much of a dog person. Then Dad had put her on the front seat of the car and taken her on one last trip to the park. He lifted her out and let her sniff the air and watch the ducks on the pond, but she didn't have it in her to chase after them anymore; those days were long gone.

That had been at his last school before they moved for the most recent time. It was only a matter of weeks later that Dad left for good. Harry didn't blame Shellie; she had been loyal and faithful to the very end.

He did blame Dad.

Dad had been gone for so long, he felt like more of a footnote than a presence in the house now. And yet he had been amazing, a comic book hero of a Dad with a square jaw a robot would have been proud of; a man-monster with colossal, bone-crushing, bear-like paws. Nothing beat losing yourself in his bookcase-wide chest, all puffed out like a peacock when he came through the front door, wearing his uniform, pride pinned to his chest where his medals normally perched on special occasions.

Then the Gulf War happened.

Dad had been in the SAS, the Special Air Services, famous for their covert operations all around the world: and famous also for their secrecy. Consequently, for years, Harry didn't really have a clue exactly what Dad did. All he could suppose was that Dad's life was like something out of the pages of a thriller and it was awesome to think that he was most likely off parachuting somewhere dangerous behind enemy lines, while other children's Dad's worked in factories or sat behind desks shuffling papers.

But when he came back from Iraq, he was... different.

It was immediately apparent to everyone; even to the mind of a teenager, usually so notoriously self-obsessed and jammed full of screaming hormones and impenetrable angst to even be aware of other people's problems... but Harry knew.

Of course, Dad couldn't talk about it and that only made things worse: the sudden angry outbursts and then long, unbroken sullen silences. It was unbearable and, slowly, the germs of resentment started to shoot. Then, one night, Harry woke up and thought he heard something... at first he thought it was outside; a cat mewling mournfully or the wind howling or *something* and then the awful truth hit him like a double decker bus: it was Dad, crying.

Crying!

Harry's heart froze as he quietly peeled back the sheets and tiptoed onto the landing. He could hear Mom's consoling voice, cooing like a pigeon and then Dad spoke in a hushed whisper and broke the precious code of silence he had always held so sacrosanct. Slowly, he began to unravel his nightmares and tell her all about *Operation Desert Storm*- the Coalition's attempt to win back Kuwait after Saddam Hussein's foolish invasion back in the early 90's. He told her how, although Britain's main involvement was in the air, knocking out their tanks, military installations, missile dumps and so on, he had been sent in behind their lines to send back vital information on troop movements and the like. Suddenly, it went quiet and Harry could sense Dad was getting to the crux of the matter.

"What *is* it?" Mom hissed, *"What's turned you into this stranger since you came home?"*

Harry heard Dad sigh with a weariness that was able to permeate through the wall itself before beginning again. Only this time, in reverent whispers he told her of Highway 80: Highway 80 was a six-lane highway stretching between Kuwait City and the border town of Safwan and then on again, all the way to the Iraqi city of Basra. It had been used by the Iraqi Army during the invasion as it was by far the most direct route into Kuwait. When Dad arrived, it was being used for their hasty and humiliating retreat. Dad and a handful of other SAS had, apparently, been in the area a few weeks, radioing in to headquarters on Iraqi movements and they had just moved into the path of Highway 80 near the end of February 1991.

The sight that met his eyes was utter carnage.

Hidden in a rocky outcrop overlooking a stretch of the road they watched on, appalled and helpless, as Allied forces effectively blocked off both ends at the bottle-neck near the Mutha Ridge Police station, sent in the bombers and incinerated everything and everyone inside those two points. Eventually, Dad said he could take no more of the mindless slaughter and simply closed his eyes on the living nightmare and put his hands over his ears until it was all over.

When dawn broke upon the horrific scene of total and utter devastation, the road was littered with the charred shells of abandoned tanks, destroyed trucks, mutilated armoured cars; even stolen Kuwaiti fire trucks. But, of course, that was not the worst of it. Soldiers hadn't been the only ones fleeing. Hundreds of bodies, soldiers and civilians alike, lay beneath him, scorched and face down in the sand; some still reaching out, in agonised death, against the relentless hail of bullets and engulfing fire, all blackened and pitiful against the backdrop of the merciless sun. From that moment on, Highway 80 became known as the *Highway of Death.*

Dad had whispered to Mom that he hadn't joined up for this. Perhaps he had been too idealistic, but he wasn't naïve- he knew he might witness atrocities, but not on this scale and not from *his side.* He had informed his superiors after the attack; told them of the brutal murders of hundreds of defenceless civilians... women, the elderly, children... all simply trying to get to safety. But nothing had been done. He had been told to keep quiet; it was not good PR for the War effort and the government needed to keep the public on side, especially when it was costing the taxpayer billions of pounds. Mom said he couldn't continue to let it eat him up; she knew it was wrong, knew it was hard, but he had to let it go for the sake of his sanity... for the sake of his family. He said she hadn't seen it with her own eyes... it just wasn't that easy to forget.

Of course, it had turned out that Dad simply couldn't let it go. It had gnawed away at his insides, entering his very marrow and filling him with a cold malaise that enveloped his mind with a sad mist. So, in the end, the Army let him go. That only made things worse. He couldn't find another job; or, more accurately, didn't try. Instead, he sat around the house all day staring at the silent moving pictures of the television screen or drinking. He became more distant; more embittered; more apathetic and less and less like the Dad he remembered. Or the husband his Mom remembered, Harry presumed. Until, one day, Harry came in late from a Chemistry test to find him gone. Mom was seated at the kitchen table, her jaw squarely set against the onset of tears. She didn't offer an explanation why and he didn't ask; he just put the kettle on and held her hand. In some ways, it was a blessed relief. Harry understood his Dad's grief and frustration, of course he did, but there seemed little to do when he had allowed it to become his whole life.

***

A few months later Nan moved in. Mom was struggling to cope financially on her own and Grandad had died a couple of years earlier, so Nan was rattling round a big empty house feeling lonely and useless. The pair of them decided they could sell her house and, with the proceeds, make life a little easier for all of them. It made perfect sense. So she moved into the spare bedroom and, overnight, become a second mother to Harry... and he loved her dearly for it. Chasing the tail of Dad's career and its subsequent impact on his opportunity to make and sustain friendships, meant Nan was the next best thing he had to a best friend. Mom was always at work, but Nan... Nan always gave the impression she had nothing better to do than sit and listen to even the most inconsequential of his gripes and worries.

"Dinner's ready!"

Mom's voice bounded up the stairs like an eager puppy and Harry put his thoughts on pause and pushed himself off the bed. In the kitchen, the window was steamed up and saucepans boiled busily as Harry slid into his normal seat while Nan dished up.

Mom surveyed him critically through the mist coming off the surface of a cup of tea.

"How was school?"

Harry shrugged. The less said about today was most certainly the better: Mom had a knack of picking up on a lie at a hundred paces, so it was wise not to let the sniffer dogs of her curiosity out of their kennel.

Luckily, Nan had just finished piling sausages, thick clouds of mash, and veiny ferns of cabbage onto their plates and told everyone to tuck in.

The food, as ever, was hot and tasty. Nan was a great cook and loved to share the gift; no microwave meals since she moved in. Harry tucked in gratefully.

"You were back late today," Nan said, turning a statement into a question.

Harry nodded and shoved some mash in his mouth to give him time to think.

"I called in the shop for... a chocolate bar, then I got talking; that's all."

"Chocolate! Before tea! You'd better not leave anything after I've spent all afternoon slaving over a hot stove!"

Nan was fond of hyperbole. She was also fond of the expression 'waste not, want not'. Harry smiled to himself as he thought about what a terrible hoarder she was- she couldn't *bear* to throw anything away. Even carrier bags. There was a drawer in the kitchen full of the damn things; all neatly folded and pressed down to fit in. Harry wondered if it was because she'd had nothing as a child growing up in Germany, so didn't want to waste anything now. He didn't know much about her childhood, but she'd grown up during the war, so he supposed rationing had a lot to answer for her attitude, even now.

"Got talking to who?"

Harry swallowed nervously; the dogs had got the scent of blood...

"An old man, actually, called William. I walked home with him; he only lives a couple of streets away."

Mom and Nan exchanged dubious glances and raised eyebrows. Harry jumped in quickly to diffuse the potentially embarrassing turn the conversation might take.

"Mom! Don't look at me like that- he wasn't a pervert or anything... he was... kind. Besides, he was ancient- I think I can look after myself against an old duffer like him!"

"All right, all right," his Mom said, holding both hands up in submission, "we're just looking out for you."

The rest of the meal passed uneventfully in merciful silence. Harry found his mind drifting back to his Dad. He hadn't seen him in months now. He wondered where he was living, whether he was still depressed or if he'd pulled himself out of the fog of his destructive self-pity and had sorted himself out. Perhaps he even had a new family now and had forgotten all about them. It seemed unlikely. One of the last things his Dad had said to him was, "In Russia, they don't have a word for 'optimist'- perhaps they know something we don't." That summed up Dad in the end.

Months after Dad had left, Harry had looked up whether there really *was* a word for optimist in Russian.

There was.

Typical, he'd thought.

CHAPTER FIVE

LESSONS LEARNT BEHIND THE BOILER ROOM

'Friendship...is not something you learn in school. But if you haven't learned the meaning of friendship, you haven't learned anything.'

Muhammad Ali

September 1938,
Friday lunchtime, a school in the heart of Berlin.

Rachel and Wolfgang and Ariel were cosily squeezed into their little hidey-hole behind the school Boiler Room, oblivious to the slow passing of time around them. It had only been a couple of weeks since their chance meeting in the park but it was already obvious that they would be the firmest of friends forever. And lunchtimes had proven a perfect time to share secrets and laugh at each other's foolishness, now they had found this perfect escape from the playground hubbub and the prying eyes of stern staff.

"What shall we do this weekend?" Rachel asked excitedly. Friday held such anticipation: two whole days of freedom away from the restrictive confines of the classroom; especially in such an Indian summer as this.

"Let's go to the Ufa-Palast and watch a movie... something funny!" Ariel suggested.

"Yes, lets!" Rachel agreed delightedly.

Wolfgang felt his heart sink. There was nothing he would love more than to go to the cinema with his best friends; especially Rachel. In the two weeks of knowing her, her beauty had by no means diminished in his eyes; instead it had increased ten-fold. The last time he had gone to the cinema, sneaking in with his friends back in Munich, they had seen *Algiers* with Hedy Lamarr and, as he sneaked a sideways look at her now, it occurred to him that she looked even more dark and exotic than the film star on the screen had when she stood on the deck of the ship, as the brilliantly-named Pepe le Moko called after her in vain. She was *so* beautiful: beautiful as exotic sunsets, beautiful as sunken palaces in the Mediterranean Sea, beautiful as the coppers and golds of autumn that snared in her hair and set her eyes ablaze.

"I can't go," he whined unhappily, "I've got to go to camp."

The other two groaned and rolled their eyes.

"*Again?*" moaned Ariel, picking idly at a scab on his knee just below his short trousers. Wolfgang had already teased him about the state of his legs: they were so skinny his kneecaps seemed to bend inwards so they almost touched. His short socks were always dirty and his shoes were seemingly only held together by the laces. The slightest knock caused him to bruise or bleed instantly but, despite all his obvious shortcomings, he took all his jibes in good spirit.

"I know, but father insists and I can't say no."

"I think I should like to go to one of these camps," announced Rachel, "it sounds like fun. What do you do all day?"

Wolfgang shrugged.

"It's all right *some* of the time, I suppose," he agreed, "I like the camping outside, cooking around the campfire... putting on the gymnastic displays is fun too- you should see us make a giant pyramid! But..." he paused and looked down awkwardly, "I *hate* all the marching and the talks are *really* boring."

"You have to go to lessons... *on the weekend*?" Rachel said, appalled.

"Not *lessons* as such," he explained, "more... *talks*."

As soon as Wolfgang had reached the age of ten, Christian Wirth had enrolled his son in the *Deutsches Jungvolk*. He had hoped it might toughen him up for, although he was as straight and supple as a young elm, he lacked confidence and a killer instinct. The physical exercise, the boxing lessons... they would surely supplement the blonde hair and blue eyes and make him a better example of the type of young man they were looking for to lead the Third Reich's glorious future into the next generation.

Wolfgang sighed and looked up at the line of spindly trees, like sentinels on the hilltop flanking the school's south approach, and wished his friends *could* accompany him; but he knew that wasn't possible. The 'talks' he attended spoke of an Aryan master race and a coming New World Order in which there seemed to be no place for Rachel and Ariel... and that was both confusing and embarrassing. Consequently, he had not told them the nature of these talks and shied away from talking about it now.

Ariel came to his rescue, changing the subject.

"My mother announced she's pregnant yesterday," he said, showing neither pleasure nor concern at the prospect of another sibling in the Koplowitz household.

"*Again?*" said Rachel, "how many is that already?"

"It'll be eight; including me," he grinned.

"*Eight? You have seven brothers and sisters?*" Wolfgang exclaimed, "I haven't got any!"

"Not brothers *and* sisters," Ariel sighed, *"just sisters!* I have six elder sisters- Leah, Rifka, Devorah, Esther, Hodaya and Lilly. And then there's me. I hope this new baby is a boy... give them someone else to fuss over."

Wolfgang and Rachel laughed as Ariel rolled his eyes and shook his head in mock despair.

"Mother has a book to help her choose a name for the baby; it has all the meanings of the names in. I looked us up," he announced smiling mischievously.

The others looked at him suspiciously.

"Go on then," said Rachel dubiously, "what does *my* name mean?"

"*Female sheep!*" said Ariel before bursting into hysterical laughter having clearly been waiting eagerly to deliver this marvellous punchline. Wolfgang rolled over onto his side too, similarly helpless and lost in gusts of laughter as Rachel reddened and folded her arms huffily.

"Oh, very funny, I *must* say!" she scowled.

"You'd better watch out if you're a sheep, or Wolfie will eat you all up!" scoffed Ariel, sniggering even more and wiping the tears from his eyes.

"Is that what Wolfgang means then?" she asked, sceptically.

Ariel nodded.

"Pretty much. Fairly self-explanatory really. 'Wolf' means wolf and 'gang' means 'path' or 'journey'. So you can interpret it like 'Wolf's way' or 'journey of the wolf'."

Rachel looked at him with a smile on her face and Wolfgang looked back uncertainly. She was so hard to read, like a water mark; a hidden face on a banknote only visible from a certain angle, in a certain light. What was she thinking? What did she think about *him?*

"Sounds like you're used to getting your own way, Wolfie," she smiled.

"Or he's going on a long trip. Any holiday plans?" Ariel chipped in.

"Not beyond this weekend," he shrugged, but he couldn't help thinking he would go to the ends of the earth if Rachel asked him to.

"Anyway, conveniently, you haven't told us what Ariel means yet," he added.

Ariel grinned smugly.

"'Lion of God' or 'Angel with a mission of Peace'."

Wolfgang snorted, "*Lion? With those knees? More like sparrow!*"

Now it was Rachel's turn to fall about laughing and she did so with appreciative gusto.

"You can laugh," Ariel shouted over their derision, "but I always suspected I had a greater purpose, a mission in life. This confirms it. I just don't know what it is yet."

"Well, let us know when you figure it out, won't you?" grinned Wolfgang.

Ariel looked at his watch.

"Bell's going to go soon. When do you go to camp, Wolfie?"

"First thing in the morning."

"Well, why can't you come to the cinema tonight then? Before you go?" Rachel implored.

"I have to pack and father insists I get an early night before camp; save my strength," Wolfgang replied, raising and lowering one shoulder in a half-hearted shrug.

"Do you *always* do what Daddy says?" Rachel teased, raising an eyebrow mockingly.

Wolfgang felt himself redden.

"No," he replied, unconvincingly.

"Good!" Rachel smiled triumphantly, "then that's settled. Sneak out about nine and we'll meet outside the Ufa-Palast at about a quarter past. Yes?"

Ariel pulled himself to his feet and shook out the stiffness in his legs.

"Not me," he announced, "like you two want me around playing gooseberry for your first date!"

"What?" exclaimed Rachel, a little too forcefully "what on earth are you talking about?"

Ariel laughed.

"Don't think I haven't noticed!" he grinned, before turning to a Wolfgang already blushing like a traffic light. "Bell's going any minute- I'd suggest you kiss her before Algebra starts!"

Then, before another word could be spoken, he had disappeared around the corner and was gone.

Their sword-tongued friend gone, Rachel and Wolfgang stared at the floor, completely at a loss as to how to proceed. Then, suddenly, Rachel moved a little closer, turned her head, closed her eyes and pursed her lips. Wolfgang's eyes widened as his heart left his body and proceeded to turn somersaults among the clouds. This had all happened so adventitiously... he would be a fool to let this perfect opportunity pass by unfulfilled. On this most perfect of sun-kissed days of childhood, in the times before everything got spoiled, he leaned forward... and kissed her.

The kiss seemed to last forever... the way a moment can hang in the air and float, hovering like a hawk hunting prey, for so much longer than a moment. And then the bell sounded, making them both jump and break, guiltily, apart.

CHAPTER SIX

MAGGIE'S ADVICE WHEN DEALING WITH THE MOB

'Was this the face that launched a thousand ships
And burnt the topless towers of Ilium?'
Doctor Faustus

Christopher Marlowe

'The mob has many heads but no brains.'

William Golding

'He who has learned to disagree without being disagreeable
Has discovered the most valuable secret of a diplomat.'

Robert Estabrook

June 1999
Monday lunchtime; almost. Harry's new school in the Midlands.

So far, Harry had been able to circumnavigate his enemies.
So far.
But he knew it was only a matter of time. Form was easy enough as it consisted of little more than a register, a handful of inane announcements from his form tutor, Mr. Murdoch, and some small talk about the weekend, football and TV. Thus, he had already been sat eagerly in Maths before anyone had even had a chance to corner him. Then, at break, he'd loitered the whole time with Mrs. Tansley, pretending to be catching up on all the missed work from the week before. That meant he could go straight to Art the nanosecond the bell went and still continue to avoid them.

But, as he sat in Art staring forlornly at the clock on the wall, the countdown was surely now on. It was almost lunchtime and it would be nigh on impossible to find a suitable place to secrete himself for almost an hour when they would, undoubtedly, be searching for him. Perhaps it would be better, he considered, if he just let them find him straight away and get it over with; one way or the other. His stomach lurched and sloshed at the prospect, breakfast suddenly feeling like bilge water splashing against the insides of the hull of an ancient ship as it churned on a stormy sea.

In the meantime, Harry was determined to take his mind off things- and there was no better way to do this than cast sideways glances in the direction of the delectable Maggie McGuire.

Maggie McGuire... his pulse rose a little higher at the very mention of her name.

She was in a number of his classes and he doggedly took that as a sign that, since they were interested in the same subjects, they were, therefore, more or less soulmates. But choice of options weren't the only thing they had in common. *Oh, no.* Harry had noticed that, when she was seated at the back of the class, she would take out a pair of tortoiseshell glasses and gaze thoughtfully at the board in them, leaning her chin on her hand like Rodin's *Thinker*, while making tidy notes in her un-graffitied exercise book. Harry observed her, this wonderful vision viewed from the outer corner of an eye and couldn't help but think that she looked a picture of studious intelligence, which was wholly appropriate because she *was* clever... and funny and witty and fiercely independent and loudly bored when she grew tired of a subject; all of which made Harry smile to himself. And *he* was clever; teachers in at least a dozen different schools had told his mother so at the only Parents Evenings she had attended before he changed Year groups and moved on again...so, surely, *they were a match made in heaven?*

Her tastes in music and fashion were stylishly eclectic and she didn't care what anyone else said about them. She complimented her school uniform with scuffed brown brogues and no jewellery except a jauntily oversized watch that looked comical on her slender wrist. All in all, she was pretty much perfection; as teenage girls went. Harry blew out his cheeks and contemplated the haphazard eccentricities of the human gene pool that made certain individuals irresistible whilst others...effectively invisible. Her effect on him was both encaptivating and immensely disconcerting.

There was, however, a minor problem on this sun-splattered romantic horizon.

Unfortunately, there was absolutely *no* chance she would fancy *him.* To say she was out of his league was an understatement; it was doubtful they were even playing the same *sport.* Plus, he considered dolefully, in novels, the heroines always went for the dashing, chisel-jawed hero... not the kid who got beaten to a pulp by a couple of thugs and then had his pockets ransacked afterwards.

He consoled himself in the knowledge that most love stories were, if you really thought about it, a crock of crap. Take Helen of Troy for example. Greeks and Trojans were supposed to have gone at it tooth and nail for a decade based on her legendary beauty, but historians had since proved that, when the Trojan War was fought, Helen would have been way too old for Paris to have even been interested in her. Unless he liked older women, of course. *Much* older... like old Mrs. Anderson who had taught RE since the Seventies, never married, and had a funny eye that followed you round the room like a painting in a haunted house. Harry allowed himself a smile at the thought of Paris and Hector propping up the bar in some Trojan taverna on *Grab-a-Granny-night*! No, it was simply a plot device; a reason for the conflict, an excuse for Hector and Achilles to go toe-to-toe and write their names in the annals of history.

Anyway, forget Helen, Harry thought. If anyone had a face that could launch a thousand ships, it was Maggie.

He sighed and tried to focus on copying the curve of an empty wine bottle that Mr. Raymond had placed in the centre of their table for them to copy. He seemed to have a lot of empty wine bottles on the shelf of the classroom and Harry wondered if he had drunk all of the contents himself. The red-rimmed tiredness around his eyes suggested this bottle may have been finished off as recently as last night...

Shaking himself free of his thoughts, Harry was slowly aware of the teacher talking. Mr. Raymond was pointlessly telling everyone they could start to pack away... over the hubbub of a class full of students already cramming their rucksacks and holdalls full of dog-eared books, chewed pens and graffitied pencil cases. Harry joined them reluctantly and racked his brains for a plan. He could always jump the fence and run home... but what would he say to Mom and Nan? And, as his Dad used to like to tell him when he didn't solve a problem, he only delayed it, which was merely kicking the can further down the road. Fine advice from a man who had now been kicking one particular can down a motorway for a *very* long time... Still, the advice itself wasn't flawed; just his Dad's inability to take his own advice. No, better to head for the canteen and whatever happened next... well, happened next.

He didn't have to wait long to find out. Half way down the DT corridor on the way to the canteen he found his path cut off by Adam Kellerman, Kurt Smalley and, of course, ringleader Paul Harris. He stopped and, instinctively, thought about turning and running... until he heard more noises behind him and turned to face the sick grins of Rob Kellerman, Ian Pardoe and the obnoxious leer of Tania Tonks. Harry sighed and waited for them to close in on him; like ancient stone walls in an *Indiana Jones* movie, seemingly about to imminently crush the intrepid hero and with absolutely no feasible route of escape. *What would Harrison Ford do now? Well, for a start, he'd probably have a revolver and a whip, so he was already at something of a disadvantage!* Harry started to feel increasingly crushed as his thoughts all led to dead-ends. All out of options, he braced himself, his brain whirring and ready to pick each word with the utmost care. He knew only too well from previous experiences with bullies, any hint of weakness was a drop of blood in shark-infested waters. He would have to play this one very carefully...

"So what was all that between you and the old bloke?" Paul said, his voice betraying nothing of his intentions.

Harry considered how to play things.

"He er... helped me."

"What do you mean?"

"I got caught nicking stuff and he covered for me- said it was for him."

Paul and the others took this in, still leaving no gap in the net through which he might slip.

"So what you nick?" Ian demanded.

"Some cheese," Harry admitted, suddenly feeling foolish.

"*Cheese?*" laughed Paul, "that wasn't very *mature!*"

The others howled inanely and Harris let the laughter die down before continuing.

"Let's have it then," he said, holding out his hand expectantly.

Harry hadn't been expecting that; *did he think he walked around school all day with cheese in his pocket?* He blinked, regained his composure and replied "I don't have it; the old guy took it. After all," he added by way of explanation, "he did *pay* for it."

Paul nodded and shrugged.

"Well, I guess you'll have to do something else then, won't you?" he concluded.

Harry shook his head vehemently.

"*No way!* I already did an initiation- in fact, it was probably worse for me because I got caught and Mr. Sandhu was threatening to call the Police-"

"But we've only got *your* word for that haven't we, Robinson?" interrupted Harris, "for all we know, you had a nice chat with this old bloke, walked him home carrying his shopping all the way like a real Boy Scout and made him a cup of tea to top it all off!"

Again, the others laughed heartily at his expense. Harry felt his face redden and the bile rise in his throat. *Bullies were such arseholes! It would give him the greatest of pleasure in punching him in the face and watching the look of absolute shock on his face... but, of course, he had his entourage in tow, the back up every bully requires to hide their own inadequacies.*

"I am *not* doing anything else!" he stormed angrily, regretting his words the seconds they had exited his lips.

Before he could even think about retracting them, the Kellerman twins had him pinned against the wall, his legs dangling pathetically as they lifted him on either side. Paul Harris leaned in close so he could see the angry acne erupting on his forehead.

"You will do exactly what we tell you to do," he hissed, now leaving no doubt as to his intentions.

"Mr. Broom's coming down the corridor!" said a voice that Harry immediately thought he recognised.

The gang parted in surprise and there was Maggie McGuire hovering a little way down the corridor, looking worried and skittish and indicating over her shoulder with the quick jerk of a thumb.

"You sure?" Kurt Wharton demanded.

"Just passed him," she shrugged diffidently.

Harris nodded and the Kellerman's dropped him unceremoniously on the floor. Harry could hardly have been more humiliated! He was the poor cowboy forced to dance to the rhythm of ricocheting bullets on a saloon floor, while the real gunslingers stood around and laughed; all while the love of his life watched on. Nevertheless, it was a stroke of good fortune: if there was anyone in the entire school guaranteed to put the fear of God into Harris's gang- or anyone else for that matter- it was Broom. Towering over all of them like a basketball player and with his muscles rippling under his shirt like wind through a sail, he taught PE and made a pretence of teaching Geography as a second subject and had a fearsome reputation. Harry had only been a pupil at St. Josephs a short time but, already, he had heard the whispered rumours. Legend had it that, a couple of years ago, a sixth former had made some sarcastic comment to him that he had taken offence to; Broom was not noted for his sense of humour. Mr. Broom had allegedly offered him out and the sixth former, fancying his chances, had agreed to meet him behind the bike sheds after school. The result was a bloody mess and a sixth former who changed schools shortly afterwards.

Harris ran his tongue over his teeth anxiously.

"Come on," he said, leading the gang away down the corridor. Just before he turned the corner he shouted, "we'll see *you* later!"

Maggie came up to him and stretched out a hand. Cheeks sizzling like sausages at a fairground, Harry allowed her to help him gingerly to his feet.

"I'm Maggie," she announced.

"I know," he replied, before catching the surprised raise of an eyebrow, "I mean… you're in some of my classes."

He glanced up at her and tried to tear his gaze away from the saucers of her eyes and the cute constellation of freckles spreading across her nose and cheeks.

"Piece of advice," she volunteered, "keep away from those brainless idiots."

Harry smirked.

"Easier said than done. They appear to have taken a liking to me; want me to play in their gang and everything!"

Maggie smiled and Harry's problems suddenly felt a little more manageable.

"Want me to have a word with Mr. Murdoch? He's not too bad, for a teacher, I mean; won't let on it's come from you."

Harry shook his head.

"Grassing's not gonna help my situation."

Maggie stared at him a minute, then shrugged and smiled.

"OK, suit yourself, but…try and be…*diplomatic.*"

"Diplomatic?"

"Yeah, a little brains rather than brawn; it'd make a pleasant change around here."

"I'll do my best," Harry smiled.

Maggie smiled back and, nodding, turned away and began to walk back the way she'd just come.

Suddenly, something occurred to Harry.

"*Was* Broom coming this way?" he called after her.

Maggie turned back and grinned, shaking her head, "*like I said, brains over brawn, Robinson… brains over brawn!*"

CHAPTER SEVEN

THE KINDNESS OF STRANGERS

'Three things in human life are important.
The first is to be kind.
The second is to be kind.
And the third is to be kind.'

Henry James

June 1999
Friday evening. At William and Gabriel's house.

Harry walked down William and Gabriel's street. It was the most perfect summer's evening and someone somewhere was probably having a birthday party as Harry could see a single balloon way up in the distance, lodged in the roof of the sky. He watched it disappear into the heavens and smiled ruefully.

As he walked up their pathway, he couldn't help but wonder if he was making a huge mistake. Sure, the old guy had helped him out, but he'd walked him home, thanked him... what more could he expect or even want?

Having said that, he couldn't help but feel that there was unfinished business between the two of them. He'd promised to come and meet his friend, Gabriel and, he suspected, they probably didn't have a lot of visitors so he'd be doing a good deed that might go some way towards undoing the bad he felt over his abortive theft. But it was more than that. There was something unusual about William, something different about him, something really...*elusive*.

Harry didn't know why or how, but he sensed William could... *help* him somehow. Help him more than just atoning for his weakness in the corner shop; help him *in life*. It sounded really stupid when he ran it through his head but... it was a feeling he just couldn't shake.

His thoughts were interrupted by an emaciated figure suddenly standing before him on the doorstep. Harry went to speak but was too taken aback by how old and frail this strange man looked. Instinctively, he knew that the intricate grooves and knots of his face told the story of a life full of turmoil and tragedy.

"I'm guessing you're Harry," said a voice surprisingly more spritely and full of vitality than the body it was housed in might suggest and, while his frail frame made his clothes hang off him like a child playing dress-up giving him a vaguely comical look, there was a tolerance and an inner strength about his eyes that made Harry trust him immediately and implicitly.

"Erm, yes," he mumbled, still at a loss at what to say to this enigmatic stranger before him.

"Well, don't stand on ceremony, young man, come on in," he smiled, stepping to one side to allow him to come inside. Awkwardly, Harry followed him down a dark, tiled corridor and into a high-ceilinged sitting room where William sat on one of a matching pair of large red leather chairs. The room was sparsely decorated but homely nonetheless and spotlessly tidy.

"You came," William smiled, the surprise evident in his voice.

Harry smiled and shrugged.

William gestured for him to sit on a matching settee and he sank into its deep cushions, suddenly feeling under close scrutiny; like a contestant on '*Mastermind*'.

"How was school?" William asked and Harry knew it wasn't meant as a polite enquiry about his day.

He shrugged.

"They still giving you a hard time?"

He shrugged again.

"It's all right," William smiled, "I don't mind you not telling me. It's OK to have secrets. I meet people all the time who go about their daily lives with no secrets at all and they're morons... robots. They never *think* about anything deeply enough to generate secrets. It's just..." and he paused to meet Harry's unbroken gaze, "some secrets are good to share- it helps; a solution can often be found through the sharing of the secret." He grinned and shrugged, adding, "of course, other secrets should be locked in a chest, thrown off the deck of a ship in the midst of a terrible storm and allowed to sink to the bottom of the ocean, never to be spoken of again. Some secrets should be the secrets of ghosts. You have to decide which kind of secrets you have."

Harry looked at the old men quizzically; he really didn't know what to make of them. He knew what William meant though about secrets and shallowness. He was always suspicious of people who never thought about death, for instance. It was like stepping off the pavement every morning without bothering to look either way first. Sooner or later you were going to be squished by a big articulated lorry and then these people would moan how they hadn't seen it coming. Harry thought it was way better to consider the nature of your mortality every once in a while; even if that meant it waking you in the middle of the night in a cold sweat from time to time. It showed you were *alive*; had some deeper thoughts going on in your head than whether Team A had beaten Team B on a Saturday afternoon. It also made you *live* life to the full a little more; you did things *now* if you weren't sure absolutely sure you were going to be around tomorrow to do them then. It gave life a refreshing sense of *urgency*. Nevertheless, he wasn't sure this was a particularly healthy and normal approach to life for a teenager and he certainly wasn't ready to reveal all his innermost thoughts to these two strangers just yet.

"I can handle them."

"Really? What *exactly* do you plan to do about them then?" William pressed.

"Not much I can do against nine or ten of them is there? What do you suggest- go undercover and pick them off one at a time on their way home from school with a Bowie knife?" Harry replied defensively.

"Cowards always buckle under pressure; fact. You can't not do the right thing just because it's difficult."

Harry felt himself smart at the bluntness of his assessment of Harry's predicament.

"Very philosophical; not so easy in practice," he muttered.

William and Gabriel looked at each other and burst out laughing.

"What's so funny?" he asked bemused.

Gabriel nodded in William's direction, "you have inadvertently hit upon William's career- he lectured at the University in Ethics and Philosophy! So he does tend to wax philosophical on a more or less daily basis!"

Slowly, Harry felt himself start to relax into this alien environment; muscles he hadn't even realised he'd tensed started to unfreeze and eventually unravel. Finally, he let out a long sigh as his breathing eased and he resolved to try to actually *enjoy* himself. As he listened to William's laid back lilt, Gabriel went into the kitchen and quickly returned with soft drinks and a home-made lemon drizzle cake. He cut two generous pieces for Harry and William and then sat down satisfied.

"Don't you want a slice?" Harry asked, already greedily harpooning a large chunk with his fork.

"It's all I can do to get him to eat a slice of toast most days," William smiled.

"Why?" Harry mumbled, his mouth full of zesty sponge and icing, "it's absolutely delicious! Did *you* make this Gabriel?"

Gabriel smiled and nodded.

"He's a fabulous cook, Harry; he was the Head Chef at *Elmer's* in town for years, but getting him to eat his own wonderful creations is a very different proposition. Something to do with feeling guilty for enjoying food when others are starving in the world."

Gabriel suddenly shot William a reproachful look and William held up his hands in guilty submission.

"Anyway, tell us about yourself," said Gabriel, quickly changing the subject, "Who do you live with?"

"My Mom and my Nan," Harry explained.

"And your father?" Gabriel enquired softly.

Harry raised and lowered one shoulder nonchalantly.

"He walked out on a while ago," he explained, "he was in the army and it made him... bitter. When he walked out, Gran moved in to help out; she's been there ever since."

William and Gabriel exchanged a knowing glance.

"That must have been difficult for you," Gabriel smiled softly, "what was he like- your father?"

Harry blew out his cheeks; it was hard to say really. How could you sum up both Jekyll and Hyde in a single sentence?

"When I was smaller, he was great. I can remember kicking a football around with him and him teaching me how to ride a bike and rolling about on the bed with him in fits of hysterics as Mom murdered the Top 40 in the shower. One time, we went sledging and snow got in my wellies and my toes froze solid. It was so painful, I cried and cried. So Dad carried me to the car, took off my socks and put my feet on his belly. It was wonderful and agonising all at once as I got thawed out and got that horrible 'pins and needles' feeling. I suppose it was then I knew he really loved me- cos that's what Dad's do... they do whatever it takes to keep their kids safe and happy."

He smiled sadly at the memory before adding "but then, much later, I can also remember the silences that lasted for days; with him sitting in the conservatory in some angry fog with nobody daring to go in to disturb him, as if he was some grumpy bear in permanent hibernation. By the end, it was easier him not being there and not having to tread on eggshells all the time."

Harry suddenly felt jaded; old beyond his years. Travelling the continent tracking Dad's career had been wearisome and he'd had to grow up faster than other teenagers. It had made him street-smart and mature for his age, but also a little cynical and bitter. It was difficult to see the world as a place where good things happened to those that deserved them and the bad guys got their come-uppance; that had *not* been his experience so far.

"And your grandmother?" William asked, suddenly leaning forward in his chair, "what's *she* like?"

Harry raised an eyebrow and mulled it over. It wasn't a question he considered very often: she was just *there;* his comfort blanket; his anchor.

"Nan's great," he concluded, "I don't think Mom could have coped without her."

"Yes, but what's she *like?*" William persisted, "is she happy? Does she tell jokes? Does she miss your Grandad?"

"William!" Gabriel interrupted, "stop interrogating the poor boy!"

William scowled across at Gabriel and looked as if he might argue the point, but caught himself in time and sat back in his chair with a reluctant sigh.

"Of course, you're right, I'm sorry, I don't mean to be rude; I'm merely... *interested.*"

A pregnant pause followed that ate into the very air around them. Harry studied the paintings on the wall- watercolours of foreign landscapes and city scenes, pen and ink sketches of a young woman: beautiful and exotic-looking with long dark hair and an enigmatic smile- and noticed they were all signed by the same person; William.

"It's fine," he smiled at Gabriel, "I don't mind. Nan doesn't talk much of Grandad and, to be honest, the only distinct memories I have of him are how his false teeth rattled in his mouth when he laughed and how he used to pretend to steal my nose when I was little and then pretend it was his own thumb stuck between his fingers. He was kind and funny; nice. I guess they were happy... she's never said otherwise." He blew out his cheeks and mused on their lives now, "Nan's very... *organised* now; obsessively so. I somehow can't picture her as a young girl with pigtails and white socks skipping down some tree-lined street, sucking on a lollipop or a gobstopper. Did they even have gobstoppers back then? I dunno. But she's there to do my breakfast when I get up and she's there to do tea when I get in from school and she's the rock of our family and, pretty much, my only friend since Dad left and Mom works so many shifts to make ends meet."

Another long pause followed before Gabriel added.

"We're your friends now."

Harry looked at him, surprised, then smiled and shrugged.

"She sounds a wonderful woman," William added, "and they *did* have gobstoppers when she was young... I ate them all the time!"

****

William stood on the doorstep with Harry shaking hands.

"I'm glad you came," he announced, a hint of pride in his voice.

"Me too," Harry admitted.

"Will you come again? Keep us informed how things are going at school? Perhaps there might be something we can do to help? You never know, *old* doesn't mean *of no use*, you know."

Harry raised and lowered one shoulder.

"I guess," he agreed, "though I feel you have higher expectations of me than I can fulfil. I have no idea what I'm going to do or how I'm going to avoid getting another kicking."

William laid a firm hand on his shoulder.

"You start off by doing the right thing," he advised, "everything else follows on from that."

CHAPTER EIGHT

CRY OF THE HUNTERS

'To talk without thinking is to shoot without aiming'

William Golding

'Like the base indian threw a pearl away
Richer than all his tribe.'

Othello
William Shakespeare

'And Peter remembered the saying of the Lord,
How he had said to him,
"Before the rooster crows today...
You will deny me three times."
And he went out and wept bitterly.

Luke 22:v61-2
The Bible

5th November 1938
Saturday evening, Berlin.

The distant insinuation of thunder had quickened Rachel and Wolfgang's pace. Now, they ran laughing down the street as the rain bounced off the pavement and their clothes stuck to their skin like glue. Quickly ducking into a shop doorway, Wolfgang pulled Rachel close to him and kissed her. Once he had experienced the buzz of electricity from their first kiss behind the school boiler room, he had become addicted to the sheer shock that made every extremity in his body tingle with each fresh union of their lips; and Rachel didn't seem to have any particular objection either!

In the weeks following the start of their relationship, Wolfgang found Berlin was rapidly growing on him: a city of dark secrets shared in the shadows of seedy cabarets; of lauded aristocrats and corner-begging paupers; of wide avenues and winding labyrinthine backstreets... perfect fodder for an exciting date brim-full with the potential for adventure and romance.

"Where does your father think you are tonight?" Rachel whispered in his ear.

"At Martin's house," Wolfgang smiled, "studying for a trigonometry test!"

Rachel's laugh echoed around the doorway before being drowned out by the roar of engine as a Horch 853 sport cabriolet in fire red zooming by; a flash of white-walled wheels, bug-eyed headlights and the glistening swathe of wet chrome.

"We'll drive around in a car like that, one day, when we're older," Wolfgang announced happily.

Rachel looked at him with a mixture of pity and sadness in her eyes.

"No, we won't," she said softly.

"Of course we will," he retorted, "my family are loaded! When I'm older, I'll go to university and get a well-paid job and... and..."

"And what, Wolfie?" Rachel insisted.

Wolfgang had wanted to say *'and we'll be together forever and I'll buy you whatever your heart desires';* but how could a teenage boy say all of those things to a teenage girl he'd only known for the blink of an eye, especially when he had no more than a handful of pfennigs in his pocket.

"Where does your father think *you* are tonight?" he asked instead.

She smiled sadly.

"At Ariel's house helping his mother make cakes for Esther's birthday. *You see?* It's hopeless. My mother hates the Germans because they made her leave her job at the hospital and father hates them because they make him wear a yellow star on his overcoat and add the name *'Israel'* to his own name, so no-one can be under any illusions as to his Jewishness. *Your* family would never let us be together because we *are* Jews and somehow inferior in their eyes. How long do you think it will be before someone sees us and tells? Then it will all be over. Don't you see that?"

Wolfgang could feel the electricity dying like the thinning rain as the thunderclouds passed leaving the sky smoky and dark. He didn't want to have to confront Rachel's doubts: he was besotted with her and that was enough for now: children should be allowed to indulge their fantasies and not have reality smack them in the face, he concluded.

He kissed her again.

"You worry too much; *typical girl!*"

Rachel wriggled free of his embrace, "Well, you won't want to be stuck with a *typical girl* on a Saturday night then, will you?" she smarted, "I'll go home and let you have a *much* better time with your *boy*friends at your precious weekend camps!"

"Very funny!" Wolfgang scoffed, a little bemused at her quick change of mood but happy at least for the subject to have veered away from the squirming awkwardness of their faiths and families, "You know I wouldn't want to spend the evening with anyone but you. Besides, I've used all my pocket money to get us tickets for the new Marx brothers' film; be a waste to miss it now."

Rachel scowled at him for a moment, then shook her head and relented.

"Wouldn't dream of it!" she smiled, taking his hand and pulling him out of their shelter and into the fine drizzle. Arm in arm they strolled contentedly past rows and rows of shimmering newly-wet parked cars: expensive Opels and Daimler-Benzes and large

Wanderer saloon cars, cheap DKWs and extortionate Horchs; none of which he promised to buy her in the future.

***

Wolfgang emerged from the Ufa-Palast movie theatre into a beautiful star-kissed night, but with the reassuring anchorage of Rachel's hand in his to stop her floating away from him. She had giggled her way through *Room Service* and the foolish exploits of Groucho, Chico and Harpo and now she flitted around him as they walked through the foyer, re-enacting lines from the film, moth-like and ethereal in her exuberance. Now he had her grounded and tight in his grip all the way home.

Anhalter Bahnhot railway terminal, near Potsdam Platz, ran through the middle of three vast arches. Their footsteps echoed as they took the shortcut through, the sounds bouncing back towards them ominously off the black emptiness of the high vaulted ceilings. Rachel lived on the other side of the train tracks and it was already late; a shortcut might just keep her out of *too* much trouble with her father.

The lights and sounds of the street had almost faded to nothing when Wolfgang noticed the brief flare of red appear and fade before them: someone had lit a cigarette.

Some instinct told him to quicken their pace and he tried to encourage Rachel to hurry, but she was still in her own little haze of happiness and continued to dawdle as a dark shadow of figures emerged, blocking their path. Wordlessly, they surrounded the bemused couple and Rachel suddenly felt her deliriously happy mood quickly being bludgeoned into submission.

"Identity cards?"

Hitler Youth! Wolfgang felt a terror flicker in his heart as his mind searched desperately for a way to wake him wake from this unexpected nightmare.

The tallest member of the gaggle of Hitler Youth stepped closer to Wolfgang and thrust out his hand aggressively. He was probably a year or two older than Wolfgang and he recognised the type immediately; the sort who bullied the weaker members on camp and who was actively encouraged by the instructors to do so: *weed out the weak and make the strong stronger.* That seemed to be the philosophy. Wolfgang passed over his papers trying not to let his hand shake. The older boy gave them a cursory glance, all the while keeping his piercing eyes firmly on Rachel.

"German, yes?" he demanded and, flustered, Wolfgang reached again into his shirt pocket taking out further papers.

"Of course, of course, I have just been promoted from the Deutsches Jungvolk and start in the Hitlerjugend next weekend when I next go to camp. Here is my Leistungsbuch."

He handed over his Performance Booklet and smiled meekly, while the leader pushed a blonde lock of hair out of his eyes and allowed the corner of his mouth the slightest of sneers as he scoured the lists of Wolfgang's rather average accomplishments.

"And you are with this *Jew*?" a second, shorter, boy asked, having already checked Rachel's papers with obvious disgust.

Wolfgang stared at the floor and said nothing.

The leader shoved his papers into his chest and pinned them there with the flat of his hand.

"Does your family know you are a *Jew lover*?" he hissed.

Again, Wolfgang stared at the floor and did everything possible to make himself inconspicuous; withdrawing into himself to the extent he became as one with the rapid beating of his heart, the exaggerated rise and fall of his chest.

"I think," the leader continued, though Wolfgang was barely listening as self-preservation had completely taken over by now, "that you just happened to be walking along the street next to this Jew but that you don't actually know her. *Isn't that so?*"

Wolfgang stuffed his identity papers back into his shirt pocket.

"*Isn't that so?*" the leader repeated, prodding him with a thick finger on each syllable.

"Yes," Wolfgang mumbled, "I just met her."

There was a mumble of assent from the remaining members as they nodded their acquiescence. The second boy held out Rachel's identity papers but, when she reached for them, he let them slip from his fingers and flutter into the heart of a black puddle before she could grasp them between her fingers.

"Ah, how foolish of me!" he mocked, as the others laughed openly.

Wordlessly, Rachel bent down, wiped the papers on her coat sleeve and squirreled them safely away.

From the blackness they heard something scurry past, its nails scratching the floor as it went. Rachel felt a shiver shoot up her spine and prayed they would let them past soon. A terrifying silence ensued as if the gang leader was deciding whether he would, indeed, let them past or escalate things to an even more terrifying climax but, eventually, he gave an almost imperceptible nod, after which they parted and let Wolfgang and Rachel pass silently through and leave them behind, laughing and muttering to themselves in the enveloping darkness.

****

Neither of them spoke for the rest of the walk back to Rachel's door: firstly, for fear they were being followed and then, because there was nothing to say. When Wolfgang turned to face her, she turned away from him, hiding the burning stripes of her tears.

"Three times," she whispered, "three times you were asked. I told you it could never work; perhaps now you'll believe me."

"Rachel, I'm-" Wolfgang began, but he knew he had no excuse and no reason for her to ever forgive him.

Rachel was half way up the stairs when she turned to face him.

"Don't speak to me or Ariel at school on Monday; I think it is for the best."

Wolfgang tried to gulp back down the rising bile that had already reached his throat and, when he looked up again, her door was already closing.

CHAPTER NINE

THE NIGHT OF BROKEN GLASS

'Friends show their love in times of trouble, not in happiness.'

Euripides

Wednesday November 9th 1938
Kristallnacht

Rachel had blatantly ignored him for three days now, while Ariel kept glancing across guiltily; although he knew better than to go against Rachel's express wishes.

For Wolfgang, it had been the worst three days of his life.

If he had thought moving from Munich to Berlin had been a painful experience, nothing could have prepared him for the endless torture of wanting to speak to the girl he loved more than any other on the planet, only to be looked through as though he were invisible. And it was all his own doing. Of course, he had tried: notes passed in class had been derisively screwed up without bothering to open them; visiting their spot behind the boiler room only emphasised his loneliness after finding it pitifully devoid of waiting friends; even attempting to sit by them in the dinner hall only resulted in them moving tables without a backwards look. Each day had felt more hopeless than the one before to the extent he was beginning to even find coming home to the distant and efficient running of the Berlin house a merciful release from the relentless rejection.

But that evening was different somehow…

The moment he walked in from school and draped his schoolbag over the end of the bannister as normal, he instinctively sensed the nervous tension in the air. A pair of servants were whispering animatedly at the door leading to the dining room and Wolfgang stared as their nervous chat skittered across the space between them but faded infuriatingly before it reached his ears. Dismissing it, he had gone up to his room to sulk and wait for the call for supper but, surprisingly, it had not come. Eventually, the growl of his stomach forced him back downstairs where, to his amazement, the servants were still hurrying here and there, in a state of animated confusion.

What on earth was so urgent?

Why did their faces seem to encapsulate so many different emotions simultaneously… from surprise to concern to…well, to outright *fear*. His mind started to work overtime and fill the lack of knowledge with terrible possibilities:

Did they know about him and Rachel?

Wolfgang sighed at the infuriating secrecy of the maids. He had always been so friendly and relaxed with the maids back in Munich, Bridgitte and Hannah. In fact, he had grown up with them, been bathed and dressed by them, comforted by them when monsters under the bed invaded his nightmares. They were his older sisters and mother all rolled into one. But these two were virtual strangers; he wasn't even sure he could remember their names... Gretl was it? And perhaps the other was Rebecca? Either way, like Brigitte and Hannah, they were Jewish and, until the rising tensions between the Germans and the Jews, would have been treated more like extended family than servants. All that felt different now though, with an invisible barrier apparent between both sides that seemed impossible to breach.

Wolfgang wondered too whether it was not beyond the realms of possibility that, being Jewish, they might have overheard something in their neighbourhoods of his illicit relationship and were concerned. *Why? Because his father already knew and they didn't want to be accused of withholding information?* Or because they intended to *tell* him and were feeling sorry for him for what agonies he was about to suffer? His mind swam with unanswered questions bumping together like plastic yellow ducks waiting to be hooked at a fairground.

He was just contemplating going over to them to attempt to initiate a polite interrogation when Lt. Helmut Tanzmann strode out of his father's office, puffed up like a peacock. Wolfgang bridled the moment he clapped eyes on him and the two maids quickly flitted away like tiny birds escaping at the approach of a sly cat. He had taken an instant dislike to the Lieutenant from the very first time he had met him. There was an arrogance and a cruel streak that ran all the way through him like a stick of rock in him and, worse than that, he was everything his father desired in an Aryan youth and everything Wolfgang felt he could never be: tall, muscular, blonde-hair styled in a severe parting and with SS uniform polished and preened to perfection... and, of course, totally ruthless. Normally, Tanzmann gave little away, appearing apathetic to life in general and unresponsive to an emotional impulse; rather like a shark showing no pity in its' daily extermination of ocean life. But tonight he uncharacteristically appeared... well, *excited.*

"Have you heard?" he said crisply, the fire of ambition burning brightly in his eyes.

"Heard what?" Wolfgang replied, after recovering from the shock of being directly addressed by Lt. Tanzmann of his own free will; instead of out of grudging respect for being the son of his commanding officer.

"Tonight is when the Jews get what's coming to them!" he announced triumphantly, not really looking at Wolfgang, but rather giving the impression he needed to say the words out loud for them to become actually real to him.

Wolfgang felt his stomach lurch and the blood chill and then freeze in his veins.

"Wh…what do you mean?"

"Haven't you heard? Some impudent Jewish teenager had the sheer gall to murder a German official in Paris! Can you believe it?"

He shook his head at the unbelievable audacity of the news.

"Well now they will learn the error of their ways! They will pay many times over for the outrage they have caused- Goebbels has sent the word through: take revenge on the blood-sucking Jewish scum! Burn their synagogues! Loot the businesses that have robbed the Fatherland for generations! Take back the jobs they have stolen from our youth!" Tanzmann held court like Hitler on a balcony overlooking tens of thousands of adoring supporters, a distant look of zealous ambition in his eyes. "Tonight it all begins: *the beginning of the end for the Jews!"*

Wolfgang barely heard the last syllables of Tanzmann's tirade, hurriedly excusing himself and disappearing into the kitchens. The room was devoid of all activity so he slipped silently through, opened the back door and followed the winding path that led between the dark undergrowth of the garden. He didn't want anyone to know he had left in case they came looking for him. Hopefully, he deduced, in all the furore engulfing the entire household, no-one would think to check the bedroom of one insignificant teenage boy.

The gardens were long and sprawling; all creepers and vines and creatures scurrying in the undergrowth. But, as unwelcoming as the ominous outlines of grasping branches were, Wolfgang would have happily stayed there all night rather than exit the back gate into the

Hell that waited beyond. Pausing by the ornate summer house on the very far edge of a neatly manicured lawn bordering the tree line, Wolfgang waited and listened. Danger seemed to exist in the very air; not close by, (this was a German district) but in the distance where he could already hear shouts and cries drifting on the wind, he could smell burning and, most clearly and eerily of all, he could hear the shattering of glass...

Wolfgang decided to try for Rachel's house first. He had to warn her and her family: her parents Benjamin and Ruth, her sisters Esther and Elizabeth, he had to explain to them about the tornado of hate that was spinning their way... if they didn't know already. Although she had point blank refused to talk to him since his abject behaviour in front of the Nazi Youth, he knew in that moment he would do absolutely anything in his power to protect her; including willingly giving his life for her. *But was he already too late?*

The back gate opened out onto a quiet side street; an avenue of silver barks, bare in the early winter dusk, their white trunks mottled and spotted like the wrinkled hands of an aged aunt. Wolfgang crept past silent houses, curtains drawn and plunged in darkness, and a smattering of patient cars, idly kicking their tyres until the morning rush hour. A mongrel lolloped past, his hind legs doing their very utmost to outpace the front ones. Wolfgang hugged the shadows all the way to the main street then took stock. The road ahead in both directions was eerily quiet, but Wolfgang couldn't help but feel that every step from this point on would be like walking the plank to a highly unpleasant end.

Turning right, he moved quickly and stealthily through a German district, past houses and shops, honing in as quickly as he could on Alexanderplatz. As he turned the corner, the sight that met his eyes made him gasp out loud in surprise. *Everywhere was unrecognisable.* The bright market places were full of gangs of men and youths: shouting, chanting, punching fists in the air and clasping burning brands. The toy store, where Wolfgang had recently admired the tin-plate toys: monkeys banging cymbals together jollily, aeroplanes and money boxes shaped like open-mouthed heads that swallowed pfennigs whole, was cheerfully ablaze. The glass had been shattered by half a dozen well-aimed large cobbles, so that the shop owner's name was nothing more than the odd remaining syllable now. The wooden toys: Noah's Arks, jigsaw puzzles, a large and very grand doll's house... they had gone first and provided fuel to the fire. The monkey's smile was just starting to ooze down his sad little face when Wolfgang pulled himself away.

From the deep doorway of the pawn shop two doors down, Wolfgang watched in horror as Mr. Adelstein was pulled from his shop door and thrown into the street. Whenever they passed his shop, Rachel always said '*Good morning Mr. Adelstein*', in a polite sing-song voice and he always smiled back and waved and, occasionally called them over, disappeared inside for a moment before returning with a treat... a sweet, or a fig, or a small slice of cake. The force of the shove and the frailty of the old man sent him sprawling to the floor, not having time or the reactions of youth to break his fall with his hands. When he was pulled upright by two youths, yanking him carelessly to his feet, Wolfgang could see blood gushing from his mouth and matting his white beard as he pleaded with them for mercy. Shamefaced, he retreated further and further back into a shopfront as their laughter echoed around the square, followed by the dull thuds of their relentless punches and kicks...

****

By the time Wolfgang reached Rachel's steps, his mind was in a frenzy. Dozens of shops had been broken into and hordes of vandals were brazenly carrying away armloads of stolen goods. He had passed two synagogues newly set alight; at the second of which, dozens of people were standing around throwing stones through the stained glass windows, while still more brought the Torah scrolls from inside and burned them in front of the weeping and helpless congregation of Jewish onlookers. Wolfgang hoped to God Rachel and her family had managed to barricade themselves safely inside their house and were doing the only thing they could do: pray for the healing light of morning.

Bounding up the stairs to her front door three at a time, Wolfgang rapped on the wood, firelight playing on its lion-headed knocker, while nervously glancing over his shoulder to make sure no-one had followed him. No reply. He pushed open the letterbox and shouted into the dark corridor.

"Rachel? Are you there? Mr. Braverman? Is anyone home?"

The silence hung there and was met with no response.

Wolfgang looked around for another way of entering, but this seemed to be the only entrance and there was no way of getting around the back. Were they inside hiding pretending not to be in? It was what he would probably do. Yet something about the house suggested it was empty. He decided to go to the only other address he knew in Berlin apart from his own... Ariel's house.

****

The journey to Ariel's house was equally fraught and littered with traps and snares. A huge house, not unlike his own, had tongues of flame licking greedily at every window sill and flower pot. The ground floor was totally ablaze: the floor where the servants... cooks, gardeners, chauffeur... and, of course, his grandmother, (who could no longer make it up the stairs with her arthritis) would be housed. He wondered how many people had inhabited the ground floor of the blazing house that he had watched burn from across the street.

Wolfgang then imagined the flames methodically working their way through the rest of his house: bounding up the wide wooden staircases sweeping up to the second and third floors-to the living quarters, his father's private study, his mother's dressing room and on to Wolfgang's own bedroom. The owner of this house must be a wealthy merchant- one of the many goldsmiths in the city, perhaps- to have so impressive an abode, Wolfgang considered as the flames began to overwhelm every window on the fourth floor and disappear in orange wisps among the stars. Wolfgang sent a little prayer up with them whispering how he hoped the family had all been away on business, or the children at boarding school, or *anywhere* but inside when the rioters had begun their wanton destruction. Mercifully, he could hear no screams over the crackle and hiss of the flames.

Wolfgang was breathing heavily by the time he reached the entrance to Ariel's courtyard. There was so much chaos swirling around him in a maelstrom of feverish hate, he now felt able to move between the havoc as easily as a ghost. Maybe his face had been blackened and disguised from the continual billowing smoke of burning shops, synagogues, homes... even some of the beautiful Opels and chrome-splashed and white-wheeled Horchs were now little more than blackening bonfires.

And, most of all, every pavement seemed to sparkle and crunch underfoot from the star-studded carpet of broken glass.

Most tragic of all though, were the number of motionless bodies Wolfgang ghosted past, slumped over against lampposts or lifelessly rag-dolled where they lay. But he had been in far too much of a hurry to find Rachel or Ariel to even dare to look more closely or investigate further. Even in the darkness, he could feel his cheeks burn with shame of his passing by on the other side, but he tried to convince himself he simply couldn't save everyone...

****

Darting into Ariel's courtyard, he ran headlong into something enveloping and damply cloying. Wolfgang resisted the temptation to scream; it felt like he had run into a giant spider's web but, as his senses fought to take control, he realised he had run headlong into a bedsheet, hung out to dry on one of the washing lines that crisscrossed the courtyard. He shrugged it off him and briefly smiled at the sheer ridiculousness of the situation... *all the devils of hell had been released and were running wild through the city and he had been scared by a bedsheet!* He bit his lip... maybe his father was right: he was not the right person for such an expedition... heroism did not coarse easily through his veins... he was still little more than a child. What was he thinking? He had been foolish to even consider he had the strength of character to see this through and rescue his beloved...

Suddenly, something stirred in the shadows bringing him back into the present. Wolfgang jumped back, his heart pounding and wishing he'd paused long enough at home to grab some kind of weapon to take with him. A shape emerged from the shadows...

Frozen to the spot, he was still trying to reason with himself which instinct it were better to follow: fight or flee... when Rachel fell into his arms weeping and squeezing him so tightly for a moment he couldn't speak until he had untangled himself from her grasp.

"*Rachel! You're safe!*" he gasped at last.

She looked as pale as a corpse, her eyes sunken into the sockets like wet black pebbles in the depths of a dark pond.

"I don't know where Mother and Father are... or Esther and Elizabeth... no-one was there when I got back," she blurted out, struggling to get the words out between sobs.

"So you came to Ariel's?"

She nodded.

"No-one here either I presume?"

She shook her head, the tears welling up again. Wolfgang saw the fear and confusion in her eyes, not just for herself but for the safety of her missing family.

"It's probably an awfully good sign they *weren't* there as that means they've found somewhere safer to hide," Wolfgang argued, trying to convince himself as much as her. "Or perhaps they couldn't make it back when all hell broke loose. Either way, they would want you to find somewhere safe too. You need to come with me…"

Wolfgang put his arm around Rachel, as if it were a cloak of invisibility, as he led her out onto the main street. He had no idea where he was going but, instinctively, began retracing his steps towards home: *But he could hardly take her home to his parents, could he?*

Then a vision of the summerhouse popped into his mind. It was far enough away from the house to be seen and wouldn't be used for at least another six or seven months. *It was perfect.*

***

The journey back home was slightly less fraught than the search for Rachel had been. Wolfgang wondered if you could become immune to absolutely anything if you were exposed to it for long enough?

The crowds were more sporadic now… it seemed most of the obvious targets had already been destroyed and many had seemingly started for home deeming the evening a job well done. However, a hard core still remained, unwilling for their night of revelry to be over. Wolfgang found if he strode confidently, grinning openly at anyone with whom he made eye contact, he could convince them he was one of them: a co-conspirator; a fellow barbarian at the very gates of Rome… and so successful did this strategy prove that, not once, did they look past him at the face of his silent companion, hidden behind a headscarf and trembling with fear.

****

To Wolfgang's delight and relief, he was soon leading Rachel down the coal-black side street that led back to his own house, their echoing footsteps the only noise to disturb the unearthly silence.

Wolfgang lifted the latch and showed her into the garden. After her recent ordeal, to Rachel, it now seemed she was entering a magical kingdom.

"Stay here!" Wolfgang whispered, as he opened the door to the summer house and perched her on a bench inside. Rachel closed her eyes and tried to ignore the images that had been burned forever onto her retinas that evening. Shaking, she grabbed him, imploring him not to leave her; not even for an instant.

"I need to go up to the main house," Wolfgang explained, "to get some blankets and pillows... and to make sure I haven't been missed. I won't be long."

Rachel seemed unsure but finally nodded in agreement. Wolfgang acknowledged her bravery with a kiss before taking her hands in his own and looking steadily in her eyes.

"I love you, Rachel Braverman and, when I return, I promise you I will *never* leave you again!"

Then he turned on his heels and Rachel rose and stood looking through the cobwebbed-panes at his silvery silhouette as it sprinted across the moonlit lawn. Despite the wild improbability of his rash promise, she couldn't help but smile at the sincerity of the sentiment.

The kitchen was still shrouded in darkness, but dark outlines on the surfaces suggested evidence of a meal having being recently consumed. Wolfgang could see plates piled high, some with the greasy remnants of bratwurst and sauerkraut or dumplings on them. The scene was most surprising. Dinner was normally a formal affair and dishes were certainly not left to fester until morning. It all smattered of a wolfed-down meal, eagerly devoured to feed an appetite for bigger prey.

Peering out onto the hallway, he saw a clear route ahead and skittered across the tiled floor with the nervousness of a new-born foal, forcing himself to tiptoe as he scaled the wide staircase up to the second floor.

"Wolfgang? Is that you?"

His Mother's voice rang down from the next floor up.

Wolfgang froze like one of the sculptures outside in the moon-kissed gardens. His heart was pumping. He did not want her investigating too closely; she always knew when he was lying.

"Just getting a glass of water," he replied in as casual a tone as he could muster.

Pausing long enough to be confident that no footsteps were making their way towards him, he quietly opened the door to his bedroom and slipped inside. He was about to start stripping the bed of its' bedding when he thought better of it: if someone happened to open the door and discover the bed stripped bare, they would raise the alarm. If, however, the bed was merely unmade and Wolfgang missing, there was a reasonable chance they would think he had gone to the bathroom or for a glass of milk. Quickly, he mussed up the bedsheets and opened the blanket box at the bottom of his bed before taking out pillows and thick blankets. Then he tiptoed back down the stairs, careful not to wake his ever-vigilant mother.

****

Lt. Tanzmann was physically shaking with the adrenaline pumping around his body. He had only returned to the house ten minutes or so ago and had surprised himself with the bubbling venom that had so easily come to the surface and spilt over the cauldron of hatred and vitriol he had kept hidden inside all these years. When he had walked back with the others to drink schnapps and toast the success of their evening, he had barely been able to contain himself. Yes! Helmut Tanzmann, who kept his heart under permanent lock and key, had been forced to come into the garden in order to smoke a cigarette and try to reel in his thrashing emotions...

He looked down at his outstretched hands: they were battered and bruised and the bloodstains looked black in the moonlight. His clothes stank of smoke and soot and the smell brought back vivid images of the last few hours. He had lost count of how many blows he had rained down; how many kicks he had aimed at midriffs; how many punches landed on hands pathetically attempting to protect faces; at balls of human flesh, made small and compact as hedgehogs in a vain attempt to minimise the pain, but really looking more like human footballs perfectly made for the boot of star striker Helmut Tanzmann.

It was all as clear as rainwater to him now. *Why hadn't he seen it before?* He had been born two years after the end of The Great War; two years after the humiliation of the *Treaty of Versailles* and the humbling of people like his father; heroes who had served the

Fatherland with distinction and who were left destitute as their reward. Helmut had grown up as a young boy in the Depression of the Twenties and Thirties, watching his father slip further and further into the pit of depression, becoming a shell of the decorated war hero, presented with his Iron Cross from the Kaiser himself. That man had slowly faded away in the hard times that followed defeat and the harsh imposition of reparation. But not everyone had suffered equally. *Oh no.* Some had preyed on the weak, on those who had fallen on hard times, and profited from it. *The Jews!* Young Helmut had stored away those years of frustration and anger, his bile growing with his impotence at being unable to rectify the injustice. But now he had a new father figure to replace the one he had lost: Adolf Hitler, who stood up for the ordinary German and would return to them everything that was rightfully theirs... *with interest. A new pound of flesh was to be taken now!*

****

Tanzmann was stubbing out his cigarette in the soil of an ornate garden urn when he saw the kitchen door open not twenty yards away from the patio he now stood on. Mildly curious at first, he watched with increasing interest as the boy of the house- a sad excuse of an off-spring compared to the greatness of the father, surely one of the Third Reich's next leading lights- steal across the lawn curiously laden down with blankets and pillows. Tanzmann wondered what on earth he might be doing with such objects and on such a glorious night as this? Playing some childish camping out game? Tanzmann snorted to himself, shaking his head in disbelief... that would be just like that Wirth boy; to be playing games when the most momentous night in recent German history was passing him by outside these very garden walls! Nevertheless, his curiosity was sufficiently pricked to follow him at a discreet distance and find out for sure what the young fool was up to.

Peering from between two trees, he watched Wolfgang light a lantern, then make up a bed from the cushions taken from the furniture dotted about the spacious summer house. Then he draped the blankets over his makeshift mattress and... suddenly, a figure reached up and kissed him, put her arms around his neck and pulled him lower and out of sight! Tanzmann started in surprise; *he had underestimated the boy!* He thought for a moment: he had only caught a glimpse of the girl, but he was sure it had been sufficient to know her identity. He didn't know her name, yet, but he had gone to school with her elder sister, Esther... her elder sister, *the Jew!*

Tanzmann's eyes narrowed. He had been looking for a way to ingratiate himself with SS Sturmbannfuhrer Wirth and, further down the line, feather his own nest and here an opportunity had fallen into his lap as fortuitously as a chick falling from its' nest into the stalking path of a cat. But, like the tender offspring, the news was delicate, fragile... would have to be imparted with tact and subtlety and at the precise moment, to avoid the messenger being shot for the delivering of unwanted news. Yes, he considered, as he stole back towards the noise of conversation and the smell of cigar smoke drifting through the open patio doors, this would require a *great* deal of care; his mind already quik-silvering a plan as unstoppable and beautiful as the iridescent flow of liquid mercury.

CHAPTER TEN

'DER GIFTPILZ'
('The Poisonous Mushroom')

'War is peace,
Freedom is slavery,
Ignorance is strength.'

Animal Farm
George Orwell

'Two plus two equals five.'

Winston Smith
'1984'
George Orwell

Thursday 10th November 1938,
In the summerhouse, Berlin.

Wolfgang didn't know how to feel as he walked to school that morning. Last night had felt like the end of the world; a time when anything was permissible because there might never be another tomorrow again.

But the stars, like old, rose-cut diamonds had given way to a tomorrow that had formed into a crimson dawn bleeding mournfully into the horizon; while Wolfgang's promise to Rachel had been broken even before breakfast.

Rachel had woken first to find herself still wrapped warmly in Wolfgang's arms and, for a fleeting moment, she had felt wonderfully, deliriously happy. Then the faintest of breezes blew in through an open window, playing pianissimo in the leaves... and it all came horrifically flooding back. She sat bolt upright with a gasp, causing Wolfgang to roll off their precarious arrangement of pillows and bang his head off the cold tiled floor.

"Ow!"

"Oh Wolfie! I'm so sorry!"

Cradling him in her arms, she kissed the offending bump on his crown, then kissed his forehead... his cheek....his smiling lips.

"I can forgive you *anything!*" he whispered.

"Then you must forgive me leaving now."

It was Wolfgang's turn to sit bolt upright.

"What? No! It's not safe! I forbid it!" he added desperately.

Despite everything, Rachel burst out laughing.

"Oh Wolfie, you know so little of love, and yet, in other ways, so very much!" she grinned mischievously, making Wolfgang blush furiously. "But I must go and find my parents and sisters, I must know that they have safely returned home; they must be sick with worry about *my* whereabouts too! You must see that?"

Wolfgang couldn't argue with the logic of her argument and, despite all his protestations, she insisted she went alone and promised to see him at school later to share what news she had managed to find out.

"We must try to give the impression of some sort of normality, so as not to raise suspicions about where we spent last night... though these are as far from normal times as it is, perhaps, possible to get," she added, before kissing him gently on the lips and leaving with a backward glance through the back gate.

****

That had been a little over three hours ago and, since then, Wolfgang had returned all the incriminating evidence to the blanket box, dressed and appeared downstairs for breakfast as if nothing out of the ordinary had happened. He had kissed his mother goodbye, picked up his packed lunch and left the house as though this surreal world he found himself immersed in was all perfectly normal...

Hurrying to school, he barely noticed the regular crunch of glass underfoot with almost every step. But, as soon as he entered the school gates, Wolfgang knew something was dreadfully wrong. The playground resembled a ghost town.

Where the hell was everybody?

Wolfgang hurried across the creepily empty school yard, normally buzzing with life and activity as students milled about, laughing and gossiping; perhaps idly kicking a ball or playing games chalked on the playground floor. Quickly, he strode down the corridor towards his classroom and was surprised to see the class already seated at their desks. *What was going on?* His teacher, Herr Beckmann saw him gawping through the glass of the door and opened it briefly, signalling for him to enter and take his normal place. That was when something even stranger occurred to him: about half of the class were missing and it was immediately apparent which half were missing- the *Jewish* half.

"Come in, come in, Wirth; hurry up and take your seat boy!" said the stern schoolmaster, puffed up with his own self-importance and clearly irritated at being interrupted, mid-flow. He seemed so excited about something he could barely contain his delight.

Wolfgang sat down and glanced around at his remaining classmates. Most looked bemused and a little scared at this bizarre turn of events and, doubtless, from the scene of devastation and carnage that had greeted them on their walk to school. Forlornly, he glanced at Rachel and Ariel's empty desks and girded himself for the news Herr Beckmann was so keen to impart.

"Our glorious Fuhrer, Adolf Hitler," Herr Beckmann beamed, "has decided in his ultimate wisdom, that Aryans and Jews will be educated separately from this day forward."

A couple of students gasped and many exchanged anxious and confused glances. Others looked on with smug, satisfied sneers and folded arms.

"And to celebrate," Herr Beckmann continued, "the Fuhrer has generously provided us with *brand new books* to start our new studies."

As he spoke, he strode up and down each row, keenly observing the slightest hint of dissent as he distributed a brand new exercise book to write in and two new reading texts to each child. Out of curiosity, Wolfgang risked a sneaky look inside his own desk. Lifting it only a crack he bent down to peer inside... *it had been emptied overnight*! All previous work had vanished. His new education was clearly meant to replace everything that had gone before...

He looked doubtfully at the first book the teacher had proudly laid before him, like an offering to the Gods. It was entitled *'Der Giftpilz.'*

"*'The Poisonous Mushroom'?*" whispered Gerhard from the desk behind, "sounds really boring!"

Wolfgang smiled and nodded his agreement quickly while Herr Beckmann had his back to them, distributing the last of the books. He shushed them irritably, then turned to face the class with a flourish.

"Open *'The Poisonous Mushroom'* first," insisted Herr Beckmann, "we will be having a 'Jewish lesson' every day," he explained, "starting today."

The boys obeyed and were greeted with a picture of a young boy, Franz, picking wild mushrooms in the woods. Wolfgang smiled briefly at the memory: it was something he had done on a number of occasions with his own mother- along with picking raspberries and strawberries and wild flowers- and was one of the few happy memories he had of her back in happier times in Munich... It harkened back to a past when she'd actually made time for him and seemed to love him completely; a time before she was totally devoted and consumed by being the perfect Nazi wife, hosting perfect functions for the perfect Fatherland. Just as the moment when the inextricable linking of the words 'career' and 'soldier' had been the moment when he undoubtedly lost his father so, when his mother had stopped taking him into the countryside as a child, was the time when he stopped having a mother that took that particular role seriously.

Wolfgang was brought back down to earth with a bang by Herr Beckmann slamming a ruler down hard on his desk.

"*Are you listening, boy? Have you even considered how much your Fuhrer has done for you today? Righting the wrongs of generations in a single night! It is nothing short of a miracle!*"

"Yes sir," Wolfgang mumbled, staring at the open page of the book, with little Franz still smiling innocently up at him.

Herr Beckmann regained his composure and went on to explain how Franz's mother showed him how several varieties of mushrooms were edible, while some were poisonous. The boy listened attentively as his mother compared the good mushrooms to good people and the harmful mushrooms to bad people. Just like the poisonous mushrooms are hard to distinguish from the edible, so the Jews are hard to spot from Non-Jews, as they take many forms, she explained. Horror-struck, Wolfgang followed the ways to recognise a Jew as described in his new text book: A Jew is a flat-footed devil, with long arms, thick lips, dark hair and a shifty look. He is bulky and misshapen with a sloping forehead and a crooked nose, heavy beard, bulging frog-like eyes...

Wolfgang looked around at his classmates to see if they were falling for this abhorrent nonsense. Worryingly, some were looking wide-eyed at the images as though they were finally having their eyes opened to the terrible truth about the children whose birthday parties they had attended and who they might have played hopscotch with only the day before. Wolfgang pictured the beautiful, raven-haired girl he had just spent the night with and smirked at how utterly ludicrous it all was. He smiled... *but knew it wasn't the slightest bit funny.*

In contrast, of course, the book ended with images of Aryans: upright and handsome; blond and well-muscled; bare-chested and courageous. Irritatingly, many of them looked a lot like Helmut Tanzmann, except they were all smiling and Wolfgang had never seen him smile... not once.

Before break, they also read the second book, which was called *Reinhard the Fox*. Unsurprisingly, the second book followed a depressingly similar vein; the long snout of the fox being likened to the protruding nose of the Jew. At break, the other boys were tenser than usual and looking for an outlet for their anxiety. They knew massive upheavals were taking place but didn't really understand the full ramifications of what was going on and how it might affect them, so they mercilessly taunted a boy named Ronan Fuchs. Unfortunately for him, the translation of 'Fuchs' was 'fox'... which was easily enough to make him stand out for abuse after what they had just read.

"Are you sure *you* aren't a Jew, Fuchs?" Hans laughed, nudging Gert, while others whispered and sniggered behind cupped hands.

"If you are," warned Gottfried, "don't sleep too soundly in your bed tonight!"

Fuchs turned puce as he stewed in his impotent rage and embarrassment. He had always received a certain amount of ribbing from his classmates because of his unusual Christian name. The rumour was that his father was German but his mother hailed from a family of travelling gypsies; although this was something he strenuously denied, to the point of getting into a number of fights defending the dubious honour of his family tree. Now, unfairly it seemed, this was one more slur that would probably result in more fisticuffs.

"Don't worry about me," he snarled angrily, "if I come across any Jews tonight... *I'll kill them myself!*"

As he made his threat, he drew his finger across his throat as if to emphasise his intent. Shocked, everyone fell silent and, even more unsettled than before, reluctantly began to drift back to class.

****

The remainder of the day was torturous and, seemingly, endless. Normal classes continued after break and on into the afternoon, but Wolfgang couldn't concentrate and had no interest in Trigonometry and History when far more important questions remained agonisingly unanswered: *where was Rachel and was she still safe? What about Ariel? Had their families got caught up in last night's chaos?*

The moment the bell went, Wolfgang snatched up his school bag and ran...

CHAPTER ELEVEN

THE STRAW THAT BROKE THE BULLY'S BACK

'He that seeks trouble never misses.'

William Golding

'Use only that which works, and take it from any place you can find it.'

Bruce Lee
Tao of Jeet Kune Do

June 1999,
Tuesday morning, Harry's new school.

Mr. Murdoch finished the register and closed his mark book with a sigh of resignation. Harry had thought of little else but his conversation with William and Gabriel and was no nearer deciding what he was going to do when confronted by the bullies again with their criminal ultimatum; he supposed he'd just have to play it by ear.

"There are no notices today," Mr. Murdoch announced glancing at his watch. "I need to have a… quick word with another member of staff for a minute, so silent reading until I return please."

Mr. Murdoch then grabbed his *'Best Teacher in the World'* coffee mug and hurried off. Harry looked back anxiously; he would now be left unprotected for as long as it took the kettle to boil.

Murdoch's footsteps had barely faded down the corridor in the direction of the staffroom, when the scrape of Adam Kellerman's chair behind him alerted Harry's attention. Out of the corner of his eye, he caught sight of Tania Tonks' sneer and instinctively knew what was coming…

Kellerman turned a chair round and drew it up to Harry's desk. He plonked himself down on it noisily and rested his chin on the backrest. The sharp spike of panic registered in Harry's brain as he tried desperately to stay calm.

"Tonight," Kellerman hissed, "you can do it tonight. We know an old dear on the estate who teaches piano to nice little boys and girls. Her last lesson is at nine o'clock and then the old biddy goes straight to bed. Give it twenty minutes, then break in through the ground floor window; she always leaves it open in the summer- probably to get rid of the smell of rotten granny! We know this because we often kick a football up against her wall until she phones the Police or comes out to chase us away! Steal whatever you find that's worth flogging and meet us round the back of the *Spar* to hand over what you've got. Got it?"

Harry had listened patiently to the whole plan without interrupting. It had given him time to think whilst also allowing him to hear the entirety of what they had in store for him. It proved to be the final straw in his decision-making process.

"No," he announced simply.

"No?" Kellerman replied, the first crease of doubt crossing his forehead as he tried to determine which part of the plan he was rejecting: Meeting afterwards? Or handing over his loot?

"No to what?" he muttered, seeking clarification.

"No to all of it," Harry shrugged, the sudden resolve in his voice amazing even himself. "I'm not doing it and I'm not joining your poxy little gang- got it? So you can pass that on to Harris and the rest of his hangers-on."

Kellerman actually *snorted*, he was so surprised. Then he got to his feet and his expression changed to one of violent intent.

"What you say to me?" he sneered, his fingers already curling into expectant fists, his legs bending slightly at the knee, poised to spring forward and land the first blow.

Tanya jumped up and clambered onto her desk, gleefully anticipating a fight.

"You're gonna get it now, dickhead!" she squealed, her little piggy eyes glinting, her spotty cheeks so flushed the yellow of her zits seemed to glow phosphorescent, as though they would all, simultaneously, spontaneously combust.

Harry pushed his chair back and stood up, preparing himself for whatever would come next. Suddenly, Maggie sprung up out of her chair and called across to Kellerman, fear etched into the grooves of her forehead.

"Pick on someone you own size, you big bully!"

Harry looked across in surprise and gratitude, but simply smiled back at her, a strange calm spreading over him like some kind of cape of invincibility.

"You're wasting your breath;" he explained to her, "you can't reason with an idiot- they removed his soul to make way for extra bully!"

Adam Kellerman looked bemused for a second while he processed this surprising turn of events and desperately tried to think of a witty retort. When he failed to come up with anything, snarling like a feral animal, he resorted to what he did best... mindless violence.

****

The fight unfolded like some kind of Bruce Lee movie in surreal slow motion. Harry saw Adam coming for him and, grabbing the first thing that came to hand, picked up his chair. One second he was *thinking* of hitting him with it, the next the chair was making a satisfying crack as it broke into pieces from the impact on Kellerman's skull and shoulders. Pieces of wood shattered everywhere, leaving him holding two legs and half a broken seat. Adam Kellerman hit the deck like a floored boxer out for the count of a hundred, let alone ten! Tanya Tonks' mouth gaped open so wide her chewing gum rolled right off her tongue and splatted inaudibly on the wooden floor. Then, screaming like a banshee, she leapt off the desk and went for Harry herself; nails poised like talons and fire shooting from her eyes...

What she hadn't seen was Maggie leaning out from her desk. As she flew past, Maggie stuck out a leg and Tanya was sent sprawling into three or four desks in a cacophony of confusion and shrieks of fury.

"Not so fast, *bitch*!" Maggie muttered under her breath as a dazed Tania lay rag-dolled on the floor.

Into this utter carnage walked Mr. Murdoch, cradling a steaming coffee in one hand, the door handle still gripped in the other. Like a driver hitting the brakes but knowing without a shadow of a doubt that he's not going to stop in time, everything that followed only took seconds, but felt like hours to Mr. Murdoch. First, he felt the coffee cup slip from his grasp and the contents start to spill from the cup, even before the handle on his *'Best Teacher in the World'* mug snapped off as it made contact with the floor. Then he began to break into some sort of a haphazard jog, but found himself zigzagging between the unconscious Adam Kellerman, a zen-like Harry still holding onto a chair leg, and a woozy Tania groaning from underneath a table...

Eventually, he summoned up enough wit to grab Christopher Strainrod, a quiet, mousy boy miraculously still in his seat at the back of the class and screamed at him:

"Get the head! And a First Aider! Run, boy, *run*!"

CHAPTER TWELVE

SAD VIOLINS IN THE BANDSTAND

'Look before you leap,
For snakes among sweet flowers do creep.'

Proverb

'Anticipation is the carrot suspended before the jackass to keep him moving forward.
Horror is what he would see if he took his eyes off the carrot.'

'The Walking Drum'
Louis L'Amour

June 1939,
The Bandstand, Berlin.

Wolfgang and Rachel sat in the bandstand looking out at the beautiful summer's day spread out tantalisingly before them and oblivious to the stormy war clouds gathering behind its' summery façade.

"Remember our first meeting in this park, Wolfie?" Rachel smiled, glancing over at him.

Wolfgang winced.

"Don't remind me; you must have thought me such a baby!"

"Of course not!" Rachel shook her head, "I was concerned for you, that's all."

"Concerned they'd let a little cry baby out all on his own!" Wolfgang protested.

Despite herself, Rachel giggled and Wolfgang shook his head, embarrassed at the still vivid memory.

The months between *Kristallnacht* in the early part of November and now had been both difficult and wonderful for the pair of them and they reflected on the cataclysmic changes to their lives as they talked in secretive whispers in one of the few places they could still meet in relative safety. Often, Ariel would join them, like in the old days back at school but, on this particular day, he was being kept busy doing chores for his father, so they sat alone; hand in hand.

****

After Wolfgang had ran out of school that first day after *Kristallnacht,* he had sprinted all the way to Rachel's house and found her on her front step with Ariel, disconsolate and crying onto his shoulder. As soon as she caught sight of him, she leapt to her feet and sprang into his open arms, laughing and crying at the joy of the three of them being back together but also distraught at the horrible day she had experienced. In a whispered gabble she recounted everything that had happened since she had left him with only the dawn's opaque light for company. Running with the breaking morning chasing at her heels, she had miraculously bounded straight into her frantic father near the Charite Hospital, wringing his anxious hands and pacing the streets like an expectant father, looking everywhere he could think of for his lost daughter. In desperation, he had tried the local hospitals, unsure whether to hope she was there and not too badly hurt or whether to dare she had found safe haven through the carnage elsewhere.

Overjoyed, he clasped her hand all the way back to their home, explaining how they had been out visiting her sick Aunt Zelda when the first signs of trouble flared. It soon became clear the Jewish neighbourhoods were being targeted and it was simply too dangerous to attempt to get back home. Mother had been frantic about Rachel, but father explained how he had to ensure the rest of his family were safe before he could start the search for her.

"It was the hardest thing I have ever had to do, but Mother was convinced you had a Guardian Angel looking over you keeping you safe, just like during Passover," he shrugged and smiled down at her, "I had to believe in *her* faith to keep *me* sane."

Rachel nodded and smiled back to show him he had done the right thing.

"So, we headed for the Albrechtsen's in the Wilmersdorf District. We've been friends for years and I trust Jakob with my life. As I'd hoped, he took us in, fastened the shutters and hid us in the cellar, just in case anyone came calling. Once everyone was settled, I borrowed some of his clothing and, without my yellow star, came to look for you."

Benjamin Braverman stopped in the street and took his daughter in his arms and wept.

"I searched all night but couldn't find you. I was afraid to go back to Albrechtsen's; *I swore to your mother, I wouldn't come home alone.*"

****

Once the family were reunited, the harbingers of bad news arrived one following the other in a grisly procession retelling the awful night's events in shocked whispers: the murders; the looted shops; the burnt synagogues and destruction of the holy Torahs...

The eerie stunned silences throughout the whole of the Jewish District were punctuated only by the sporadic cries of grief as news reached people of the brutal death of a loved one. Rachel and Ariel were also told of their expulsion from Wolfgang's school by a proclamation delivered in the city square before being subsequently told to report to the temporary building that would serve as their own schoolroom from that day forward. Rachel had silently wept all day long, fearing she had already seen Wolfgang for the final time.

****

The terrible night that followed, Thursday November 10th 1938, was at least as debauched as the previous one; if not worse. The Braverman's and Koplovitz's sheltered in their cellars, holding hands around a lighted candle, praying and putting their faith in the Almighty. There was little else to do. Mercifully, he spared them a second time; but nothing could have prepared them for the events that would unfold over the following days and weeks. Tens of thousands of German Jews were arrested and sent to work camps; Ariel's uncle Barzillai was forced to fire the Jewish workers in his shoe-making factory and then the Nazis forced him to sell the business that had been in the family for six generations to a non-Jewish German for a fraction of its worth. The final insult was that the only job he could secure was as a lowly paid worker in the same factory he had so recently owned. Many Jews found the humiliations too much to endure and committed suicide; others naively thought it couldn't get any worse and tried to see it through...

On November 12th, the Nazi's imposed a fine of a billion Reichsmarks on the Jewish community and a demand they make reparation. However, they were also barred from collecting insurance for the damages. Thousands of Jews tried to leave, packing what they could and vanishing into the night under the cold shield of darkness.

The Braverman's and Koplovitz's decided to stay...

****

When Wolfgang and Rachel met up, they usually arranged their illicit liaisons for straight after school. Between them, they had invented a plethora of fictitious after-school activities: revision sessions, sports teams, Art club, exam preparation, Drama club... anything that allowed them to spend precious hours together without arousing the suspicions of watchful parents. And even those opportunities were further restricted following the imposing of the curfew on Jews, which meant Rachel had to be back home before nine o'clock each evening and couldn't leave the house until six the next morning. Rachel joked how she was like Cinderella, but with a particularly strict Fairy Godmother!

Still, the bandstand remained a firm favourite: a beautiful little pagoda and an oasis of tranquil civilisation, flanked on all sides by oblongs of flowerbeds in regimented rows. And, in amongst it all, two figures, kissing and talking in hushed whispers beneath the spider-webbed shadows, stockpiling memories while they still could...

Rachel broke away from a lingering kiss and sighed. Her lips felt almost rubbery and numb from the sheer volume of kisses they had shared in the last half an hour and she could taste Wolfie when she ran her tongue over her upper lip. But there was no point delaying telling him her news any longer; he needed to know.

"Mother and Father are seriously thinking of leaving," she blurted out, unsure how he would react.

Wolfgang's eyes narrowed a little as he contemplated this unexpected news, before he attempted to put on a brave matter-of-fact face.

"They've been saying that on and off for months!"

He leaned forward to kiss her again but, this time, although she allowed him in, it was different. She was holding back, determined he would hear her out and she had sealed off her emotions from him as clearly as if an invisible layer of wax lay between his lips and hers. He broke away; hurt.

"What is it?"

"They're serious this time. They've already written to my aunt and uncle in England; asked if they will put us up for a while, until we can find our feet."

Wolfgang felt his blood chill and solidify in his veins. He couldn't lose her; *not now*. He had almost lost her once and that had broken his heart into as many pieces as the shards of glass broken on *Kristallnacht.* He wasn't about to let it happen again.

"Then let's run away together!" he announced, "elope- like Romeo and Juliet!"

Rachel put her hand over her mouth and stifled a giggle.

"And where would we go? You've no job, no money." Then, as an afterthought she added, "besides, Romeo and Juliet didn't elope...

he got banished and they both ended up committing suicide; not the greatest of examples, Wolfie!"

Wolfgang blushed and shrugged.

"Well, you know what I mean," he mumbled.

She took his head in her hands and smiled, "yes, I do. I know exactly what you mean," and she kissed him. Instantly, Wolfgang knew the invisible wax separating them before had melted away from her lips...

Silently, Rachel took him by the hand and led him down the bandstand steps and into the densely wooded area that skirted the rear of their lover's nest. Night, who had been germinating silently in the shadows, was now spreading her shadowy fingers across the manicured lawns and neat flower beds and, soon, they would be lost to anyone who might care to come looking for them.

Together they lay under the star-strewn sky with the soft moss for a bed and, with almost telepathic synchronicity, forgot the world beyond their gaze. To Rachel, they were two leaves dancing round the park to a wind unfelt by anyone else. To Wolfgang, they soared between the stars, tearing the very sky asunder with their comet's tail, so that even angels lost their footing and fell through the cracks in the floor of Heaven.

Afterwards, they lay silent and untroubled by conversation, alone in the absolute certainty that love provides.

Except they weren't alone...

If they had only dragged their eyes away from each other for a moment, they may have seen the viper slithering through the undergrowth of their Eden, enviously watching their every caress, eavesdropping in on their adolescent scheming.

Lt. Tanzmann had bided his time and his patience was about to be rewarded. Hidden, subtle as a stick insect on a branch, he had overheard Wolfgang's romantic gesture of elopement, and took it as gospel. *Now* he had something to report back: he had discovered their affair and would feel obliged to tell Sturnbannfuhrer Wirth before his son could flee in the night and bring even more disgrace to the family name. And then he would be justly rewarded. He was sick of being at the cat's table at meal times, furthest away from importance and unjustly neglected. Oh no. Now he would be seated at the Captain's table and his previously underrated talents fully appreciated from now on…

Softly, he withdrew, already spinning his words of revelation into a web of ruination for them all…

CHAPTER THIRTEEN

ONE STEP FORWARD, TWO STEPS BACK

'In life, I regret the things I didn't do
Far more than the missteps I made along the way.'

David Stanley

June 1999,
Tuesday, after school; the Headteacher's office.

Harry sat in the Headteacher's office zoning in and out of her seemingly endless droning on and focusing instead on the neat layout of her room and what he could deduce from the random contents. Mrs Butts had seemed kinder than most of the Heads he'd had the brief misfortune to be ruled over. Her eyes betrayed an empathy with the children, even though the smart suit, shoulder length bob and perfectly manicured nails betrayed her ambition and desire to be taken seriously in what was still very much a male-orientated world; once you reached the heady heights of Headteacher, at least. Her desk was minimalist. With a big note pad laid dead centre, like a giant ink-blotter from olden days, while everything else- pens, stapler, post-its- were arranged in perfect symmetry to that central start point. It was room Feng Shui in miniature. Behind her, three filing cabinets stood like bouncers guarding the school's precious data and, above them, trophies for football, netball, rugby, cricket... even one for tug-of-war, stood in freshly gleaming rows, reflecting the sporting as well as academic prowess the Head was keen to imply. But how would all those psychological deductions reflect in her attitude to his violent outburst, Harry wondered?

He tuned back in to the frequency of her voice and listened in to see how things were going so far. To be fair, he had been expecting far more of an angry tirade than he was getting; in fact, her voice was surprisingly conciliatory. Still, it was doing little to ease the furious glare on the face of his mother and, even worse, the look of disappointment etched across every muscle of Nan's face. To the side of them perched Mr. Murdoch, looking a mixture of anxious and faintly embarrassed; probably concerned that his neglect of his charges to satisfy his caffeine addiction was going to come out sooner or later and he would be hauled over the coals for being AWOL from his classroom when the fight had broken out.

"...and whilst it has been brought to my attention that Adam Kellerman, Paul Harris and a number of other students at this school, have been exerting pressure and threatening violence against Harry in order to force him to commit criminal acts..."

As he listened in, he had to stop himself smiling. It seemed bizarre to hear the Head recount the events of the past couple of weeks. It didn't feel real somehow; as though he was watching the news, rather than hearing events that had directly involved him. Harry deduced it had probably been Maggie who had told either Murdoch or the Head about Paul and his cronies; *he* had certainly said nothing, it usually only made things a lot, lot worse.

"Why on earth didn't you tell me?" hissed his Mom.

He sighed and glanced around the room as the first flush of crimson filled his cheeks. *Because you'd come up the school and try and sort it and end up making things ten times worse.* But he couldn't say that, could he? He glanced again at Mr. Murdoch whose expression was unfathomable, so he went back to analysing the contents of the room and waiting for it all to be over.

"...would normally be an automatic permanent exclusion..."

Harry heard his Mom and Nan audibly gasp in shock at the unthinkable prospect.

"...given the mitigating circumstances and, whilst this degree of violence cannot be tolerated, no matter how justified Harry may feel he was..."

Harry was suddenly aware of a communal holding of breath as everyone awaited the Head's final judgement; like a TV court drama when the Head Juror stands up and announces their final verdict... *guilty or not guilty*? It was excruciatingly agonising and yet, Harry was surprised to note, he felt a strange thrill at the excitement of it all. Besides, the worst case scenario wasn't *all* bad news... If he were to be permanently excluded, at least his troubles with Harris and his minions would be over... although his mother and Nan would never let him forget it and make his life a living hell for, at least, the next decade. Their never-ending shame would doubtless be chiselled onto their tombstones so he could continue to feel guilty every time he lay flowers on their graves! It was difficult to know which was the lesser of two evils...

He noticed Mrs. Butts was speaking directly to him now, so quickly tuned back in...

"Nevertheless, this is out of my hands. There is a Governors' meeting next week. Your position as a pupil of this school will be discussed at that meeting. Until then, you are suspended."

With that, Mrs. Butts sat back in her chair and sighed. She was done. A stony silence ensued as everyone took on board her words and waited for something to happen. It was Nan who, surprisingly, galvanised them into action, rising from her seat and announcing loudly:

"Thank you for your time, Mrs. Butts and for being most fair with our Harry. Have no fear that he will be punished for his part in all of this, but I trust you will also do your best to fight his corner at the Governors' Meeting next week, considering the atrocious treatment he has had to face at the hands of members of *your* school community."

Harry and Mom blinked at her sudden and erudite speech, which had ended in more of an instruction than a request. They both rose with her, as did a relieved-looking Mr. Murdoch, who got the door and showed them out.

Not another word was spoken until they were well off school premises and had walked almost halfway home. Mom had set off at a furious pace in front, clearly trying to work out some of her anger before they got home, while Nan was breathlessly trying to keep pace a few steps behind. Harry had wisely let them go; his shadow dawdling idly behind him in no rush to get back home for the inevitable re-trial that would be played out around the kitchen table, along with the apportioning of guilt and enforcement of suitable punishments.

When they did eventually walk past the end of William and Gabriel's house, Harry wondered what they would make of his actions. He would find out soon enough, he decided, promising himself he would go and see them as soon as possible. He had a sneaking suspicion they would probably think doing something, *anything,* had been better than doing nothing at all...

CHAPTER FOURTEEN

TANZMANN AT THE CAPTAIN'S TABLE

'War is what happens when language fails.'

Margaret Atwood.

June 1939,
The Wirth household; dinner time.

Apparently, the grand old Berlin house the Wirth family currently resided in had, until recently, been the home of a very well-known cabaret star, whose reputation and exploits, both on and off stage, were the stuff of legend amongst the Berlin gossip columnists. Perhaps in keeping with the wild and extravagant nature of her life, her death had been equally tempestuous, having been found strangled with one of her own silk stockings in her theatre dressing room; the gaudy bulbs bordering her mirror backlighting her dead body as perfectly as any Lighting Director could have managed. As Wolfgang sat at the dining room table, he couldn't help but wonder what scandalous conversations might have soaked into the wood-panelled walls over the years and whether any of them could match the conversation that was so clearly brewing to a kettle-screaming climax this very evening...

Sturnbannfuhrer Christian Wirth was apoplectic with rage and, despite his attempts to conceal it by, thus far, adhering to the social conventions of a dignified dinner, absolutely everyone knew it. The serving staff, Katarina and Susanna knew it, as did the Head Butler, Kurt; hence the tiptoeing around taking extra special care not to spill a single drop of vintage earthy Bordeaux or carelessly ladle a spoonful of butter beans into anyone's lap, thus presenting a perfect excuse for the bubbling over of his seething wrath. Mother sat with a typically pained expression, putting on a brave front and pretending against all logic and evidence that nothing untoward was happening. Wolfgang pushed his food around his plate wishing that whatever was going to happen would get on and happen so they could all get it over with.

Grandmother and Lt. Tanzmann made up the quorum; Grandmother seemingly oblivious to everything other than the asparagus soup three inches from her nose... and Tanzmann: Tanzmann, who sat with a supercilious smirk on his face that Wolfgang couldn't decipher; other than the fact he was always smug and self-congratulatory, whether there was a good reason for it or not.

"Not hungry, darling?" Mrs. Wirth enquired, hoping to deflect her husband's anger by a change of subject and by defiantly pushing the corners of her smile even further out towards her ears.

Wolfgang shrugged one shoulder sullenly and pushed a mouthful of food through barely parted lips in a half-hearted attempt to appease her.

Christian Wirth took a big gulp of wine and eyed his son distastefully.

"You should appreciate your food more, Wolfgang. When you find yourself out in the field with only a handful of rounds of ammunition left and a mouthful of food left in your pack, *then* you will appreciate every morsel and rue the day you wasted precious food when it was in plentiful supply."

"I can't help it if I'm not very hungry," Wolfgang replied petulantly, unwilling to be rebuked in front of Tanzmann and his relentless sneer. He was no longer the child his father despaired at- let his father's rage come... he *dared* it, because there was a resolve burning within him that awed and even frightened him now and which craved to be given a voice.

"We will *all* need to be hungry to prove ourselves worthy of the Fatherland!" his father announced, already growing red in the face in his burgeoning frustration, "war is coming- war on many fronts and on a scale greater even than The Great War!"

"Well, who says I'm joining the Army?" Wolfgang taunted.

That proved to be the straw that broke the Sturmbannfuhrer's back. Wirth slammed his fist down on the table so the wine glasses danced a jig on the tablecloth and then spilt their full-bodied contents in red bloody stains beneath. Kurt rushed forward but Wirth sent him back with a dismissive wave.

"But that *is* where you are wrong!" his father shouted, "did you think I was going to let you embarrass yourself and drag the family name through the mud a moment longer? I *know* what you have been doing with that Jewish slut and it ends *now! Tonight! I have enrolled you into the services of the Fatherland... and you leave first thing in the morning!*"

The table fell into a stunned silence for what seemed an eternity... then everything erupted simultaneously! Wolfgang felt his mouth fall slack and the grip on his knife and fork tighten as his mind whirled… his mother gasped and brought her hands over her mouth as tears spilled from her eyes…grandmother looked up from her soup, spectacles a little steamed up and completely bemused as to the sudden chaos… and Tanzmann sat back in his chair delightedly and watched it all unfold like a scene in a movie.

"He's too young!" Mother cried out, rising to her feet, her napkin falling to the ground beneath her seat, "he's still a child!"

"If he is old enough to sneak around behind his parents' back, he is old enough to attempt to restore some family honour."

Mother looked around the table for support and, finding none, did the unthinkable: *stood up to her husband*: "he cannot go, I … *forbid it!*"

Christian Wirth moved with the speed of a jackal. Before Wolfgang could even react, he had risen from his chair, and brought the back of his hand across Mother's face, sending her sprawling to one side, grabbing the tablecloth as she fell. Every remaining un-spilt glass tottered and fell, shattering or spilling their contents, while the plates closest to her followed her over the precipice of the table's edge. Wolfgang rose and found the knife still in his grip. He moved towards his flushed father, spittle caught on the old man's chin…and then he caught sight of Tanzmann's expression… and suddenly *realised*. It was *Tanzmann* who had betrayed him to his father, not some local gossip spread by servants… *Tanzmann, that baboon-blooded, deceitful scoundrel*! And it also occurred to Wolfgang, with a sudden and startling clarity, like a beam of light bathing him in understanding and wisdom, that this loathsome creature would love nothing more than for him to sever the last strands of the pitiful relationship he held with his father, so he could swoop in like a cuckoo, and take his place. *No, he decided, he would not give him the pleasure.*

Fighting back his anger, he resumed his position at the table, as Kurt and Katarina and Susanna swept in to clear up the mess and help Mother back onto her seat, her hand still pressed to her cheek; a look of utter shock on her face; a trickle of blood escaping the corner of her mouth and dripping onto the fur collar of her extremely expensive dress.

"Childhood is a disease," Father was saying, "a sickness that, thankfully, the Army can cure you of. Considering the urgency of the situation the Fatherland finds itself in, I have secured permission for you to enlist immediately with my old regiment. You leave for Basic Training at dawn, so I suggest you go to your room and pack."

With his heart pounding so loud he found it hard to believe the rest of the table could not hear it, (like in that Edgar Allan Poe story and, surely, *he* was going mad too) he stood deliberately and dropped his napkin onto his plate of half-eaten food. The maelstrom of emotion roaring in his ears was deafening but, as he passed Tanzmann, he calmly made a promise to himself: he would get revenge on Tanzmann for this, *no matter how long it took.*

CHAPTER FIFTEEN

A GLOW-WORM OF HOPE

'Praise bounteous providence if you will
That grants even an ogre
A tiny glow-worm tenderness encapsulated
In icy caverns of a cruel heart.'

'Vultures'
Chinua Achebe

'We are all worms, but I do believe
I am a glow-worm.'

Winston Churchill

June 1999,
The Robinson household.

Hannah Robinson stood with her hands in a bowl of washing up and stared out the window into the shapeless black of the garden. The harsh bulb over the kitchen table bounced back her reflection in a tired unflattering light. She sighed. She looked exhausted, she concluded; old before her time... and most *definitely* at the end of her tether.
It wasn't supposed to have panned out like this... a single mother, struggling to make ends meet, questioning every decision she made, reliant on her mother to keep her sane. How easy it had been, all those years ago, when she had spotted Mark in a pub, playing pool, strutting around the table, laughing and joking with his mates, swigging from his pint of lager between shots, glancing over at her and smiling when no-one else was looking. He had looked so perfect in his uniform... strong, lean, with right on his side somehow... she had been swept up in the image, not considered the long term... the months alone when he was on a Tour of Duty, the sleepless nights imagining him being blown up by some roadside IED...

Still, she'd loved being a new Mom... the little white baby-grows; the warm baked bread smell of the top of his head as he lay sleeping on her stomach; the way hers and Harry's little eyes locked while he slurped greedily on his bottle. She smiled as she pictured him now: tiny mouth slack, arms flung back, hands tightly bunched into little clammy fists as he slept in his cot

But it hadn't been easy for Harry... for either of them: moving from base to base and then, when Mark went to War and was involved in all those... covert operations... she had effectively become a mother of two; an introverted teenager and a shell-shocked husk of the man she'd once loved. She'd tried to bring him out of it, of course, tried to make allowances... God knew she had... but he was lost at the bottom of some deep ocean and her words couldn't permeate so many fathoms down. When he had left, she had fallen apart, but Mother had stepped in, picked up the pieces, put the jigsaw back together and even added in some glue to the puzzle. But now *this...*

What should she do with Harry?

She felt an overwhelming disappointment that he hadn't felt able to confide in her; that she didn't know what her son was going through or what, seemingly, he was capable of. She had always tried to be there for him but missing out on a father figure must be tough for him.

Was that why he had gone off the rails so badly?

Was she exaggerating the situation? After all, he had been a victim in all of this too; only she hadn't known the full extent of it then. She should have realised when he wouldn't let them call the police... but she was so overwhelmed with everything as it was... the long hours at work, money worries, fear of being on her own for the rest of her life.

Perhaps if she'd met someone else, someone who could have taken an interest in Harry, taken him up the football...he might have cheered up, settled down more, made friends... She had, briefly, tried dating, but the one short relationship she'd half-heartedly begun had quickly fizzled and died. It was blatantly obvious that Phil was no keeper. He had been a mere tourist in their lives and, in Harry's case, not a very welcome one at that. Even Nan had not seemed very keen. She had always liked the fact that Mark was a soldier; there was something honourable about such a profession. Phil, on the other hand, sold poor quality second hand cars at exorbitant prices from a garage just off the ring road that had flags hanging outside it like it thought it was some kind of castle. The whole affair had lasted a fortnight.

She blew out her cheeks in exasperation. Was that why he had felt the need to assert himself with those bullies? He thought himself the man of the house now and had to act accordingly? And, if she had known what was happening in his life, what *could* she have done? Complained to the Head? That would probably only have made it worse... keep him off school? What- *forever?* She felt like screaming! Why did being a parent have to be so bloody difficult? One thing was clear though: she couldn't let him use violence to solve all his problems and he was going to be grounded for at least eternity while he learnt that lesson. Finishing off the washing up, she sighed and turned to face her mother.

"What do *you* think I should do, Mom?"

Her mother looked up from the coffee she was cradling at the kitchen table.

"He's not a bad boy," she smiled reassuringly, "but, like most teenagers, he likes to think he's slippery as an eel smothered in butter; so we need to keep a tight leash on him and stop him having any contact with those boys in future."

Hannah nodded and smiled, he *wasn't* a bad boy. She had to keep that thought in her head. Feeling slightly more relieved and with a new sense of determination and purpose, she went to the foot of the stairs and shouted up for Harry to come downstairs. For a moment nothing happened, then his music went silent and his reluctant footsteps could be heard shuffling down the stairs.

"All right, Mom?" Harry asked, looking warily from one arm-crossed woman to the other.

"What do you think, young man?" his grandmother replied.

Harry bit his lip and waited; absolutely no point answering that rhetorical question.

Mom went to the fridge and reached in for a half-drunk bottle of rose, a cork loosely wedged in the neck. She got a wine glass from the cupboard and let it glug out until it was almost full. Harry thought to himself how Mom only ever used to drink at Christmas and Birthdays... now it seemed to be almost every night.

"You're only supposed to have two or three units a week, you know Mom," he mumbled.

Mom paused mid-gulp and glared at him angrily.

"Two or three glasses a night might seriously reduce my chances of grounding you forever, so I'd keep quiet if I were you. Besides, we're not talking about me, we're talking about you." She paused and glanced across at Nan who nodded her support, "Your Nan and me have decided that, while you are excluded from school, you will also be banned from leaving this house-"

"But, Mom..." Harry interrupted.

"No buts," his mother continued, "it's the only way we can be sure you're not getting into any more trouble. But don't think you'll be sat watching telly or playing on your Playstation all day, oh no, this is a *punishment,* and it should feel like one. So, you'll be doing our own individually tailored form of *community service."*

"Community service?" Harry asked dubiously, "and what *exactly* will that consist of?"

"Washing, ironing, cleaning your room, hoovering, washing the car..." said Nan, still with her arms folded and leaning on the kitchen table like a presiding judge with a coffee cup for a gavel, "pretty much any task we need doing and which you normally take for granted... *you'll* be doing instead!"

Harry scratched the end of his nose pensively and considered his predicament. All of a sudden, school didn't seem so terrible a prospect; bullies and all. Then he had a brainwave....

"What about William and Gabriel?"

"Who?" asked his Grandmother.

"You know, I walked home with William and he... helped me in the shop when the kids at school were pressuring me. If I'm going to have to do odd jobs as a punishment, I'd like to do something for them... to say thanks."

The two adults looked at each other in surprise, sharing a raised eyebrow.

"Well," mother began, "I suppose that would be OK... but I'll come and meet these two gentlemen before we agree anything; you're not pulling the wool over my eyes again!"

CHAPTER SIXTEEN

KILL OR BE KILLED

'It is forbidden to kill;
Therefore all murderers are punished
Unless they kill in large numbers
And to the sound of trumpets.'

Voltaire

November 1941,
The Siege of Leningrad; the Eastern Front.

Wolfgang shifted the weight of his rifle slightly and tried to stretch out the aching muscles in his right arm. His trigger finger felt frozen solid; fat lot of use he would be if the Russians attacked again right now, he cursed. He let his right arm drop for a minute, flexing his hand and fingers in a half-hearted attempt to lose the numbness and start the tingling sensation as life, painful and raw, slowly returned to his thickly-gloved digits. His rifle still rested on the ridge of the trench, waiting for the inevitable. Straight ahead of him a small church bore the scars of war in every foot of its walls, while the irregular gaps in a row of houses made Wolfgang think that a malevolent God had taken a greedy mouthful out of the helpless buildings.

Wolfgang turned his attention to his fellow occupants in the length of trench he found himself in: an entire company shivering and cowering, shoulder to shoulder, soldier to soldier, a mound of dirt all that separated them from ten thousand Russians and certain death. Reiner saw him looking and Wolfgang tried to offer a smile of encouragement. He gazed back in bemusement: no-one had smiled for months now.

Since his father had sent him away, Wolfgang's life had been a whirlwind: basic training, an immediate posting in Western Europe in 1939, before helping to push back the disastrous British Expeditionary Force all the way back to Dunkirk and then boot them back across the channel in May 1940. Then, at the intervention of his father, he had been enlisted to take part in *Operation Barbarossa*: Hitler's invasion against Stalin's Soviet Union, and he had consequently been moved to the Eastern Front in order to 'prove himself'. Initially, all had gone well for Germany, and Hitler's vision of Russia as a home for the expanding Germanic Empire, while Russians were banished to Siberia to starve, was looking increasingly likely as Wolfgang spent the summer of 1941 encircling and destroying Soviet Armies at Minsk, Smolensk, Uman and Kiev.

But then they had reached Leningrad.

Leningrad and the armies of the Leningrad Front had been cut off within four days when Lake Ladoga fell in the east and, surprisingly, Hitler changed tactics. Instead of pausing to destroy the city, as he had done before to such great effect, before moving his juggernaut on, he chose instead to lay siege to it; as though they were still in medieval times. Thus, while Hitler's blitzkrieg raced on towards Moscow, Wolfgang and his legions stayed on to slowly strangle the life out of an already gagging Leningrad.

Wolfgang and the others had scoffed at the prospect of Russian resistance. Sat in their billets in the outskirts of the city, Jurgen had given them a month at best; Hartmut said it wouldn't even be a fortnight -they simply didn't have the provisions. Logically, it wasn't possible, *was it?* But there was nothing logical about Russians. Rumours abounded... they had introduced rations... rations had been cut...rations were fast running out... they were supplementing their diets by boiling up wallpaper and leather and putting them into soups, or making bread from cardboard and sawdust. As pitiful as it was, these rumours consoled Wolfgang and the others: their hardships *must* hasten their surrender.

But hold out they did, so Wolfgang and his friends were forced to wade through line after line of defence, through anti-tank ditches and barricades, defend wave after wave of counter-attacks, fight metre by metre, house by house, street by costly street. By November, Wolfgang had lost Heinz and Detlef; Tomas had been blown up by a hand grenade, Axel was picked off by a sniper. Siegried was bayonetted through the heart in the bloody cut and thrust of close combat; his blood spattering Wolfgang's uniform shortly before that of the blood of the Russian who had killed his unfortunate friend.

Then winter fell like a boulder down a cliff side taking many innocent souls in its wake.

It was one of the most ferocious, unforgiving winters in living memory. Four thousand Russians were dying every single day, finally overwhelmed by the bitter twins of starvation and exhaustion; their bodies left to become frozen sculptures amidst the rubble of the streets. Yet still they fought on: fought on when oil and coal supplies ran out; fought on when cruel winter snapped the water pipes so they lost their supply of drinking water; fought on when the temperature hit minus thirty five and trams froze in their tracks and ground to a squealing halt.

And so they found themselves in this never-ending stand-off. A never-ending purgatory. Each night the Russians whispered to each other that Troy had fallen, Rome had fallen but Leningrad would *never* fall. They needed that hope to survive. Those that lost sight of it committed suicide or were found the following morning, stone cold under their blankets; their bodies having given up the fight.

Wolfgang didn't use the thought of victory to keep him alive, he had Rachel.

When night came and the threat of death slunk back into the stinking shadows, that was when he allowed Rachel to appear, bright and beautiful in this barren wasteland and smiling serenely at him. As he slipped into sleep, nightly she took him by the hand and they walked through the park, sat and giggled in the bandstand and behind the boiler room at school, lay in each other's arms in the summerhouse. Every night, she kept him warm and safe until the pale sepulchral light crept in, pulling him slowly but ruthlessly back to the here and now; a fist of steel wrapped in a velvet glove allowing no refusal.

Wolfgang looked across at Manfred as he held up his binoculars and stared across the tiny gulf between them and the Russian front line.

"See anything?" he whispered.

Manfred shrugged, "they're like rats; you don't know they're there until they're biting you on the ass!"

Wolfgang smiled and squinted into the dirty white that made up the uninspiring view. It had snowed overnight, briefly stripping the world back to nothingness, but it never lasted; the world always forced its ugly way back through. He scanned the horizon. For once, it was deathly quiet; a brief hiatus in the almost relentless air and artillery bombardment. And when the guns and bombs did mercifully fall silent, it was eerily quiet because there were no trees left for the wind to blow through, no dogs left to bark, no horses to neigh. Anything with a pulse had been added to the pot months ago. There were stories that owners had swapped cats and dogs with their neighbours so they wouldn't have to face eating their own pets.

Wolfgang scanned the shells of buildings opposite for any signs of life. The dead, of course, were everywhere. Countless bodies lay sprawled in the dead zone of No Man's Land between them, body upon body, German and Russian hand in hand, intertwined in death in a way they never could be in life. But the buildings seemed strangely still. Then Wolfgang thought he saw a shadow cross the bullet-riddled square of a window... Quickly, he held out his hand to Manfred, signalling for him to pass him his binoculars, before focusing in on the building again. Once, in another world, it had been a café; now the only signs of its' previous existence were a shabby green awning, shredded by bullet holes and tattered on the fringes, and an advertisement for a brand of washing powder, painted directly into the side of the brickwork and faded almost beyond recognition. Wolfgang moved his focus up to one of the upstairs windows where he thought he had first seen the shadow. In front of it, slack telephone wires were draped across the barren street like a child's skipping rope but, behind it, there was nothing; just the faintest movement of a wisp of tattered curtain in the breeze.

Then he saw it: the glint of glass. Someone else was looking through binoculars and that meant only one thing.

"*They're coming!*" he hissed, passing the binoculars back to Manfred and raising his rifle in grim expectation. The buzz quickly passed down the line and Wolfgang was aware of demoralised moans and nervous shuffling as everyone readied themselves.

Then came the cry: a tumultuous banshee-cry from the barbarian horde as they appeared from every shell hole, every doorway and every alleyway simultaneously. Wolfgang felt his heart heave and lurch hideously then pound like the pistons in a steam train as the whole German front line opened fire in a furious fusillade. Bodies fell like dominos, adding to the tangled mounds of the already fallen. But these demons were refusing to depart without taking German souls with them: Ulrich fell backwards into the trench, his sightless eyes no longer seeing the low-moving clouds scudding overhead. Paul and Erwin fell too, slumping over their rifles to take no more part in the desperate defence.

Wolfgang hurled a stick grenade into a pack of Russians not fifteen feet away and ducked down as it exploded. Brief screams could be heard then were lost in the mad hubbub. Wolfgang knew they were getting closer with each assault and, surely, this was the time they would finally be overrun and massacred. Peering over the edge again, the enemy were now so close he could see their eyes, wide with fear, anger and starvation in equal measures. He fired, reloaded, fired again...it was impossible to miss at this range and in such numbers and the bodies spun and fell before him.... *But still they came.*

The first Russians to break the line fell into their trenches, some already dead, others firing their old and largely unreliable rifles, probably picked up from a dead comrade only seconds before; it was common knowledge they didn't have sufficient for one each and sometimes charged at enemy lines with nothing but the fear of being shot by their own men if they turned back.

Wolfgang spun around to find himself faced with a Russian machine gun, with the round barrel clip that slotted in underneath, pointing right at him. Diving to his left, he felt the bullets whistle past him, then heard the click as the machine gun jammed. The Russian looked helplessly at his useless weapon and then his eyes widened as Wolfgang fired from bottom of the trench and the man collapsed, dead, at his feet. Hauling himself up, he glanced behind him and realised the terrible truth: *the Russians had got behind them!* Manfred had been right, they *were* like rats and hid in the sewers so they could appear behind enemy lines and catch them unawares. Wolfgang had learnt the hard way, not just to look forwards for the next attack, but *behind* them as well!

"They're behind us!" he screamed, up and down the trench, "we must go forward! *Attack! Attack! Attack!"*

Another Russian dropped into the trench beside him, using all his force to lunge at him with the bayonet fixed to the end of his wooden-shafted rifle. He fired... but nothing happened! *Out of bullets!* Again, Wolfgang reacted quickly and instinctively, batting it away with the length of his own rifle, when he noticed his spade still protruding from a pile of frozen earth. German spades folded for easier transportation but, when they were screwed together, they made an extremely useful weapon. Wolfgang plucked it from the earth and, in one smooth swinging motion, smashed it across the soldier's face; blood and teeth spattering from the man's mouth as he fell to the floor of the trench, instantly unconscious. Wolfgang tossed the spade to the floor, scooped up Ulrich's rifle and urgently reiterated the need to advance. His mind was working overtime and it rapidly came to the single conclusion that might keep them alive: the only way out of this was to break through the Russian assault ahead of them, veer off to the side and try to re-join the German front line somewhere further down, where the Russians hadn't broken through and encircled them yet.

The others around him had heeded his advice and he found himself dodging bullets and advancing Russians alongside Jurgen, Manfred, Reiner, Hartmut and several others. Bombs were exploding everywhere, sending bodies flying up into the air like trapeze artists and falling back to earth like crash test dummies. Armed with the element of surprise, Wolfgang and the others managed to punch a hole through the Russian advance and immediately swung off to their left, sticking close together and trying to maintain a relentless barrage of fire on all sides. Wolfgang realised they were now, effectively, running down the centre of what would have once been a main street; though it was so densely littered with rubble, chunks of masonry, burnt out tanks and armoured German half-tracks, not to mention the endless horizon of dead bodies, it was struggling to retain anything of the normality it once had.

Wolfgang led the way, picking off surprised Russians as he went. When Ulrich's rifle also ran out of bullets, he turned to his luger and carried on with that until the clip of that was empty too. Then he just ran. They were cutting a swathe through the Russian line that seemed to go on for ever and Wolfgang knew they had to veer off somewhere. There were pockets of sterner German resistance but, it seemed to Wolfgang, they were being largely overrun. Up ahead, he saw a side street and signalled to the others to follow him. He sprinted off to the right, down a quieter street that was a warren of shuttered homes in the Old District. He took another left down a narrow alleyway and paused for breath to look over his shoulder in the dank staleness.

He was all alone.

Jurgen... Manfred... Hartmut.... They were all dead; only he had made it this far and no-one seemed to have seen him duck into this alleyway. Struggling to hold back the tears for his dead comrades, he tried to force himself to think what to do next. Somehow, he thought, he had to carry on westwards. The Russians couldn't have broken through the entire length of the line; they had always been repelled before when they had tried to lift the siege and, if he could get far enough along, he could sneak back across to his own lines again. That was the theory anyway.

He crept to the opposite end of the alley, stopping on the way to take a machine gun from a long-dead German lying slumped in the doorway of a house and rotten as a decaying drunk. He checked to see of it was loaded and was pleased to find more than half a clip left; whether it still fired would only be known when he was next called upon to use it... he couldn't risk trying it now and drawing attention to himself.

From the end of the alley he found he was at the entrance of another street with a similar alleyway opposite. Checking both ways like an obedient schoolboy, he crossed the road and started down the next alley. The sound of fire was more intermittent here; though it was hard to tell what that meant. The Russians may have been forced to retreat but, equally, they might have killed everyone in sight and be establishing a new front line. Wolfgang could only hope it was the former.

At the end of that alley, Wolfgang looked out onto a cobbled square, its snow-covered floor criss-crossed with cart and tank tracks and overlaid with the smoking corpses of several Soviet T34 tanks and at least two hundred dead soldiers. A couple of craters, acrid smoke still drifting upward into a battleship grey sky broke up the pattern and provided Wolfgang with some slight hope. If he could make it across the square, he could see if it was safe to head off south again. The tanks would provide some cover and he could also dive into the craters if a sniper was in one of those buildings that overlooked the square so ominously.

Taking a deep breath, he slipped out of the alley and, keeping to the overhang of the awnings of the nearby shops, made it to the first tank. He waited and listened. Nothing. But then a sniper wouldn't give away his position so easily. When he had first started moving East, his first Oberfreiter, (a vastly experienced soldier who'd enlisted as a teenager and knew everything there was to know about war,) always used to volunteer to go across a space like this first. His men loved him for it; thought it demonstrated his bravery, showed them he was not asking them to do anything he was not prepared to do himself. But, one night around a camp fire, when everyone else was asleep, he confided in Wolfgang and admitted he always chose to lead the way *because a sniper would use the first soldier to pinpoint where the enemy were coming from and the second soldier to be the victim of his first shot.* Unfortunately, Wolfgang had nobody behind him to take the attention away from him; if a sniper was out there, he would be ready for whenever he moved again.

He knelt at the edge of the burnt out tank, crouching low beside the huge wheels and cogs; the upper skeleton of the turret blown to bits and the tank commander almost certainly blown to smithereens inside. Taking off his stahlhelm, he balanced the steel helmet on the end of his machine gun and eased it into view. Nothing. He blew out his cheeks. Either a sniper had figured out his trick or there was no-one watching. Setting himself like a sprinter, at the sound of an imaginary pistol he set off for the crater about twenty feet ahead of him. He had covered fifteen of those body-strewn feet when he heard the crack of the rifle. With a desperate lunge, he threw himself headlong into the crater as a bullet ricocheted off a cobble by his feet.

Landing heavily, Wolfgang skidded and rolled to the bottom of the crater, landing face-first in a dirty puddle with a splat. Choking and gasping for air, he pushed himself upwards and took in a few deep gulps of fairly rancid air. Then he was aware of a strange sight... a Russian soldier facing him but with his sagging head bobbing like a ventriloquist's dummy. He tried to scrabble amongst the mud for his machine gun, but noticed it wedged halfway up the slope of the crater and agonisingly out of reach! Then he stared more closely at the Russian... he was leaning at a steep angle down the opposite length of the crater when, suddenly, his head lolled back and Wolfgang could see he had a bullet hole right between the eyes! Then he noticed the legs and torso *behind* the dead Russian... someone was attempting to *hide* behind the dead man's body!

Despite the mud-caked uniforms, Wolfgang could see enough grey to recognise a German uniform from a Russian.

"Don't shoot!" came a frightened voice from beneath the dead man.

"It's all right, comrade, I'm German," Wolfgang whispered, scanning the rest of the crater to make sure no-one else was loitering, unseen, in the mud.

A filthy face peeked out, shivering and nervous as a moth... *a face Wolfgang recognised!*

Wolfgang felt his jaw go slack and his blood freeze.

"*Tanzmann!* What the hell are you doing here?"

Tanzmann looked at him uncomprehendingly for the longest time before a flicker of recognition, then a look of misapprehension, registered in his eyes. He rolled the lifeless body off his own and revealed himself more fully. Immediately, Wolfgang couldn't help but notice a bandage tied around his upper thigh and a dark crimson ring staining the centre of it.

"Am I hallucinating?" the wounded man hissed, looking at Wolfgang in utter disbelief, the pain etched in deep creases all over his face.

Wolfgang couldn't speak... all the hatred welled up inside of him like a volcano and, despite his perilous situation, his mind was full of nothing but Tanzmann's betrayal and how he had vowed revenge; there had been room in his heart for little else for these past few months; except for the nightly spectral visits of his beloved Rachel.

How beautifully ironic it was, he considered, *how this man of all men, without whom he might even be sat with Rachel right now, was in his trench, wounded and needing his help. It would be so easy to kill him now and no-one would ever know.*

The two men stared mutely at each other, as if Tanzmann could read Wolfgang's thoughts and only now realised the imminent danger he was in. Finally, Wolfgang ducked down and crawled over to his side; his adversary noticeably flinching anxiously as he neared.

"How bad is your wound?" he hissed, and Tanzmann sighed and relaxed a little.

Gently, Tanzmann lifted up his bloodied hand allowing Wolfgang to lean in closer and take a look. Cautiously, he lifted up the bandage and tried to see the wound. It was caked in dry blood on the fringes but still bleeding at the centre, so he couldn't make out much. Reaching into the basic First Aid kit in his pack, he pulled out a fresh bandage, scissors, gauze and alcohol. He poured the alcohol over the wound, causing Tanzmann to wince and bite down on his lip, then he looked at the wound again. He could see the dark circle of the entry wound clearer now and, as gently as he could, rolled his leg to one side to see if he was bleeding underneath. There was no exit wound; which meant the bullet was still inside him. Wolfgang couldn't be certain but he suspected that was marginally better than if the bullet had passed straight through: at least there was only one wound for him to bleed from.

Wolfgang pressed fresh gauze against the wound then wound clean bandage round his thigh, tucking the end in at the top. Then he sat back and thought. He looked up at Tanzmann: he had his head back and his eyes closed now, as if standing the pain from being freshly bandaged had taken all his strength temporarily. He looked pale and there were dark circles arcing his sunken eye sockets. How long had he been lying there? How much blood had he lost? He needed to get him out of the trench and to a medic that much was obvious; who knew where the bullet had lodged? It could have been a lot worse than the thigh, he concluded.

"Can you walk on it?"

Tanzmann opened his eyes wide, "are you crazy? There's a sniper out there; we wouldn't get three feet! And that's if there's only one!"

Tanzmann had a point, but Wolfgang didn't know if Tanzmann would last until dark when they would have a better chance, or if he wanted to spend any more time in this hellhole than was absolutely necessary; *especially* with Tanzmann. He worried that the longer he stayed with him, the harder the temptation would be not to kill or, at the very least, abandon him.

"You want to die here or take a chance, Tanzmann?" he asked.

Tanzmann said nothing, glancing in surprise at the very different man Wolfgang had become to the boy he had last seen leaving the dining table back in Berlin.

"What are you doing here anyway? I figured you'd have some cushy desk job in Berlin by now thanks to your handy work." Wolfgang continued, sneering angrily up at his enemy in a world where they were surrounded by unseen enemies he hated far less than this all-too-visible one.

Tanzmann scoffed bitterly. "Initially, it worked in my favour. Your father rewarded my efforts with promotion and a posting in Holland. He said he needed men like me; men who would know what was best for the Fatherland."

"What happened?" Wolfgang asked, his curiosity getting the better of him.

"Your *mother* was what happened," Tanzmann said, spitting out the syllables bitterly. "It seems she blamed me for your... *exile* and she must have worked on your father; either that or she had connections of her own who were able to make my life...well, less comfortable than it had been and, eventually, to take her revenge."

Despite their situation, Wolfgang couldn't help but laugh to himself. It was the first even vaguely amusing thing that had happened in, at least, three months.

The pair of them stared at each other for the longest time before Tanzmann spoke again.

"Do you have a plan in mind?"

Wolfgang sighed deeply.

"Not a plan so much as an act of desperation. Do you know where our front line is?"

Tanzmann nodded. "We were advancing into this square when we were ambushed. They were all around us... in the buildings, picking us off ten at a time. We were bloody sitting ducks. As we were pulling back they counter-attacked." He nodded towards the glassy-eyed Russian still staring blindly at the darkening skies. "This guy came at me with his bayonet. Got me in the leg. We fell into the crater and I fired as we fell. He was dead before we hit the ground. I hit my head as I landed and fell unconscious. By the time I came round, we'd fallen back and they'd disappeared into the shadows. But it seems they left a present behind."

Wolfgang nodded. "The sniper. Do you have any stick grenades?"

"Two," Tanzmann confirmed, "in my backpack. Why?"

"Well, I'm just an ordinary soldier, not some sharp shooter; I can't take out a sniper while holed up in a bomb crater from God knows what distance. All we can hope to do is distract him for long enough to get us both out of here. I've got three grenades and I'm hoping that, if we throw them all out simultaneously, in different directions, the blasts might act as cover or disorientate him for long enough for us to get out of range. With a bit of luck, he might think he's under attack and pull back. Can you get on my back?"

Tanzmann physically wilted, "What? *Right now?*"

"Or we could wait here for you to bleed to death; I've got to be honest, I'm really not bothered either way."

Tanzmann thought about his options for a few moments and nodded glumly. Wolfgang reached into his pack and took out the stick grenades and did the same with Tanzmann's pack. Then he went over the plan with the stricken man.

"Right, we'll throw all five in different directions and as far as we can. I'll throw them towards the buildings over there," he pointed off to the right, "and you throw these two straight ahead. The second the last one is out your hand I'll lift you in a fireman's lift and run like hell!"

With a nod to synchronise their timing, Tanzmann and Wolfgang tossed all five stick grenades, one following hard on the tail of the last; both men watching them fly high into the air. Before waiting for the explosions to begin, he dragged Tanzmann to his feet, ignoring his grunt of agony and, bending down, flung him sideways over his left shoulder, so that his left arm was clutching Tanzmann's right hand and his left hand was gripping the back of Tanzmann's legs. In this awkward position, he took a run at the side of the crater and dug his boots in deep as he scaled it in five energy-sapping steps then, as the first grenades started blowing debris dangerously close by, he began running towards the far side of the square, Tanzmann bouncing on his back as he went.

Although German provisions were a universe away from the Russian diet of yeast soup made from fermented sawdust; or meat jelly made from boiling bones and calf skins; or toothpaste; or cough mixture; or practically *anything* that contained calories, Wolfgang was still weak with hunger and that made Tanzmann feel like a grand piano strapped across his shoulders. Beads of sweat were already forming on his forehead despite the freezing temperatures and his knees were starting to buckle; not helped by the uneven surface of cobblestones, rubble, discarded weaponry and frozen bodies.

He kept his head down as he manoeuvred through the debris, not looking up or even allowing himself to consider the frightening number of broken windows on all four sides of the square offering so many easy kills for a skilled sniper. The dust was settling now behind them and Wolfgang braced himself for the inevitable shot that would surely ring out and still be echoing eerily as his life was ended.

But it hadn't come yet... and the far side of the square was looming ever larger... he could see the route Tanzmann and the others must have taken when they advanced and then again on their subsequent rapid withdrawal... there was a street straight ahead, a bottleneck littered with many German dead... if he could only make it through there, he could turn the corner and be out of view....

The street was only twenty feet away now... then fifteen...

Wolfgang heard the shot and Tanzmann's cry almost overlapping it. The disadvantage for Tanzmann was that, slumped as he was over Wolfgang's back, he acted almost as a shield for Wolfie, blocking the bullets from finding their intended target.

Wolfgang kept going. It was less than ten feet to the end of the street and, now he was so close, he could see the end of the road ahead... see the barricades and sandbags of the German front line! He was almost there; almost taste freedom! He didn't know how badly injured Tanzmann was, or where he'd been hit, but he was clearly still alive as he was screaming out in agony with the painful jolt of every footstep.

The last few steps were especially treacherous because of the log jam of bodies and the smouldering wreck of a German half-track blocking the way. For a moment, he turned briefly to negotiate the smallest of gaps through to the Promised Land and, as he did so, two further shots rang out; one after the other in quick succession. The first pinged off the side of the half-track and ricocheted harmlessly away...

The second struck his head just below the steel helmet...

The pain rose like a temperature gauge, reaching the top and bursting through the glass in an excruciating crescendo. Wolfgang was aware of the sensation of falling... was vaguely aware of the fading noise of German voices shouting from his own lines ahead of him... then Nature's anaesthetic, shock, kicked in and the world went black...

Wolfgang and Tanzmann fell to the ground and lay there unmoving. The dust rose in a grey billowing mushroom cloud and finally settled in quiet benediction over the bodies of the fallen.

CHAPTER SEVENTEEN

UNORTHODOX, BUT EFFECTIVE!

'The nation that will insist on drawing a broad line
Of demarcation between the fighting man and the thinking man
Is liable to find its fighting done by fools
And its thinking done by cowards.'

Thucydides

'One must have chaos within oneself
To be able to give birth to a dancing star.'

*Friedrich Nietzsche
Thus Spoke Zarathustra, prologue*

June 1999,
Early Friday morning, on the way to William and Gabriel's house.

It was still early, barely gone eight, but a blue sky dotted with clouds as fluffy as *Angel Delight* already filled the heavens. Mom had come in at seven and announced that, since he had completed all his chores at home over the previous two days, she would take him round his *'elderly acquaintances' house and see if they can find something suitably back-breaking and hopefully nauseatingly tedious to keep you busy with.'*

Harry had jumped at the chance; anything was better than the frequent disappointed head-shaking and teeth-sucking he had been subjected to by his grandmother for the past forty-eight hours.

Soon they found themselves on William and Gabriel's doorstep. Mom was dressed ready for work, Harry slouched next to her in jeans and a sweatshirt, listening to *'Roll with It'* by *Oasis* on his Walkman. *Appropriate,* he thought, suddenly aware of a sharp nudge in his ribs:

"Take those damn things out of your ears!"

Reluctantly, he clicked the *STOP* button and, winding the headphones around it, held it patiently in one hand. Within thirty seconds, Gabriel had appeared at the door, in a paisley dressing gown over striped pyjamas and with slippers flapping on his pale, thin feet.

"Oh..." mumbled Mom, suddenly acutely aware that, perhaps, it was rather early for visitors, especially at the house of retired people who had no reason to get up early and that she should probably have been well advised to call first. "Are you Mr. er... William, is it?"

"No, *I'm* William," a voice announced, as William appeared over Gabriel's shoulder and smiled broadly when he caught sight of Harry. When he saw his Mom standing next to him, Harry was surprised to see his smile waver briefly and some emotion that Harry couldn't quite identify fill his eyes when he met her gaze so unexpectedly.

"You must be Harry's mother," he said, quickly regaining his composure.

"Erm, yes, that's right: Mrs Robinson... Hannah, how do you do?" she replied, belatedly holding out her hand. "I'm sorry to have called on you so early; it was thoughtless of me..."

"Not at all," William interrupted, shaking her hand warmly.

"...but Harry has talked about you so much I really thought I ought to come and meet you... and, being truthful, he was wondering if you might be able to provide a suitable *punishment* for him to fill his time over the next couple of days?"

"*Punishment?*" said Gabriel quizzically, "I'm not sure I understand."

"Well," Mrs. Robinson continued, glaring across at Harry briefly as though having to explain his atrocious behaviour to strangers brought back all of her disappointment and frustration all too vividly, "unfortunately, Harry has been excluded from school for fighting. Hopefully, it is only a temporary measure but, in the meantime, his grandmother and I don't want him to think he's on some sort of little *holiday*. Consequently, he is not allowed out of the house and needs to work off some of his *aggression* doing something more productive. He suggested that you two gentlemen may be able to find him some useful chores to do? If it's not too much of an inconvenience, of course."

Harry waited impatiently throughout his mother's biased account, desperate for her to finish and set off for work so he could explain to both of them what *really* happened. Gabriel and William exchanged meaningful glances and Gabriel gave a little nod.

"I'm sure we can keep him fruitfully employed and out of trouble, Mrs. Robinson," William smiled. "How long do you want him... *entertained?*" he asked.

"Oh, I wouldn't want to impose too much..."

"No trouble at all," insisted William, "the back garden is a veritable jungle, and Gabriel's knees and my back are simply not up to the effort any more. Young Harry would be doing us an immense favour if he could possibly hack away at the undergrowth for a few days."

Mrs. Robinson glanced at her watch, acutely aware that her bus left in exactly three and a half minutes; she really didn't have the time to debate and it was something of a relief that they both seemed nice and apparently normal. "Well, if you're sure you don't mind?" she added as a parting shot.

"Not at all," beamed Gabriel already stepping aside to let Harry through.

"OK, then," she said, shooting Harry an expression that spoke volumes before hurrying away with a nagging feeling in the back of her head that, somehow, she had been conned...

****

Half an hour later, the three of them were sitting in the lounge nursing steaming cups of tea and tucking in to generously buttered slices of toast. Harry had pretty much recounted the whole story admitting for the first time to being beaten up by the two thugs; then explaining the ultimatum set by Harris and his cronies; to William's timely intervention stopping him from being prosecuted as a common thief; through to, eventually, his fight with Adam Kellerman and subsequent exclusion.

Both men listened without interrupting; taking an occasional sip from their tea or polite nibble on the corner of a piece of toast. When he was finished, they both nodded sagely, inwardly digesting everything he had told them. Eventually, it was Gabriel who broke the silence:

"So, it would seem the problems have not yet been resolved; only put on temporary hold, yes?"

"Well, yeah, I suppose," Harry agreed, "if I get permanently excluded, I won't ever have to see any of their ugly mugs again; which is *almost* worth it, but I'd struggle to get a place in another school and what kind of future would I have with no qualifications? Plus, I can't get away from the nagging feeling I keep getting that they'd have *won* if I did that."

"Precisely," Gabriel nodded, "what did the Head advise to rectify your situation, should you be permitted to return to your studies? She seems an eminently sensible individual, from what you've told us."

Harry rolled his eyes, unconvinced.

"That I should ignore them, report anything they say or do to a teacher, and that, if I don't show that they've got to me, they'll leave me alone. Ironically, if I was at school *now* I wouldn't have a problem because *they're* all excluded until the Governors' Meeting as well."

"Sensible advice which you would do well to heed," Gabriel said, nodding vigorously and wagging a finger in a way that reminded him of his Nan.

"What utter nonsense!" scoffed William, "you did *exactly* the right thing. You *must* stand up to bullies or they will never change. I'm sure the Head is a charming woman who means well, but those words were clearly meant to placate your mother. I can guarantee it has been a very long time since *she* has been on the other side of the tracks, walking the playground as a pupil not as an adult with nothing to fear. Bullies don't stop unless you *force* them. You take a chair to a bully and he thinks twice before doing it again," William grinned, winking at Harry as he took a sip of his tea.

"I'm sure William is not advocating *violence* as an appropriate course of action for Harry, *are* you?" Gabriel interrupted, looking across at his oldest friend pointedly.

"Oh, come on Gabe," William frowned, "fight fire with what? A piece of paper? The pen is mightier than the sword and all that? You know as well as I, *if not more so*, that peacefully standing by and hoping it will all work out for the best is naïve at best, foolish at worst." He smiled at Harry encouragingly before concluding, "so, overall, I'd say your response was unorthodox, yes…but ultimately, highly effective!"

Harry laughed, feeling hugely vindicated; it was like a refreshing zephyr washing over him, filling his lungs with sparkling oxygen and making his laugh even more full-throated because, if the truth were known, his actions had kept him awake the last few nights and, while he knew he had gone way over the top, he felt a sense of relief that William could at least understand his desperation and thought, to a degree, he had been justified in defending himself. William got caught up in his infectious laugh and soon joined voices with it, laughing so hysterically until even Gabriel couldn't help but smirk and look away at their unbridled mirth.

The chorus of laughs echoed around the room until, suddenly, William's transformed into a hacking cough. He brought out a handkerchief, holding it over his mouth as he continued to splutter until blood-speckled spit stained the purity of the monogrammed whiteness. Small strawberry-shaped patches could be seen appearing and spreading like wine stains. Harry looked across anxiously at

Gabriel who was staring equally fretfully at William. William was staring stoically at the newly-made stains on his handkerchief and considering whether he could craft the spots and splodges into some form of Rorschach test result; deciding finally that he could possibly make out a Victorian gentleman with a curling moustache. He smiled to himself, wondering exactly what a psychologist would make of his current state of mind...then noticed the concern etched on the worried faces opposite him and dismissed them quickly with a nonchalant wave of his hand.

"I'm fine; don't fuss, the pair of you!"

An awkward silence arrived and settled on the room like a mist. Eventually, Gabriel sighed, reached for his tea, took a sip and the spell was thankfully broken.

"I take it you are very much in the bad books of your mother and your grandmother?" he remarked.

Harry blew out his cheeks in exasperation. "You could say that; I think Mom has now branded me the official black sheep of the family."

"That will pass," he suggested. "Time has a unique knack of smoothing the edges of hurts and grievances. You may be the black sheep right now but, in my humble opinion, almost everyone is, at best, *off*-white..."

Harry grinned; whilst their conversation hadn't exactly come up with any solutions as to how to solve his problems if he were ever actually allowed to return to school yet, he hadn't laughed out loud for what seemed like months... and it felt good.

When they'd finished their tea and toast, William levered himself noisily to his feet and led Harry through the kitchen and out into the garden. Considering what had been told to his mother, Harry was fully expecting a sprawling wilderness. What he was actually confronted with was a neatly trimmed lawn fringed with ordered flowerbeds! Harry's mouth fell slack in surprise. As he turned to face William, he was met with a sheepish grin and a shrug of the shoulder.

"So I may have exaggerated somewhat!" he said with a knowing wink.

Harry shook his head smiling: it appeared the next couple of days wouldn't be too arduous after all!

For a little while the pair of them stood on the patio looking out at the garden and beyond. The back garden sloped away to a shed at the bottom and a fence that ran along the length of the far end. But, beyond it, lay the rest of the estate condensed before them: rows and rows of little boxes scattered like building blocks in different shades of tan and rust-red and grey; like dirty sugar cubes. Further off in the distance rested a low range of hills and, above them, streaks of cloud and a sun slowly heaving itself out of the tallest treetops. It was surprisingly beautiful and Harry felt remarkably at ease with these people he really barely knew.

"You should listen to Gabriel," William announced eventually, as Harry jumped slightly at the long silence being broken.

"I like your advice better," Harry admitted.

"Probably so," William replied, "but I was always the hot-headed one and it is not always the one quick to anger that achieves the best results. I admire your guts in standing up to your bully, but now you must tread a little more carefully and use your *wits* rather than your *fists* to come out on top in the end."

Harry sighed morosely.

"Sometimes I wish I was... older, you know, *retired* like you guys."

William swung around and looked at him with genuine surprise on his face.

"No, I mean, it must be *easier*..." he explained, "you know, no school, no stress at work... no bullies. You can do whatever you like."

William reached into his trouser pocket and pulled out a pipe and a pouch of tobacco. After pressing a wad into the bowl, he lit it and took a few ruminative puffs while he considered Harry's words.

"Let me tell you, Harry, inside every old person is a small child staring in the mirror wondering what the hell happened!" The smoke coiled up from his pipe, thinned out and vanished into the blue sky. "Life is too precious to wish away. When I lectured at the University, I used to teach a module on Nietzsche. Nietzsche said that you must have chaos within you to give birth to a dancing star."

He looked across at Harry to gauge his reaction. Harry was creasing his forehead and giving no indication he was comprehending the relevance of his words of wisdom.

"Chaos is change," William explained, "chaos brings change to order; to the way things are now. If you have chaos in your heart, you will always strive for something different, for something *better*. So don't wish your life away; things never stay the same for long- sometimes they get better, sometimes worse and you long for the situation you had before. But always remember- a little chaos in your life is a good thing; just try to *channel* your chaos and don't let it dictate to you and get out of control; like it did at school." He gave him a steely gaze. "Understand?"

Harry raised and lowered one shoulder.

"I think so," he said, mulling it over, before adding, "clever dude that Nietzsche, wasn't he?"

William smiled and nodded in agreement, "indeed he was Harry, indeed he was." Slowly he walked back to the house before pausing and turning. "You know, it takes a lot of graft to get a garden looking this good... so don't get *too* complacent!"

CHAPTER EIGHTEEN

THE FINAL SOLUTION

'If you win, you need not have to explain...
If you lose, you should not be there to explain!'

Adolf Hitler

December 1941,
Wolfgang's house, Berlin.

The tree-lined streets of Berlin were heavily-laden with the translucent lights and baubles of fast approaching Christmas as Wolfgang walked tentatively towards home. The cold seemed to delight in pinching his cheeks tight like the fingers of an over-enthusiastic Aunt, until they felt red raw.

Wolfgang picked his way carefully along the hard frost that glittered beneath his feet as if the whole surface was littered with diamonds just begging to be plucked from the icy pavement with a Swiss Army Knife. It was not even four in the afternoon but, already, soft twilight was caressing the darkening streets and the solemn moon was a faint lantern barely rising between the thumbprints of black cloud overhead.

It had only been a few short weeks since he had been cut down on the desolate streets of Leningrad and he knew he should be grateful to be alive... but it was difficult to feel gratitude when the ghosts of Manfred and Reiner, Detlef and Paul and so many others visited him in his dreams every night. The sense of emptiness and waste was all-encompassing.

Later, when he had awoken on a canvas bed in a dressing station with a rough blanket tucking him in and a saline drip attached, he discovered he had been rescued by troops on the German front line who had heard the sniper's rifle and seen his fall and had run to gather their limp bodies and carry them behind their lines and to safety. He learnt his life had tilted so finely in the balance one way then the other, to the extent that the doctor said he would not have gambled a weeks' salary on his surviving until, finally, the scales had fallen on the side of life over death. The bullet, he was told, had not affected the brain delivering, in effect, more of a humiliating backslap than a knocked-senseless punch but, by the time he was lying on a table before a doctor, his massive loss of blood had been the doctor's biggest concern. It also transpired that Tanzmann had not survived and Wolfgang felt a strange numbness to the news; a feeling that mirrored how he responded to most news these days.

As he walked, the stitches in his head still felt tight when he squinted at the misty horizon and the medal on his chest made a tiny thud like a heartbeat on his chest with every step. A captain in the front line had watched his heroic attempts to save Tanzmann through his binoculars and had mentioned the incident in dispatches. When he had arrived back in Berlin the previous day, he had been instructed to report to Command Headquarters *where the Fuhrer himself* had pinned the Iron Cross on his chest, making the briefest of eye contacts before moving down the line to the rest of the heroes...

Now he was returning home to recover fully until he was deemed fit to return to active service. His footsteps made a hollow echo as he turned into his empty street. Out of the diaphanous mist emerged the outline of the house and Wolfgang felt a sudden surge of trepidation. He hadn't seen or spoken to his parents since that night at the dining room table... what would he say to them? Did he even *want* to see them? It was his father's fault he had been forced to abandon Rachel a second time, without even the chance to explain. He felt the bile rise in his throat at the very thought of it. He had written to her every day since they had been cruelly torn apart and she had never once replied. Was it because he had been almost constantly on the move and her touching replies had never made it up the line? It seemed unlikely... other troops had received mail. Or was it because she didn't want to know him anymore? He felt his hands clench into furious fists at the very thought... he refused to believe she could forget him so easily, as if it were possible to turn emotions on and off like the twisting of a faucet. Either way, now he was home, he was determined to find out the truth, no matter how painful that truth might prove to be...

He climbed the stone steps and pressed the doorbell. He could hear the chimes echo down the hallway and thought he could hear the excited rustle of whispers from behind the solid oak door. After a brief hiatus, the door was swung open and the warming light from the hallway lit up the most wondrous sight imaginable to the war-weary soldier who stood outside in the cold: the whole household had been lined up to welcome the hero home! Butlers, maids, cooks, gardeners, chauffeur... all were resplendent in immaculate uniform, lined up in two rows spreading from the door to the grand staircase, where his parents had begun walking down the centre with all the pomp and ceremony of the Kaiser and his consort!

His mother flounced to the bottom of the stairs in a long black gown, finely sequined and trailing along the floor behind her and, rushing over to him, took his icy hands in her own silk-gloved ones.

"My poor boy! My poor *brave* boy! Thank goodness you are home at last!"

Then she saw the scar running like a railway track down the side of his skull; still angry and clearly visible where his hair was yet to grow back and cover it. She gasped theatrically and placed her hand delicately over her mouth in horror.

"Oh my! What have they done to my poor sweet boy? My brave soldier! I will never let you out of my sight again!"

"All of this was really not necessary, mother…" Wolfgang mumbled, feeling the flush rise in his cheeks despite himself.

His mother still held him tightly in her grasp as his father neared, in full Gestapo uniform. He leaned in for a better look at the son's Iron Cross and smiled in a satisfied manner, before shaking his hand firmly: *so this is what my father's approval feels like then,* Wolfgang thought to himself. He had finally come up to his father's standards of what was expected of a specimen of prime German manhood. To his surprise, he suddenly came to the realisation that he no longer *cared* whether he came up to the mark or not. Respect was a two way street: if he did not respect his father's opinion, it mattered not what he thought of him, he realised. The qualities he valued as important in life, were certainly not what Wolfgang deemed important.

"You have returned home on a most auspicious day," his mother remarked quietly, leaning in and whispering in his ear, "Herr Eichmann and Herr Heydrich are here to confer upon your father a most prestigious promotion."

It was only then that Wolfgang noticed the *other* men standing at the end of the line, almost at the entrance to the dining room, with their arms clasped behind their backs watching the unfolding performance put on by his parents. And that's when he realised that was exactly what it was: a *show* to impress their important guests, not a real expression of love for the lost sheep who had found his way home again.

His mother linked her arm in his and led him over to meet the interlopers into his party.

"Wolfgang- allow me to introduce SS Obersturmbannfuhrer Eichmann and SS Obergruppenfuhrer Heydrich. Gentlemen- my son, the *decorated war hero* just back from the Russian Front."

Both men put out their hands curtly and Wolfgang shook them without a word. Of course, he knew the reputations of both men and, eighteen months ago would probably have wet himself to have even had to be in the same room as them... but he was a very different person nowadays and only mild curiosity permeated his apathy. Surreptitiously, he eyed the infamous Adolf Eichmann while his father made small talk with him, laughing obsequiously at his every comment, and he couldn't help but think how much he looked like a Jew to him. His pointed nose and receding hairline cowardly deserting the forehead; his ears that stuck out like antenna and his supercilious smile... how it reminded him of the pictures he had been confronted with in the books he had been forced to read on that first day after *Kristallnacht* and in the months beyond. The irony made him smile, causing Eichmann to glance at him curiously from behind his thick black-rimmed glasses. Heydrich, on the other hand, had a longer face, like a horse, but with small piercing eyes, his thin hair cut short and parted high on his forehead. His Iron Cross was perched on his breast pocket just like Wolfgang's and he couldn't help but wonder what he might have done to deserve it.

With his welcome apparently concluded, everyone started drifting through to the dining room, which was seemingly being used as a meeting room. His father indicated for him to follow; which he reluctantly did. The moment he entered the room he found himself engulfed in an oppressive fug of noise, cigarette smoke and stale body odour that hit him full in the face like a steam train. As his eyes adjusted to the cloud of thick cigar smoke, he saw the room was already full of high ranking officers; eating, talking, smoking and laughing. Seemingly, they had been waiting for the guests of honour to arrive before beginning the meeting in earnest and had been gorging themselves in the meantime.

Everyone stood smartly when Eichmann and Heydrich entered and took their places, alongside Wolfgang's father, at the far end of the table. Along the length of one wall, a fabulous spread had been laid out and partially devoured: hors d'oeuvres, cooked hams, piles of dumplings, basted turkeys... clearly, big appetites needed to be sated before big decisions could be made, Wolfgang concluded.

Wolfgang seated himself at a spare seat halfway along the line and tried to blend in. The table's surface was littered with papers, boldly embossed with the swastika and the eagle. Wolfgang could guess their tenor: whilst he had received little news from home, other Berliners in his unit had received regular updates and some had been secretly sympathetic to the treatment of the Jews and had filled him in on the latest developments. Jews were now compelled to wear the Star of David at all times and were forbidden from leaving Germany. Only a couple of months ago, news had reached him of Jews being taken from their homes in Berlin and transported to camps somewhere in the east... but no-one seemed to know where exactly... or for what exact purpose. Wolfgang was straining to read some of the titles on the documents spread before him with a growing sense of unease when Heydrich cleared his throat and began to speak.

"Gentlemen, now the rough work has been done, we begin the period of finer work. We need to work in harmony with the civil administration. We count on you gentlemen as far as the final solution is concerned."

The final solution? What could he mean?

Wolfgang started to look again more closely at the folders that were now being opened and scrutinised by high-ranking officers all around him. His brow furrowed as the strange images... drawings and plans came into focus. Then he caught sight of a telling phrase and the slow-dawning truth began to sink in and chill him to the very marrow of his bones. The phrase was: *Lebensunwertes Leben...to exterminate life unworthy of life.*

Then in a terrible rush, he realised what the camps were for; what the Final Solution must be. His mind told him the truth, but he still couldn't bring himself to believe it. Not Germany. Not his own people. Were they capable of such thoughts? Of such unimaginable deeds? Were these educated men sitting around a table really planning the extermination of a whole race of people as though they were nothing more than cockroaches?

His head began to spin and bile began to fill his mouth as Adolf Eichmann spoke again, drawing their attention to references in their folders; explaining complexities and organisational details; speaking in a matter-of-fact monotone as if he were talking about a temperamental boiler or a problematic washing machine. Except he wasn't. He was talking about killing: mass murder on a scale Wolfgang couldn't even begin to imagine or believe he was hearing. He tried to look from face to face, sure he would see the same disgust he felt etched on every muscle, the horror behind each eye... but he saw nothing on the faces emerging through the cigar smoke but studious concentration and the satisfied murmurings of a job thoroughly researched and well presented.

The pictures were nothing short of incredulous... plans of camps that would be constructed, springing out of the soil like nightmares from some lower circle of Dante's hell, with chambers made to look like showers that would be used to trick the Jews to voluntarily go to their deaths like dumb sheep. He heard names he had never heard before: Treblinka; Belzec; Sobibor... these would be pure extermination camps where Poland's Jews would be killed almost immediately upon arrival. Then Auschwitz; Birkenau; Majdanek... where the gas chambers would be only one component of a larger labour camp complex. He listened, aghast, as Eichmann recounted the early teething problems... the initial idea to use gas vans producing carbon monoxide in exhaust fumes... but how this would be insufficient to keep up with demand, so they had moved on to Zyklon B. Again, the mutterings of general approval rippled around the room...

Just when Wolfgang thought he was beyond surprising, that his threshold for loathing and revulsion had been exhausted beyond what was humanly possible... he was proven wrong.

The door opened and another man was shown inside. Clean-shaven and innocuous, he was welcomed in by Eichmann and invited to sit at the end of the table with Heydrich and his own father. Heydrich put out his cigarette in an unfinished plate of dumplings and introduced their newest arrival.

"Gentlemen, allow me to introduce SS Gruppenfuhrer Otto Wachter, who will be the first Governor of Belzec Extermination Camp!" A ripple of applause spread around the room. "Otto- I believe you are acquainted with most people around the table... Dr Wilhelm Dopheide, whose experiments at the camp will doubtless prove enlightening over time; Obersturmbannfuhrer Richard Thomalla, who will oversee the construction of the camp; SS Hauptsturmfuhrer Gottlieb Hering and, of course, our gracious host and Camp Commander directly responsible to your good self... SS Sturmbannfuhrer Christian Wirth."

The gasp that escaped Wolfgang's lips was, luckily, covered by a second trickle of applause as his father nodded his appreciation, while the darkness and smog of the interior of the room covered the shock and tears that welled and brimmed in his eyes. *This was the wonderful promotion that his mother had gushed about in the hallway? To be Chief Executioner? To be the one signing his name to the daily death count? Reporting back to Wachter on the efficiency of his murdering operation and puzzling over how to improve efficiency still further? Did his mother even have the faintest idea of what her husband would be calling his profession from this day forward? Of course not! Her sensibilities were far too delicate for such cold truths and she was too wise to probe too deeply.*

Richard Thomalla was on his feet now, explaining the intricacies of setting up the camp:

"We will site the camp between the Lublin District and the German Distrikt Galizien, so that we can process Jews from both regions- *kill two birds with one stone, eh?*" he grinned, as loud guffaws echoed round the room. "Polish villagers and Jewish slaves will be used to construct it and I anticipate it should be ready by the spring of 1942."

But Wolfgang wasn't listening. He was totally numb and coping with this maelstrom of emotions in the only way he knew how... by floating out of this room and away to a happier place, a happier time. He did what he always did when the real world was too difficult to exist in: he flew to Rachel over the grey moon-shimmer on frosted rooftops and found her in a secret garden where they could be undisturbed till morning.

Rachel!

It suddenly occurred to him that he had been incredibly selfish! Here he was wallowing in his own grief at the knowledge his father was even more of a monster than he had ever imagined and he had completely overlooked the fact that, soon, *very soon,* the Jews he had once thought of as his school friends; neighbours; teachers; doctors... they would all be loaded onto trains and never seen again.

He had to warn Rachel and her family... and he had to do it quickly.

CHAPTER NINETEEN

THE SEARCH FOR RACHEL

'Even the biggest failure,
Even the worst,
Beats the hell out of never trying.'

Meredith Grey
'Grey's Anatomy'

'It is only through labor and painful effort,
By grim energy and resolute courage,
That we move on to better things.'

Theodore Roosevelt

December 1941,
Berlin.

Wolfgang had lain awake all night, his mind a whirlwind of conflicting emotions. On the one hand, he was disgusted by all he had heard that previous evening and even more appalled by the central role that his *own family* were about to play in it. The shame he felt burnt his cheeks and caused him to flip the pillow several times throughout his restless night. However, he was back in Berlin at last and couldn't help but feel the guiltiest twinge of excitement at the possibility of seeing Rachel again; of having the possibility of explaining himself to her, face to face, as he had in so many of his letters, and of finally discovering how she truly felt about him now.

Nevertheless, more important even than that, was the urgency with which he needed to warn the Bravermans before it was too late. Last night, Heydrich had reported that the first thousand Jews had already been sent East on the 18th October to the Lodz ghetto in Poland before travelling on to certain death at Chelmno. They had been told they were going to be deported because the leases had run out on their apartments; Wolfgang wondered if they were naïve enough to believe that fairy tale or just resigned enough to accept any brazen lies the authorities came out with as they simply could do nothing about any of it.

Since then, the Nazis had turned the Levetzow Street synagogue into a transit camp as well as various other synagogues and old people's homes and, now, many more had been taken to locations in Riga, Minsk and Kouno. Once the new camps were built, the steady trickle of trains leaving from Putlitz Street railroad station would become a biblical flood and it was only a matter of time before the knock on the Braverman's door came and they too were told to pack their bags.

Wolfgang had got up sometime in the bleak portentous hours before dawn and wrote Rachel another as-yet-unanswered letter outlining the mortal danger she and her family found themselves in. He warned them to leave as quickly as possible and by any means possible. Failing that, he told them they should hide; find a family they could trust and hide themselves away for the duration... *anything but get on that train*. His letter also asked her to go warn Ariel's family too before they made their escape. He ended the note with a P.S. *'I have and always will love you.'* Then he retired to his bed and whispered his urgent pleas to Eos, Titaness and Goddess of the Dawn, to open the gates of Heaven and let the warming rays of the sun rise at last...

Wolfgang decided to wait until after breakfast to try and find Rachel. Eichmann and the others hadn't left until the early hours and he suspected no-one would be up particularly early the following morning. He didn't want to raise suspicions and have awkward questions to answer, so he decided he would have breakfast before casually telling his parents he was going for a walk. Then he would head for the Jewish Quarter, visit Rachel's house and... well, who knew how the rest would pan out?

****

Breakfast had been a solemn affair. No-one had spoken much; his father was seemingly a little the worse for wear and bleary-eyed, while his mother seemed anxious and preoccupied. Wolfgang made the most of the distractions to excuse himself as soon as the dishes were being cleared away and slipped out the front door unnoticed.

As he walked the familiar streets of Berlin, his mind raced back to the last night he had spent pacing these pavements: when he had rescued Rachel from the shadows and hidden her in the summerhouse. It had been the most terrifying night of his life up to that point, but he could hardly have imagined the horrific sights he would see in the months and years that would follow; sights seared into his grey matter and catalogued in his nightmares forever. There was little doubt, he had left the city a naïve young boy and returned to it now a war-weary man; and the whole process had only taken a matter of months.

Some cities change little over time, retaining the atmosphere that makes them distinct and recognisable despite the passage of time, but Berlin over the last eighteen months was no longer one of those cities. The soul had been sucked out of the place; the people wandering through the crowd-cluttered streets dragged and shuffled their way from shop to shop, not making eye-contact, as though fearful of the people they once called their neighbours; as though the joy that used to fill the air had melted and flowed down the gutters to be replaced by the rancid stench of the sewers below. Even the cats looked threadbare, stalking the shadows suspiciously, while the long-flared faces of horses looked miserable as they wearily pulled carts of coal or milk churns.

There was much that was unfamiliar about the architecture of the city too: when Wolfgang passed shops that had once been owned by generations of Jewish families, the shop fronts had changed and, whilst the stock inside looked similar, the names aboard the windows were wholly German now. Worse still, as he neared Rachel's house, he was shocked to find a barricade with barbed wire separating his progress to his destination any further. On the road ahead was a checkpoint guarded by a pair of soldiers; machine guns slung menacingly over their shoulders. Wolfgang was in his uniform, so approached the nearest soldier with the confidence of a man with the whole weight of the Third Reich behind him.

Immediately, the soldier eyed the stripes on his shoulder and the medal on his chest and stiffened to attention.

"What is all this?" Wolfgang asked, waving a dismissive hand towards the check point in an air of what he hoped appeared mild disinterest.

"It's the entrance to the ghetto, sir," he said, clearly puzzled that Wolfgang wouldn't recognise such an obvious feature of the city.

"I see," replied Wolfgang tentatively, "and how does one... enter the ghetto?"

This time both soldiers looked puzzled, raising their eyebrows simultaneously in surprise.

"Anyone crossing into the Jewish Quarter needs a permit... like a truck driver taking in food supplies... but, generally, this checkpoint is to stop the Jews getting *out*, not to prevent people getting *in*, sir," the first man smirked.

"Of course," he muttered, "I haven't been... home for a long time, that's all," he added by way of explanation.

The soldiers saluted again and Wolfgang turned on his heels and withdrew to formulate a plan. Walking the length and breadth of the next few streets he quickly established that there was no way in or out of the ghetto besides the entrance he had first approached. So, what to do? How to get his message to Rachel and Ariel? Slowly, the shadow of an idea formed, the vague contours taking shape into the pleasing certainty of a fully-formed plan: it seemed unlikely that he could either sneak or talk his way in, so the only sensible option seemed to be to bribe a lorry-driver to take the note in for him, find the address he would give him and deliver the note personally to her house.

The plan was, of course, fraught with risk and uncertainty: most obviously, the driver could inform on him to the authorities. Helping Jews resulted in almost as harsh penalties for the perpetrator as for the Jews that were attempting to help. Equally, the driver could simply pocket the bribe while lying about delivering the letter, or he could be searched by the soldiers and the incriminating evidence discovered. As he walked, Wolfgang considered all of these points and decided that, no matter what the risk or the probable outcome, it was surely better to try and fail... than not to try at all.

Wolfgang sat at a table near the checkpoint and ordered a coffee. He sipped at the strong thick liquid and watched, looking for a likely messenger... Several trucks passed by with officious, stern-faced individuals behind the wheel, splashing their way through puddles the colour of pewter. Wolfgang continued to wait. After forty minutes, a cart turned the corner with a jovial-looking individual perched on the edge of his seat gently frisking the reins he held in his hands to coax his ancient nag forward. He had the bushiest of moustaches and rosy cheeks so his physical appearance made Wolfgang think he should be a figure on a poster advertising a foaming jug of beer. Wolfgang nodded to himself and moved quickly. Intercepting the man before he was in sight of the guards, he stood in front of the horse and pretended to show an interest in the tired old mare. Smiling, he stroked the piebald mane as the horse whinnied gratefully at such rare attention.

"Ah! You like Griselda, I see," said the man with delighted surprise.

"Yes," Wolfgang replied, "it's nice to see a horse still being used for a purpose other than to pull artillery." He shook his head sadly. "I saw thousands of poor horses give their lives for the Fuhrer on the Eastern Front."

The beaming smile slipped instantly from the man's face and his thick moustache drooped like a sad boomerang. "Damned Russians and damned snow!" he cursed, spitting into the road as if to emphasise his disgust.

Wolfgang nodded in agreement.

"You go through to the Jewish Quarter every day?" he ventured, testing the water.

The man's eyes narrowed. "I do: somebody has to take them supplies or they will starve. I am adequately rewarded for my pains though."

That was good enough for Wolfgang: he had not immediately bemoaned his lot at having to deal with stinking, lying Jews and had, instead, only justified his involvement with them as an afterthought.

"What's your name, friend?" Wolfgang asked.

The man paused, considering whether he could tell the character of a man through the intensity of his gaze.

"My name is Ulf," he said, deciding you probably could.

"Well, Ulf," Wolfgang said, "I have a friend beyond those barricades who needs more than food, she needs my help. Only I can't help her." Reaching into the inside of his jacket pocket, he brought out his wallet and withdrew a thick wedge of notes. Then he took out the envelope with his note for Rachel inside. "But *you* could help and you will also be *adequately* rewarded… in this world and the next."

Ulf glanced all around him then, quickly, took the money and the note and stuffed them inside his pockets giving a large sniff of satisfaction when the task was completed.

"The address is on the envelope."

Ulf nodded and clicked his teeth gently. Griselda flicked an ear to one side and broke into a slow walk.

"When will you return?"

Ulf shrugged, "a few hours, give or take."

"I'll wait for you."

****

The day passed as if Wolfgang were on a never-ending treadmill, forever going nowhere. He tried to pass the time by revisiting the places he had been with Rachel and Ariel but, when he stood in the bandstand in the park and looked out over the ice-coated earth, he struggled to make the connection between this barren wasteland and the world in which he had laughed and kissed and loved in with

Rachel. The outline was there but the fire, the passion, had died; it was like gazing at long dead volcanoes decked in ice but still billowing plumes of grey, vanishing sorrowfully into the upper atmosphere.

Besides, he didn't dare be away for too long in case Ulf returned early and he missed him. So, by lunchtime he was back at the same café, only this time inside looking out, as the sky turned granite grey and the heavens opened. He nursed a couple of beers and some bread and sausage for the next two hours, glancing continually at his watch like an expectant father, until Griselda finally trotted into view, her head bobbing like a cork in water. Wolfgang resisted the acute urge to run over until the horse and cart had turned the corner into the square and away from the suspicious eyes of the guards.

Then he did run. At a sudden parting of the darkness, the rain ceased and the sun broke through and Wolfgang was filled with an irrational hope that Rachel was well and had missed him like he had missed her and that Ulf had a love letter stashed in those rough woollen trousers of his, laughingly held up with a thick coil of rope... and he was filled with that hope right until the moment he met Ulf's stare. Then his heart sank, for this was no Mercury, messenger of the Gods, bringing great tidings in his winged helmet and sandals; these were times when good news was in pitifully short supply.

Ulf shook his head sadly and reached into his pocket.

"I went to the address you said, but the house was empty."

"Well, did you push the letter through the door anyway?" Wolfgang asked urgently.

Again, Ulf shook his head, "no point; they've gone. There's a notice on the door informing them their lease has run out and that the house is to be re-appropriated for a German family once the ghetto is fully emptied."

He held out the note and the money.

Wolfgang shook his head. "No, you keep it," he said, pushing his hand away.

"But I didn't..." he began.

"No, you did your part," Wolfgang interrupted, forcing a smile, "get some apples for Griselda from me."

Then he turned and walked away as the clouds closed over the sun once more and the rain began to pour.

CHAPTER TWENTY

A SMALL SQUARE OF STARS

'To live is the rarest thing in the world.
Most people exist, that is all.'

Oscar Wilde

December 1941,
Berlin

If Wolfgang had passed his note to Ulf a mere fortnight earlier, Rachel or Elizabeth, Esther or one of their parents, may well have opened the door but, instead, his beloved lay on a lumpy bed and stared through a skylight at the same square of stars that had been her view for the last twelve days: Orion hunting them down for the dirty Jews they were, his bejewelled knife glinting through the clouds like a permanent reminder of the constant danger of discovery they faced. Of even greater bitter irony was the physical closeness Wolfgang was to Rachel and her family- *just two streets away*- as he sat at that café and wondered at the fate that had befallen his precious love.

Since he had last seen them, it had been an increasingly difficult couple of years for the Braverman family and, if Mr. Braverman ever stopped worrying long enough to really think about it, he would have regretted not getting them all out of Germany when he had the chance. Taken them to England like they had talked about so many times... but chances come and go in the blink of an eye. A spin of a wheel. A roll of the dice. And now it was too late. Now they were forbidden from leaving; which seemed incomprehensible to Rachel as they were clearly despised by the Germans who, one would have logically thought, would have been glad to see the back of them. Apparently not. So, they had struggled on. Until the day had rolled around for *them* to take the train to oblivion and father had put his plan into action and..., well, here was where they had ended up.

Here was the attic space above Mr. Sankt's shop. Mr. Sankt had worked for years with Mr. Braverman learning the jewellery trade under his kind and skilful eye until, with her father's blessing, he had branched out and established his own successful business. They had remained friends ever since and, crucially, he was German through and through: Aryan ancestry as far back as could be traced. The kind of friend every Jew needed...

For months, rumours had infiltrated and spread through the ghetto like an icy draught, freezing the blood like overheard whispered nightmares and starting almost as soon as the first people began being transported East. The optimistic were willing to believe they were being re-settled in new Jewish communities somewhere in Poland or Russia and went willingly; after all, *anywhere* had to be better than *here*, they argued. But Mr. Braverman was no fool. If they were being re-settled, why was nothing more heard of them again? *Any* of them.

Not a letter, not a postcard, *nothing*.

Some feared the worst and committed suicide, rather than be forced to leave the homes of their forefathers for... only God knew where and, apparently, he wasn't saying. Others hid: hid in cellars, in secret compartments behind walls, under floorboards, in attics, in wall spaces, in the most implausible of holes barely suited to a cat... the choice of location was often as varied as the ingenuity and invention behind it.

Mr. Sankt had made a pact with Rachel's father back in early 1940 that, when the time came, he would help him and his family in recompense for all the help and kindness showered on him and his own family over the past thirty years. And so it came to pass. One day, remarkable only for its very ordinariness, Mr. Braverman came home from the munitions factory where he now reluctantly worked, to find the eviction notice hammered on the door and, without panic or tears, immediately went up to his room and began packing; as they all did, as they had rehearsed many times in the weeks prior to that day. Then they waited patiently for night to fall and cover their escape.

Under the blanket of a moonless sky, Mr. Sankt arrived in his van and, one by one, they slipped noiselessly into the back, before undertaking the heart-stopping journey to his shop and climbing the stairs to their new home.

The attic.

It had been split by Mr. Sankt into two rooms: parents in one room, Rachel, Elizabeth, Esther and the baby in the other. The barest of possessions to offer comfort and solace: two double beds (one shared by Elizabeth and Esther), a single bed and an extended cot beneath a single bulb and the goldfish bowl of the skylight. A table and chairs; kitchen utensils, plates and food; and a few boxes and drawers to store clothes and personal items. A handful of finger-worn books, a radio and an ageing pile of newspapers Mr. Sankt or his morose teenage son, Walther, brought up to keep them informed of the seemingly inching progess of the war.

Ah, yes, the *baby!*

Rachel had found out she was pregnant shortly after Wolfgang had disappeared.

Of course, she had been so angry with him at first: How could he leave her without a word after those precious, wondrous few months they had spent together... after that final night in the bandstand making their own mystical music? She had waited for him to come around, to contact her... but nothing. Finally, in desperation, she had gone to his fine house, sneaked around to the servants' entrance and waited for one of them to come out. Casting nervous glances all around her, the girl, Katarina, had told Rachel he had gone to war and didn't know when he would be back. Rachel sensed there was more to it than that, but the girl refused to be pressed. Frustrated and confused, she had no choice but to return home and wait until she received some news, some sign, that he still loved her... that he was still alive. So she waited...

And then Felix came; a symbol both of joy and shame.

In normal times, she would have been sent away to have the baby; forced to have it adopted, or worse, while the subject would never have been spoken of again. But these were anything but normal times. Restrictions on movement meant she couldn't have been sent away even if her father had demanded it. As it was, he considered it for a while and decided, much to the amazement of everyone else in the household, to view the child as one tiny source of salvation in a world full of endless hurt and loss. Thus, they let nature take its course and, if the truth be told, Felix's innocent smile had been the only thing that had kept all of them going through many of the dark, bitter days that followed.

When not staring into the innocent eyes of her young son, Rachel had spent countless more hours trying to discover the truth of what had happened to her beloved. She became convinced Wolfgang must have been forced by his father to enlist- *why else would he have not told her he was going before he left? Or even come to say goodbye?* She slowly became equally convinced that he would write and explain. But, as the weeks turned to months, her excitement drifted into doubt, then disappointment until, finally, her grief deepened and settled and, when she eagerly questioned her parents each day on her return home from school as to whether *she* had any post, her mother would simply shake her head and turn away. Slowly, she had to accept the previously unthinkable possibility that Wolfgang had joined up to *escape* her: a way out from the humiliation of being weighed down by association with a Jew. Then the baby came and there was so much to do... who knew being a mother was *so exhausting?* Wolfgang was never forgotten, but she had to direct her love to the one who needed it most; who couldn't survive without it... the one who was *there*.

As she gazed up at the skylight, her father appeared soundlessly beside her. Rachel didn't start; they were used to moving about the place as secretly as ghosts: who was she kidding? They *were* ghosts. They didn't *exist* anymore- they had left everything behind... school, work, friends, home... nothing existed of their old selves. They were shadows; ciphers; nonentities... ghosts.

"What are you thinking about, my child?" he whispered.

Even at night they had to creep about and whisper. The hunt for Jews was zealously embraced every minute of the day *and* night. They could be below them right now, creeping up the stairs, or with a stethoscope pressed to the wall, listening for the tell-tale heartbeat of life.

In truth, Rachel had been thinking about Wolfgang when her father stole into her thoughts, but she knew if she said that, he would not be able to hide his sadness; and he had enough to be upset about without her adding to his woes. She looked across at him and smiled at his earnest expression and little round glasses perched on the end of his nose. Despite their situation, he still retained a smartness about him in his collarless shirt, waistcoat with the gleaming hint of a pocket watch, thick corduroy trousers and snow-white hair loosely parted atop a face wind-lashed and worry-worn: he was down but not beaten and Rachel loved him for that.

"How long do you think we will have to stay here father?" she asked.

He smiled sadly and sat beside her on the edge of the bed. He pointed up at the skylight above their heads.

"Last night," he said, "I came in here to look at you while you slept and, as I glanced up, a shooting star blazed across our little square, unzipping the night sky in its brilliance and I made a wish on that star. I wished that we would all leave this place, together and in peace." He took her hand in his and stroked it with his own rough fingertips. "I don't know how long it will take- that will be however long the war lasts, and which side eventually emerges victorious, of course- but I do believe we will emerge from all of this alive and well and ready to put this hold on our lives behind us; ready to start a new chapter where we have a future again."

Rachel lay back and closed her eyes. She had no idea if her father truly believed any of what he had just told her... but it was lovely to let herself dream it; even if only for a little while.

CHAPTER TWENTY ONE

TOO COOL FOR SCHOOL

'Being uncool is being pretty much the coolest you can be.'

Rufus Wainwright

'Rather be dead than cool.'

Kurt Cobain

June 1999,
Friday morning round William and Gabriel's house.

Harry had spent most of the morning mowing the lawn and weeding the edges, and had found it strangely calming and satisfying. It was a welcome world away from the pressures and stress of trying to avoid getting your head kicked in or permanently excluded. Whilst William had wildly exaggerated the overgrown state of the garden, he certainly had not exaggerated the amount of attention required to maintain its bowling-green-like perfection. All morning, Gabriel had been informing him as to the names of the flowers he had pruned earlier and he was now familiar with everything from the magnolias to the clematis that crawled beautifully up the side fence. Gabriel was currently trimming back various bushes and shrubs and burning the pruned back branches in an old oil drum when they both heard the phone ring inside.

After a small pause, William appeared at the back door.

"Erm, it's for you," he smirked, indicating for Harry to follow him inside.

Harry wondered what the smirk could possibly be about; it had to be either his Mom or Nan... nobody else knew he was there. Still, he picked up the receiver and spoke tentatively into it.

"Hello?"

"Harry? Hi, it's Maggie," the voice at the other end of the phone announced.

Harry felt his stomach plummet like a lift with its cable cut and, in an instant, his mouth went as dry as sandpaper.

"Oh, erm, hi. How did you know I was here?" he mumbled, then immediately regretted it, not wanting to sound as if he were interrogating her.

"I looked your home number up in the phone book, then your Nan gave me this number."

Harry tried to think of something to say... of *anything* to say but the only sound was the booming bass drum in his head.

"I just phoned to see if you were all right?" Maggie said after an eternity, "Mr. Murdoch said you'd been excluded and I just think that's so unfair! I told him so too in no uncertain terms!" she added with a little chuckle to herself.

"Oh, thanks," Harry replied, looking up to find William gesticulating wildly at him. "Hold on a minute," he told Maggie, before holding his hand over the receiver. "*What?*" he hissed.

"Invite her over, idiot!"

Harry blinked and blushed. He stared at William mutely, then sighed resignedly. He put his ear back to the receiver to find Maggie already speaking.

"...you still there Harry?"

"Yeah...sorry. Thanks for calling, it's really made my day."

Harry felt he could almost sense Maggie's smile on the other end of the line and grew in confidence slightly. He decided to go against his every instinct and chance his arm...

"Listen, my Mom's grounded me for, like, *ever* and I'm going out of my mind with no-one under the age of forty to talk to. How'd you fancy coming over after school to keep me company?" he blurted out then, when he was met with silence on the other end, he quickly added, "I mean, if you'd like to."

Harry bit down hard on his lip to force himself to shut up and wait for her response. Thankfully, he wasn't kept waiting long.

"I'd love to."

Harry blinked in surprise then punched the air like he'd just scored the winning goal in the World Cup Final. William grinned and gave him the thumbs up sign as he gave her their address and said he'd see her later. The line went dead and Harry found himself engulfed by William in an unexpected and extremely embarrassing bear-hug!

"All right, all right, take it easy!" Harry laughed, "I don't know why you're getting so excited; she's just coming round after school to hang out, that's all."

"From small acorns..." William grinned just as Gabriel walked in, taking off his gardening gloves and leaving them on the side. He went to the fridge and started pouring them cold drinks.

"Harry's gone and got himself a date!" William announced like a proud father.

Harry threw his hands into the air in mock horror.

"You two are *ridiculous!* You're too old to be getting so excited about this!"

Gabriel snorted in derision, "We're not old; you just need to add a little for postage and packaging to our ages that's all. Besides, love transcends age."

"You're wasting your breath anyway," Harry argued, "I'm hopeless with girls, always have been. I'm not... *cool.* When she comes round later I'll blow it, I know I will. It'll be a miracle if she's even speaking to me by the end of today."

Gabriel raised an eyebrow at William and, handing him a glass of ice-cold lemonade, put a protective arm around Harry.

"If I could go back in time," he began, "and sidle up to my teenage self; all spotty, and self-conscious; gangly as a human bicycle and squinting at the blackboard from behind jam-jar spectacles, know what advice I'd give that nervous mess of hormones? I'd tell myself to *bloody well relax!* Take a break from worrying about the inconsequential things- the belly button fluff of life; the things that really don't matter when you really stop to think about it." He paused to look Harry in the eye, "Think of it like this," he added, "there are six billion people on the planet... whatever the hell we do with our lives, however we embarrass ourselves, whatever failures we may experience...in the grand scheme of things, none of it really matters. So don't worry about making a fool of yourself- go with the flow... and have some *fun* while you're still young!"

Harry smiled, "I guess you're right," he conceded, "it's just there's a fine line between being 'mean and moody' and just coming across as 'monosyllabic and morose'. I'm not sure I'm very good at walking that line, or even knowing where it's drawn in the sand."

William picked up his glass of lemonade and motioned for them to join him outside.

"Come on," he said, "I think better in the sunlight."

****

Outside, the sun was still streaming down in thick shafts, warming their very bones as they sat on fold-out chairs and basked in the pleasantness of it.

"What is this Maggie like?" asked William, his eyes closed and head tilted upward to get a full face of sun splashing down onto his wrinkled features.

"She's... smart and cool... and gorgeous. She seems to know what she wants and isn't afraid of what other people think; she's sophisticated and... she's everything I'm not, basically."

William nodded. "In that case," he said, "my advice is this: if begging is your lot in life- only knock on the doors of the big houses."

Not for the first time, Harry looked at him utterly bemused.

"William- what on earth are you talking about?"

"What I mean, foolish boy, is that if you're going to go down in a blaze of glory, do it with somebody *worth the effort!*"

Gabriel opened his eyes briefly and nodded sagely, then went back to sunbathing. Harry stared straight ahead at the view: The trees at the bottom of the garden seemed suddenly full of great bursts of life; leaf after leaf crowding in on one another on beautifully burgeoning branches. Suddenly, life seemed full of possibilities... possibilities that *might* have happy endings, possibilities worth taking risks for. For the first time in a very long time, Harry felt... *optimistic.*

CHAPTER TWENTY TWO

A CRY IN THE DARK

*'Now I know what a ghost is.
Unfinished business, that's what.'*

*Salman Rushdie
'The Satanic Verses'*

August 1942,
Berlin.

The summerhouse was dark but the moon, luminous through the black panes of glass, gave it an ethereal glow. Wolfgang was kissing the back of her neck and she could feel the tender touch of the tips of his fingers sending spider legs running up and down her spine. Her skin was strewn with goose-bumps but she wasn't in the least bit cold. This was the best time of the night... past the leaden tolling of the early hours, but still some way off morning; so even the birds had not yet even begun the opening strains of their dawn symphony. Wolfie had his arms around her and she felt perfectly happy and perfectly safe. He was whispering in her ear now... too faint for her to decipher... She strained and mumbled for him to speak more clearly, but it was still indistinguishable. It seemed to be more of a cry... a gurgle... She felt puzzled. Wolfie was holding her tighter now... squeezing her arm... she opened her eyes...saw a square of stars...

...and Elizabeth standing over her.

"Quick. Felix is awake."

She pushed back the sheets and rolled out of bed on auto pilot but with an innate sense of urgency bred from being in almost constant danger. Felix had stirred and was bleating, half awake, half asleep, like a little lamb.

At the very same time Rachel gathered him up, still swaddled in his blankets for warmth, in the hallway two floors below, a German soldier removed the stethoscope he had pressed to the wall and turned to face his commanding officer with a triumphant smile on his face. He nodded curtly and the officer smiled back.

"So the boy was telling the truth," he hissed, referring to Walther Sankt who, as a member of the Gestapo Youth and disgusted that his *own parents* had sheltered Jewish scum, had happily signed all of their death warrants...

The officer turned and nodded in the direction of the open doorway that led directly onto the street. Behind him, the tailgate at the back of a truck parked on the pavement swung down and half a dozen soldiers, machine guns in hand, jumped down and began pounding up the stairs, the heart-stopping thuds of their jackboots preceding them; stealth no longer their main concern.

The noise of the Gestapo reaching the top of the steps above the shop and breaking into the apartment below, then the cries of Mr. Sankt's wife, Angelika, as she was dragged from her bed, was more than sufficient to wake Ruth and Benjamin Braverman; even before their three daughters hurried into their room, tears running down their cheeks in wet rivulets and visibly shaking with absolute unbridled terror. Rachel held Felix close to her breast and tried not to scream. He seemed to be the only one oblivious to their imminent fate, having dozed off to sleep again in the warmth of his mother's embrace. Mr. Braverman swung his feet out of the bed, his shaking hand clutching for his spectacles from the top of the upturned fruit box that stood by the side of the bed and served as a makeshift bedside table. He had just managed to get between his family and the door when the Germans unceremoniously crashed in; Walther at their shoulder, showing them the secret entrance behind a sliding bookcase and pointing the way like a modern-day Judas.

Everyone paused for the briefest of moments, like the stand-off in the second before a gunfighter draws his gun in a flash, or like circling boxers sizing each other up in the ring, before the candle flickered and died where it stood on the fruit box and the spell was broken. The Captain pointed a gun at Rachel's father and spoke more loudly than anyone had in that room for over eight months.

"We can do this the easy way Mr. Braverman, or the difficult way: get your family together and come with us."

Rachel saw her father's shoulders slump a little and a chill resignation seep over him like melting snow. But Rachel set her jaw defiantly against the Nazis lined up in front of her. She was not going to let this moment be the moment of surrender; the moment she gave up on life. Kissing the top of her sleeping baby's head, she offered up a silent prayer that she hoped was strong enough to pierce at least the cellar of Heaven with the strength of her prayer, *for she was not done living yet.* As she said the words, she felt herself suddenly filled to the brim with a resolve so potent and powerful that every fibre of her body told her this was not going to be the end of the line: she still had unfinished business with life, with Felix and with Wolfie and this ghost would hide herself away fearfully in the rafters no longer.

CHAPTER TWENTY THREE

KEEPING THE CANDLE ALIGHT

'In three words I can sum up everything about life:
It goes on.'

Robert Frost

'She girdeth her loins with strength and strengthened her arms,
She seeth that her merchandise is good;
Her candle is not put out by night.
She putteth her hands to the wheel,
And her hands handle the spindle.'

Proverbs, xxxi: 17-19

August 1942,
On the train to Belzec Extermination Camp.

For the two days following their discovery in the Sankt's attic, Rachel and the rest of the family had waited in agonising purgatory at the Levetzow synagogue; which served as a holding station until there was space on a train. They had been half-heartedly fed and watered and slept on makeshift beds in rough rows arranged the length and breadth of the synagogue; the otherwise empty building long since stripped bare of furniture and anything else of value. Still, at least the religious images that adorned the walls and ceiling offered some kind of solace to Rachel as the benevolent eyes of saints looked sadly down on them from above. Despite the crush of people, it was still relatively cool inside and far preferable to being outside in the sweltering summer heat.

The room was a buzz with rumour and counter-rumour: what country they were to be taken to; what conditions would be waiting for them; whether they would be housed in a new Jewish community and left alone to start afresh or whether they were to be set to work in Work Camps to aid the war effort.

Everyone had an opinion.

Everyone except father.

From the moment they had been piled into the back of the truck and driven here, surrounded by the soldiers who had captured them, he had barely uttered a single syllable. It was as if he already knew their fate was sealed and there was nothing left to do to rectify the mistake he had made not evacuating his family when he had the chance and now there was nothing to do but await their fate. His last chance had been to squirrel his family away, like precious jewels or gold bars hidden under the floorboards until the War was over and, hopefully, the Nazis had tasted bitter defeat. Only then could they emerge, like tiny hibernating creatures blinking in the rubble, and start again. But he had missed his opportunity; he'd had a chance to save them all and he'd let it slip through his fingers.

Mother fussed round him and pressed his rations (as well as half of her own) into his open palms, laid loosely open on his lap, but he was already in a place too far away for any train to reach.

On the morning of the third day, they were abruptly awoken by whistles and shouts and the insistent barks of alsatians. They were told to gather their possessions together as they would be leaving in five minutes. Everyone obeyed, setting about the task with clumsy urgency, throwing items into battered suitcases daubed with the names and addresses of their owners in white paint, or even scratched on in chalk. Others pulled on winter coats and wrapped scarves around their necks despite the heat for, surely, where they were heading was far away in the frozen East and they would freeze without them.

Running the gauntlet of two unbroken lines of soldiers, everyone was jostled along at uneasy haste towards a long line of cattle carts that seemed to stretch endlessly away from them, starting from the platform and ending somewhere in a vanishing point far down the tracks. The fireman and engineer leaned lazily out of their engine, both staring stone-faced at the dismal procession that passed by a few feet below them. Rachel had no baggage because they had been given no time to collect their belongings from the attic, so she had simply girded her loins and pulled Felix tighter to her bosom, half-hidden as he was beneath the woollen folds of her coat. She tried to keep pace with her mother and sisters, but was continually being swayed and shoved this way and that, forcing her to submit to the eddying undercurrent of the crowd.

The urgent throng throbbed and surged, lapping against the railings to their left that offered no hope of escape; only their cries seeping through the barbed wire and slipping away to freedom on the traitorous wind. One young man carefully placed his suitcase on the floor then, suddenly, made a break, like a fox bolting from its hiding place as the hounds honed in, diving the opposite way, onto the tracks and rolling under the train itself, before scrabbling to his feet on the other side. He was spotted almost immediately, shouts rising from furious guards, as the dogs jumped up and strained at their leashes, eager not to be left out the game. Half a dozen guards left their place in the line to clamber between the wagons, (many of which were already stuffed with human cargo), appearing on the far side and scanning the middle distance for signs of the escapee.

The runner was already halfway down the length of the train, heading in the direction the train would shortly go; as if he were eager to beat it to its unknown destination. Three or four soldiers took careful aim. A volley of shots rang out, a few making pinging noises as they ricocheted off the metal track or thudded into the soft forgiving wood of the wagons... but two found their mark.

The man was stopped dead in his tracks as the first bullet struck him full in the back, sending his arms flailing upwards, as though in futile surrender, before the second embedded itself in his shoulder, the impact spinning him round like a top before he crashed to the floor in a dusty heap.

Two of the soldiers ambled up to him, smiling with satisfaction at each other, before planting two more bullets in his head; as if to emphasise their displeasure at the sheer gall of the man daring to try to avoid their iron will.

Rachel was now at the entrance of a cattle truck. Its door was already slid open and the crowd were in the urgent process of tossing their suitcases ahead of them into the void of the dimly lit space before clambering in after them. Even from her place in the heart of the queue, a rancid stench of sweat and urine emanating from the truck filled the air; which seemed odd to Rachel as this was, after all, the *start* of their journey, not the *end*. But she didn't have long to contemplate this mystery as screams behind her violently gripped her attention and squeezed at her pounding heart.

"*No! Please! Please! Hurry! Hurry! Move inside the truck! Please!*"

The pleas were punctuated with cries of undisguised agony. Rachel craned her neck to see the source of this desperation and caught the briefest glimpse of steel raised in the sunlight. With a horrified gasp, she realised the source of their panic: the *Germans were bayonetting the stragglers or clubbing them with the butts of their rifles in a cruel and vicious effort to hurry them on board.* Rachel felt her jaw go slack...each time she believed she had seen every horror this war had to offer, it found new and unique horrors with which to surpass her expectations.

A guard stood impassively to the side of the wagon, counting them on as they ripped nails, scuffed knees and pierced their palms with splinters in their mad desire to get on board the foul-smelling hellhole. As Rachel hurried past him, she heard him muttering under his breath:

"Sixty-seven, sixty eight, sixty…"

Rachel was past him now and pushing up as best she could while still trying to protect Felix. Her tights laddered and tore as they pulled on the rough floorboards. She was shoved from behind from those desperate not to feel the sharp end of a bayonet and fell inside, hitting her head as she stumbled, as she stubbornly refused to lose her grip on Felix. Dragging herself back to her feet, she forced herself forward until she was as far inside the carriage as she could manage; whereupon she quickly found her face pressed against the musty shirt of the man in front of her as ranks closed in all around her and pinned her there. There must have been close to eighty people crammed in the rank semi-darkness. Rachel tried not to retch at the claustrophobic hell she found herself in, packed in so tight she felt it would soon be impossible even to exhale, while she had to hold Felix above her head for fear of him being smothered to death against her own breast. Others held their arms aloft too; such was the crush, making it impossible to even stand shoulder to shoulder.

When it seemed so cramped that even a cat couldn't have wound its way between the forest of legs, the doors slid shut and the wagon was cast into an eerie darkness but for the thin strips of light running in parallel lines along the sides of the coach. A morbid silence fell upon the praying congregation within; with the notable exceptions of the low moans and cries of those wounded from the bayonet's point and still bleeding.

Outside, the last carriage was finally filled with the remaining dregs of men, women and children to be encased in their moving tombs and slammed remorselessly shut.

The conductors signalled *'All aboard'*, the brakemen waved their lanterns, and the engineer opened the throttle. Slowly, the train pulled out the station and began to pick up speed.

A soldier glanced at his watch and noted it was right on time…

****

Almost three days and nights had passed since the train had left Putlitz Street station and, if Rachel had thought the smell of the wagon had been fetid and disgusting then, it was utterly beyond description now. Within hours, the first victims started falling foul of the exhausting conditions and began to collapse onto their equally exhausted neighbours: an elderly woman, sweating profusely in a fur coat, who had been complaining of a pain in her chest for some time to anyone who would listen, suddenly gasped like a fish for air momentarily and, without warning, stopped breathing. Such was the closeness of the inhabitants, she didn't even fall to the ground but was, instead, suspended in vertical death between her appalled neighbours, her head lolling grotesquely this way and that as the train shuddered and swayed on the endless tracks.

A few miles out of Berlin, others in her compartment had started calling out to try to determine if friends and relatives were trapped in the same carriage alongside them; it was simply too dark to see past the immediate circle of pinched and anxious faces. Rachel soon did the same.

"Mother? Elizabeth? Esther? It's Rachel... *can you hear me?*"

A muffled cry came from somewhere over her shoulder.

"Rachel, it's me- Esther... I'm behind you... I can see Felix in your arms. Are you both all right?"

Rachel cried out in a gasp of relief.

"Yes! Yes! I'm tired but we're fine."

Then Elizabeth and their mother called out and the four of them could at least communicate, even if there was no possible way of moving closer to each other. They called out repeatedly for father... but no reply had come.

After a time, people in the wagon began to ask questions of those on the periphery, looking out through the cracks between the planking of the wooden walls: *What could they see? Had they recognised anywhere? What about the names of stations?* But they confessed they could see only fleeting glimpses of greenery or industrial landscape and only occasionally could they catch the odd name of a station as they sailed right through it.

The train did not stop once.

Later still, people cried out that they could wait no longer to relieve themselves. A man replied saying that, by his feet, there were two buckets: one full of water, one empty, which he presumed was to be used as a toilet. Murmurs of relief and disgust echoed around the darkness in equal measure and individuals urged him to pass the empty bucket over to them... but he confessed be couldn't bend down to pick it up.

After a protracted argument, a plan was hatched to pass the bucket along by kicking it along from person to person, from muddy boot to scuffed shoe until it reached a person in desperate need. It was an incredibly time-consuming and painful process. The Germans seemed to have worked out the absolute maximum number of people that could fit into a single carriage and had left no room for leeway. Like the black slaves in the holds of cargo ships, they were nestled as close together as the space between sheets of paper and, like those sea-sloshed slaves, they too did not know their final destination or the fate that awaited them when they reached it.

For a few of the lucky ones closest to the man with the buckets, they were able to position themselves astride the bucket and relieve themselves into it, but the more people that did so, the heavier it became, sloshing over trouser legs as they tried to shuffle it along until, eventually, all attempts were abandoned out of sheer exhaustion and a reluctance to move the stench any closer towards them. At that point, when people could wait no longer, they simply had to relieve themselves in their clothes; there was no other choice. A handful managed to slither and slide and squirm their way to their knees and thrust their heads into the bucket of stale water, lapping noisily at it like dogs while everyone else wailed bitterly at the unfairness of it all while their throats burned with thirst.

****

By the middle of the third day, Rachel was no longer standing; she was merely being propped up by the throng. The throats of the tortured passengers were so parched and bone dry, all words had long since died on their chapped lips, while Rachel's legs burned with lactose acid from standing for so many relentlessly unbroken hours; as though she were a martyr permanently being burnt at the stake while the flames refused to travel higher than her thighs and finally end her misery.

During the first day, Felix had cried and whimpered and moaned, begging Rachel for food and water when she had none to give him.

She had been unable to hold him above her head for long, before being forced to lower him onto her shoulder and the shoulders of two men whose backs were almost in her face. They complained at first but, seeing her distress and understanding the nature of the situation, accepted there was nothing else to be done and shouldered the tiny burden without further complaint.

Throughout the second day, Felix seemed to sleep more and more. Rachel knew this was from exhaustion and dehydration rather than any comfort she was providing, and she repeatedly tried to moisten his chapped little lips with her own spit, only to find her own mouth a barren wasteland in which no refreshing sustenance could be found.

Rachel was barely aware of the dawning of the third day. All through the journey there had been no water provided. No food. No toilet. No ventilation. An unknown number of people had died now; it was impossible to say how many as all still remained standing, in a silent mockery of death. As glints of sunlight flashed like diamonds in the slivers between the flaking and sun-bleached slats of wood, groggily, Rachel slowly became aware of a tiny imbalance in the way Felix was suspended across her shoulders. He suddenly felt different... no longer helping in his own little way to help ease the burden by shifting ever so slightly to give a break to a numb patch of shoulder blade by shuffling a few centimetres along; a tightrope walker across bones, before finding a new resting place.

Now he was perfectly still.

A dead weight pressing down on her mercilessly.

Rachel pushed her hand upwards from her side. Her whole arm was so numb, she could not even feel the fingers still dangling on the end of it. Bringing her hand up through the swell of bodies was like pulling it free of quicksand and inching it upwards like a new shoot trying to break to surface of the soil, and the sweat formed on her forehead in glistening beads as she worked it higher, inch by agonising inch. Eventually, she pushed through the seemingly never-ending mass of conjoined limbs until it sprung out, limp as a jack-in-the-box. Rachel struggled to gain control over it, flexing and un-flexing it until she could place it on Felix's cold head. Fighting back the tears, she moved it down to his face and held it suspended there... praying for the slightest hint of breath on her palm.

There was none.

Rachel put her head back, opened her mouth and screamed a silent, horrific cry of grief that died before even leaving her parched throat. Her eyes filled with tears that stung as they ran down her face. Her exhausted mind drifted to the thoughts that had filled the countless hours since they were loaded aboard once more: were her mother and sisters still alive? What had happened to her father? What was worth living for now that Felix was gone? She wondered where the resolve was that she had felt so strongly until so very recently, the fire that had looked the Nazis in the eyes and demanded they do their worst... and she wondered what had happened to her dear Wolfie, who had not been there when she needed him more than ever... *more than ever...*

CHAPTER TWENTY FOUR

VISIT TO CAMP BELZEC

'All that people have they will give to save their lives.'

William Golding

'War does not determine who is right-
Only who is left.'

Bertrand Russell

19th August 1942,
Belzec Extermination Camp

The camp was in a state of heightened panic because Obersturmfuhrer Kurt Gerstein was visiting to report back to Adolf Hitler himself on the efficient running of the camp. The sky was still grey as pigeon feathers as Wolfgang yawned blearily and watched them all, scurrying around like disorientated ants, animatedly pointing here and there, and double checking every insignificant cog in the camp's smooth operation.

Wolfgang had been posted to his living nightmare almost five months ago but, to him, it felt like he had been trapped in this ghoulish otherworld for an eternity.

****

After returning home from his fruitless search for Rachel back in the icy mists of December, his mother had been waiting for him and anxiously intercepted him the moment he walked in through the door. Refusing to be deterred, she had sent him straight through to his father's study, where he had been waiting patiently for him, sat upright and stiff as a piano and pristinely turned out, as though about to conduct some formal interview.

To Wolfgang's utter horror, he happily informed him that, due to the fact he had finally proved himself on the field of battle and had lived up to the almost unattainable expectations required to be a Wirth, his father had pulled a few strings and, not only he was to be promoted, but he was also to be permitted to work *alongside him when he left in the spring for Belzec camp!* Wolfgang's jaw fell slack and, momentarily, he was dumbfounded. When he did find a voice, his anguished protestations that he would rather return to almost certain death at the Russian Front fell on deaf ears. His father was not for persuading and interpreted his outburst as little more than simple misguided bravery... his desire not to have a cushy posting with no risk to life and limb. Unsurprisingly, mother was immensely proud and relieved: her two boys would be working together for the brighter future of the Fatherland and in a place far from the front line where they would be safe and sound... though whether she had any clue as to the nature of their 'heroic undertaking for the Fatherland' remained unclear.

****

What followed was a bizarre and utterly surreal Christmas in which Wolfgang repeatedly tried and failed to convince his father to arrange a posting somewhere else... *anywhere* else. While everyone else decorated Christmas trees and sang carols and welcomed in the New Year, in *his* strange parallel universe he found himself watching the celebrations unfold around him, whilst being totally numb to the sights and smells of Christmas.

He thought seriously about deserting... *but where would he go?* It seemed the whole world was at war and nowhere could offer sanctuary from the conflict. Also, he couldn't help thinking he didn't *deserve* to be shot as a deserter if he was caught either...he *had* fought bravely on the Eastern Front... even though the shame his desertion would heap down upon his father *almost* made it seem worthwhile. No, he still had unfinished business before he died... *he still had to find Rachel.*

Thus, the only other energy he found he had the will to exert, was to daily walk the streets of Berlin making numberless enquiries into the fate of the Braverman family. Despite the dogged nature of his search, he could discover only that, one day, Mr. Braverman had returned home from work as usual but, that night, they had all simply vanished and no-one had the faintest clue where they had gone. Wolfgang prayed it was far, far from Berlin.

Eventually, Wolfgang's physical wounds were fully healed and springtime brought with it both new life and fresh horror as he and his father packed their bags ready to commence murder on a scale almost unimaginable. In First Class compartments, they travelled to Belzec, retiring to their berths in the sleeper carriage at the end of each exhausting day staring from the window at the passing countryside.

During the final lunchtime, his father informed him they would soon be pulling into the nearby railroad junction of Rawa Ruska, where a car would take them the rest of the way; it would be unseemly to arrive on the same tracks as the Jews arrived for extermination. Wolfgang nodded mutely and stared out of the window. They were being served a meal of roast beef, spring onions, potatoes and a mustard gravy with a rather fine dry burgundy made from the very best Pinot noir grapes and followed with a selection of cheeses, including some magnificent l'ami du Chambertin; whose sharpness contrasted perfectly with the milky burgundy. All of this fascinating detail regarding his meal was provided through the unrequested running commentary from his father as he ate and drank enthusiastically, eager to start at his new post and to make a good first impression.

Wolfgang wasn't listening to a word, however, wondering instead if every mile they moved away from Berlin was a mile further away or closer to Rachel... if she was even still alive, that was. He looked down at the plate in front of him and pushed the food away apathetically...

****

The first four months of the camp had been an unmitigated disaster.

The first Jews had begun arriving from Lublin and Lvov and Krakow, but the original gas chambers, (wooden with double walls, disguised to resemble shower barracks,) were hopelessly inadequate to deal with the tens of thousands that were arriving every week for 'cleansing'. Consequently, the showers kept breaking down and the chaos that caused, with Jews having to be kept even longer on the trains or even held, weeping and moaning, in the shower barracks themselves, was nightmarish and horrific.

In July, however, they were demolished and new ones, constructed of bricks and mortar were erected and his father could delightedly report back to Berlin that, now, they could successfully kill one thousand people at a time (in the six chambers fully insulated with thick cement walls,) with beautiful efficiency.

Wolfgang found there was only one way to survive the daily abominations he witnessed and that was to lock his emotions away... deep, deep down, Kraken-deep, where he could feel nothing and see nothing and, from which, it was almost impossible to awake.

His job was to oversee the safe and swift movement of the Jews from their arrival through the first phase of Camp One as far as *The Tube*. To help him achieve this, he had SS Scharfuhrer Fritz Irmann positioned on a podium as the Jews disembarked from the trains in the reception zone, reassuring them in calm, dulcet tones that this was a transit camp and that they would be showered and de-loused before movement to a more permanent destination at a later date. They were aided in this deception by a number of SS guards and Sonderkommando (a Special Detachment of Jewish prisoners, hand-selected as they stepped off the trains to act as extra guards and to hurry them along in undressing when they reached the showers; particularly the young and the very old while, all the time, deceiving them with talk about life at the Camp.)

Then they were someone else's problem and, at least Wolfgang didn't have to witness their actual deaths; though it was impossible not to hear their cries, no matter where you were.

The Sonderkommandos themselves were not so fortunate. They also had the pleasure of burning the bodies in huge funeral pyres after their extermination and burying the remains. Little did they know that one day, without any warning, they would join their fellow Jews in a shallow grave before being replaced by new, unsuspecting accomplices.

Wolfgang had been stationed at the camp for about two months when, purely by chance, he had been dragged from his self-induced torpor when he thought he'd caught a momentary glimpse of a familiar face stepping off the platform and staggering forward in absolute exhaustion and malnutrition... Quickly, he'd reached for the field glasses he kept permanently around his neck when a train was arriving and scanned the seething mass of fragile life for confirmation.

He passed the magnification quickly over the sea of faces, then doubled back on one pathetically scrawny-looking and dejected figure... *it was Ariel!*

His heart had pounded like a piston as he had scrabbled down from his position trying to keep his eye on one particular cluster of the new arrivals as he pushed his way through. To his repeated horror, he had searched through the effusion of people pouring onto the platform and saw and lost sight of Ariel several times. Eventually, he had managed to grab hold of Erich, one of his guards, and pointed out Ariel through the crowd.

"Fetch me *that* man," he'd demanded, "We need another Sonderkommando... and I want it to be him."

Erich had looked at him quizzically, not overly keen to fight his way through the swarm of fetid human bodies; most of whom could arguably be said to be virtually dead already.

"But we were due to change the..."

"*That's an order!*" Wolfgang had shouted and Erich had, wisely, questioned him no further, hurrying off instead and retrieving Ariel without further complaint; surprised at the unusual outburst from his normally distant superior officer.

Later that night, Wolfgang had sneaked over to the block where the Sonderkommando were stationed and had ordered Ariel outside. There, in the shadows at the side of the block, well out of view of the sentry patrols with their dogs and the guards in their lookout towers, they had both embraced and wept at this most unlikely of reunions and Ariel had thanked him for saving his life.

It was then that Wolfgang had filled him in on the bitter reality of the camp and the fact that the SS regularly killed and replaced the Sonderkommandos (or Totenjuden, the 'corpse unit' as they were affectionately known,) before they could think of organising a revolt or telling anyone else about the camp's real purpose. Smiling bitterly, he told Ariel he would do everything he could to protect him but, in time, he might grow to wish Wolfgang had left him to the same fate as his fellow passengers. He also couldn't help but wonder to himself whether he had saved Ariel to help preserve what little remained of his *own* sanity as well... as for Ariel's sake.

***

One other surprising event had briefly pulled him from his self-induced coma over the last four months: the shock appearance of Ronan Fuchs.

Wolfgang could honestly say he hadn't seen or even thought of his old classmate since that day at school when the boy had hinted at his own vitriolic hatred of the Jews; that, clearly, bubbled away constantly below the surface and threatened to overwhelm him entirely. If he had ever stopped to consider the kind of man he had grown into, he would have hoped the hatred had dissipated without the stimulus of taunting children to add fuel to his passion. Unfortunately, as soon as he caught sight of him again at the camp, Wolfgang realised that, if anything, the venom had travelled deeper beneath the skin, and was now coursing faster and faster around his veins until it had seemingly infected his every waking thought.

Wolfgang had met him in the canteen, trying to decide if his stomach could overcome the smell of roasting flesh that clung rebelliously to the hairs on the inside of his nostrils, when Ronan had tapped him on the shoulder and attempted a shark-like smile.

"Fuchs? *Ronan Fuchs?* Is that really you?" he had gasped in reply.

Fuchs had bowed curtly and clicked his heels together in a little salute. It wasn't clear if he was in earnest or if this was some feeble attempt at a joke.

"SS Hauptscharfuhrer Ronan Fuchs at your service," he'd replied.

They were both served with something bland and tepid and had sat together to eat. Wolfgang didn't want to talk about school while Fuchs had seemed happy to stare at him in a rather menacing silence. Searching the recesses of his mind for the lost art of conversation, Wolfgang had finally managed to shape his reluctant lips into words:

"So, what exactly is your job here?"

"Operator of the Gas Chamber," he'd replied simply.

"You mean you actually-"

"Conduct the exterminations? Yes, that's right. We have a diesel internal combustion engine and the exhaust fumes produced kills them in minutes."

"Ronan, I'm sorry-" Wolfgang had stammered.

"Don't be," Fuchs had interrupted again, "I volunteered for the position."

Wolfgang was speechless. He looked deeply into his unblinking and stone, stone cold eyes and saw no hint whatsoever of a soul within.

****

Obersturmfuhrer Gerstein arrived on time to see the first train of the day pull into the station. Christian Wirth guided him round the camp while he took on the role of a lap dog, his bald head nodding vociferously as he agreed with every whispered observation. His little moustache also twitched every now and again at what, Wolfgang could only presume, was a criticism that would be reported back to the Fuhrer upon his return.

The camp itself was effectively divided into two sub-camps: Camp One included the barracks for the Ukrainian guards and the workshops and barracks of the sonderkommandos, the reception area and the two undressing areas. Camp Two contained the gas chambers themselves and the open ground beyond, where the bodies were buried. Wolfgang and the other guards were housed in two cottages outside the confines of the camp itself and across the road.

The wagons were being unlocked as Gerstein and his father came to the viewing platform to get a better view.

"Forty five wagons means approximately six thousand seven hundred Jews- although many will, of course, already be dead from the journey," Christian Wirth noted, waving a hand over the fragile life spilling from the train into the 'processing' zone. The sonderkommandos formed two lines with their truncheons forcing them to funnel forwards while Irmann had already begun his spiel of comforting lies over the loudspeaker.

Gerstein gave a curt nod, apparently satisfied.

Wolfgang forced himself to watch as grief banked up on all sides, looking for a means of escape and finding none; human potential processing, oblivious, into the afterlife. Over the hubbub of the crowd, a woman emitted the guttural assonance of a pain-laden cry and, instinctively, Wolfgang lifted his field glasses to his face and followed the sound. Zoning in on the woman, middle-aged and drained of all colour, he watched, spellbound, as Ariel gently approached her and, taking her hand momentarily, whispered something that seemed to calm those darting panic-filled eyes so she met his gaze, nodded, and resumed walking calmly on. Then Ariel resumed his position in the line, offering words of encouragement to all those who needed it.

"We'd better wait until they've exited Zone One," Wirth commented, "as you can see, the 'processing' zone is divided into two sections, shielded from one another by a high barbed wire fence and camouflaged by a row of fir trees. From here, they are forced to run through a narrow corridor we call *der Schlauch-*"

"Why do you make them run through this *'Tube'*?" Gerstein interrupted.

"It is best if they do not settle. They are already disorientated from being confined for so long, we convince them this is a mere stop-off point and hurry them through to the two undressing and hair cropping areas before they can consider any ulterior motive or consider rebellion," Wirth explained.

The 'processing' zone was empty of all living Jews now.

A couple of upturned suitcases lay abandoned... a shoe had been left behind, stuck at a jaunty angle in the mud... a coat lay spread-eagled near the tracks as though the owner were a magician who had suddenly and mysteriously vanished and it had drifted, body-less, to the floor to rapturous applause.

The Ukrainians had stayed behind and were starting to remove the dead bodies that inevitably spilled out as the living emerged, as well as pulling the dead bodies that congregated inside the wagons; while a couple of others waited with hoses ready to rinse out at least some of the putrid and festering stench, ready for the return journey. A diesel-filled breeze, like the hot flap of the Devil's leathery wings, washed over Wolfgang's hot face as he stared dismally at the scene he had done his best to avoid for so many days and weeks. Surreptitiously, he wiped away a tear before his father and his illustrious guest noticed. His job done, Wolfgang turned to retreat down the steps, hide himself away in the cottage and drink as much as it took to forget. As he passed, his father laid a hand on his shoulder.

"Join us on the rest of the tour," he said, looking towards Gerstein as he added, "I don't believe I've had the opportunity to introduce you to my son, Obersturmfuhrer?"

"Ah, a great pleasure," he replied, offering his hand and shaking it firmly, with all the ease and enjoyment of a man stood in the smoke-filled room of some Gentlemen's Club. Wolfgang said nothing, but reluctantly followed them down the steps and through the *'Tube'* marvelling at how some men's capacity for witnessing horror clearly knew no limits.

They were able to bypass the Jews now, as they were being prepared for the chambers, allowing the three of them to take up a position next to Fuchs above the shower barracks before their imminent arrival. Below them, they could hear snippets of conversations, as women and children were separated from the men shortly before the freshly-disrobed new arrivals were run to the gas chambers themselves and bustled inside. Wolfgang tried not to listen, but the clamorous notes of fear rose quicker than the hushed susurrations of mothers attempting to comfort their softly crying children.

Then disaster struck!

The diesel engine refused to choke and splutter into life!

Fuchs fussed and flit around it nervously, but his quiet curses were deafening compared to the unexpected silence of the huge engine. Wirth wrinkled his fat little nose and Gerstein made a show of checking his watch. An engineer was called for- one of the Ukrainians who had worked in a factory making tractors before the war- who arrived promptly and set about twisting hot screws and bolts with an oily rag, as the whole thing boiled and bubbled like a giant cauldron. Wirth muttered something to one of the guards, who hurried away purposefully. Soon after, he returned with Ernst Hackenholt, who carried a bucket filled with some small items that Wolfgang couldn't quite make out. He held the bucket under the nose of Gerstein as if he were a horse about to eat the contents.

"*Teeth*, Herr Gerstein," he announced proudly, "each one has a gold filling in it!" He shook the bucket so it rattled hollowly, "*and these are only from yesterday!*"

Gerstein nodded but, clearly, hadn't been distracted by this diversionary tactic. The Ukrainian added more oil and, eventually, nodded at Fuchs to suggest he hoped he had fixed it. They powered it up and... the engine finally coughed and spluttered into life.

Gerstein checked his watch again.

"Thirty minutes, Herr Wirth."

Commander Wirth glowered furiously but said nothing.

In silence, the four of them waited, and listened while the Jews below them screamed, begged, cried, moaned and, finally, took their last breaths on this earth. By Gerstein's watch, after twenty-eight minutes, only a handful were still alive. By thirty-two minutes, all were dead.

Commander Wirth led Obersturmfuhrer Gerstein away to his office, apologising furiously all the way. Wolfgang was finally free to return to the cottage and begin his daily futile attempts to rest.

As he trudged back, Ariel came out of one of the barracks and caught his eye. Wolfgang nodded back and motioned for him to walk a little way with him.

They walked in silence for a while, before Wolfgang stopped and turned to face him.

"Why do you bother, Ariel?"

"Bother with what?"

"Why do you bother to comfort them? Tell them it'll be fine when you know very well that it won't."

Ariel stared up at the grey sky pressing down on both their heads.

He gave a little sigh, "no-one plays a bit part in the story of their own life, Wolfie. I try to give them the end of the story they would like to hear; a happier ending... for a little while at least. It's all I can do for them; so I do all I can."

CHAPTER TWENTY FIVE

MAKING THE MOST OF THE TIME GIVEN

'Nothing very very good and nothing very very bad
Ever lasts for very very long.'

Douglas Coupland

June 1999,
Friday afternoon; on the way to William and Gabriel's house.

Maggie McGuire walked towards William and Gabriel's house with a nervous spring in her step. She had noticed Harry the first day he had been brought into class halfway through the academic year, standing awkwardly in the doorway avoiding eye contact with everyone, while the school secretary introduced him and Mr. Murdoch told him to sit in the spare seat next to Nathan Clegg. He hadn't looked across at her, but she had been unable to keep her eyes off him. She knew then there was something about him that was irresistible to her.

Maggie was impatiently fifteen. She liked to think of herself as independent; a free spirit; someone who read more a little more widely than *19* and *Just Seventeen;* whose topics of conversation stretched further than her favourite member of *Take That*, make-up, and the contents of the latest episode of *Friends*. She wasn't like the likes of Kerry Anderson, or Julie Wilkins, or the rest of them for that matter, who wouldn't be seen out in anything but the latest brand name; who never considered the world outside of school, the shopping centre and the nightclubs in town. She thought more deeply; was more eclectic, more unique, she wore what she liked, watched the *actual news* and thought things through before making up her *own* mind. And there was something about Harry that was familiar to her... a shared attitude and approach to life. She recognised a kindred spirit in him. But there was something *darker* about the aura he gave off too. He was more troubled, more enigmatic somehow, and that made him interesting; attractive; *dangerous even*. From what little she knew of his story, she wanted to know more and, potentially, to be a part of the chapters that followed.

****

Harry, on the other hand, was feeling somewhat more anxious than excited. He had worked in the garden until mid-afternoon when Gabriel had come out with a glass of blackcurrant juice and an invitation to go wash up before Maggie arrived.

"What time does your school day end?"

"Three fifteen."

"Well," Gabriel said, pointing at his grimy hands, "That gives you about thirty minutes and, in my limited experience, girls aren't overly enamoured with boys who hold their hands with grubby paws that have dirt under their fingernails."

Harry's stomach lurched suddenly and a nausea washed over him like a sickening tide at Maggie's imminent arrival. He had tried to keep his mind busy all afternoon and, when he had allowed himself to briefly consider her coming round, had tried to convince himself she was just keeping him company; a *friend* coming over to hang out, but girls *never* came over to hang out with him and he wasn't sure what he was supposed to do if they did. *What if she leaned in for a kiss? What if she was waiting for him to kiss her? The whole thing seemed a logistical minefield...*

"I'll go and get washed."

****

The doorbell rang and Harry sprang to his feet like a jack-in-the-box. William motioned for him to sit back down again.

"I'll get it. You sit back and try to look..." he searched for the right word, "*cool.*"

Harry flung up his arms in despair.

"Yeah, right," he scoffed, "I'm really good at that!"

Gabriel grinned and shook his head, highly amused at Harry's discomfort.

William appeared in the doorway with Maggie behind him.

"Your guest has arrived," William announced with a curt bow, affecting a mock upper-class English accent; like some butler to the aristocracy. Maggie stuck her head out from behind William and waved shyly.

"Why don't you kids go and sit in the garden and make yourselves at home?" Gabriel suggested.

Harry nodded and led the way through the kitchen and out into the bright sunshine. They sat on a couple of recliners and stared at the same view he had stared at with William and Gabriel just a couple of days before. The nerves had really started to kick in now, and Harry suddenly found himself utterly incapable of being perfectly still. Either his leg tapped incessantly on the stone patio in some bizarre Morse code aimed at waking the worms embedded in the lawn, or else his fingers tapped on the arm of the chair, like he was suffering from some acute form of OCD.

Maggie glanced at him from the corner of her eye.

"For someone so cool and aloof in school... you certainly seem nervous now."

She smiled at him and raised her eyebrows as if to say *he needn't worry, she was on his side.* Harry grinned sheepishly and abruptly gained control of his infernal tapping.

"You think I'm cool and aloof?" he laughed, looking at her incredulously, "you clearly don't know me as well as you *think* you do."

"I know not many people would have stood up to a gang of bullies the way you did."

Harry raised his eyebrow; he hadn't thought about it like that.

"Everyone at school is still talking about it…"

"About what? Talking about how I'm going to get my head kicked in when I go back? If I'm even *allowed* back in; which appears unlikely at best."

"No," Maggie smiled, "how you were brave to stand up to them and that everyone is sick of Kellerman and Harris and the rest of them and it was about time somebody stopped letting them do whatever they want round school."

Harry raised his eyebrows in surprise; somehow he didn't see himself in the role of vigilante... a cigar-chewing Clint Eastwood of the classroom.

"Guess you might have started something," she added, shrugging.

"If I remember rightly," Harry grinned, *"you* more than played *your* part with that sneaky trip on Tania Tonks!"

"Oh," Maggie grinned mischievously, "you spotted that, did you?"

Harry raised an eyebrow and they laughed contentedly.

They stared at the view again, far more at ease this time, as the sun started to droop in the sky like an overripe orange. Harry suddenly wondered if *the* moment was fast approaching. His heart suddenly beat faster at the very thought of it and he noticed his hands were starting to get ridiculously clammy.

"I was wondering," ventured Maggie, interrupting his thoughts in a sort of sing-song voice that told him some kind of invitation was coming, "if maybe you'd like to go to the cinema? Maybe tonight? Or tomorrow?"

Harry's heart sank.

"I'd really love to but..."

"But?" Maggie interrupted, the disappointment immediately evident in her voice.

"But my Mom has grounded me until the next Ice Age... I'm only allowed over here because she thinks William and Gabriel are working me like a slave."

"And are they?" she asked.

Harry grinned, "Nah, they're great actually. I've done a bit of gardening, painted the shed, mowed the lawn... mostly they feed me and we chat. It's nice actually."

Gabriel appeared almost on cue with fresh drinks and a knowing wink at Harry from behind Maggie's back.

"You kids all right then?" he asked pointedly.

"Fine, thanks," Harry scowled.

"Good, well, in that case," Gabriel said, "how would you like to stay for dinner, Maggie?"

"What? *Here*?" Harry spluttered, completely caught off-guard by this sudden turn of events.

"Yes, here... I did cook for several of the top restaurants in the city for the best part of thirty years, even had a *Michelin* star at one point... I think I can rustle you up something edible. Plus, what's the alternative? Skulking around in the shadows trying to avoid your Mom seeing you? Sitting on the wall outside the *Spar* looking freezing and miserable? I've seen them on a Friday night, gangs of them...never understood the logic in that, I must say, looks like absolute torture!"

"I'll have to phone my Mom; check it's all right," Maggie shrugged, before looking across at Harry and adding, "I mean, if you *want* me to stay, that is."

"Er... no, I mean yes, of course, that'd be... great," Harry stumbled awkwardly.

Gabriel clapped his hands together delightedly, "Well, that's settled then. I'll cook and William can serve as Head Waiter. It'll be fun! Trust me! So, what culinary delight would you like to be presented before you this evening?"

Gabriel waited with baited breath. Harry thought for a moment.

"Erm... burger and chips?"

"Philistine!" he snorted and stormed off back into the kitchen, while Harry and Maggie attempted to stifle their laughter until he was safely back inside the house.

CHAPTER TWENTY SIX

THE BLAMELESS AND THE WICKED

'God destroys but the blameless
And the wicked.'

William Golding

'A short time ago death was the cruel stranger,
The visitor with the flannel footsteps...
Today it is the mad dog in the house.
One eats, one drinks beside the dead,
One sleeps in the midst of the dying,
One laughs and sings in the company of corpses.'

Georges Duhamel
(French doctor serving at Verdun in the Great War.)

17 March 1943,
The Guard's cottage, Belzec Extermination Camp.

Wolfgang shuffled abjectly from his small room upstairs down to the table in the kitchen, with a thick head that throbbed and pulsed like a stormy sea. Like most of the other guards, he had become a heavy drinker on most evenings after his shift had finished; just one more futile attempt to block out the nightmare that refused to leave either his waking or sleeping hours. None of them ventured into town unless it absolutely couldn't be avoided, because that would inevitably involve the locals asking about the nefarious activities taking place behind the mysterious barbed wire and tall sentinel trees that guarded the camp's perimeter. So, they ordered in supplies from town and then one of them would go wait outside, meet the local on the roadside and unload their beers... wine...schnapps... whatever was available, it didn't really matter, and take it directly into the cottage.

Already seated around the table were Erich, Fritz and Werner; looking equally the worse for wear. They had been muttering about something as he'd come down the steep narrow steps and had shut up quickly, looked up guiltily as he entered, but they sighed in relief at seeing Wolfgang's bleary face and soon resumed their conversation.

"Thought you were Fuchs for a minute," Fritz muttered, half under his breath.

"I think I heard him go out earlier," Wolfgang yawned.

"Yes, can't wait to get back to work, that one," said Werner shaking his head in disgust.

"In his '*iron determination to fulfil the Fuhrer's dream*'," added Wolfgang, quoting verbatim the words Fuchs had once said to him about their work at the camp.

Wolfgang reached for a plate and looked at the breakfast selection on offer: some brotchen with poppy seeds sprinkled on top; honey; jam; and a selection of sausages and salami. He pulled apart some bread, spread a little jam on and reached for the coffee pot.

"We were saying we don't know how much more we can take of this," Erich hissed, "a man cannot do this without it leaving an imprint on his soul."

Fritz nodded, "I was overseeing the sonderkommandos the other day with Josef. They were emptying the chamber when one of the Jews came across the corpse of his wife. He took his cigarette out of his mouth to tell me this was the body of his wife, then he carried on smoking as if nothing had happened. I swear, we'll all go insane in this place!"

Wolfgang looked round the table, "insane is the best thing to be here- you'll fit in perfectly."

"But what are we to *do*?" Werner insisted, "I can't sleep, eat... I keep thinking about how utterly ashamed I will be when I try to explain to my parents what I have been doing after we return home."

"I know, Werner, but what choice do we have?" bemoaned Erich, "You do what the Nazis say or you join the Jews in the line to the gas chamber. Which side of the fence do you prefer to be on? Well? Either has got to be preferable to sitting on the fence and getting splinters in your arse like you!"

Suddenly, Fuchs burst in through the back door, cutting their conversation dead.

"Train's going to be here in less than fifteen minutes," he announced eagerly, "better get the men in position, sir."

This last remark was aimed at Wolfgang as the main officer in charge of the German guards. As such, his father had tried to get him to take a room in his own quarters further outside the camp, but he had decided the least amount of time he had to spend with his father, the better.

Wolfgang sighed and pushed his chair away from the table, leaving his breakfast still barely touched. "Very well. Gentlemen, time to go."

****

Within five minutes, Wolfgang was in position on the platform with Fritz, who held his loudhailer loosely by his side in reluctant readiness. All along the platform, the sonderkommandos and the Ukrainian guards were forming their two rows, tapering away so as to squeeze the mob inside its hideous embrace and down into *the tube*. Wolfgang heard something and looked down the line, before realising what he had mistaken for the distant approach of the train was, in fact, a roll of thunder. He glanced up at the sky; the grey drizzle quickly became a black downpour, as if the sky itself was mourning the death of the sun. Wolfgang pulled up the collar on his overcoat and retreated his head further into it.

The plume of smoke from the engine stack was now visible, sending smoke signals skywards as the train came into view. The ground started to become a quagmire as the rain fell in tiny daggers and Wolfgang's heart sank to his boots as he waited for the inevitable out-spilling of pitiful humanity. Almost as soon as the train stopped and the steam was still flaring out from between the wheels, the sonderkommandos had the wagons unlocked and the dazed occupants disgorged onto the wet earth. Dead bodies that had been propped against the doors by the crush fell out first, lying in heaps like collections of rags, quickly trodden and lost underfoot.

The pulsing mass of bodies ebbed this way and that like a shoal of fish; confused, exhausted, almost delirious with hunger and sleep deprivation. Wolfgang tried to look away but found himself drawn to the macabre sight. When he had first moved to the camp, he had been surprised how easier it had been for him to face bullets, all straining to burrow their way inside of him and eat away at his life blood, than it was to watch these strangers herded to their deaths; but now that fact didn't surprise him at all. It made perfect sense. There was, at least, honour in battle: the pitching of a soldier against his foe on, relatively, equal terms. There was no honour to be found in this ceaseless slaughter. And, unlike in battle, where battles were either lost or won, here there could be no end to his torment...bar merciful death, and that could not come too soon. He felt trapped in a room, desperately holding on to a key, only to find there was no door in the room; let alone no lock.

He watched their haggard faces, filled with an overwhelming sense of pity but unable to offer any consolation: An old man, ancient as Methuselah, hunched over a stick and tried to keep up with the flow (Wolfgang was staggered he had even survived the journey); a woman stubbornly clutched a tiny bundle to her chest, but all reason said her child was already dead; older children tugged at their mothers' skirts like hungry sparrows while, all the time, Fritz told them monstrous, audacious lies and filled the desperate chasms of their hearts with tiny stalactites of hope.

The platform was almost empty now as the sluggish clouds refused to pass over and the rain continued to soak the dark earth. Wolfgang was about to turn away and return to the dubious solace of the cottage when something caught his eye. He thought he saw somebody wave at him! He turned back and scanned again the much diminished numbers and, suddenly, caught sight of Ariel's face looking up at him, his hand raised in the air in what was neither a wave nor a salute.

What on earth was he doing?

Didn't he realise how foolhardy he was being drawing attention to their friendship like this?

Absolutely nobody knew they even knew each other and that was the way it had to stay... if Ariel harboured even the tiniest glimmer of hope of staying alive.

Then, even from the distance that separated them, he saw the look in his eyes. Immediately, he knew it could mean only one thing... Rachel!

Wolfgang hurried down the steps and joined the guards following the stragglers into the tube. Dodging and weaving through the Ukrainians, he made his way over to Ariel and waited for him to speak.

"I've just seen Rachel..." he whispered in a tone of utter disbelief, *"I've just seen Rachel!"*

Tears filled his eyes and he smiled the first true smile that had crossed his lips since the day Wolfgang had saved his life. Wolfgang grabbed him by the shoulders.

"Show me!" he hissed.

Bypassing *the tube*, they cut through the side of Ariel's barracks and came out by one of the two undressing barracks, set immediately before the six new concrete gas chambers, so cunningly disguised as shower rooms.

The area was crowded and both men frantically scoured the sea of faces swarming before them. Wolfgang tried to see those eyes he knew he would recognise anywhere...but every pair of eyes he settled on were either darting everywhere, like hunted animals, or were as glazed over and unseeing as the blind eyes of statues.

Rachel was nowhere to be seen.

Suddenly, a woman broke from the crowd and made a bolt for the far fence. She was screaming and pulling at her own hair as she ran; suggesting an act of hysteria more than a serious attempt at escape. As her fingers closed around the wire, a single shot rang out and, for a moment, she danced a silly jig, like a puppet on a string, before falling motionless to the ground. Slowly, her blood seeped out into the mud like Indian ink bleeding into a glass of water.

"It's no use, we need to get higher!" Wolfgang hissed. "Stay here and I'll point her out to you!" he added before running up the steps to where Fuchs waited like the Angel of Death.

Fuchs blinked when he saw him turn the corner and stand overlooking the carnage below. Wolfgang imagined for a second the leathery opening and closing of the eyelid of a lizard, shivered, then put the image out of his mind.

"You don't normally come to witness this part of the process," Fuchs observed calmly.

"No," he replied, not taking his eyes off the crowd for a single moment, "today's different."

He could see Ariel below, moving round the fringes of the crowd as they were herded inside to get changed: men being separated from women and children, many with such terrible fear painted on their faces that it reminded him of the faces of the damned on a medieval stained glass window he had once seen, where devils forced the sinners' naked and chained bodies into the jagged-toothed open mouth of Hell. Suddenly, Ariel pointed, he followed the line of trajectory of his finger... *and he saw her!*

Taking the steps three at a time, he pushed through the crowd and closed in on her. Ariel approached her from the other side in a clumsy pincer movement. She was near to the door of the chamber and Wolfgang knew he didn't have much time. Already, he was so close he could hear the pleas of those who were starting to doubt they would ever leave the building in front of them if they dared to cross the threshold. He saw a woman try to hide her baby under a pile of her clothes as a member of the sonderkommandos forced her to take him in with her, even though she tried to convince him the disinfectant would sting his eyes. A man approached one of the SS guards at the entrance to the showers and told him the names and addresses of those he knew were still in hiding back in Berlin. The guard calmly took out pen and paper, noted down the details before nodding to a Ukrainian who shoved him inside with the rest.

Finally, Wolfgang was at her side. Whilst utterly filled with dread that Rachel was seconds away from being inside the chamber, he could not help but experience a brief sensation of utter elation: this was a moment he had all but given up on. The urge to sweep her up in his arms and take her to a place of safety was compelling, but hopeless. He was right by her side, *but she still hadn't seen him! He glanced ahead and saw she was only a few stumbled footsteps away from stepping inside the chamber and the door closing on her forever. He had to act fast!*

Reaching out, he put his hand onto her arm. Slowly, her head began to turn... he caught a glimpse of two pale emeralds veiled behind a shadowy light; of a cheek, white and fragile as a bone picked clean by jackals; of the sad corner of her mouth, down-turned into tiny arrow-heads; then he saw a flicker of recognition somewhere deep within those green eyes...

"*Wolf-*" she began.

Without a word, he took out his luger, and struck her hard across the face with the butt of it.

CHAPTER TWENTY SEVEN

DATE NIGHT

'One good thing about music,
When it hits you, you feel no pain.'

Bob Marley

Some might say they don't believe in heaven
Go and tell it to the man who lives in hell

Oasis

June 1999,
Friday night, at William and Gabriel's house.

Both Maggie and Harry had phoned home and got permission to stay for tea, so Gabriel had ushered them into the lounge to watch TV while he clanged about in the kitchen and William disappeared into the garden on some secret mission.

Although Harry had spent most of the afternoon with the heartbeat in his head pounding like some drum of destiny, drowning out almost every other sound, he was finally starting to calm down. They had talked more about school and about things that really drove them crazy, and about what they wanted to do when they left school... and they seemed to have an encouraging amount in common.

"What music do you like?" Maggie asked.

Harry shrugged, "Indie stuff mainly: *Oasis, Pulp, Suede, The Manics*. In other words, pretty much nothing that's in the charts right now! I *hate* boy bands so much!" he scoffed.

"I know! Me too!" Maggie laughed, "every time you put *Top of the Pops* on, *Boyzone* or *Westlife* or *The Backstreet Boys* are number one... I grew out of all of that *ages* ago!"

"Glad to hear it!" he grinned, warming to his subject, "best film seen recently?"

"*Cruel Intentions*...went a couple of months ago with Becky from class. You?"

"*The Phantom Menace* was well cool, but I'd have to say *The Matrix*. Went in the Easter holidays."

"Who'd you go with?" Maggie asked tentatively.

Harry paused and felt a slight flush to his cheeks, "I went on my own," he shrugged, "it was that or go with my Mom."

"Well, not anymore," Maggie grinned, placing her hand on top of his, "*The South Park Movie* is out the end of the month, we could go together... if you want."

"And if my Mom has finally forgiven me by then," Harry joked, before becoming more serious and adding sheepishly, "but, no, that'd be great. Thanks."

Their eyes met and Harry was struck by the sudden feeling that this was the moment he had been waiting for... this would be the absolute perfect time to kiss her...

Edging closer, his mouth suddenly inexplicably parched, he leaned forward and began to close his eyes as...

"Dinner is served on the patio!" William announced as he burst into the lounge, wearing an apron and with a tea towel comically draped over one arm. Harry and Maggie both jumped up guiltily and then tried, failing dismally, to look relaxed and casual.

"Oh, *sorry,*" William grinned, "haven't interrupted anything, have I?"

Harry just glowered as they followed him out into the garden... *where both their jaws fell open in delighted amazement.*

The cast iron patio table and the two chairs had been moved to the centre of the patio, and a tablecloth had been spread across it, complete with cutlery, pads, crystal glasses, a lit candle and a single rose, snipped from the bush climbing up the back fence, in a thin vase. Even more than that, William had strung up some fairy lights in the branches of the apple tree and there were burning torches set at intervals around the edge of the lawn. The whole effect was magical and Harry and Maggie looked at each other and shook their heads in wonder.

"I can't believe you've done all of this for us, William... I'm speechless!" Harry whispered.

"Consider it payment for all the unpaid labour you've put in this week," William smiled pulling out a chair for Maggie to be seated at.

"I feel totally underdressed now!" she sighed, looking down at her school uniform in despair.

"*You* do!" moaned Harry, "I came dressed for a day of gardening... not a first date!"

He suddenly realised what he had just said and they shared a shy smile as Harry also took his place.

"Now- drinks," continued William, seemingly not having noticed their communal embarrassment, "I don't think your parents would approve if I got you drunk, so grape juice will have to suffice!"

Taking a bottle from the centre of the table, he unscrewed the top and poured them both a glass. They smiled and lifted their glasses, clinking them together before taking a sip.

"Fizzy!" laughed Maggie.

"Your starters, monsieur et mademoiselle," said Gabriel, appearing from the kitchen with two plates delicately decorated with salad and something Harry couldn't quite identify from a distance.

"Fried goat's cheese with grapes and hazelnuts and a rocket salad," Gabriel announced as he placed the plates before them with a flourish. Harry looked up at him impressed.

"So you weren't joking when you said you could cook!"

"Of course!" Gabriel replied, pretending to look offended.

Carefully, he put a fork into the grilled cheese and took a little taste. Gabriel stood close by with one eyebrow raised in patient enquiry.

"That is *delicious*!" he announced smiling up at Gabriel, who nodded in satisfaction.

****

At that point, William and Gabriel had left them in peace, William returning shortly afterwards to collect their finished starter plates, before they both emerged a third time with two main dishes hidden under gleaming silver domes.

"Wow," said Maggie, "thank you so much for doing this, Gabriel; you're amazing!"

Gabriel blushed and William grinned in amusement.

"Your main course, mademoiselle," he said, ignoring Harry's smirk as he laid the dish in front of her and lifted the lid artfully, "herbed pork tenderloin with mustard-roasted apples and potatoes, and for sir..." he added, withdrawing the second dome with an exaggerated flourish, "*burger and chips!*"

Harry looked down at the plate in front of him: it could, indeed, claim to be burger and chips, but it was also the most gourmet version of the dish Harry had ever seen with delicious looking sides of onion rings and battered mushrooms with a sour cream dip! He clapped his hands together in genuine appreciation and Gabriel gave a curt bow.

****

Pudding was apple tart with maple cream, eaten by the light of the twinkling stars of the fairy lights, as a beautiful, pale, phantom moon rose above the trees. The two teenagers turned their chairs back to face the setting of the sun and sat in perfectly contented silence, sipping on their grape juice. Maggie reached over and pulled his hand across to her lap, before enclosing it in both of hers and, without thinking, Harry leaned across and kissed her soft cheek. She turned and met his gaze and, this time, there was no-one to interrupt their first, wonderful, tender, fireworks-in-the-sky, kiss...

****

Harry was still floating on air as he walked home.

Maggie had phoned home on William's insistence and her Mom had picked her up half an hour later, but not before he had written her phone number on the back of his hand. Then Harry had set off for home himself, after thanking William and Gabriel for what he could honestly profess to be the most fantastic evening he had *ever* experienced.

The air was alive with traffic and laughter spilling out from the open door of the pub on the corner, its cadences swelling and falling, reflecting the buzz of a weekend really starting to gear up. The excitement of it all reflected his own mood perfectly; in fact, things couldn't really have gone any better. He realised he had a song going round and round his head: *Some Might Say* by *Oasis*. The refrain in particular had got itself stuck on a loop and refused to move on:

Some might say we will find a brighter day
Some might say we will find a brighter day

He turned the corner and into the alleyway that would bring him out halfway along his own road. He whistled the tune as he stared at the ground, watching only the path and his own footsteps growing darker as he strayed farther from the streetlamps, thinking of nothing but how ridiculously elated he felt right now.

With absolutely no warning, a figure stepped out from the shadows, placing itself right in front of him. The whistle stalled in his throat as he was forced to stop abruptly in order to avoid walking straight into him. He looked up but the face was still masked in blackness as a punch to his abdomen left him suddenly gasping for breath and utterly disorientated. He could hear voices over the desperate rasping noise he made as he tried to force air into his lungs.

The first voice spoke in a hiss drew closer until a large shadow loomed over his face and spoke into his ear: "you didn't think we were just going to let you get away with it, did you?" Then other voices joined in over his shoulder; mostly male but with a female's shrill call in there as well, standing out above the rest like a gull's shriek, crying out: *"Get 'im, Adam! Get 'im! Kick 'is 'ead in!"*

Harry vaguely remembered falling to the floor... was even less aware of boots flying towards his face and body... but was aware of the refrain playing over and over in his head as he lost consciousness...

Some might say we will find a brighter day
Some might say we will find a brighter day...

CHAPTER TWENTY EIGHT

LETTING RACHEL GO

'One word frees us from all the weight and pain of life:
That word is love.'

Sophocles

'If you love somebody, let them go, for if they return,
They were always yours.
And if they don't, they never were.'

Khalil Gibran

'We don't live alone upon this earth.
We are responsible for each other.'

J.B. Priestley
'An Inspector Calls'

17 March 1943,
The woods behind Belzen Extermination Camp.

In the dark heart of the wood, Wolfgang and Ariel stood amidst pine cones and the mulchy undergrowth with Rachel lying between them like a bloodied sleeping Titania.

After Wolfgang had struck Rachel, she had crumpled like a rag doll to the ground and, before Wolfgang could even turn to call him, Ariel was at her side and sweeping her into his arms. People in the immediate vicinity had turned to look, but it was almost out of curiosity than any great horror; there was not a man, woman or child among them that hadn't seen atrocities far worse than this in the last six months and, frankly, they all had other things to worry about. Within seconds, they had turned away and paid no more attention. Wolfgang was more seriously concerned about the other guards seeing what had just happened and coming up with their own interpretations.

"Follow me. *Quickly!*" he had hissed and pushed his way through the crowd and past the shower blocks, the cremation pyres and ash pits, (where that heaving throng that could still be heard clamouring behind them would be buried, or scattered to the winds, before the end of this very day,) then on to the woods that fringed the back of the camp.

Once they were out of sight of prying eyes, Wolfgang hissed, "Wait!"

Ariel stopped in his tracks and turned to face his old school friend, his eyes wide with terror, their best friend in all the world lying limp in his arms, her head lolling back, blood from her forehead already staining his sleeve, as he hurried over the uneven earth, farther and farther from the cries and complaints of the soon-to-be-dead.

"Let me carry her," he whispered in a hushed tone holding out his arms as if about to take a baby from him. Ariel smiled softly and handed her over.

They carried on at a walk now between tall trees, the sun barely breaking through the shielding arm of the canopy overhead.

Wolfgang noticed how Rachel felt so frail; almost as if he were carrying nothing more than her bones in his gentle caress. He blinked back the tears from his eyes and, reaching a clearing, laid her softly on the damp undergrowth. Her left eye was already beginning to swell and her forehead was red and angry as the blood started to congeal. He leaned in close to press his cheek to her mouth; he could feel her shallow breathing, light as birds' wings. He silently thanked God she was still alive!

"What do we do now?" Ariel whispered, the fear dripping off every syllable.

Wolfgang nodded, "it's all right, Ariel- I have prepared for this day."

"*What? How...?*" Ariel stammered, "How could you? You couldn't possibly have known Rachel could arrive here... now... how could you... plan for this?"

"Not for *her,*" Wolfgang replied, "for *you.*"

Ariel's mouth came up to his mouth and tears filled his eyes.

"I don't understand," he mumbled.

"Ariel, I told you the day I first saw you and made you a sonderkommando... it was not going to be a job for life. Every few months, they replace you; worried you might grow sick of killing and do something stupid... lead the others in a revolt... try to warn them before they go to the gas chambers. So you are killed and the terrible cycle starts again with new guards. But it would be a little too obvious to take you to the ash pits and ask you to jump on. They try to be a little more subtle: get you to take some 'troublemaker' from the train into the woods, to execute them away from onlookers; nip a riot in the bud. Only *you* get executed too."

Ariel felt his legs go weak. He let himself sink to the ground beside Rachel and took her frail pale fingers in the filthy hands he no longer even recognised as his own. *Suddenly, he noticed, in the damp earth beside them, an exposed ribcage sticking up out of the moss!* His predecessor? Or, at least, one of the many, lying there waiting to be found, like a fossil, coiled up and forever at rest in the cool grass where nobody could hurt them now. Ariel almost envied them, whoever he or she was.

"So what happens now?" he said, so faintly Wolfgang was unsure whether he had actually said it or it had been whispered by the wind.

"I made contact with the Polish Resistance several weeks ago. One of the men who delivers our supplies... he knows the truth about what goes on in here. I was getting him photographic proof to send to the British in the hope they will do more... more *quickly*... when they see the... *nightmare*." His voice trailed off and then he steeled himself again. "I'm not a traitor, you understand, but this... this is not *War*."

They shared a knowing stare for a moment, then Wolfgang pulled himself away from his thoughts. "I digress," he said quickly, "and we don't have a lot of time. In return for the pictures, I asked him to get you out of here... out of the country... somewhere *safe.*"

Ariel wept and furiously scrubbed at his eyes with the heel of his hand, angry at his own human frailty.

"There is an old woodman's hut, back there," he nodded further into the trees, "about a hundred yards. You go and hide in there until someone comes for you. I'll tell the other guards I killed you both, then I'll organise a delivery for later today so I can let the resistance know the time has come. They'll come for you under the cover of darkness."

Ariel nodded numbly, stroking Rachel's hair without even realising he was doing it. He struggled to his feet, wiped his palm down his striped trousers and held it out towards Wolfgang. Puzzled for a second, Wolfgang realised his intentions and shook it.

"Like the first time we met," Ariel smiled.

Wolfgang nodded and caught the first tear with his thumbnail, sweeping it away.

"Goodbye old friend."

"We *will* meet again," Ariel insisted.

Wolfgang nodded again and reached into his holster for his luger.

"You need to go," he whispered.

Ariel carefully scooped up Rachel again as Wolfgang fired two shots into the air. Then Ariel turned and hurried off into the trees. When he was a few feet away, it suddenly occurred to Wolfgang he hadn't kissed Rachel before Ariel had taken her from him.

"*Ariel*!" he hissed. Ariel turned. He paused and thought better of wasting more time, "...tell Rachel... tell her I'm sorry... and I love her."

Ariel nodded, turned and was soon lost among the trees.

CHAPTER TWENTY NINE

THE STUFF OF NIGHTMARES

'Sleep is when all the unsorted stuff comes flying out
As from a dustbin upset in a high window.'

William Golding

June 1999,
Sunday morning, 5.33am

The door shuts with a dull thud and the bar is slid across, clicking into place with dreadful purpose and finality. There is a pregnant pause and he can almost hear the metaphorical penny dropping moments before the clamour starts. It starts off as a dull thud, a tentative knocking, a double-checking of the handle from the inside... followed by a panic that rises swiftly to an ocean roar: the incoherent rush of screaming; banging; hammering; scratching; scuffling; sobbing; dragging; moaning.
And so it goes on, for an eon of endless minutes until the last croak: a final, weary, exhalation. Softly, an ear is placed to the door to listen for the sound of any remaining solitary sigh of surrender...
But it is not over yet.
Oh no.
That would be too merciful; too brief a punishment to sate the revenge of so many, many victims...
The bar slides back into its start position, the door draws back like a curtain on the most macabre of freeze frames imaginable: a mountain of jigsaw-piece limbs and twisted faces; eyes wide as saucers, captured in stunned discombobulation and horror; a ladder of limbs and torsos that rises higher than the doorway, as the futile surge to escape, to clamber over everyone else in that primal urge to survive, kicked in.
Slowly, guards unpick them, an arm here... a leg there... are they connected? No... More tumble out with them, interlocked in death, slack-jawed and silent, as they are yanked apart and slumped into wheelbarrows like naked guys on a hellish Bonfire Night.
Bonfire Night! Ah! The smell of the wood, the glow of the flames warming your face, the stomach-rumbling ache from the stirred pots of something hot and tasty.
But this stench of burning is very, very different.
The endless piles of emaciated bodies... gaunt stubble still visible on the taut skin of the men, a blood-flecked white beard, all naked so every rib stands out in curving arcs, lie burning in the relentless flames. Mosaics of taut skin, tenter-hooked over white bone, flake

away. Eyeless sockets stare and skeletal fingers point accusingly. Ashes swirl in the wind, still warm from the embers, flying like locusts into his mouth, gripping his larynx, choking the breath from him; this is their verdict; their revenge... let him choke on them, choke on the very thing he has done...

They gather round him, their hungry teeth bared to bite into his unguarded flesh... when he sees a figure walking away through the crowd. He is carrying a girl... her head lolls in his arms. He calls out to him, ask him to turn, so he can see her face again, he can say the words he loves her again; but the figure does none of those things. He walks on, toward the sinking sun into a horizon of grey-pewter dusk leaving him to his agonising fate...

****

William sat bolt upright with a gasp. The sheets beneath his body were soaked in sweat and beads had formed on his body like raindrops. His sandpaper throat ratcheted painfully as he tried to swallow, as though a single cough could rip his throat in two; straight down the middle. He looked across at the curtains: dawn was barely breaking through, like a guttering candle on a window ledge. He reached across to the bedside table and took a sip of water, wiped his damp forehead with the sleeve of his pyjamas.

It was always the same: the horrific nature of the nightmare. Always the same torture of re-living that hell every night and always the worse torture of all: watching as his precious Rachel disappeared out of his life... the agony of losing her again every night, over and over and over...

The door opened softly and Gabriel's head appeared.

"Everything all right?"

He nodded.

"I heard a cry."

He nodded again.

A pause.

"Well, good night, then."

The door gently closed and, lying back down, William rolled over and returned... returned to the world he would never be able to leave, a world re-imagined in detail fine as fish scales, where they always waited patiently for him... waited for him to return to them... *all those he sent to the chambers...*

CHAPTER THIRTY

RESISTANCE IS FAR FROM FUTILE

'There are causes worth dying for,
But more worth living for.'

Albert Camus

August 1943,
Naliboli Forest, German-Occupied Poland.

Ariel was awakened by the growl of his stomach and opened his eyes to find himself lying in an unbroken sea of green. Tall grasses, ferns, flowering weeds and mossy undergrowth filled his eye-line on both sides in a beautiful natural mosaic. A caterpillar's many legs straddled a leaf that bent under the inching weight, but did not break. Stretching, he rolled over and looked up at an expanse of pale blue sky snared between the towering ash trees; they were so tall and beautiful, he noted, with their silver grey barks the colour of old men's hair, some marbled with green moss that hinted at their ripe old ages. He yawned and sighed and felt he could happily lie here for ever...

He put his hands behind his head and reflected on the past five months: it seemed like an eternity since he and Wolfgang had said their hurried goodbyes in the woods behind the camp, but he had been predictably true to his word and, that night, a quiet knock had come on the door of the woodsman's hut, that was the start of a journey taking them both to safety.

****

During the anxious hours of waiting, Ariel had tried to revive Rachel but, whether it was the force with which Wolfgang had struck her with his luger, or the sheer exhaustion that she had finally succumbed to, he could not bring her out of her semi-conscious state and was reduced to cradling her in his arms and kissing her soft cheeks and, every so often, leaning in and listening to the soft wheeze of her breathing.

Three men had come for them that night.

One led the way through the rest of the woods, with Ariel following and the other two bringing up the rear and carrying Rachel like a lifeless corpse between them. Squeezing between a jagged square they had cut and peeled back in the barbed wire, the stony-faced leader led them silently to a truck, where he signalled for Ariel to clamber beneath the tarpaulin stretched tight over the back of it. He did so and the two men hauled Rachel aboard and followed him inside.

They drove for an hour or so without speaking until the truck came to a stop and the two men lowered Rachel down from the back and began to carry her towards a non-descript cottage, a thin wisp of smoke curling up from the chimney the only sign to suggest it was inhabited. Ariel made to jump down and follow but the leader appeared around the side of the truck and signalled for him to stop where he was.

"What's the matter?" Ariel hissed.

"*She* must stay here," he replied simply.

"But we're... friends," he pleaded, noting how faintly ridiculous he sounded. "We need to stay together."

"She is hurt; she needs medical attention," he shrugged by way of explanation. "There is doctor here. Is better if we split you up. If Germans figure out what happened, will be looking for two people; is safer this way."

Ariel couldn't argue with the cautionary sense of their logic but accepting it was heart-breaking nonetheless. Ignoring the leader's hissed complaints, he clambered down from the truck and ran over to Rachel before they could carry her across the threshold and out of his life. An old woman in a headscarf and an impenetrable expression, with a face as craggy as a rock face, waited in the doorway to receive the motionless cargo. Ariel leaned over to her, still seemingly lifeless in the arms of the two men, and kissed her tenderly on the forehead, a single tear dropping down his cheek and onto her own as he did so.

"Tell her... tell her Wolfgang says he loves her and he's sorry," Ariel pleaded with the two men. "Will you do that for me? Please?"

The older of the two men, a haggard-looking individual with greying stubble shrugged in vague agreement. Ariel turned and faced the leader.

"What will happen to her now? Will I see her again?"

The leader was already clambering back into the truck and turning the key in the ignition.

"We will see how she recover then try to get her out of the country; nowhere is safe in Poland now. Where she go depend on what she want... if she have relative, friend somewhere... America perhaps."

"She's got family in England," Ariel interrupted.

"That is good. Much safer in England," he replied, almost attempting a smile. "If she like, we have people in England, can get message to family."

Ariel smiled, slightly reassured. If there was one thing he could wish for when this would be over and, one day, who knew how many years it would take but, one day, it *would* all be over... he would wish that Rachel were safe.

"And what about me?"

****

Ariel's future turned out to be a simple choice: *fight or run*.

After he was taken to his own safe house, given a bowl of steaming stew, that tasted better than anything he had eaten for years, and downed three shots of vodka that made his head spin like he was back on The Devil's Wheel during *Oktoberfest*, his options were laid out before him: He could be given safe passage out of the country and try to start a new life somewhere else, like America, or he could join them and help fight the Germans and win the War; or die trying.

Ariel smiled. He thought back to the boy he was in school... that timid, scrawny, bullied boy scared of his own shadow, who would avoid confrontation at all costs. The thought of that boy picking up a gun and fighting was, frankly, laughable.

But he wasn't that boy any more.

That boy had died in the camp as surely as the rest of the family he had got separated from: his mother and father; his sisters Leah, Rifka, Devorah, Esther, Hodaya and Lilly; his baby brother, Chaim. Named so because it meant 'life' and new life, new hope, had been so precious in the dark days surrounding his birth. But precious Chaim, the brother he had so longed for, had lived a little less than three years of that precious life before it had been so ruthlessly snuffed out.

No, he was not the same boy anymore and, as he slaked his thirst with another vodka, he realised he had a far more burning thirst... the thirst for revenge that far out-weighed the burning vodka slipping down his throat.

As he raised his glass in a toast to his saviours, he told them he would stay and fight.

****

They let him rest over the coming weeks; allowed him to regain his strength through sleep and regular meals. They also told him Rachel had recovered and would be leaving the country soon, bound for England as soon as safe passage could be arranged. It was a blessed relief to him knowing she could see out the rest of the war in relative safety, even if they wouldn't allow him to visit her before her departure.

Slowly, he was allowed to go out with them on missions.

They were sabotage missions mainly. They knew they couldn't defeat the enemy by themselves, but they could make life unpleasant as possible: disrupt his supply lines, ambush his deliveries, blow up his railway lines... do whatever they could, until the Russians pushed back and freed them from their slavery.

It was during one of these night raids that they got caught out. Following a well-worn plan of attack, they were hidden in the undergrowth on either side of a deserted stretch of road in the hope someone might pass and give them the opportunity for an ambush.

Although it was early April, spring seemed to have abandoned this God-forsaken part of the world and snow still lay on the ground in thick drifts that showed no signs of melting. After an hour of crouching in wait, their bodies numb with cold and their teeth chattering in their skulls, they heard the distant noise of an approaching engine. Hurrying to stretch the piano wire across the road before it came into view, they eagerly waited...

A German motorcyclist came into view and never stood a chance. As he sliced into his invisible obstacle, the motorcycle shot from under him like a horse that had scared and bolted, while the soldier was dead before he had hit the ground; cruelly garrotted by the wire. Quickly, they reached for the satchel strapped across his back. Single riders were often dispatch riders carrying important messages and they had discovered some of their most useful information in this way; information they also passed on to other resistance units and the advancing Russians.

Just as they were taking the papers from the dead man's body, the roar of several engines sent them scattering. The unexpected appearance of a whole convoy on the road ahead, froze them in terror, like rabbits in the proverbial headlights! They were hopelessly outnumbered and outgunned! They opened fire and tried to find cover, already knowing this was a hopeless cause. An armoured vehicle was upon them like a jackal, its machine gun strafing the treeline as they ducked behind fallen tree trunks and returned sporadic fire. Then a truck screeched to a halt behind it and the spidery shapes of soldiers spilled out, one after another; their shouts visible in icy clouds in the truck's headlights, as they methodically fanned out and began the process of trying to encircle their foe.

The gunfight was brutal but brief; the smell of cordite soon heavy on the chill wind. Ariel saw several Germans fall, but they were like cockroaches...for every one that fell, three more seemed ready to take his place. Ariel sensed the gunfire weakening around him and heard the cries of fallen comrades but could see little in the darkness. He knew it was only a matter of time before he too would be picked out by a rifle or grenade... so he turned and ran blindly into the dark clutches of the trees.

As snow crunched and creaked under his fleeing feet, Ariel was briefly aware of a pain, shooting up his leg from below the knee; but the adrenaline kept him going, farther and farther into the undergrowth, until the sound of machine gun fire was less than the cold rasps of his breathing searing through the freezing night air. Slowing to a walk, Ariel then became aware of the blood that was steadily filling his left boot, so that it squelched with every step. As the immediate threat of danger receded, so the pain increased proportionately, but Ariel knew he couldn't stop... if he tried to rest he ran the risk of freezing or bleeding to death or being captured by the Germans.

He had to press on, but where... he knew not.

****

Ariel walked all night, stopping only long enough to tear a strip from his shirt sleeve to make a temporary tourniquet and stop the bleeding in his leg. When morning broke, he continued on, moving as silently as he could; though more afraid his blood-spattered footsteps in the snow would betray his escape route to the Germans more than any sound he was making; should they still be tracking him.

In the afternoon, he walked across fields of icy clods and stole food from a barn, but mainly he kept to the woods, weaving in and out of the thick trunks; pedestals for out-of-reach birds' nests. *At least they are safe from this remorseless, cruel world below*, he thought to himself bitterly.

It was almost dusk of the second day, when Ariel came across them: the dead bodies. He knew he was somewhere deep in the Naliboli forest but, apart from that, he had not a clue as to his exact whereabouts. But, despite being in the middle of nowhere, he was no longer alone: six bodies lay in the snow, slumped like ventriloquist's dummies, their grins pared back over skin-tightened skulls. The one immediately in front of him was propped up against a tree trunk, and right between his eyes... was a black bullet hole. He edged closer, noting the German uniforms and wondering what they were doing out there.

"You don't need to fear them; they've been dead for weeks."

Ariel spun around and found himself facing the barrels of half a dozen machine guns.

"And who might *you* be?"

Ariel looked from the barrel of the gun to the face beyond it. The face of Tuvia Bielski.

****

That had been three months ago and, now, he was a fully-signed-up member of the Bielski partisans. Ariel pushed himself up on his elbows and surveyed the camp from his vantage point on the floor. He could have chosen to sleep in one of the zemlyankas (or underground dugouts the group had built) but, it was summer now and there was something comforting about sleeping under the stars; especially after those months spent in a stinking barracks with a group of hacking, wheezing, quietly weeping sonderkommandos.

After he had introduced himself and convinced Tuvia sufficiently to be blindfolded and taken back to their camp, he was taken to the infirmary, the bullet removed from his leg and his wound dressed.

"What ...*is* this place?" he had mumbled, staggered by the sheer scale and number of buildings he had passed in the last few minutes, and was quickly even more staggered when told the full story by Ehud; the stranger who had been bandaging his wounds as he lay on a makeshift bed.

"This camp is the sanctuary provided by the four Bielski brothers- Tuvia, the eldest, and a handsome and a rugged man- I believe you have met him already?" he began.

Ariel nodded and Ehud smiled, before continuing his story in a hushed and suitably reverent tone:

"And his younger brothers Zus, Asael and Aron- they are our saviours. They are God's Angels who fight, not with guns, but with the slingshot that David used to bring down as mighty a warrior as Goliath. So shall we bring down as mighty a foe as the Third Reich!"

"How is all this possible?" Ariel asked, amazed by this oasis in the middle of the dense forest.

Ehud smiled and nodded, "Well you might ask, for what they have achieved is difficult to comprehend; impossible to imagine if you have not seen it for yourself, in fact. They *had* been millers and grocers in Nowogrodek before the war then, during *Operation Barbarossa,* the Germans invaded and Nowogrodek became a Jewish ghetto. Soon after, the slaughter started and the brothers lost pretty much everyone…their parents, wives, other family members…" he shrugged, "it was pure luck they were away from the village when everyone was either rounded up and taken away, or shot on the spot. If you want to call that luck. There, you are done," he smiled, the bandage secured with a firm knot that made Ariel wince. He swung his legs off the bunk he had been lying on to sit upright as the man continued his fascinating story.

"They managed to flee to the woods and hide. At first, there were only a handful of them, maybe a dozen or so, hiding like mice in the Penelaz Forest, but their numbers quickly swelled and Tuvia would turn no-one away- women, children, the old and infirm- all were welcomed, fed and offered his protection."

Ariel looked at him in amazement; *could such a man exist amidst all this chaos and hatred?*

"But this is Naliboli forest. We are a long way from Penelaz. What happened?" Ariel asked, surveying the doctor's completed handiwork as the old man stood wearily, took his glasses from the end of his nose and rubbed his tired eyes.

"You are right, young man. Initially, the brothers only searched for food, or took it by force from peasants who were conspiring with the Germans but, after a while, they refused to cower and die in ditches like slaves, and decided to fight back. About eighteen months ago, the partisan combat group was formed and they set about disrupting German supplies and intercepting messages from High Command to pass on to our friends in other Brigades."

"We were doing the same thing," Ariel nodded, "when we got... overwhelmed." He looked away quickly, thinking suddenly of the men he had fought alongside who had nursed him back to health and who were now, almost certainly, dead.

"Well, you will know well enough then," Ehud nodded sympathetically, "that the Germans do not appreciate their Aryan supremacy being questioned in any way. They sent troops into Penelaz to destroy the camp. We had sentries stationed on the edge of the forest who got word to us when they were close by, but we had to leave immediately and so many valuable things had to be left behind." He shook his head ruefully. "Still, we escaped with the most precious gift of all: our lives, so I suppose the rest was a small price to pay."

"And you came here?"

"Yes," Ehud agreed, "Tuvia sent Zus to scout ahead and find a suitable new base... and, out of the wilderness we came to settle in this, our new Zion."

****

Asael wandered over to where Ariel still lay slouched on his elbows in the long grass, thoughtfully reminiscing.

"Planning to lie around all day?" he grinned, giving his foot a playful kick. In the few months he had been at the camp, it was Asael who had become his closest friend. The youngest of the four brothers, he had retained a twinkle in his eye and a positive attitude that simply refused to be subdued. It was infectious and Ariel had found himself drawn to him.

"Let's at least have some breakfast first!" Ariel laughed, hauling himself to his feet and following his nose to a large vat of porridge that was cooking over a fire in the heart of the camp. Around him, hundreds of people were emerging from zemlyankas as well as from the kitchen, the mill, the bakery, the bathhouse, the tailors, the shoemakers. Children were on their way to the schoolhouse. Shmuel Oppenheim was shuffling across the leafy floor into his metalworking shop, where he spent all day repairing damaged pistols, rifles and machine guns or making new ones from the spare parts.

The scale and ingenuity of it all was simply unbelievable.

As the myth of the Bielski Brigade had spread, more and more had sought refuge with them, so now they numbered over a thousand and, while most did not ever leave the camp and fight, everyone had a job to do; a role to play in the continuation of the legend.

Ariel picked up a bowl and joined the queue. Breakfast was always supplemented with things found in the forest to stretch it ever further, but no-one complained. If they had stayed in the ghetto, they would be dead now, everyone appreciated that grim reality; so, hardship was, by far, the lesser of two evils.

Perching on one of the long logs positioned in parallel lines to provide organised seating, he talked through the plans for the day with Asael. Sometimes they hunted: wild boar, rabbits, deer, even wolves, if they tried to attack. Other times they would leave the camp for days, maybe weeks, to stake out targets, ambush small convoys, report troop movements back to the advancing Russians.

Life was hard, there was no doubt about it.

All that sleeping rough took its toll; especially in winter. Ariel permanently ached; everyone in camp was sick most of the time and he usually smelt as bad as he looked by the time he returned to camp. Clothes hung off him that he would never even have fit into before the war.

Only the trigger of his gun seemed to fit as snug as it ever did.

And that was what was so satisfying about his life with the Bielski Brigade: it was *real*. He was no longer living a lie, telling people what they wanted to hear in what he had tried to justify as a final act of kindness but which, all too often, had felt like a futile consolation before their inevitable, painful, scratching, clawing death. But now he was *doing something about it*. It didn't matter if it was a tiny, toffee-hammer blow for justice and freedom, it was *something*.

He was fighting back...

CHAPTER THIRTY ONE

NEW BEGINNINGS

'O diva...
Seves iturum Caesarem in ultimos
Orbis Britannos.'
*(Oh Goddess,
Safeguard Caesar as he sets off for the remotest region
Of the earth: Britain.)*

Horace

Give the ones you love
Wings to fly,
Roots to come back
And reasons to stay

Dalai Lama

December 1942,
St Pancras station, London.

Rachel stepped off the train into a flurry of bustling activity and plumes of steam from the trains lined up like snorting stallions on the start line of the tracks of the station.

She had been glued to the window all of the seventy-seven miles from Dover to London and, before that, had been transfixed on the windswept deck of the boat that had brought her all the way from France. Her first impressions of England had, so far, been positive: the sea had shimmered like fish scales glinting in the winter sun, and the white cliffs had loomed up before her like ancient monolithic gates barring the way to some mythical kingdom. Even the miles of twisted and barbed sea defences and grey pill boxes had failed to dampen her enthusiasm; although it was tinged with both nervous anticipation and incomplete grief. She had never met her relatives in England and was excited at the prospect of finally meeting those aunts and uncles whose letters she had read with interest but, conversely, she had also had very little time to adjust to the dreadful reality that the family she had loved and laughed and cried with and nursed... were all now dead.

Absent-mindedly, Rachel ran her finger over the small scar that still stubbornly remained on the side of her forehead as she thought back to the events of the last few months...

****

After two days slipping in and out of consciousness following her blow at the camp, she had finally come round to find herself in a small room lit only by a candle on the bedside table next to her. The blankets felt coarse and itchy, tucked in as they were around her throat, but she was warm and comfortable and still utterly exhausted. She closed her eyes and tried not to panic. *Where was she? How did she get here?*

She tried to recall the last thing she could remember... the first and overriding memory that burst into her brain was of the horrendous train journey she had endured; then the floodgates opened, and emotions washed over her in agonising waves as more and more of the nightmare came back to her- starting with the most horrendous part of all... *Felix was gone.*

She opened her eyes and didn't even bother trying to stop the tears streaming down her face; it was only right she should mourn for her lost, innocent child.

But there were still so many unanswered questions... and she couldn't allow herself to fully grieve just yet... not until she had the answers she sought. *She* was alive, but what of her sisters? And her parents? Were they here with her...and where exactly *was here*? Wiping away the tears, she forced herself to concentrate... what else could she remember? She screwed up her eyes tight and concentrated... and the memories started to return in sudden flashes, like a light being turned on and off, plunging her back into darkness as she tried to remember. She knew she remembered the aching in her arms and the shooting pains up the back of her legs and back... the remorseless feeling that the torment would never end and then, when she was barely even conscious... her mind filled with the sound of the rattling of locks and the drawing back of the doors... the sudden invasion of grey light, fresh air on her face, and rain.... teeming rain soaking her clothes, her skin...

Screwing up her eyes tight, so pinpricks of light danced on the surface of her eyelids, she recalled falling out of the wagon with the heaving mass of everyone else; both the dead and the living. Stumbling over bodies, she knew she had allowed herself to be taken wherever the swell pointed; as she lifted her head to the heavens, closing her eyes and letting the rain soak her parched mouth and lips. Despite everything, it was a few brief moments of paradise. She gasped. It was then she had let go of her son; had stumbled and felt him taken away from her, felt him swept away on the tide of pitiful humanity and lost forever. The tears came again, trailing down her cheeks and forming in little pools on either side of her face, where it met the pillow.

The need to know battled with the need to grieve: she presumed her family had been in that same throng and could hear shouts all around her but the whole effect was such pandemonium she couldn't even try to make sense of it.

Then... then she thought she remembered looking up and... and seeing...

"Wolfie!" she screamed, sitting upright in the bed, and throwing her arms around herself in a desperate attempt to provide comfort in the absence of anyone else to provide it for her. Suddenly, the door flung open and an ancient-looking woman scuttled in, muttering something while trying to ease her back down onto her pillow. Rachel tried to speak but the woman had put a finger to her lips and, for the moment, she gave in to the woman's wishes and her own physical and mental exhaustion...

****

Over the coming weeks, the picture had slowly become less hazy, although there were still a number of unanswered questions. The old woman was of little help as she was Belarussian and spoke no German, but there was a doctor who came two or three times to treat her who had been there the night she was brought to the house:

"But *who* brought me here?" she had asked.

"I do not know," he shrugged, "you arrived in the back of a truck with another Jew-"

"Another Jew?" she interrupted, "male or female?"

"It was a man," the doctor said.

"What was his name?"

"I'm sorry, I do not ask questions, I simply treat the sick and wounded. It is better not to know too much."

"But how did we get out of the camp? Me and this man?" she insisted.

"Presumably, he must have had a contact inside the camp," he smiled gently, "we don't share information. I just treat the wounded and the sick;" he re-iterated, "our resistance fighters mainly. It is better not to know more than you have to know to survive."

Rachel tried to take all of this in.

"Was the contact a German do you think?" she asked.

The doctor scoffed. "I wouldn't have thought so, would you? Murders people all day, but randomly selects you and one other person to live?"

It was then he had taken her hand and explained to her the whole horror of the camps and the reality that everyone who had been on that train with her was already dead. The doctor had put his arm around her to comfort her but, when he left, she didn't even notice...

****

Rachel looked up and down the length of the platform. The station was cavernous; arcing above her like the vaulted ceiling of a cathedral. As she walked with the flow of the crowd, she saw soldiers in uniform on leave, their packs slung jauntily over their shoulders and shuddered as she thought of the Germans in their uniforms, pushing them into the cattle trucks; bayonetting the unfortunate ones at the back. This time *she* was in control of the destination. She took the ticket stub from her pocket and checked the Departures Board. The train heading for the Midlands left in fifteen minutes.

With the ticket stub in one hand and a small suitcase in the other, she strode purposefully towards Platform 3. Despite everything that had happened, no, *because* of everything that had happened, she had to be brave; had to live a life worth living for the sake of all those who'd had their opportunity taken away. For the sake of all those nameless individuals who had nursed her back to health, had contacted her family in England, had obtained a forged passport, forged travel documents, given her clothes and money and passed her across borders like a relay team passing a baton... through Czechoslovakia, Austria, Switzerland, into France and, now finally, into England and freedom.

Rachel pushed past the Pullman cars, with their elegant interiors and ornamental table lamps and linen table clothes. The smell of food was already wafting through the open carriage door and a waiter in a white waistcoat smiled at her as she passed. No, First Class was not on her itinerary, but she cared nothing for that. She had a chance that some stranger had presented her with, had risked much to save her from the gallows of the gas chamber and, as she swung open the carriage to Third Class, she resolved to be happy; to start afresh; to live her life... for *him*.

CHAPTER THIRTY TWO

MISERY MOVES FASTER THAN JOY

'No one loves the messenger
Who brings bad news.'

'Antigone'
Sophocles

June 1999,
Early Saturday morning, Maggie's house.

Maggie was still half asleep when she heard the phone ring downstairs. Yawning contentedly, she turned over and started to doze back off. She had been dreaming about her date last night and was keen to see if she could pick up where she had left off. But before she had really slipped back into that lovely world somewhere in a hinterland between clarity and sleep, she was woken with a violent start by her Mom bursting, uninvited, into her bedroom. Sitting bolt upright in bed, she was met with an expression that was alternating disturbingly between shock and pity.

"What's happened?" she stammered, knowing full well she wouldn't want to hear the answer and with a thousand awful possibilities ricocheting around the inside of her head.

Mrs. McGuire bit her lower lip and stared at the way the sun lit up the patterns on the curtain.

"*Mom?*" she cried, jumping out of bed, so she could stand directly in front of her mother.

"It's your friend...Harry, is it? Who you went round to see yesterday?"

Maggie had a sudden feeling of immense dread that he was actually *dead*. She felt her stomach disappear down a ravine and her brain spontaneously combust, sending globules of grey matter splattering on the backs of her eyeballs. Her lower lip began to tremble and she bit down hard on it: she point-blank refused to let people see her inner emotions. It was a sign of weakness and Maggie did not *do* weakness. She could be on the verge of tears and then catch her emotions in mid-air, freeze-framing the moment so no-one could have the satisfaction of seeing her reduced to a gibbering mess. She forced herself to speak.

"What about Harry?" she whispered.

"I'm so sorry darling, he's in the hospital."

Maggie heard the words but couldn't make them fit in with the reality as she had known it only a handful of hours ago. Her legs first turned to stone and then to rubble as she felt herself go light-headed.

"But... I was only with him last night... I don't understand."

"He was beaten up on the way home; someone found him in an alleyway."

Maggie was already grabbing up clothes scattered on the bedroom floor and pulling them on in a chaos of fumbling fingers and thumbs. Suddenly, something occurred to her.

"*Who was that on the phone? Was it William or Gabriel?*"

"No, Mags, it was the hospital. Apparently, Harry had no ID on him... but he had your phone number written on the back of his hand. I gave them his name and they were going to phone his Mom now."

Each word pierced Maggie's heart.

"So William and Gabriel *don't even know yet?*" she said, pulling on a pair of converse trainers and heading for the stairs.

"I...suppose not," Mrs. McGuire called after her, "where are you going?"

"To tell them... *and to go see Harry*!" she replied as the door slammed shut behind her...

CHAPTER THIRTY THREE

GOD CREATED TOMORROW SO WE CAN MOVE ON FROM YESTERDAY

'ne tessum possum vivere, nec sinete'
(I can't live with you- nor without you.)

Martial

'Every new beginning comes from
Some other beginning's end.'

Seneca

July 1948,
Outside a set of factory gates in the Midlands.

Rachel blinked and shielded her eyes with a cupped hand as she walked through the open gates and out into the blinding sunshine of a picture-perfect English summer's day. Inside, the factory was lit only by long strip lights of jaundiced yellow and, as she started her shift at six in the morning, she travelled to work in the dark and stepped outside after each day's work like a newly-freed prisoner into the disorientating light of afternoon. But her delight at being outside might imply Rachel was unhappy with her place of work, and that would have been some distance from the truth; it had been a wonderful few years, full of hope and healing...

****

Auntie Florence (or Flo as everyone called her,) and Uncle Arthur had been incredible from the first moment she had stepped off the platform at Moor Street Station. They had hugged her like she was the long-lost daughter they had always wanted and, shortly afterwards, she had taken her first journey on a British red bus; replete with Ticket Inspector and a view through the window of average people living relatively unconcerned lives. Rachel gawped through the window in amazement; to her, it looked as if the war was already over. It had certainly shifted on its axis; that much was true. Hitler had been repelled in the Battle of Britain, bitten off more than he could chew in Russia and was now starting to be pushed back, mile by bloody mile...

Slowly, hope was flickering where before, all had been darkness. It surely wouldn't be long before the Allies started taking back huge swathes of France and could begin the final phases of this hellish conflict. The normality of it all and the rare feeling of safety had been intoxicating for Rachel and she drank it in greedily.

Flo and Arthur had been appalled by the waif-like stray that had stepped off that train and had a simple solution to almost any ailment: strong tea and big portions. They lived in a terraced house in the middle of a street in which the houses were crammed together like cigarettes in a pack. Within a month she had been introduced to every living relative within a fifty mile radius and put on half a stone.

They heard her cry in her room at night and made the decision early on that she needed to grieve in private. Only once did Uncle Arthur relent and allow his pity to get the best of him. He came into her room, with his dressing gown wrapped tightly over his striped pyjamas, and his round glasses perched on the end of his nose. Settling his considerable bulk on the end of her bed, he asked her if she had wanted to talk about it and then waited patiently for a reply.

Rachel didn't know what to say; where to begin. Ashamed, she stared at the flowery bedspread and whispered that she had loved a German boy called Wolfgang and that she had given birth to his child. She told him that she had lost that child, along with every single member of their family. She told him that she had thought she had seen the boy working in the camp that killed every one of her family; although she couldn't be sure it was really him. Then she waited patiently for his response.

Uncle Arthur hadn't said a word through all of this and, when she finished, she glanced up from staring at the bedspread to see his eyes wide as saucers. The resistance had told him of the demise of his cousins and nieces and nephews in Belzec and other camps and they had wept rivers of tears for them already. The rest- Rachel's unplanned birth at the hands of a German soldier- was a shocking revelation to him. Quickly, he had pulled himself together, cleared his throat and offered his summation of all he had heard:

"So he got you pregnant, abandoned you *and* was a bloody Nazi? I'd say you're better off without him! If he ever dared to show his face round 'ere, I'd give 'im the same treatment we gave that bloody 'itler when he tried to invade Britain!"

Rachel wanted to explain it wasn't that easy... and that she would always love that German boy despite everything... and that... Suddenly, she saw with crystal clear clarity that to try to explain was hopeless...you had to have lived it to appreciate how any of them felt. So, she decided to not even try. She couldn't think of a single thing she could say that could make him understand; help him to see the beautiful but flawed world they had inhabited and appreciate the brief, wondrous happiness they had once held in their hands.

So she sat still and said nothing. He had meant well enough, had her best interests at heart and really cared about her. So she had put on a brave face, smiled and leaned over and kissed him on the cheek. They never spoke of her life in Germany again. After a few months, when she was ready, they encouraged her to think about what she wanted to do with the rest of her life and she decided she wanted to help the War effort. She got a job in a munitions factory and, when the War ended, the factory diversified and began making cars instead of bullets and so did she.

****

Rachel had not even reached the corner of the street before Guy pulled up level with her on his bicycle.

"How was your shift?" he asked, smiling shyly as he meandered alongside the pavement, slowly turning the pedals and swerving left and right, to control his speed and not out-pace her.

"Fine," she shrugged, "they've got me training up the new lads at the moment."

"That's because you're the most skilled person on the whole shop floor... course they're going to get you to show them how it's done!"

Rachel smiled; Guy was sweet. He had been in the British Expeditionary Force back in 1940 and had been invalided out of the War after being seriously injured in the humiliating retreat from Dunkirk. Apparently, it had been touch and go whether he lived or died and, if his friends hadn't carried him on their shoulders into the waves under almost constant attack from the Luftwaffe and got him safely onto a boat, he almost certainly would have done. Rachel thought that must say something of his character; his friends clearer considered him worthy of risking their own lives for in order to save his. After several months in hospital, he had been released and got a job in the munitions factory to 'still feel useful'. He had been one of the first people Rachel had been introduced to when she had started working there and she had caught him glancing across at her surreptitiously in the canteen on a number of occasions.

It was obvious he liked her but, for a very long time, the thought of opening her heart to someone new seemed absolutely impossible; a betrayal even. But she began to accept that, wherever Wolfgang was, if he was still alive, he would be getting on with his life and he would want her to get on with hers.

"I was wondering," he began tentatively, and Rachel smiled at the awkwardness of his advances: "whether you'd like to, perhaps, I mean if you've nothing else on... and as it's such a lovely day... whether you'd like to go for a walk over the hills this afternoon?"

She looked across at Guy and smiled. He grinned happily and dismounted from his bike to walk alongside her.

Perhaps, she thought, *at some point, you have to accept that you are never going to put all the shattered pieces of your life back together again exactly as they once were and, at the realisation of that moment, the best thing you can do is to leave them scattered on the floor and simply walk away.*

Rachel smiled at Guy again and carried on walking without once looking back...

CHAPTER THIRTY FOUR

SOMEONE TO WALK AWAY WITH

'The only way out of the labyrinth of suffering
Is to forgive.'

John Green
'Looking for Alaska'

July 1948,
View from a hillside somewhere in the Midlands.

Rachel closed her eyes and let the sun settle on her face like a warm towel. She was sat on a gently sloping hillside overlooking the estate and the factories and the canal network and the fields all stretched out beneath her like a tablecloth and, at long last, she didn't look at it all in the way a stranger looks at an unfamiliar landscape; she looked at it as if this was her home. Gradually, as the years had drifted by, she had come to the realisation that the sun was the same; that the same kinds of clouds scudded above the fields of England as they did the tree-lined avenues of Berlin; and, after five long years, that it was time to put the past behind her and move on.

Guy was lying beside her, his hands behind his head, eyes closed and basking in the sunshine contentedly. Sprawled there, Rachel thought amusedly, he looked like a seal sunbathing on a beach. He had called for her after she had gone home from the factory and changed into a wonderfully light summer dress with a simple floral pattern on it: red roses trailing up her torso, coiling provocatively around her waist. She had felt so very happy as they walked together; like she was dancing down the narrow terraced streets, which soon gave way to countryside once they had cut through the alleyway and climbed the stile into the fields that spread out before them like the start of an adventure. Guy had a rucksack slung over his shoulder and, when they came across a thick wall of blackberry bushes, he reached into it and withdrew two empty jam-jars. Rachel had looked at him, bemused.

"We used to do this when we were kids, before the War; I thought you might enjoy it."

Rachel shrugged and smiled and, together, they filled their jars with juicy blackberries till they were overflowing. Then Guy pulled out a pair of knitting needles and, passing one to Rachel, showed her how to squash the blackberries down until the contents were a delicious-looking purple pulpy mess. Guy then brought a little sealed tin of sugar out of his rucksack and heaped in several spoonfuls before mixing the gloopy contents together. Contentedly, they ate the whole sticky, sweet mess with spoons as they walked and talked all the way to the top of the hill.

When they reached the summit, they had stared out across the view, not looking at each other as Guy continued to gently quiz Rachel all about her life in Berlin and, at last, she had felt able to tell someone... well, *almost* everything. It was a big step forward, when she considered how she had felt unable to tell her new family almost nothing of the life she had lived before she stepped off that train in the centre of Birmingham.

But now it all came out in a cathartic outburst: she told Guy of Wolfgang and Ariel and of falling in love. She told him of *Kristallnacht* and how it was the start of everything falling apart. She told him of hiding for months in the Sankt's attic and of being betrayed by Walther Sankt, pointing the finger and counting his silver as the Germans burst in the door. She told him of being in the camp and the mystery of her rescue; her recovery in the safe hands of the Resistance and her eventual passage back to England.

She neglected to tell him about Felix or about her strange recurrent dreams about who she had thought she had seen just before she had been struck in the camp; or of the most horrible of fates that she had escaped by a matter of hours but which her family had undoubtedly suffered soon after: some things simply were almost too painful even to be thought of, and certainly too horrific to be spoken out loud. Nevertheless, every memory she shared felt like a balloon floating on the wind, taken off that hillside and whisked far away from where it could continue to torture her.

Throughout, Guy had listened attentively, firstly, dragging a long stick he had picked up along the ground meditatively or along the tops of hedges, and then with his hands thrust deep in his pockets as he looked over the streets and canals and factory stacks, but never once did he interrupt her. It was as if he sensed this was a time of cleansing for her; that he was being told things that she was saying aloud for the very first time... and he was immensely grateful that she had felt able to share it all with him.

He had been in love with her for three years and, it wasn't so much that he had been scared to ask her out; it was more that he had *sensed* that she wasn't *ready*. She was a flower that had been destroyed by frost and he had to wait for the thaw and the first green shoots of recovery to show themselves. Lately, he had begun to get the impression that things were changing; nothing overtly encouraging; no dramatic change in personality... but she seemed *happier*, he actually caught her *smiling occasionally*, or laughing when he cracked a joke. He knew he had seen terrible things in the war but he guessed she had seen things ten times worse and, if he was to win her heart, he would have to learn to be patient.

"Guy?" Rachel whispered.

He rolled onto his side to face her, shielding his eyes with his hands.

"Are you having a good time?" he asked, immediately attentive.

"The best time I've had in ages," she admitted.

Guy sensed grey clouds foaming ominously on the beer glass rim of the horizon: *had it been too soon after all?*

"I just don't want to... lead you on, that's all."

Guy could feel the blood pumping in his ears and saw Rachel had suddenly flushed; and it was nothing whatsoever to do with the heat of the sun beating down on them.

"Please don't misunderstand me," she explained, "I like you... a lot. In fact, you are the first person I have felt really comfortable with since, well... since Wolfie; and that makes me happy. I *want* to have a future as well as a past. But I *loved* Wolfie with all my heart and soul and opening my heart to someone else feels like..." she searched for a suitable metaphor but could only come up with, "like I am reducing his memory to the size of a passport photo and losing it in the folds of an old wallet."

Guy sighed in relief. "I understand totally," he smiled. "You feel guilty." He reached out and took her hand in his own. "I would never do anything to rush you, please believe that, and I know you don't love me the way that I love you... yet. But I am prepared to wait. Remember, Rachel, God created tomorrow so we don't have to permanently regret yesterday."

Rachel shot him a surprised look. There had been no inkling that he was going to say he loved her... She wondered how she felt about it. She *thought* she liked the idea... and she liked the idea that she had climbed that hill emotionally alone, but would descend it with someone she could depend on; someone to walk away with when it all got too much. Yes, she concluded, that was *definitely* something to be happy about.

CHAPTER THIRTY FIVE

IN STASIS

'A hospital alone shows what war is.'

Erich Maria Remarque

June 1999,
Saturday morning, a hospital car park.

Maggie and Gabriel pulled into a parking space, jumped out of the car slamming the doors shut behind them, and raced through the sliding glass doors of the hospital.

****

After her mother's shocking revelation, Maggie had run all the way to William and Gabriel's and knocked furiously on the door. She had just been about to give up and make her own way to the hospital, when Gabriel had answered it, still pulling on his dressing gown; hair all spiked up laughably on the top of his head. But no-one was laughing. His hand had gone to his mouth automatically as she told him about the brutal attack on Harry and he beckoned her inside to wait fretfully while he hurriedly dressed.

"Is William still in bed?" she had asked, only for him to call down to tell her he had already gone out earlier that morning.

"Where?" Maggie pressed, coming to the foot of the stairs and pacing the tiled floor like an expectant father. "We need to let him know what's happened!"

Gabriel had shrugged as he descended, biting down on his lip anxiously and flattening down his hair with his palm, "I don't know where he is. After you left, we went and sat outside with a couple of single malts, watched the stars twinkling overhead and generally felt quite smug at how the evening had panned out for you two young love birds!" He grabbed a coat from the bannister at the foot of the stairs and slammed the door behind them. "We fell fast asleep and woke up shivering at about three in the morning. I went to bed and, when I took him a cup of tea in the morning as I always do, he had already dressed and gone out." Gabriel paused and shook his head. "He does this sometimes... goes off by himself and won't tell me where he's gone."

Maggie had looked at him in surprise, but there hadn't been any time to think on it further. Quickly, Gabriel pinned a note to the front door telling William to get to the hospital fast, before they jumped in the car and sped off.

****

"Harry Robinson?" Maggie blurted out at the front desk, making the receptionist blink in surprise as she looked up from a pile of papers in front of her.

"What's the matter with him?" she replied.

"He was... beaten up," Maggie replied, the words sounding alien even on her own tongue. How could it be true? Just hours before they were kissing and now he was lying in a hospital bed somewhere in this very building... so close by and yet so very far away. It was all too much to comprehend.

"And when was he brought in?"

"Sometime in the early hours of this morning apparently."

"A&E sounds like your best bet then," she replied, "they'd take him there first, then into triage before eventually allocating him to the right department."

"You mean you don't actually *know* where he is? *Really?*" Maggie said, exasperated, feeling her rising panic might spill over at any moment into a massive emotional meltdown right there in the hospital reception. In her frantic imagination, the couple of dozen people currently milling around reception were already turning around in shock and embarrassment as she screamed and pointed and demanded to know where Harry was, before collapsing to her knees and pounding the floor with her fists. Gabriel saw her rising panic and wisely intervened.

"You don't have his name on some list?"

"It doesn't work like that," she replied, eyeing them coolly over the top of her glasses.

"Could you point us in the direction of A&E then please?" Gabriel asked, endeavouring to maintain his calm exterior.

The receptionist gave the pair of them terse directions and they hurried off; a cursory thanks still hanging in the air as they ran down the broad corridors, their footsteps echoing behind them. Maggie was vaguely aware of passing hurrying nurses and hobbling patients; bustling doctors with stethoscopes draped loosely from their necks like a hangman's noose; a man, older than Time himself, attached to a drip and heading for the exit with a packet of cigarettes clutched in his free hand... The whole place smelt of disinfectant and urine and a launderette and she felt hideously nauseous.

A&E was straight ahead according to a sign that had so many arrows and directions, it reminded her of the one at Land's End: *New York 3147 miles, John O'Groats 874 miles, Australia 12000 miles, A&E about twenty feet straight ahead...* and, as they pushed through a door, they were stopped in their tracks by the vision of a large imposing man seated behind a desk.

"Can I help you?" he asked, sounding a lot less scary than he looked.

"Harry Robinson," Maggie gasped, breathless with nervous tension, "we're trying to find out where Harry Robinson is."

The man nodded and tapped away at a keyboard in front of him before squinting at the screen.

"Ah, yes," he sniffed, "admitted at 3.23am." He paused and seemed to hold his breath before he looked up from the screen. Maggie saw it in his eyes before he spoke: something was horribly, terribly, awfully wrong. "He's in Intensive Care," he admitted eventually. "He's been put into an induced coma."

Maggie felt her head swim suddenly and her legs give out from under her. Gabriel was at her side, taking her awkwardly in his arms moments before everything blacked out...

****

Hannah Robinson sat by the side of the bed looking but not looking; sandwiching his hand between hers and letting each new flood of tears drown out the last. Harry was a human car crash: a freak show of drips and catheters, heart monitors and ventilators. She rubbed her bleary eyes and blew her nose on her sodden tissue.

She had been there less than half an hour, since the Police had phoned and told her he was in the hospital, but she hadn't slept a wink all night worrying about where he was; pacing the kitchen floor and crying into her mother's arms, phoning hospitals in a futile search for him...*when, all the time, he was lying in a pool of his own blood less than five minutes' walk away.* She had even turned up at William and Gabriel's house at two in the morning- but the house was in cloaked in darkness and nobody had answered her urgent rapping at the door.

Walking home again, hugging herself hard against the wind, she hadn't gone back home through the alleyway. She had paused at the entrance and squinted down its tunnelling black. But it was dark and foreboding and she had always told him not to go through there because it oozed danger at night. Naively, she had convinced herself he would have listened to her; he wouldn't have been stupid enough to cut through such a place just to save five minutes... and neither would she.

Together with Nan, they had sat opposite each other at the kitchen table, nursing a continual flow of strong coffees as they waited for the dawn to break and bring with it the news they both feared. When the phone did eventually ring, she had driven straight to the hospital, leaving her mother to get out of her dressing gown and follow behind in a taxi.

Now, the scene before her was like something out of a science fiction film... her boy, the thing she cared about more than anything in the world, was lying there like an astronaut put into stasis and sent out into the far reaches of the universe.

"Where are you now Harry?" she whispered to herself, *"come back to me, son, please come back to me."*

Slowly, Hannah became conscious of a knock at the door. She turned as two people quietly slipped into the room. After triage, Harry had been stabilised and moved to a side room in Intensive Care. At least she could weep in private; her sporadic sobs and the infernal bleeps of the machines the only sounds before the sudden knocking. Hannah blinked the tears from her eyes and found she recognised the man who entered first: he had been one of the two she had spoken to on the doorstep. *Gabriel? Yes, that was it. An unusual name that stuck in the mind.* Then a girl followed. She was pretty but looked pale and drawn. There were black circles around her eyes and she had recently been crying. *So this is the Maggie he has been so coy about lately.* Hannah felt herself smile despite herself; there was something about her she instantly liked... instinctively she knew her son had made a wise choice.

"I don't mean to intrude..." Gabriel began, his voice trailing off as she signalled for them to come in. Maggie's eyes roved helplessly from the pads on his chest connected to the monotonous bleeping of the heart monitor... to the ET tube down his throat... to the drips in his arms linked by slack tubes to saline in bags hooked on a pole... and bit down hard on her lip to stop herself from crying or screaming.

"I'm so sorry," she managed to mumble as she stood helplessly by the bed, looking in horror at the angry bruises and dried blood still caked on Harry's face. Gabriel walked to the back of the room, pulled up two plastic chairs and sat on the first, indicating for Maggie to sit on the other.

They sat in silence for several moments before Hannah turned to Maggie and forced a smile.

"You must be Maggie."

She nodded and smiled weakly.

"I would say I've heard so much about you but you know what teenage boys are like; keep their cards close to their chests. Still, the change in his mood these last few days... he couldn't hide that... not from his mother."

Maggie blushed and said nothing. She sneaked a look at Mrs. Robinson out of the corner of her eye: her eyes were red-rimmed and puffy and she looked exhausted. A woman on the edge if ever there was one. Last night, she had talked to Harry for hours during and after Gabriel's culinary banquet and he had opened up about his parents and the breakdown of their marriage. Maggie could imagine their life since 'Dad' had left: Mrs. Robinson working every hour God sent, pushing away any male interest, apart from one brief disastrous foray into the dating world. Harry trying to step up...be the man of the house. Things had been tough for them. And now this had happened. The final nail.

She looked again at Harry's motionless body. She thought she could see his eyes flickering behind his eyelids. Was that a good sign? Should she say anything? She felt she was somehow embarking on a war... a ferocious battle against Death, she felt her resolve hardening... *this was one battle she was going to win, no matter what the cost.*

Suddenly, the door flung open and an elderly woman burst in. Her grey hair was tied back in a bun perched securely on the back of her head, while the creases around her eyes and the corners of her mouth gave away her advancing years like bird tracks in snow. Yet one person in the room still looked at her through eyes that forever saw a teenage girl with shimmering black shoulder-length hair, parted down the middle, and dark exotic looks... just like Hedy Lamarr. He sat on his chair, blushing furiously and saying nothing.

Meanwhile, ignoring everyone else in the room, the old woman rushed over to the bed, taking in all the wires and tubes and her unconscious grandson in a single glance.

"Dear God! What have they done to you?" she exclaimed.

Hannah Robinson was unsure if she meant his attackers or the doctors.

"He's in an induced coma, Mom. The doctors say it's the best way for his body to heal."

Nan looked bemused.

"How does putting him into a coma help? Normally you want people to come *out* of a coma, don't you?" she muttered, unconvinced.

Mrs. Robinson racked her brains trying to remember exactly what the doctors had said while her mind had been somersaulting inside her skull. She closed her eyes and repeated the words the young man had said to her in such an earnest voice; at the time she had clung on to his words desperately, keeping her afloat just about in what had appeared a hopeless situation.

"They… whoever did this to Harry… they kicked him in the head and he might have brain damage… there might be swelling in the brain" she repeated. "Putting him in a coma reduces the amount of energy the brain needs, it… shuts off blood flow to damaged areas of the brain… which is a good thing, gives it time to heal…that's what the doctors said anyway," she finished with a tired sigh, opening her eyes again after such an exhausting burst of enforced concentration.

Everyone sat in silence, trying to digest and come to terms with what Mrs. Robinson had said. Then Gabriel cleared his throat and shuffled to his feet, keeping his head low while simultaneously trying to take Maggie by the elbow and guide her to her feet.

"We should give you some privacy…" he began, trailing off in a hushed tone.

Hannah looked up and silently berated herself.

"How rude of me, Gabriel, I'm so sorry, and you too Maggie," she said, smiling bravely. "Mom- this is Harry's girlfriend, Maggie, and Gabriel, one of the two neighbours who's been so kind to Harry since he's been excluded."

Despite being distracted, Mrs. Williams rose to her feet and, extending her hand, met Gabriel's stare for the first time. With a gasp, the outstretched hand moved with exaggerated slowness to cover her open mouth, the disbelief apparent in her wide-eyed expression.

"*Ariel? How...*"

Ariel Koplowitz stood before her and smiled meekly.

"Hello, Rachel, it's been a long time."

CHAPTER THIRTY SIX

HIGH ABOVE THE CLOUDS

'You wanna fly, you got to give up the shit
That weighs you down.'

'Song of Solomon'
Toni Morrison

June 1999,
Somewhere in the ether, floating a little way above his hospital bed...

Some might say we will find a brighter day
Some might say we will find a brighter day...
   Harry felt the blows raining down like confetti. He covered his head with his hands, curled into a ball, tried to make himself as small a target as possible... a hedgehog, unable to stop the flurry of kicks and punches, simply hoping to outlive them. Outlast their fury. Wear them down with his compliance.
   The pain of the blows seemed to lessen as his vision started to darken at the edges, zeroing in so only light remained at the pinprick centre. The noise was dulled too; like being underwater and hearing music playing above the surface. But, in the far distance, he could clearly hear a girl screaming, her venom slicing through the fathoms: 'kick 'im! Kill 'im! Do it!'
   The sound started to fade along with the picture, but the Oasis lyrics continued as the blackness briefly took over once more before being replaced with a different backdrop...
   Harry was soaring above the clouds now... a hawk; tightrope-walking the currents. He swooped and turned, slicing through cloud and leaving a razor-sharp furrow of air in his wake. Fields were far below, houses, estates... now he could see his own house! He could pass within an inch of his chimney pot if he so desired or stay up here in the upper echelons of the sky, hidden from view in the protective glare of the sun.
   But, suddenly, the clouds were fringed with black...he felt himself falling, uncontrollably spiralling to earth, a spitfire with a trail of smoke like a comet, sparking from its tail, with no time for the pilot to eject... falling, falling, the ground rising up to meet him, open armed...
   The scene changed yet again... Harry was in a car. He was a passenger in the back, Dad was driving. Mom was by his side laughing at his rubbish jokes, her hand resting on his leg. He was playing a game: how many different animals could Harry spot in the flashing fields that passed by the side windows in a blur. Harry tried to concentrate: cows, (black and white ones, brown ones, the odd,

thick-bodied bull) sheep, (some with coats dense as hawthorn bushes, others mere fragile-looking lambs, still unsteady as they stumbled after seemingly disinterested mothers), piebald horses... crows on telephone wires... pigs in a muddy field basking outside little huts that looked like Anderson shelters... but the staring was making him feel nauseous; made his stomach bubble and froth queasily. He stopped looking and closed his eyes...

...and when he opened them, the black took on new definition, became the outline of figures, forming the firm edges of details: trousers, coats, leather jackets, flat caps, striped scarves... the roar of a crowd. He was caught up in the midst of it but it wasn't sickening, like the fields zipping by, it was exhilarating! He strained to see and Dad reached down and swept him up, in one swift movement sitting him on his broad shoulders so now the pitch was laid out before him in all its splendour... floodlit and green and utterly beautiful. His team were on the attack... the ball floated into the box, a figure jumped, met the ball cleanly with his head. It was destined for the top corner the moment it left the crease of his forehead... Harry screamed at the stars, arms aloft, fists closed and eyes screwed shut...

When he opened them, he was floating over his bed; his bed in the hospital. Mom was sitting holding his hand. Nan was no longer there, but he somehow knew she had been there a minute ago, shaking her head at something as though she was struggling to accept it. He called out to them, but they couldn't hear him. Or obstinately refused to look up. He looked down at his motionless self, tucked neatly into folded back sheets, wires and drips hanging off him like monstrous extra limbs. He called out again and again... getting louder and more desperate, screaming and sobbing until his voice was hoarse... but they didn't hear him... they didn't look up... there was no way out!

Hannah Robinson had barely let go of her son's hand since she had arrived in the hospital and showed no sign of doing so now. It was as if he might slip away from her if she let him go; might float away and never return to her. She glanced up at him trying not to let herself imagine the worst, unthinkable scenario... that he might always be like this... that this might be her son's existence *for the rest of his life.*

She pictured herself visiting him every day, coming in out of the cold to this unseeing face; stamping the snow off her shoes to the background accompaniment of the endless tiny wheeze of his breathing and the torturous, relentless bleeping of the machines.

She saw her new life now in this hellish limbo: sitting by his bedside reading him stories she would have no idea he could hear; telling him about her boring day just for something to say; playing him music that he may have grown to hate by now. Actually, she couldn't decide what was worse... knowing there was an emptiness, a void, a nothingness behind those eyes... or knowing that he was fully aware of everything happening to him... the shaving of his face by a strange hand, the tube delivering fluids directly into his stomach, the indignity of bed baths and soiled sheets, the screaming at the top of his lungs that no-one, *no-one,* heard. *Yes,* she thought, *that was worse; way worse.*

No, she stopped herself angrily, *she wouldn't allow herself to think like that, he was going to be fine, the doctors knew what they were doing; this was all part of their masterplan to bring him back.*

She had to believe that was the truth, *had to*...the alternative was simply too unimaginable for words...

CHAPTER THIRTY SEVEN

THE TRUTH WILL OUT

'We fear violence less than our own feelings.
Personal, private, solitary pain
Is more terrifying
Than what anyone else can inflict.'

Jim Morrison

'A life spent making mistakes
Is not only more honourable,
But more useful than a life
Spent doing nothing.'

George Bernard Shaw

June 1999,
In the hospital carpark.

Outside, there seemed to be a sea change of bodies, as visitors made their way back to their cars at the end of visiting hours, crossing over with doctors and nurses shuffling in the other way to begin their afternoon shifts. After Rachel had found herself face to face with a man she hadn't seen for over fifty years, she had mumbled something about stepping outside to speak in private and walked to the door in a daze.

Hannah Robinson had been so distracted by the motionless vision of her son still just lying there, unresponsive and mute, she had hardly seemed to notice as the three of them slipped out of Harry's room and walked, in awkward silence, to the lift. Maggie followed them, unsure what to do: she didn't feel able to stay and share in Mrs. Robinson's pain, but didn't understand what was going on between Gabriel and Harry's grandmother either... *for a start, why was Harry's grandmother looking so shocked by the arrival of Gabriel and why on earth was she calling him Ariel?*

As the doors slid shut and the lift started to descend, she watched the pair of them in the mirrors that curved around three walls. Gabriel was staring at the floor like a naughty schoolboy blushing furiously. Maggie thought about trying to break the silence, when Rachel suddenly burst into tears and both looked across at her in surprise.

"Ariel," she sobbed, "I can't believe it's really you..." she sobbed, "I've thought about you and Wolfie *so* many times over the years... I don't understand...*what are you doing here?*"

Gabriel smiled in relief and gratefully enveloped her in his arms.

"I know," he whispered, cradling her like a child with a grazed knee, "it's crazy, I know and I *will* explain, I promise," he puffed out his cheeks, " it's just knowing where to *start...*"

As they reached the ground floor, the lift doors slid open to reveal a porter pushing a big man in a wheelchair, his leg encased in plaster and sticking out at a right angle to the rest of his body. He was dressed in a rugby strip and his free leg and strip were caked in mud.

Their eyebrows raised in surprise at the sight of an elderly man and women embracing in a lift while a teenage girl tried to look elsewhere clearly, embarrassed. Gabriel took Rachel by the hand and led them past the bemused porter while Maggie hurried apologetically behind.

Turning left, they headed for the reception and then outside; Gabriel sending Rachel and Maggie on ahead so he could use the payphone to add an answerphone message for William to the one he had pinned to the front door of the house before they left for the hospital. Maggie took in a big breath of fresh air and looked up. The sky was a delicate porcelain blue and packed full of clouds that seemed to make one shape after another just to entertain her... elephant...Viking long ship... ice cream cone. She watched them drift by, one by one, like floats in a parade as the pair of them waited on a bench opposite a gaggle of nurses smoking and laughing, the rows of visitors' cars, their bonnets glinting in the sunshine, silent behind them.

"I'm not sure I've figured out what's going on," Maggie began, "but I take it you were surprised to see Gabriel?"

A strange noise left Rachel's lips that suggested Maggie's words were something of an understatement.

"*Ariel*," Rachel corrected, "and, yes, you could say that. The last time I saw the man you know as Gabriel was in Berlin during the war over fifty years ago."

Maggie stared at her in utter disbelief, but didn't get a chance to ask any more questions as Gabriel- or Ariel, as she supposed she should think of him from now on- re-joined them. Sitting between them, he took Rachel's hand, pressed it to his lips, and then clasped it tight within his own, before blowing out his cheeks and considering where to begin his tale...

"Perhaps it's best to start with your rescue from the camp, as it was the last time you saw us," he said, staring into space as he pictured the scene as if it were yesterday. "When Wolfie hit you, I-"

Ariel felt Rachel squeeze his hands really tight and, when he looked across, she was wide-eyed, with tears already starting to form in the corner of her eyes.

"*Did you say Wolfie? Wolfie was the one that struck me?*" She shook her head in amazement. "I cannot tell you how many times I have wondered about that day, *dreamt* about it, woken up in a cold sweat with the memory of it still emblazoned on the backs of my eyelids. For so *many* years. But I convinced myself it was my mind playing tricks on me. I was exhausted; emotionally drained; I'd been struck on the head, been unconscious for God knows how long, it had all happened so quickly... but..." something suddenly occurred to Rachel, "are you saying *you* were there too?"

Ariel nodded shamefully. "I was a sonderkommando..." he turned to Maggie and added by way of explanation, "a Jewish guard in an extermination camp."

He saw the look of disbelief on her face and nodded. "It's not something I'm proud of, believe me, and I have spent many nights living with the faces of the men, women and children who I dragged from the gas chambers and placed into wheelbarrows to be buried or burnt."

He stopped as his voice wavered. Angrily, he wiped away a tear from his cheek. "Damn it! I know I have no right to any pity, but Wolfie saw me disembark from the train the same way you did and it was the only way he could save my life. It brought me a little precious time until he could arrange my escape from the camp."

He turned back to Rachel and smiled sadly. "Then, one day, *you* arrived out of the blue." He squeezed her hand and nodded. "Or should I say, you arrived out of the storm: it was a horrible day, pouring with rain, black as night...do you remember? I saw you not long after you stepped off the train and I hurried over to try to catch Wolfie's eye and point you out to him, hoping against hope he would be able to do something... a*nything.* You seemed in a daze; didn't seem to notice anything going on around you. Do you recall much of that day Rachel?"

Rachel nodded and wiped away a tear, Felix yanking at the raw strands of her memories as he so often did. Ariel noted her silent grief and picked up his story.

"Wolfie had to act fast: he strode over and hit you before you could speak or show any recognition that you knew him and end any chance of saving your life, then I gathered you up and he told me to follow him. If he hadn't, you would have been dead within the hour."

Maggie gasped in horror, trying to comprehend how it could be that this perfectly normal day was taking such unbelievable and bizarre twists... and it wasn't even lunchtime yet! Ariel stared at the floor, still ashamed at his latest revelation.

"I carried you into the woods behind the camp," he eventually continued with difficulty, "where we waited for night-time in a huntsman's hut for the resistance to come and rescue us."

Rachel looked puzzled, while Maggie perched on the edge of the bench, her mind still playing catch-up with all she was hearing.

"But how were you both able to just... walk out of the camp and into the woods and nobody bat an eyelid?" Maggie asked.

Ariel bit his lip and smiled sadly.

"Because Wolfie was a guard in the camp; an *important* guard. His father was the Kommandant."

Ariel saw Maggie's jaw fall slack and smiled.

"I know it is almost too incredible to believe but it is true nonetheless. Thus, no-one would question anything his son did. Everyone would have simply presumed Rachel had been causing trouble... kicking up a fuss, refusing to go into the shower block... and he had taken her into the woods to kill her discreetly. The woods were still within the confines of the camp. It had happened many times in the past and, doubtless, happened many more times after that day. Before he left us and returned to his duties, he fired two shots into the air... that would have signalled our execution to anyone who might have been bothering to listen. No one would have questioned it further after that."

Something occurred to Maggie.

"You keep going on about this bloke *Wolfie*...if *you're* Ariel and not Gabriel... does that mean William... is this Wolfie?"

Ariel heard Rachel audibly moan and become faint. She began to lean heavily on Ariel and he supported her as best he could.

"Rachel? Are you all right?" he whispered, turning her cheek to look into her eyes. She met his gaze, eyes wide with wonder.

"My God!" she stammered, "are you saying Wolfie is *still alive too?"*

There was a long pause before Ariel nodded slowly, acutely aware that this was a ridiculous amount of information for her to try and process in one go.

"Not only is he alive," he said, squinting his eyes and hunching his shoulders as if he were expecting an imminent explosion, "but I have lived here in England with him since 1947; it was Wolfie who I tried to phone before I just came out here."

Rachel sprang to her feet and began pacing frantically, wringing her hands like a demented Lady Macbeth and muttering to herself incoherently.

"I can't take all this in," she said, shaking her head. "How did you come to be in England? Did you already about... *me?* About my life? My family? Why didn't you come and *find me? Speak to me? Tell me you were alive? Do you know how many years I've longed to see you, to know the truth?"*

She continued pacing, turning this way and that, talking as much to herself now than the two people looking up at her anxiously. *"*The torment my mind has been through all these years. The private *hell,"* she muttered, shaking her head and staring into the far horizon of her soul.

Ariel nodded guiltily.

"I know, I know, it's all...too much, but you really have to hear it from the start for it to... for it to make some kind of *sense.*"

Rachel sighed and considered this. She forced herself to stand still, to assimilate all of this information; her darting eyes being the only movement that remained. Then she stared at him for a long time before finally shrugging one shoulder nonchalantly and answering him.

"Very well," she announced, "I've waited fifty years for the truth, I can wait a few minutes more."

CHAPTER THIRTY EIGHT

HUNTING FOR WOLFIE

"There is nothing for it but to try and see our missions through to the end,
As best we can, for until we do so, we will be permitted no calm."

'When We Were Orphans'
Kazuo Ishiguro

The end of May, 1945.
Berlin.

Berlin had finally fallen a matter of days ago and the city Ariel walked through was unrecognisable to the one he had been forced to leave three long years ago. Hitler was dead. The Third Reich was defeated. The War was over. The Western Allies and the Russians now patrolled the rubble-filled streets where the Nazis had ruled so ruthlessly, and where now Ariel cautiously picked his way crawling ever closer towards Wolfgang's house.

It appeared to Ariel that barely a single house had been left untouched. He knew the Berlin garrison had fought bravely at the end, the Russians moving house to house, fighting hand to hand, but he had also heard the rumours that the German army was reduced to boys and old men by the end and the ruthlessness of the Russians had been brutal. It was hard to feel sympathy, Ariel reflected grimly; whatever they had suffered could hardly have been any more unspeakable than *his* war had been.

****

Ariel had stayed with the Bielski Brigade for almost the entirety of the war and it had obviously been a difficult and dangerous struggle but, even with the cold and the hunger and having to repeatedly change camps when the Germans came looking for them, it had ultimately felt worthwhile. When he had left them to begin the journey home, there had been almost twelve hundred of them still sheltering in the woods. More than a thousand men, old people, women and children who would unquestionably have perished if they had stayed in the ghettos from which they fled. And, even more satisfying, they had made life hard for the Germans: ambushed patrols on dark winding roads late at night; blew up train tracks to disrupt supply lines; raided villages and took food and drink off Nazi-sympathisers; cut telephone wires and intercepted messages. They had been a colossal thorn in the side of the Germans and that had felt extremely good.

Then the Germans had begun to withdraw: Ukraine, Belarus, Poland...like the mighty Roman Empire, everything was crashing about their ears and, mostly, they were having to pull back at speed, often desperately trying to burn incriminating documents and destroy resources they didn't want to fall into enemy hands. The chaos was intoxicating. One minute, they were living like foxes in their dens then, almost overnight, there was no need to hide in the forests anymore, as the Russians were chasing them all the way back to Berlin. In the aftermath, Ariel decided to do what he had wanted to do for many months: try and find Wolfgang.

If he was still alive.

It was a big *if* too. For months after his escape, he had heard nothing of Belzec. Then they had picked up a man on a patrol in early 1943 and he had filled him in on the demise of the camp: He had also worked as a sonderkommando until its final horrific days. In hushed tones, he told Ariel that the last Jews had arrived at Belzec on the 11th December 1942. By now, the six-chambered shower block, complete with insulated cement walls, could kill a thousand people at a time: pretty much the same number as every man, woman and child living in the Bielski's camp right now, Ariel had considered grimly, *could be killed in one go*. The only problem was, they had become victims of their own success: they couldn't cope with the demand. The camp was full to the brim with corpses. The very earth bulged with them and, as the putrefied bodies swelled in the summer heat, they burst through the surface of the soil, as if the souls of the dead were rising from their graves to take bloody revenge on their murderers.

The man took a long swig of vodka, wiping his mouth with the dirty back of his hand before continuing. Along with the other sonderkommandos, he had spent weeks digging up the bodies, piling their emaciated limbs onto vast pyres enclosed in a base of railway sleepers and then dousing the whole abhorrent mess in petrol. The stench of rotting, burning flesh, he said, would never leave him.

After, the bones were collected and crushed. Eventually, in June 1943, the camp was closed, the area ploughed over and, ironically, disguised as a farm: the earth full of life again instead of putrefying death. "What happened to *you* then?" Ariel had asked. The man had grinned morbidly. "I was one of the lucky ones. They sent us to a work camp near the Russian border. I lasted a little under eighteen months then, one day, the Russians appeared out of nowhere. Caught the Germans off-guard. They were slaughtered and we were free."

****

Ariel turned into Wolfie's street. The trees that had once lined the wide avenue were now no more than blackened stumps where the Allied bombers had left their indelible mark. Ariel turned his gaze to the row of houses on the left. The street resembled an old man's mouth: some teeth were still present and in a reasonable condition but where others used to be, only dark spaces remained; the empty husks of what had once been some of the wealthiest homes in the city.

As Ariel drew level with Wolfgang's house his heart sank and he wondered whether he had wasted his time. The house had suffered from the ravages of a great fire that had completely destroyed the roof and decimated the upper floors. Below it, the bottom two floors were less affected; although the windows had pretty much all been blown out and a thick red velvet curtain blew idly out of one on the second floor. Judging by the devastation caused to the house next door, Ariel guessed that it must have been the victim of a direct hit, while the fire had seemingly spread to Wolfgang's house as it exploded and burnt to the ground.

Ariel turned into the pathway and walked up to the front door. He stood staring at the still brightly-painted red door, with his hand poised above the lion-head knocker... and wondered what to do next. It seemed churlish to knock; he couldn't imagine anyone was living there anymore, although so many had been bombed out of their homes, there had to be thousands living in much worse conditions. It also occurred to him that he had never been inside Wolfgang's house and brazenly knocking on the front door seemed, somehow... disrespectful. On the odd occasion he and Rachel had called for Wolfie to come out and spend the long summer afternoon's together, they had called around the tradesmen's entrance at the back and Wolfie had slipped out, giggling naughtily, as if he were truanting from school. Ariel let his hand fall and walked around to the back of the house.

When he reached the back, he was met with the surprising sight of a neat and tidy garden in full bloom, with an ornate summerhouse still perfectly intact at the bottom of a winding path. Ariel shook his head sadly. While the house had suffered badly, the garden had remained remarkably unscathed and looked like a slightly unkempt Garden of Eden amidst all the wanton destruction that surrounded it. Approaching the back door, he looked for a way in. Perhaps he could find an address or some clue as to what had happened to Wolfie, he mused. Turning the handle, he found it was locked, so he looked around and easily located half a fallen house brick. Wrapping his hand in a rag he similarly found lying about, he smashed the square of glass directly above the door handle and, reaching his hand through, pulled across the catch and opened the door.

Stepping inside, Ariel blinked in the half-light. The windows in the kitchen had been covered so no light escaped during air raids. He paused a few steps in, patiently waiting as, slowly, his eyes adjusted and turned the opaque darkness into the vague outlines of more distinct shapes in front of him.

Then, his eyes settled on two small circles only a few feet away…

He squinted and strained his eyes to make out the strange, unidentifiable shape more clearly. The circles seemed to have something attached to them…he followed it back as a crease furrowed his brow…two long tubes running backwards towards… two hands… and a face.

Ariel slowly raised his hands as it slowly dawned on him… *he was looking down the barrel of a shotgun.*

CHAPTER THIRTY NINE

TIME TO SAY GOODBYE

'The greatest hazard of all, losing oneself,
Can occur very quietly in the world,
Almost as if it were nothing at all.'

Kierkegaard

'I don't consider myself a pessimist.
I think of a pessimist as someone who is waiting for it to rain.
And I feel soaked to the skin.'

Leonard Cohen

25th March 1943,
Belzec Extermination Camp.

Wolfgang lay on his bunk in the cottage looking at the only photograph he owned of Rachel. It was black and white, only two inches square and showed her smiling directly at the camera while leaning out of the bandstand in the park where so much of their relationship had played out. He had taken it on the Leica camera his parents had given him for his fourteenth birthday. It was creased with little lines like leaf veins from the years it had spent snug in his wallet at school and then in his tunic pocket from the time he had left for basic training, to fighting on the Russian Front, right to this moment.

It had been just over a week since he had left Rachel and Ariel in the woods and he had waited until today to find a little time alone to spend with Rachel's photograph before he did what he needed to do; *because today was her birthday.*

He lay back and closed his eyes and allowed himself to leaf through a selection of his favourite memories of them together, stored with startling clarity in his memory, like pages in an album: their first meeting... first kiss... holding hands and sneaking glances at each other...laughing together. He screwed up his eyes really tight and tried really hard to remember the peal of her laugh. It was just one of a million things about her he would never forget and, for the first time in what seemed like forever... he felt himself smile.

Hoisting himself wearily off the bed, he squatted on all fours and squinted under the bed. He saw the dim outline of the thing he wanted and pulled it out. It was the small case that he had brought most of his personal possessions in that weren't required to be kept in his kit bag. Inside was a bottle of red wine. Wolfgang had brought it on a rare visit to the village and had kept it for a special occasion; though what he might have to celebrate whilst living in his own personal corner of Oblivion, he couldn't have begun to imagine.

Then Rachel had appeared out of the blue... well, more accurately, out of the thunder and lightning, like an angel parting the clouds and making everything clear. He *could* do something good;

even *here* and even if it were only a candle-glimmer of good in a valley of endless shadow- *he could save Rachel and Ariel.*

And he had successfully achieved his primary objective; his *only* objective.

After firing his luger into the air, he had weaved his way through the trees, fighting back the tears, kept his head down as he strode through the camp, before climbing the stairs to his room and lying on this bed, (the bed where he now contemplated his next fatal step...) and wept. He had only just pulled himself together when Fuchs had entered gleefully clasping a large jar, full to the top with extracted teeth.

"Look at all that gold!" he had exclaimed delightedly, *"and that's only from yesterday! We really could make a fortune on the Black Market, you know."*

And that was what had, finally, decided Wolfgang: he had done what little could be done, but there was no more he could achieve. How could he continue to live through this ordeal with no end in sight and knowing that he was perpetrating the most heinous crime imaginable, *every single day?* He didn't even have Ariel to console him anymore.

In fact, the more he had thought about it, the more it had seemed poetic somehow that Rachel's birthday was coming up imminently and that would be the right time to end it all.

He decided to toast her birthday with the wine he had saved; which would also take the edge off the pain of what he had in mind. Opening the bottle, he sat it next to a small glass and the thin metal blade he had taken from his razor. Pouring himself a glass, he took the first swig; it was thick and earthy and made him feel a glow in his cheeks as soon as he drained the first glass. He poured himself another and lifted it high in the air.

"My closest friend Ariel," he began, as though he sat in front of him on the wooden chair in the corner, "I thank you for being the best friend anyone could wish for: non-judgemental, funny, and the single most kindest human being I have ever had the pleasure to know."

He drank deeply, then filled it to the brim again.

"And to you Rachel, my first and my only love, I have been so blessed to have had you in my life that I can die happy knowing that

I saw you one last time and was able to give you the opportunity of a second chance. I wish only for you to take it, to have a long life after the War is over and to meet someone else and have... the life that was so cruelly denied us."

Again, he lifted the glass and drained the contents in two big gulps. There was only a small amount left sloshing in the bottom of the bottle now, and he emptied it into the glass. He felt woozy from the speed he had drunk and his cheeks burned. Swigging back the final drop, he eased himself back onto the bed and lay his head back onto the pillow. Surprisingly, a vision of being with his father at *Oktoberfest* came, uninvited, into his mind... they were laughing, a full, unforced laugh as they came down the helter skelter together, their feet tucked into a hessian sack, Wolfgang getting dizzy as they went round and round...

Wolfgang smiled to himself. It was mildly comforting to remember that his father had once *been a father. That they had shared a few happy memories together.* He wondered where it had gone wrong; if there had been a moment (because history was replete with defining moments,) when his father had gone from being a Good Man to an Evil Man? And, if that was the case, was his father *aware* of such a moment and did he *regret* that crossing of the line? Wolfgang sighed and concluded they were questions he would have to accept he would never know the answers to...

He reached across and, pinching the razor blade between his thumb and forefinger, looked at the thin slice of metal that would end his life. Such a little thing to achieve such a dramatic outcome, he mused absent-mindedly. But then again, every day, he watched hundreds of men, women and children trudge off the trains. They thought they were simply taking something as inconsequential as a *shower,* little suspecting it would be their final act on this earth.

Wolfgang suddenly became overwhelmed with a miserable malaise. The world felt like it was pressing down on him... heavier than water and thicker than blood, so that his ears seemed dulled to everything but the thudding of his heart. He felt worn threadbare with regret and exhaustion. He closed his eyes... if only he could return to that night... in the summerhouse. The most perfect night of his life. If only they could start again from that precious moment, slip away in the shadows and never return. Leave Germany behind and find a new life outside of Europe and start afresh. But life was not like that; life enjoyed showing glimpses of wonderment so the regret would be all the more keenly felt.

Suddenly, Rachel's face appeared from nowhere in the forefront of his mind. She was crying and shaking her head; imploring him with her eyes. He gasped in surprise. *What was she trying to tell him?* His resolve was still cradled between thumb and forefinger as before, like a pen ready to write the story of his war crimes in his own blood... but he felt his grip on it waver.

Was this really what Rachel would want?

What if she searched him out after the War was over and discovered the nature of his demise?

Would she think him a coward taking the easy way out? Giving up on the chance of redemption or of ever seeing her again?

He was confused... what he had been so certain about before, now seemed shrouded in doubt and confusion. He looked into Rachel's eyes and could read her mind as clearly as if she were standing right in front of him and speaking her thoughts out loud to him: *she wanted him to live; to get through this.*

If there was any slim chance he might see her again, he *had* to take it. This didn't have to be the end.

With an enormous effort of will, he let the blade slip from his pincer-like grip and fall to the safety of the wooden floorboards below. With a sigh, he laid his head back, and slept.

CHAPTER FORTY

STARING DOWN THE BARREL OF A GUN

'Relata refero. No Iupiter quidem omnibus placet.'
(I only tell you what I heard. Juve himself can't please everybody.)

End of May 1945.
Berlin.

"Turn around and get out… *now!*" hissed the voice at the end of the double-barrelled shotgun.

Ariel slowly raised his arms and spoke softly so as not to anger the voice further.

"I don't mean any trouble," he tried to explain, "I have simply come looking for an old friend."

There was a long pause while the voice considered his words.

"Who the hell are you?"

Ariel smiled. *Where to begin?* he thought. *With the 'who' I used to be, the 'who' I became or the 'who' I am today?* He puffed out his cheeks as he thought about what to tell this stranger and, with a shrug of his shoulder, decided he might as well go with the truth.

"My name is Ariel Koplowitz and the person I seek is a boy who lived here and who I used to play with as a child, a lifetime ago… his name was Wolfgang Wirth."

Ariel saw the barrels lower a little and sensed the hesitation might be concealing some information about his old friend.

"Did you know him well?" the voice asked, a fondness clearly evident in his tone.

Ariel nodded, smiling warmly.

"He was my best friend. I called round here for him sometimes," he said, indicating the door behind him, "I used to knock at that very door and wait for a servant to answer and fetch him. We weren't allowed in the house…" he added, "because of what we were."

Now the shotgun lowered completely and the previous accusatory tone changed to one of surprised recollection.

"Did you used to come here with a girl?" it asked.

Ariel smiled, "Yes, Rachel."

The voice became a shape and then a figure, who stepped forward to reveal the man behind it. He was old and emaciated and was dressed in the remnants of a white shirt and black waistcoat underneath a large threadbare overcoat and scarf, loosely draped around his scrawny neck. Bony digits extended and still curled around the trigger of the gun from the ends of fingerless gloves. From beneath white jowly whiskers, he smiled sadly.

"I remember you. My name is Kurt. Once upon a time, I was the Head Butler of this once fine house."

Ariel looked again at the lined face before him and thought he saw the shadow of the man who had sometimes sent them on their way with a treat in their pockets and a whispered warning not to let Wolfie's father see them as they walked past the front of the house.

"I remember you," Ariel whispered.

The man nodded and they stared at each other in wonder; a thousand happier times dancing in the space between them. He motioned for Ariel to come inside properly and be seated at the kitchen table. Then, he took a broom and set about sweeping up the broken glass before disappearing for a few moments. He returned with a hammer and nails and a rectangle of wood to cover the hole.

"Sorry about that," Ariel apologised, "I presumed the house was deserted."

Kurt nodded grimly, "I am the last but, even though it is but a shell of the splendour it was, it is prudent to keep it as secure as possible. Looting is rife and the Russians don't need an excuse to take revenge for what was done in their homeland."

Ariel nodded without responding.

"I would offer you something to eat," he continued, and smiled wistfully, "like I used to before the War when you looked no more than a twiglet on legs but, alas, I have nothing to offer you. The battle for Berlin was long and brutal and we were completely cut off. What rations that were left were constantly being cut and many, many people died from hunger even before the Russians broke through our defences." He stopped and bit down on his lip, unable to say any more for the time being.

"I would be honoured if you would share what little I have," Ariel said, taking his rucksack off his back and beginning to take items from it.

When the Russians had liberated the area surrounding the forests where Ariel and the Bielski Brigade had made their final camp, they had emerged from their self-imposed exile and returned to the villages and towns of their births. Those who had sympathised with the Nazis had paid a high price for their treachery and, consequently,

Ariel was able to leave with a sack full of food and drink to sustain him for the journey, as well as a purse full of money to buy more when those supplies ran out.

He placed half a dozen red apples, half a loaf of bread, a lump of cheese wrapped in a square of cloth and a bottle of schnapps on the table between them. Kurt made a show of resisting his generosity, but it was clear the man was starving and he didn't take too much convincing.

"What happened here, my friend?" he asked, indicating around him with a sweep of his hand to show he meant to the house, as Kurt fetched two liquor glasses and Ariel poured them two generous shots.

"We have the Fuhrer to thank for that," Kurt scoffed humourlessly, "April twentieth: Hitler's fifty-sixth birthday. The Russians decided to send him a present he would never forget and let loose an almighty artillery barrage right into the heart of the city, while the Americans bombed overhead. I'm not sure if it was a bomb from a plane or a cannon from behind the Russian front line that did for next door but, either way, the fire took hold and, by the time it was extinguished, it had already spread to us and we lost all of the upper floors."

"Was anybody killed?" Ariel asked.

Kurt glanced up at him from a mouthful of bread and cheese and nodded wistfully. "The mistress of the house and her mother- Wolfgang's grandmother- and four of the staff. It was my day off and I was spending it with my family." He finished his mouthful and stared mournfully at the table, his eyes wet with tears. "Unfortunately, our apartment block was bombed two days later and my wife and son were killed while I was out trying to find food for us all. So I cheated Death twice in three days; I am lucky, do you not agree?"

Ariel couldn't mistake the bitter irony in his voice and winced. What could he say? Everyone he knew had been changed irrevocably by the events of the last few years. Tragedy hung heavy like an anvil around the neck. Eventually, when Kurt had composed himself again, he plucked up the courage to ask the question he had been burning to ask the old man since he had first introduced himself:

"And what of the rest of the household?"

Kurt nodded and bit into an apple with a crunch. The juice dribbled down the edge of his mouth and he shook his head as he grinned a skeletal grin.

"I must apologise to you, young man. I cannot tell you how amazing this tastes. I have not eaten anything apart from the contents of rusty cans for weeks. Last week I managed to shoot a bird in the garden with my shotgun. When that was gone, I had nothing left." He paused to swallow, then sighed and blew out his cheeks, picking up the trail of his story again. "After the camp closed, Kommander Wirth and young Wolfgang returned home to recuperate; take some well-earned leave. We were never told what really went on in the camp but, whatever it was, it had clearly taken a toll on them both."

Ariel looked up at him but said nothing.

"The Kommander worked in Berlin for a while," Kurt continued, "then got posted to Italy in 1944. He had only been there a matter of weeks when, driving through the countryside, his car was ambushed by partisans and he was machine-gunned to death, along with his driver."

"And Wolfgang?" Ariel persisted.

"Yes, of course... dear Wolfgang," Kurt nodded dolefully, "I remember being shocked when I saw him for the first time after his return. He was unrecognisable; even from the young man who had returned from the Russian Front." He paused and thought how best to explain the change he had witnessed. "It was like a light had gone from his eyes; he was dead to everything and everyone. He cut a tragic figure that's for certain."

Ariel nodded, unsurprised. He was just thankful he had made it back home at all.

"Then what?"

"Then he had a nervous breakdown," he said bluntly, "he simply fell apart."

He noted the pain on Ariel's face and nodded, "I know, it is tough for a friend to hear. After he came back home, he refused to come out of his room for weeks. His mother tried to cajole him, the Kommander shouted at him... nothing worked. Eventually, they called for a doctor."

"What was his diagnosis?"

Kurt smiled grimly, "that he had simply seen...too much. His mind couldn't cope with it anymore. His brain started to shut down, went to a place where he could... *co-exist* with the horror of whatever it was he had been forced to do. When they took him out of here, he was strapped to a stretcher and staring blankly at the ceiling. That was the last time any of us saw him."

****

"What happened to him, Ariel? What happened to my Wolfie?" Rachel begged.

They were sat in the hospital canteen. The two of them were nursing coffees while Maggie sipped on a coke as Ariel recounted his story. They had listened in silence until this point, but now Rachel had burst animatedly into life, her eyes flashing with an overwhelming desire to know the truth.

"That's what I asked next, of course," Ariel smiled. "Kurt said that, as far as he knew, he was still in the hospital where they had first taken him. He gave me the address and I went that same afternoon..."

****

The mental hospital had, miraculously, survived the ravages of War and stood, imposing and grey as a prison, but still intact; which Ariel took as a good omen. When he asked at the reception, they confirmed he was, indeed, still a patient there and agreed he could be permitted to see him. A nurse came and led him down long sterile corridors, their footsteps echoing eerily behind them. When he mentioned the name of the person he had come to visit, the nurse stole him a glance and looked away guiltily when he returned her look. Suddenly, she stopped abruptly, nodded at the room in front of her then, without a word of explanation, turned on her heels and walked away. Ariel knocked on the door and prepared himself for the worst...

Wolfgang was being kept in a private room. Kurt had explained that, after the fire, everything from the house that had been salvageable had been sold and, after the funerals of his parents, the family solicitor had put the combined totals from their life insurance policies, the value of their various investments and the family's life savings into a trust fund for Wolfgang, as the only son and heir. He was, in fact, a wealthy young man. Thus, the best care was being provided for him. Nevertheless, Ariel had a growing fear that they had failed to make any significant progress in curing him of his malaise.

No reply came from within, so he opened the door a little and peered inside. There was Wolfgang, seated in a chair by the window, staring unblinking through the bars on a small square of cloudless sky.

"Wolfie?" he said gently.

Wolfgang did not stir so much as a muscle.

Ariel stepped inside and, closing the door after him, glanced around the room. It was white and stark. A single bed had been made with clinical precision, suggesting it hadn't been slept in by Wolfie the previous night, while a bedside table crouched beside it and a small lamp perched on top of that. A wardrobe on the far wall was the only other furniture in the room. Ariel noted that there wasn't a single personal possession in the room that could have been identified as Wolfgang's at all. *Had he brought absolutely nothing with him?* he mused, *or did they strip away everything of the past in order to begin the process of healing?*

It was hard to know...

Ariel sighed, squatted on the edge of the bed and gazed sorrowfully at his old friend. He was gaunt and pale and his blue eyes looked washed out and red around the rims. He was dressed in a hospital gown and his bare feet lay splayed out at odd angles in front of him.

"Wolfie?" he tried again, a little louder, "it's Ariel- I've been looking for you."

This time Ariel thought he saw the tiniest flicker of recognition behind the waxen expression. Reaching out, he touched Wolfie's cheek and turned his head to face him.

"Wolfie- it's me. Don't you remember?"

Wolfgang blinked and a crease of confusion seemed to scratch itself across his forehead. He opened his mouth as if to speak, then had to moisten it with his tongue as though he had not uttered a single word for months.

"Ariel?" he whispered, his voice raspy as sandpaper. *"Is that really you?"*

Ariel laughed and cried simultaneously as he gathered up the frail figure in his arms.
"Yes, Wolfie, it's me and I won't leave you again, I promise!"

CHAPTER FORTY ONE

THE GOOD SAMARITAN

'I may not have gone where I intended to go,
But I think I have ended up where I needed to be.'

'The Long Dark Tea-Time of the Soul'
Douglas Adams

'A healthy attitude is contagious
But don't wait to catch it from others.
Be a carrier.'

Tom Stoppard

February, 1950.
A University in central England.

"According to Luke's gospel, the parable of the Good Samaritan begins with an unnamed man who is attacked while travelling on the road from Jerusalem to Jericho. Left for dead, a priest happens to pass by the same road. When he sees the man, he crosses over and passes by on the other side. A little while later, a Levite does the same; also passing by on the other side."

William looked up from the sheaf of notes on the lectern in front of him and scanned the upturned faces of his students, all expectant and eager to learn, and smiled. The lecture theatre was full of life; full of *lives* still very much ahead of them and it felt good to be amongst it, in the heart of all that positive energy. He had been lecturing in Ethics at the University since gaining his degree the previous summer and was now lecturing the undergraduates while he studied for his own Masters.

"But then a Samaritan passes by," he continued, "and he takes pity on him. He pours oil and wine on his wounds and bandages them. He takes him to an innkeeper on his own donkey and pays the innkeeper to nurse him until his return. So," William said, gazing round the room and scrutinizing the faces in turn, "according to Kantian Ethics, what aspects of his actions made him a Good Samaritan?"

Several hands were raised, some more confidently than others. William selected a smiling girl, almost itching to answer.

"That the Good Samaritan acted without the expectation of reward or benefit."

William nodded.

"But wasn't his reward the knowledge that he'd *done the right thing*?" William pressed.

More hands shot up like plants flowering in an instant. William smiled and picked one at random.

"Yes?"

"He may well feel *morally* rewarded," said a blonde-haired young man who rose from his seat to answer, "but Kant says that only when something springs from a desire to do something with no expectation of recompense or reward, other than to treat humanity as an end in itself and never as a means to an end, can we say the *'goodness'* of an ethic has been received."

"Excellent," William nodded, "and why have the priest and the Levite in the story? What role do they play?"

Again, hands were raised eagerly; some tentatively, others boldly. William decided to pick a young girl named Yvonne, whose essays were always brilliant but who, he knew, would never volunteer an answer. She looked up from her notes in surprise at the mention of her name and quickly flushed as those around her turned and awaited her response.

"Er... the priest and the Levite both chose to ignore the injured man," she began nervously, "maybe because they were in a hurry, or because they were afraid his attackers were still in the area, or maybe they simply didn't care," she said growing in confidence, "but the point is that both men were considered to have high moral values but chose to ignore the man while the Samaritan had to overcome social barriers to help the other man, so the contrast between their actions and his become even more emphasised; thus reinforcing the moral of the story." As she ended, she blew out her cheeks in relief, stealing a glance at the others for the first time.

"Excellent, Yvonne, thank you," William nodded, catching her eye and smiling encouragingly. She smiled shyly in return then stared furiously at her notebook.

"I think that will do for today," he announced, looking at his watch. "I will see you all next Tuesday. In the meantime, enjoy your weekend and try to do something for somebody else without the expectation of reward... you will find it surprisingly gratifying, I guarantee it!"

Several of the class sniggered or smirked as they packed away and William gathered his own notes together and was soon joining them as they filed out of the lecture theatre and into the middle of a chilly Friday afternoon.

William hurried across the quad, weaving in and out of the meandering students. He was on a strict timetable: *he knew exactly where she would be in half an hour from now and he didn't intend to miss her.* On the far side of the campus, he jumped on a bus and sat thinking about the lecture he had just delivered as he waited for his stop. He couldn't help but wonder how Kant might interpret *his* motives in that most traumatic time of his life? He concluded that he had always tried to fight bravely on the Russian Front and had saved the lives of his comrades on many occasions. And what had he expected in return? That they would risk *their* lives to save *his* life if the opportunity arose? Possibly. But he hadn't done it for that reason alone, he was confident of that; he had done it *because it had been the right thing to do.*

He smiled grimly. If only his War had ended then…

Instead, he knew there could be no defence for those interminable months of the war he had spent the last six years trying and failing to block out; those terrible months in the camp that haunted his blackest hours nightly. *No, he had acted in his own selfish interests to save his own worthless life. There was no other way to look at it.*

He stared, flushed with burning shame, out the window at Post-War Britain trundling by, slowly readjusting to the world returning to an uneasy Peace. It had been five long years since VE Day, but times were still pretty tough, what with rationing still in place and some cities still rebuilding after the, seemingly, endless German bombardment.

But what about his actions in saving Rachel and Ariel? How would they be viewed? Had he acted selflessly? Without wanting anything in return? Had he expected to see them again, to rekindle his love and friendship, after the War? Did he save them to appease his own conscience because of the horrific things he was doing every single day? Could you balance out so much evil with two minor acts of kindness? Was he really being selfish in attempting to save the only two people he cared about in order to lessen his own loneliness and suffering?

The questions swirled around his mind like a tornado, arguments and counter-arguments flashing by like cars and picket fences plucked up by that awesome force of nature and equally as unfathomable to control or analyse. He sighed and turned from the window. There was no point beating himself up about it anymore than he already did… the important thing was to focus on what he could do now… what he *had* been doing for a little over three years: *being Rachel's Guardian Angel.*

He saw the ornate gates to the entrance of the park, rising above the rectangular boxes of terraced houses and bland shopfronts, like the curved back of a sea monster, and hurriedly got to his feet. Thanking the driver, he stepped off the bus and crossed the street, careful to approach the entrance as surreptitiously as possible.

Ever since they had arrived in England, they had searched for Rachel and, when they found her, William had watched over her as much as his work commitments allowed. *If he couldn't actually be with her, watching her life unfold, making sure she was safe, happy...as much as he could, was the next best thing.*

William took a side path through the park that led straight to the bandstand. He stopped on the fringes of the treeline and waited, pulling the collar of his overcoat up around his neck and his flat cap low over his eyes against the biting wind. William knew that Rachel worked in a factory and, as she worked on a Saturday, had a Friday off in recompense.

And most Fridays, she came to the park.

For the first couple of years she had come alone, then William had started seeing her with a handsome man. Everything about him suggested to William he had been a pilot; even his slick moustache was brylcreemed into two perfect wings atop his upper lip. Despite his best intentions, William had been eaten up with an intense jealousy that gnawed at his stomach for weeks, until Gabriel's repeated soft words had gently soothed the hurt and given way to slow acceptance that he wanted Rachel to be happy and, if this man with his limp but proud gait did that for her, *he* should be happy too.

So, he had watched Rachel be courted: the cinema; walks on the hillside; drinks at the pub; picnics in the park. *Their* park. For William had been convinced that Rachel came to *this* park because its bandstand was so similar to their bandstand in Berlin, and she came here to think of him and feel that frisson of excitement when she stood in the centre of it, as if she were waiting for him to arrive for another illicit rendezvous.

Rachel appeared at the curve of the path and William gasped in delight, before catching himself and stepping further back into the treeline. It still amazed him that she had grown no less beautiful; even after all she'd been through. He recalled the first time he had seen her after their arrival in England to find, unlike so many other memories, he had not embellished her beauty; like a Medieval court painter, only for the King to be bitterly disappointed when finally meeting his intended in the flesh, when it was already too late! No. She was bewilderingly beautiful to him and, if anything, he found her more alluring and ethereal than ever. He knew then that their hearts and souls were inextricably entwined together and always would be.

This time, as was the norm lately, Rachel was not alone. She pushed a bright blue pram with white and silver trim. *Her son.* It had only been a few months after the wedding that Rachel had fallen pregnant and, within weeks of recovering from the birth, she had resumed her weekly vigil to the park but, this time, she sometimes walked right past the bandstand and on to the pond, where the argumentative ducks waited impatiently for the bread she brought with her. William waited with baited breath... and today was no different. Rachel paused momentarily at the steps to the bandstand before striding confidently past and heading for the glint of water showing through the treeline.

Following at a safe distance, William watched as she stopped at the water's edge, then reached under the pram for the brown paper bag that was already causing several ducks to speed towards them in anticipation; heads bobbing up and down as they propelled themselves forward eagerly. Rachel readjusted the angle of the pram so the baby, (whose name was Graham, William discovered,) could get a better view of proceedings. He remained ten or eleven feet from the reedy fringes of the pond, at the top of a slope that fell away swiftly from a foot deep to at least twenty feet deep in the pond's centre, while Rachel strolled down to the water, already choppy with the blustering of several hungry ducks, and began tearing off chunks of bread.

William dared himself to get closer for a better view of them both. For him, it was part of the thrill to see how close he could get without being noticed; sometimes, he had been close enough to hear her breathing, smell her perfume... it was totally exhilarating for him to be so close to the woman he adored but to whom he could not reveal himself! *Exhilarating and frustrating in equal measures!* He burrowed his head down even further into the folds of his scarf and dug his hands deep into his pockets as he walked past, spying her out of the corner of his eye; stealthy as a submarine with sonor-heartbeat.

She looked so beautiful, smiling to herself as she picked out which duck should receive the next precious morsel... which should be the chosen one; her breath coming out in billowing misty gusts. Then, suddenly, her expression changed... her eyes widened in utter panic and, for a moment, William thought she was looking at *him*, but then he realised she was looking past him and was already turning on her heels to move in that direction. He swivelled his head to follow her gaze and saw the cause of her distress: *the brake had come loose on the pram and it had started to freewheel towards the freezing water!*

Without stopping to think, William spun on his heels and ran. Everything slowed to an agonising standstill: the world seemed to stop spinning on its axis as he tried to get his body between the pram and the water. Each step took an age as each wheel spin seemed to rotate bullet-fast. As the black expanse seemed to open up ready to swallow the pram, cavernous as a whale's dark mouth, he lunged for the handle, falling to his knees as one hand felt something solid and clung on...

The pram lurched, its front wheels teetering no more than six inches before the point it would hit the water and unceremoniously tip its contents into the jaws of its frozen trap, and came to a juddering stop. William felt a huge surge of satisfaction, followed by a stabbing pain in his left knee and, finally, a sudden sense of panic at the massively increased probability of his imminent identification.

Rachel reached the pram seconds later, tears already blurring her vision. She reached inside and, grabbing up little Graham, held him tight, suddenly unable to hold back the moans and sobs that filled the air. Passers-by hurried over with offers of help, but she was oblivious to them: she had Graham in her grasp; that was enough.

Suddenly, she remembered. She pushed the tears to one side with cold fingers and turned to thank the man who had saved her son. Turned... *and found he was already gone.*

CHAPTER FORTY TWO

THE SECRETS OF GHOSTS

'We are all ghosts...'

Elisabeth d'Autriche

'Do nothing secretly. For time sees and hears all things.'

Sophocles

June 1999,
In the hospital canteen.

"That was Wolfie? *Wolfie saved my little Graham's life?*"

Ariel stopped mid-sentence following Rachel's interruption, to see the look of utter disbelief etched across her face. He nodded meekly.

"I was *this* close to him," she whispered, showing the smallest of spaces between her thumb and forefinger to Maggie as she shook her head regretfully. "*It seems he saved my life and my son's too!*"

Ariel raised and lowered a shoulder, "I guess you could say he has been your Guardian Angel for the best part of your adult life," he agreed.

"But I don't understand," she said, "you found Wolfie after the war and came to England... to find *me*. Why didn't you knock on my door? Let me know you were alive? Anything? Didn't you think I had missed you too?"

Ariel looked at her wide-eyed, "Oh my dearest Rachel, Wolfie *did* knock on your door... the thought of seeing you again was the only thing that had kept him alive in that awful place."

"I don't understand..."

Ariel sighed, "I have jumped too far ahead... I have to tell it as it unfolded for it to make any kind of sense... I have to tell it from where we got to... back in 1945..."

****

A Mental Hospital in Berlin,
September 1945.

Ariel was seated upon the same spot on Wolfgang's bed that he had sat on at the end of May when he had first found him again, while Wolfgang was seated in the same chair; but things could hardly have been more different from that first meeting. Wolfgang no longer sat staring unseeing out of the window at the same limited square of sky, but had now swivelled his chair around to face Ariel, who could see the fire burning brightly in his eyes again for the first time in years, as he animatedly asked about Ariel's news.

Of course, it hadn't been easy... Wolfgang had sat before him like an empty shell for weeks leaving Ariel to wonder whether, if he pressed his ear to Wolfie's breast, he would hear nothing but the distant ebb and flow of his breathing: like a sea-creature gone from a shell found on the beach, the soul had long since vacated the premises. But, little by little, he had coaxed and cajoled, encouraged and humoured and, in time, he had started to come out of that shell and emerge, blinking, into the world outside of his shuttered mind again; thanks to Ariel's relentless efforts. And now he was out, there was no stopping him- *he was eager for news!*

"It's been unremitting torture whilst you have been away," he complained. "What have you managed to find out? Have you found out where she went, old friend?" he demanded, leaning forward in his chair and urging him to speak.

"Good to see you too!" Ariel grinned, then reached into his inside jacket pocket and took out a sheaf of papers, unfolding them and laying them out on the bedspread before pressing them flat. He weighted down each corner and they pored over the contents together as though they were the directions to a fantastic treasure trove. Ariel had been gone for several weeks, firstly heading back to the site where Belzec had once stood and then retracing his steps, as best he could, to the villages of the safe houses where Rachel and he had stayed before he joined the resistance and before she was transported to England.

"I found the old woman who took Rachel in," he began.

Wolfgang clapped his hands together delightedly.

"And did *she* know where Rachel had gone?" he demanded impatiently.

"No, but she was able to put me back in touch with the men who got her across the border..." he paused and looked in his friend's hopeful eyes, "and one of them, Peter, had kept a notebook hidden behind a brick in the chimney place all this time and, in it, he kept the names and destinations of every person he had played a part in helping throughout the course of the war."

He saw Wolfgang's eyes widen.

"Why did he do that?"

Ariel shrugged, "he said he didn't know why. Perhaps it was to make him feel he was doing something significant; perhaps he intended to go and find some of the people in his little black book and see if they had made it all the way home. I don't know. All I know is this-"

He pulled out one of the pieces of paper hidden under the top page spread out before him.

"*This* is where Rachel was heading. If she made it and if nothing has changed since, this could be the address that she is living in *right now!*"

****

The Midlands,
December 1945.

Wolfgang walked down the street that Rachel now lived on, his stomach twisted into a sequence of knots that would baffle the most adept of sailors. He and Ariel had only been in England a few days, but they had already booked themselves into a simple guest house in the same town as the name that was scrawled on the precious scrap of paper in Wolfgang's wallet.

Then they had spent a couple of days ostensibly getting their bearings. Really though, it had been to give Wolfgang time to pluck up the courage required to actually approach her house and knock on the front door they had already walked past several times on each of the previous days. Ariel had offered to go with him but he felt, the first time he saw her again, he needed to explain the momentous events that had unfolded over the last few years alone.

The last couple of months had been ridiculously infuriating. He possessed a piece of paper with Rachel's name on it and an address that promised so much… but there had been much to do before they could leave for England. For a start, he was a German… not the most welcome of visitors to English shores and, before anything else, he'd had to convince the doctors he was physically and mentally restored to a sufficient degree of sanity, whatever that was, to be allowed to leave the Institution. That thorny issue had ultimately been solved by Ariel discreetly passing a large brown envelope to the doctor in charge of his care on his penultimate visit. The next time he called, Wolfgang was sat on the end of his bed with his suitcase packed and sat between his knees.

Then they moved on to the next stage of their masterplan: After emptying his bank account and transferring it to currencies that were far more stable and of more use to them then the Deutschmark, they set up base in Wolfgang's old house. Kurt was immediately set to work making further connections in Berlin's thriving Black Market and, three weeks later, they had fake passports and identification papers. Wolfgang Wirth and Ariel Koplovitz were dead and William Worthington and Gabriel Cope, a couple of German-speaking Swiss with family connections in England and who had spent the war living and working in neutral Switzerland, rose from the husks of their old lives, their majestic fiery plumes shaking off the ashes of the past. Before they left, they set Kurt up in his own apartment on the American side of Berlin and with money in the bank to allow him to enjoy a comfortable retirement.

Wolfgang paused at the garden gate of the semi-detached house that rose before him as daunting as an impenetrable fortress. *What could he possibly say to her that would make everything all right again? How could he explain the multitude of feelings swirling round inside his head?* Taking a massive breath, he lifted the catch on the gate, swung it open and walked up the garden path, bordered on each side by neatly-trimmed beds of rose bushes, baring only their winter claws as he nervously approached the front door.

Gritting his teeth and with his heart bellowing in his eardrums, he rapped on the front door and waited...

At first, nothing could be heard from within, but then he heard the shuffling of footsteps getting closer and braced himself for whatever might come next.

What did happen next was the unexpected appearance of a short rotund man dressed in perfectly creased trousers held up by braces, over a crisp white shirt underneath broad red kipper tie. The finishing touch to the whole ensemble was a pair of tartan slippers. The man eyed him suspiciously, a pipe gripped tightly between his teeth and a newspaper held poised in one hand. He didn't look overly impressed at his reading time being disturbed.

"Can I help you?" he asked, squinting at him like Popeye through the pipe smoke.

"I... is Rachel here?" Wolfgang stammered, feeling like a schoolboy asking a father's permission to take a girl out on a first date.

The man's eyes immediately narrowed at the foreign accent and the paper was folded carefully and tucked under his arm in slow, deliberate fashion.

"And who might *you* be?" he demanded.

"I'm Wolfgang...a friend of Rachel's from Germany during the War," he blurted out then cursed his stupidity. *Why had he given his real name? How foolish of him... why bother to get fake documents if he was going to tell every stranger he met his real identity? And why even mention the War? It would have been better to say he had met her recently, in England. Who knew what she had told them of her experiences in the War? Too late now...*

"*Wolfgang?*" the man spluttered, spitting out the word as if it were a fly that had flown straight into his throat. A look of absolute outrage spread across his podgy features, "the same Wolfgang who got Rachel pregnant? Who worked in one of those *death camps? Who killed all her family? That* Wolfgang?"

Wolfgang stared at him, mouth agape. He hadn't banked on Rachel telling her new family *that much* about her past... about *him*... then the full extent of his words hit him full in the face...

"Did you say *got Rachel pregnant?*"

Uncle Arthur scoffed at what he perceived were this fiend's feeble attempts at denying knowledge of his disgraceful past. He took his pipe from his mouth and pointed it severely at Wolfgang.

"Now you listen to me, young man, and you listen good because I am only going to say this once: you did your very best to destroy every single aspect of that girl's life and you very nearly succeeded. But she got free of you and your evil and she built a new life here. Not much of a life, not yet anyway, she has only just begun to take a few tentative steps on that particular road, and I imagine she will have many more sleepless nights until you are totally forgotten, but there is *no way* I am going to let you enter her life again and destroy what she is working so hard to achieve."

Wolfgang stared at the fierce little man barring his path and could find no words. His heart felt like a locked safe in his chest: everything the man had said was true. He was a monster and no good could come of seeking her out and trying to rekindle what they had once had.

"Just tell me one thing," he begged, "what happened to the child?"

Uncle Arthur looked at him sceptically, his eyes narrowing again as he seemed to mull over his request. Eventually, he decided to share the knowledge on the basis that it was a further opportunity to tell this young upstart exactly what he thought of him: "He died on that hellish journey to the camp, *as if you didn't know*. How could she do anything about it when you bastards didn't even give them food or water and kept them cooped up for days like bloody animals?" He shook his head and eyed him up and down, as though he expected to find some clue to his inhumanity in his appearance: *perhaps a cloven hoof or two might go some way to explaining it?* In the end, he shook his head in despair and concluded, "I don't know how you live with yourself, I really don't," before taking hold of the door frame.

Wolfgang blinked back the tears as the door started to shut in his face.

"If I ever see you round here again, I'm calling the Police. I'm sure they'd be very interested to know we have a *War criminal* in our midst," Uncle Arthur added as a parting shot, and then his portal into Rachel's life was closed forever.

****

Rachel's eyes were wet with tears as Ariel finished his story and met her gaze.

"Uncle Arthur," she smiled sadly, "I can picture him saying every one of those words. He was like a second father to me; but he never understood about me and Wolfie. How could he?" She reached out and squeezed Ariel's hand, "You had to have lived through it to understand it, didn't you? My poor Ariel..."

Maggie sat rapt by all she had heard. Now she cleared her throat and spoke.

"So did the pair of you just... *give up?*"

Ariel smiled sadly. "If you can call devoting the last five decades of our lives to trying to look out for Rachel and her family, then you could say we gave up, yes."

He sighed and thought back; trying to picture the difficult days and weeks that had followed. "When Wolfie came back to the guest house he was devastated; an utterly broken man. I feared he would slip back into the depths of depression, revert back to the state I found him in. I couldn't let that happen. I told him that, even if he couldn't have her back, he could still be near to you. Watch over you, if you like."

"And that was enough?" Maggie asked.

"It had to be."

Maggie sipped on her coke and thought on this.

"But what about *you?*" she asked eventually, "Why did *you* stay? You could have gone back to Germany or started a new life in America? Lots of Jews went to Israel didn't they, when it became a country again?"

"I can answer that, can't I, poor, sweet Ariel?" Rachel interrupted, and Ariel looked up at her in surprise.

"You can?" he asked.

"Oh, Ariel, did you think I didn't know?" she shook her head, "Of course I knew. You didn't come all this way solely for *me*, did you?"

Ariel started to protest but, softly, she put a finger to his lips and smiled.

"Oh, of course, we were great friends and you would have done anything you could to find me, re-kindle our friendship, stay in touch, come and visit me in England. But you came here for *Wolfie.*"

She paused and eyed him with interest.

"Does he know? Does he know that you've loved him for fifty years the way he's loved me and probably asked for nothing in return?"

Ariel stared silently into his coffee.

"No, of course he doesn't," she shook her head, "for someone so damn smart, he always did miss the thing that was right in front of his nose. Didn't he?"

Ariel looked up and smiled. "You're right, I suppose. At least, if he's ever suspected, he's never said anything. But you're wrong about one thing: I didn't have to ask for anything in return, because he freely gave me his friendship and companionship for the last fifty years and if I could have those fifty years again, I wouldn't change a thing."

The three of them fell into a contemplative silence. The sounds of the hospital broke through and filled the space between them: the clink of cutlery, the low drone of a fan, laughter at a shared joke, the distant scrape of a plate, the half-finished contents being emptied into a bin... Finally, it was Rachel who spoke first.

"I need to see him, Ariel."

Ariel nodded.

"Yes," he agreed, "yes, I think it's time."

CHAPTER FORTY THREE

THE FLOWER GARDEN

'If I had a flower for every time I thought of you...
I could walk through my garden forever.'

Alfred Tennyson

June 1999,
Wolfgang and Ariel's house.

Wolfgang looked at himself in the bathroom mirror and blew out his cheeks. His heart was all papery and light, flitting around his chest cavity like a firefly at the prospect of seeing Rachel again. He held onto the basin and steadied himself: somehow, it felt more daunting a prospect than anything he had ever had to do before, and he had done nothing but fret about it all night.
The life-changing events of the previous morning had all come to light yesterday afternoon, after he had returned home to find Ariel sitting staring straight ahead at a switched-off television set. Amused, he had perched himself opposite him and asked if anything good was on. Then, in stunned silence, he listened as Ariel recounted everything that had happened that morning in the hospital; not interrupting once until he had finished speaking and leaned back in his chair again with a monumental sigh. William mulled everything over, rubbing a stubbly chin absent-mindedly.

"But Harry is going to be all right, isn't he?" he had asked eventually.

Ariel glanced across at him dolefully. "Please God he is," he muttered, gently kissing the Star of David on the chain around his neck.

Then Ariel had broken it to him that he had set up a meeting between Rachel and him for the following lunchtime.

"You mean like... *a date?*" he had whispered in a hushed tone.

"Yes," Ariel laughed, "like a date, you old fool!"

Now he stood, freshly-shaven and hair combed, wondering what Rachel would make of the decrepit old man who stood before her, so far removed from the boy she had once loved when he was so young and handsome. Of course, she had aged too, Wolfgang thought, but he had *watched* her ripen and blossom from a distance, watched her change *by degrees over time...* and, through his eyes, she was as beautiful and delicate as ever. *She was getting the whole fifty years in one shocking revelation.*

There was a tap on the door, breaking into his thoughts.

"You all right in there?"

Wolfgang smiled and opened the door: thank God for Ariel, what would he have done without him? He shuddered to think of the life that would almost certainly have been his fate had they never met again, back in that empty and hollow room in the Mental Hospital in Berlin...

"I'm fine," he smiled at his old friend, "You know me, I'm just worrying again." He sighed and looked him sadly in the eye. "Her Uncle was right, you know, all those years ago: I don't deserve to have Rachel in my life. We should have skulked back to Germany with our tails between our legs and I should have accepted my fate. I should have been punished for all the things I did."

Ariel shook his head. "You had no more choice than I did, Wolfie; you did as they said or you were the next one in the chamber; that was the bitter reality of the situation."

"We *all* have choices; if I'd had the guts, I'd have refused to go along with it from the start," Wolfgang responded angrily.

"Then you would have been court-martialled and put in front of a firing squad; even given who your father was," Ariel shrugged, "and I would be dead and Rachel would be dead and her son, Graham, and grandson Harry would never have been born. Is that what you would have preferred?"

Wolfgang was silent for a long time, then a thin smile drew itself across his lips, "*I'm* supposed to be the Philosophy and Ethics professor- when did *you* get so clever?"

"I just believe that what goes around comes around," Ariel shrugged. "You remember Ronan Fuchs? Back at school and in the camp?"

"Of course," Wolfgang nodded raising and lowering a shoulder in a weary shrug, "what about him?"

"Well, I never told you this at the time, but when I went to try to find out what happened to Rachel, I found out what happened to him too."

"And you never thought to mention it?"

Ariel looked at him with a raised eyebrow and shook his head slowly.

"Let's face it, you weren't really in a fit state mentally to deal with anything... from *that* time in our lives. And, once we got to

England, it was a part of our lives we put behind us; it was better that way. But I think you need to hear this now. Think back to school: even then, as a boy, he was *different;* you got a ... a *bad feeling* about him, like he was destined to be a killer right from the womb. Remember how furious he used to get when we teased him about his name? There was hatred in those eyes; *hatred and evil.* Then, when he was in the camp, he was clearly the only one of us who actually *enjoyed* his work; who would have gladly done it through choice."

Wolfgang nodded sadly in mute agreement.

"Well, when I spoke to the men in the village, his reputation had gone before him. They spoke of their fear and loathing towards Fuchs; they'd named him *'The Butcher of Belzec'*. Then, when the camp was closed down he'd obviously found his vocation in life and asked for a transfer to Auschwitz."

Wolfgang looked at him with utter incredulity on his face.

"He *chose* to move to another Death Camp?" he stammered, then paused before adding ironically, "is there any point to this delightful tale, Ariel?"

"Auschwitz was different to Belzec," Ariel explained, "Auschwitz was a work camp as well as an extermination camp. Many were worked and starved to death, so a lot had a chance for their hatred of him to fester for a much longer time. And he had more chance to torture them with his boundless cruelty, rather than the comparatively brief agony of the gas chambers. When the camp was liberated by the Russians in January 1945, they found Fuchs... he'd been forced into the gas chamber by the inmates and given a very large dose of his own medicine. Like I say, what comes around, goes around. You did what you could within the barriers put before you; Fuchs went the extra mile to add to the torment of those poor souls... that's the difference in my mind."

Wolfgang considered Ariel's words.

"I've tried to live a good life since," he conceded.

"Or course, you have," he nodded before adding, "and remember, *virtues hunt in packs."*

"What's that supposed to mean?" Wolfgang replied, raising a quizzical eyebrow.

"You have many good virtues, Wolfgang; they count for something in this world."

Wolfgang smiled and took his friend in his arms and hugged him.

"Thank you my dearest friend, you have always had the happy knack of being able to say the right thing at the right time. It is one of your greatest gifts. I honestly don't know what I would do without you!" he added, squeezing his shoulder gratefully before turning from him to leave.

"And don't you forget it!" he called after him as Wolfgang disappeared down the stairs and slammed the front door behind him.

****

They sat side by side on a bench facing the bandstand, the tips of their fingers barely touching. The prodigal sun poked a curious head out from behind a cloud, bathing their faces in a warm glow. Rachel held the flowers he had given her awkwardly in her free hand and glanced down at the deep red of the roses; the same shade Uncle Arthur used to grow in his front garden.

"I thought you were dead for so very many years," she whispered sadly.

"I thought it better for you if I was," Wolfgang replied, still staring straight ahead, afraid to meet her gaze, his back pencil straight against the bench and his heart pounding like a hammer on an anvil.

"Don't you think I deserved the chance to decide for myself whether I wanted you in my life or not?"

"Your Uncle made the answer to that pretty clear."

Rachel sighed and, wrapping her fingers around his, pulled him closer and turned to face him.

"You stupid old man! What *he* said and what *I* felt were not necessarily the same thing."

"No?"

"*No!*" she smiled, shaking her head, "all those wasted years…"

They sat in silence again, watching the slow passage of clouds overhead and contemplating all that had gone before them. Wolfgang glanced at his beloved from the furthest corner of his eye.

"Of course, I found out about the child," Wolfgang said.

"Felix," Rachel whispered.

"Felix," Wolfgang repeated reverently, allowing himself to savour the sound of the syllables as he shaped the words on his lips.

Rachel felt a sharp catch in her throat hearing Wolfgang speaking the name she had kept locked inside her heart for so long.

"I'm so sorry," Wolfgang said, squeezing her hand tightly.

"For what?"

"For everything," Wolfgang sighed. "'For not being there for you, for all the terrible things that happened to you that I couldn't stop when I promised to protect you. For you perhaps believing that I had abandoned you." He looked deep into her beautiful dark eyes. "Is that what you believed, my darling? That I no longer loved you?"

Rachel smiled sadly.

"Not for the longest time. But as the weeks drifted into months, and then into years without any word, I could come to no other conclusion you were either dead or had chosen to move on with your life."

"No word?" gasped Wolfgang, the frustration still evident in his voice, despite so many decades having passed. "Not a week passed by without me putting down my love for you onto the page and sending those love letters into your arms."

Rachel shook her head. "I often wondered if mother or father stole your letters... but I feared perhaps I was only fooling myself."

"What was Felix like?"

Rachel smiled warmly. "You would have loved him dearly. He was so perfect; his little fingers curling around my thumb as he looked up at me with that quizzical little expression he had. His smile was often the only thing that kept us going in those dark days."

"I wish I could have held him; kissed him; looked into my son's eyes. What colour were they?"

"Dark," she beamed, "dark as ebony."

"Just like yours, my beautiful Hedy Lamarr; exactly as I imagined they would be."

Softly, Rachel reached up and wiped away a strand of silver-grey hair from his forehead. "Look at you..." she murmured, the smile widening across her face.

"You don't have to tell me..."

Rachel shushed him with a glance and stared at him properly for the first time. When he had first strolled over to their bench trying to look nonchalant but, in reality thrusting the bouquet of flowers awkwardly in her face, she hadn't known whether to kiss him or sock him in the face!

She was so angry with him! All those years of deceit! All those missed opportunities!

But, simultaneously, she also felt more *complete* than she had done for over fifty years: they were back where they belonged... together.

He grinned foolishly under her withering scrutiny. Yes, she thought, that much was the same; the impish cheekiness in that infuriating grin! She allowed her gaze to travel over the rest of him: he had shrunk in size... he was still tall and handsome to her, but was bent over more now and his cheeks had become more sunken and sallow. And his arms... once so strong and muscly, were thin and bony like a bicycle frame. But the *eyes*... they still had the same penetrating gaze; the same childish twinkle. She smiled, glad he had not lost that.

Suddenly, she realised he was observing *her* with what looked like the same critical eye and, quickly, she looked away embarrassed. What must *he* see? She thought, the grey hair and varicose veins? The bird's egg mottled skin, fragile and so paper-thin she swore she could see her own blood coursing through her veins like water flowing under ice?

"What's the matter?" he asked, the concern evident in his voice.

"Don't look at me like that. It reminds me of what I once was."

"Ha!" Wolfgang laughed, "you're forgetting I've watched you age, day by day, for five long decades: a Golden Wedding Anniversary of spying! You're the one who must be shocked: the teenager becoming a pensioner in the blink of an eye!"

Rachel prodded him in the arm.

"No, damn you, still as handsome as I remember, just a little greyer!"

Wolfgang stared at the faded bandstand again.

"I am *so* sorry though," he sighed, "for everything: your family, your... baby... for not telling you we were here... and I don't expect forgiveness," he added hurriedly, "I don't expect *anything*... I'm just so happy to *talk* to you again..." his voice trailed off.

"You can't do penance forever, Wolfie, and Ariel has told me you've lived a good life... been a teacher, changed peoples' lives;

changed *my* life, and Graham's. Neither of us would be around if it wasn't for *you*." Rachel stopped mid-sentence as something occurred to her: "That was no coincidence you being there at the shop when Harry was... attempting to shoplift, was it?"

Wolfgang looked at her in surprise.

"Oh, you needn't look so shocked, he told Maggie everything and she told me. A proper Guardian Angel you've been to *all* my family, haven't you?" She paused and sighed when he didn't answer. "Wolfie, you don't love someone because they're perfect, you love them because they're *not*, and each flaw becomes another star in their firmament. I forgive you, Wolfie, for everything that happened that was not your fault anyway. Now it's time to forgive yourself; forgive yourself and live the rest of your life *at peace*."

Wolfgang felt the first tear trace its way down his cheek and then could do nothing to stop the flood that followed. Rachel took him into her embrace and they allowed themselves the immense comfort of crying together...

****

When Wolfgang was finally able to compose himself, he looked up at Rachel with steely blue eyes and spoke with resolve borne out of endless hope.

"Rachel, I can't lie to you: I don't want to live the rest of my life if it's without you in it. You know I've loved you since the first day you found me crying in a park... not so very dissimilar to this and here I am again, crying in front of you like a baby! There must be something significant in that... don't ask me what it is though! All I do know is that I want to make up for all those stolen years." He shrugged and held up his hands vaguely, "I'm not saying marry me or anything... not *yet*, anyhow," he smiled, "but will you come over and spend time with Ariel and me? I need to see you... all the time... the thought of being apart now we have finally spoken again, feels like losing my reason to live. Come round tonight! We can talk all night and Ariel can cook and you can stay over-"

Rachel interrupted him with a coquettish laugh. "Oh, Wolfie! I think I'm a little too old for sleepovers! Should I bring my pyjamas and some marshmallows to toast?"

Wolfgang felt himself redden.

"But you just try to keep me out of your life," she grinned mischievously, *"you just go ahead and try!"*

Wolfgang broke into a grin, leaned across and kissed Rachel and, when she closed her eyes and kissed him back, the decades fell away and, in their heads, they were back in the summerhouse, young and in love, with their lives stretching invitingly ahead of them…

CHAPTER FORTY FOUR

MOVING BETWEEN DREAMS

'He will have no fear of bad news;
His heart is steadfast, trusting in the Lord.'

Psalm 112:7

'It is a very mixed blessing
To be brought back from the dead.'

Kurt Vonnegut

September 1999,
In a hospital room in the Midlands.

Harry floated above his bed feeling as intangible and beautiful as the aurora borealis. He was wonderfully free of the clunky awkwardness of his body: the aches and pains; the heart beat and pulse of blood around arteries; the sheer *humanity* of being inside the husk of a body. Instead, he was a *glow*... a *presence*... a being that existed but had no control over that existence and, like the Northern Lights, he felt the pull of his body drawing him back; like the magnetic pull of the earth's poles causing those wondrous lights to simmer so as they reacted with oxygen atoms in the atmosphere and emitted that haunting, spectral green glow, so similar to the aura he was giving off right now...

Below him he was aware of figures circling his bed like dazed boxers in the ring. But they weren't testing each other out, looking for a weak point, a momentary lapse of concentration in order to pounce, no, they were restless out of the sheer exhaustion of constant concern. Concern and love for *him*. He knew that now; just as he knew that his body had won the battle. The pull was strong and he could return now, return to the flesh and, when he did, he also knew he would remember nothing of any of this when, shortly, his eyelids would flicker and he would be back...

****

Hannah Robinson held his hand sandwiched between both of hers, as she had done every solitary day for the past three months. Her head lay face down on the sterile sheets, breathing in the distant odours of antiseptic and disinfectant; which would forever represent the stench of fear and anxiety to her from now on. Somewhere behind her, she could hear Maggie and her mother pacing the room restlessly; Mother with her arms folded tightly across her chest, as though Harry had stayed out long after his curfew on a night spent partying with friends, rather than having lain in an induced coma all the time summer had languidly drifted into autumn.

Hannah's head suddenly sprang up from the bedsheets as she felt a slight twitch, no more than the beating of a bird's heart, in the hand she enveloped.

"*I felt something then!*" she exclaimed excitedly, turning to look wide-eyed at Maggie and Rachel behind her, who exchanged doubtful glances that questioned whether they could even contemplate daring to hope. The reason they had both been pacing the room so fretfully was because, for the last two days, the doctors had been attempting to bring Harry slowly out of his coma to see if the weeks of rest had allowed his body to self-heal. Hannah sprang to her feet and headed for the door.

"I'm going to get a doctor! I'll be right back!"

The door slammed shut behind her as Rachel took her daughter's place at her grandson's bedside.

****

Harry found himself at the end of a long tunnel… there was the tiniest pinprick of light at the end of it, and a wind at his back, probing and pushing him ever closer towards the light. The sides of the tunnel were featureless but seemed to be swirling in endless circles; spiralling, corkscrewing, taking him ever closer to his final destination and seeming to give off the finest of mists, cooling his burning cheeks. Each blink seemed to transport him faster and faster, so the light grew to a torch beam, then to a headlamp, then to a blinding sun and finally, a stelliferous night sky, as the light burst into millions of stars streaming in every direction. Harry closed his eyes and felt the rays warming and soothing every inch of his face…

****

Harry felt himself gasp and his eyes blink open.

"Harry! Can you hear me love?"

He knew the voice at once… *his Grandmother*. He tried to answer but his voice was gravel and his mouth was parched. All he could do was concentrate on bringing her face into focus and smiling up at her concerned features.

"Do you want me to go find Mrs. Robinson?"

Harry heard the voice from over his grandmother's shoulder and strained to see the source of it. Then Maggie peered over her shoulder and his smile widened as their eyes met. Maggie and Rachel looked at each other and grinned… *he was back!*

"Don't you worry my dear, I'll find her myself... you stay with my beautiful boy!" Rachel declared, turning back to Harry, planting a big wet kiss on his cheek before whispering in his ear, "we've been waiting patiently for you and, thank God, you've come back to us! I'll be back in a minute with your Mom... don't you go anywhere!"

Harry wasn't sure where she was expecting him to disappear to, but nodded in agreement anyway, before she turned in the doorway, thought about adding something, settled for shaking her head in disbelief...and then was gone. Harry turned his attention back to Maggie.

"I... hello," he managed to croak.

"Oh, how stupid of me," Maggie said, biting her lip anxiously. "You must be so thirsty."

Quickly, she moved over to the bedside table and poured him a glass of water from the jug that sat on top of it. Harry tried to prop himself up, but found he had no strength in his arms either to lean on his elbows or to take the glass from her.

"I'll bring it to you," Maggie said softly, putting the refreshing water to his lips before attempting to explain: "the doctors said you would be weak if you... recovered. Your muscles have wasted away a little from lack of use; it's normal."

Harry swallowed and looked up at her reassuring smile.

"How long..." he swallowed painfully, ran his tongue over his dry lips and tried again, "how long have I been... gone?"

Maggie looked away for a second before meeting his gaze, "three months," she whispered, biting down anxiously on the corner of her lip.

Harry's jaw fell open in disbelief but, before he could respond, the door burst open and two highly excited women hurried in, followed by a man in a white coat.

"See?" his grandmother announced to the doctor following her in, as though he had doubted the truth of her words, "I told you he was awake!"

His mother was already at his bed, his hand slotted into its usual place between hers once more.

"Welcome back, son," she smiled through the tears before adding, "and don't *ever* do that to me again! You've had us worried sick these whole three months!"

"Three *months*..." Harry mumbled and everyone exchanged a knowing look: this had been the part they had been dreading.

"I know, Harry," his Mom began, "it's a lot to take in... but the worst's over now. It's all about getting you well enough to bring you home now, isn't that right doctor?"

The doctor was already beside them, two fingers pressed to Harry's wrist while he looked at his wristwatch. He nodded in a non-committed kind of way.

"Indeed." He glanced up from his watch and checked the monitors with a raised eyebrow. "You *seem* to have made a remarkable recovery, but there is considerable rehabilitation to do. In the meantime, rest. Let your family do the talking, and you do the listening. I'll arrange for you to have a little food and get as much fluids inside you as possible."

Harry nodded and sighed, still somewhat nonplussed by the strange situation he found himself in. The doctor checked his watch again, smiled at Mrs. Robinson and left the room. Everyone turned back to Harry and stared at him expectantly. Harry's eyes followed them round the room.

"So," he whispered eventually, "what have I missed?"

The three women around his bed exchanged knowing glances and raised eyebrows.

Rachel blew out her cheeks and grinned.

"Where to begin..." she said, shaking her head, "where *exactly* to begin..."

CHAPTER FORTY FIVE

THE LORD LOOKS AT THE HEART

'But the Lord said to Samuel,
"Do not consider his appearance or his height,
For I have rejected him.
The Lord does not look at the things man looks at.
Man looks at the outward appearance,
But the Lord looks at the heart."'

I Samuel 16:7

October 1999,
Inside Wolfgang and Ariel's house.

Wolfgang came in with two steaming mugs of tea and nervously passed one to Harry. His determined young friend had only been released from hospital a couple of days, but had felt the need to come around and see him as soon as he felt strong enough. It had been an eventful three weeks since coming round in the hospital and, after he had come round sufficiently on that first day to fully comprehend what was going on around him, his mother, grandmother and Maggie had taken it in turns to fill him in on the incredible events that had unfolded whilst he had lain comatose in his hospital bed.

Over the following nights, he had whiled away the owlish hours staring at the ceiling above his hospital bed, mulling over all he had been told and trying to come to a decision about how he was supposed to feel about the news that William and Gabriel were, in fact, Wolfgang and Ariel and that they had known his grandmother for over fifty years, crossing the continent to be close to her and watch over her in bizarre secrecy.

That in itself had been mind-blowing enough.

But then he had been told of Wolfgang's role as camp guard and Ariel as sonderkommando... and he had way more time to process that additional disturbing information. In the days that followed, Harry had to stay on a Rehab Ward while his neglected limbs went through a process of regeneration; slowly doing a little more each day- walking a little further, lifting something a little heavier... It was an incredibly tedious and laborious process but one that had given him the necessary time to consider how he should view the nature of their friendship when he came to leave. Wolfgang and Ariel had asked if they could come and visit, but he had sent them news that he would visit them at home, so they could talk in private; and he now fulfilled that promise.

Harry sipped at his tea and wondered where to begin.

"How are you feeling now?" Wolfgang asked, getting in first in an obvious attempt to break the ice.

Harry nodded awkwardly, "fine, I guess; doctors say I should make a full recovery."

"That's great," William said, forcing a smile, before the omnipresent awkward silence took centre stage again.

"You could have told me you know," Harry announced, looking him in the face and noticing his red-rimmed eyes for the first time, "I could have handled it."

Wolfgang didn't know what to say, and avoided eye contact with him.

"Nan doesn't blame you either," he continued, becoming more at ease now he had begun, "you did what you had to do to survive. You tried to do good within the restraints placed upon you; what more could you do?"

Wolfgang flashed him a look.

"Do *you* blame me Harry?" he asked nervously.

"No," he replied simply.

"Even when I talked to you about doing the right thing over the bullies and the stealing? Do you not think me a hypocrite for *daring* to offer *you* advice after all *I* am guilty of?"

Harry considered this statement for a minute before answering.

"I figure you've learnt from all the terrible things in your past and that puts you in an ideal position to offer advice: learning the lessons of history and all that."

Wolfgang felt tears well in his eyes at the boy's words of wisdom and consolation and unbelievable depths of forgiveness abiding in his soul.

"Harry, I cannot tell you what comfort your words offer me… this has been a matter of deep shame and regret that Ariel and I have kept hidden in our hearts for many years: I wanted to tell you everything, of course, but there is… never a right time for such news. I feared it would forever taint your opinion of Ariel and I; and we so wanted for you to have a high regard for us… as we have for you… so you would allow us to help you through the difficulties life throws up."

At that moment, Ariel entered with a plate of sandwiches, garnished with salad and with napkins and cutlery in his other hand. As he entered, Ariel caught Harry's reply:

"If you have both taught me anything, Wolfgang, it is that you can't start the next chapter of your life if you keep on re-reading the previous ones. You've got to turn over and start a new page."

Wolfgang glanced up at him with unmasked admiration.

"You are wise far beyond your years and I am proud to know you, Harry Robinson; immensely proud."

Harry felt himself blush and they sat in silence taking in each other's words.

"You two have certainly had quite an impact on Nan; I have never seen her so... *happy!*" Harry said before adding with a smirk, "so, may I ask if your intentions towards my grandmother are entirely honourable?"

Ariel choked on a sandwich and Wolfgang burst into laughter at the boy's impudence. Then the laugh turned to a cough and he reached into his pocket to cover his wheezing with a handkerchief. Ariel quickly went over to him, fussing over him like a mother over a child with a bloodied knee.

"Are you all right, Wolfgang?" he asked in concerned tone.

"I'm fine, I'm fine," Wolfgang insisted, shooing him away with a flick of a hand, "we are all at death's door, Ariel," he quipped, "only some of us can hear the doorbell ringing!"

Ariel scolded him with a wagging finger, "nonsense old friend, you shall outlive us all."

Wolfgang regained his breath and returned to Harry's original question.

"I can't say what the future holds for your grandmother and I, but I can say I intend to make the most of every second we have been given in this most tardy of second chances. In many ways, our lives together now will always be rooted in the past...it is hard for us to keep an anchor in the present when it so easily comes loose and we drift inescapably back to the time we were happiest: the summer of 1938. But I am eternally grateful that she has found it in her heart to forgive the past and find a way to love me in the present."

The three of them sat in contented silence until Ariel next broke the silence.

"And how are things with you and Maggie? And with school?"

Harry smiled and then grimaced slightly.

"Things with Maggie couldn't be better. I guess you could say we're boyfriend and girlfriend now; as completely naff as that sounds. But we see each other every day and I can't imagine being apart from her for longer than that. School is... school. The good news is that the Governors met to discuss my place at the school and decided I had probably suffered enough. So, I'm back in on Monday. The even better news is that the Police came to interview me in the hospital and I was able to identify Harris and his gang as my assailants. The whole lot of them have been permanently excluded from school and Mom is pressing charges."

Ariel clapped his hands together in glee.

"That is the best news we could have possibly hoped for!"

Harry shrugged, "I guess so," he half-heartedly agreed.

"Well isn't it good news?" Wolfgang asked, "What is the cause of your reluctance?"

Harry raised and lowered a shoulder ambiguously, "I'm way behind on coursework and Mom's going to insist I catch up on everything I've missed while I've been off. In some respects, there's a lot to be said for being excluded!"

CHAPTER FORTY SIX

DOUBLE DATE

'Do not go where the path may lead,
Go instead where there is no path
And leave a trail,'

Ralph Waldo Emerson

'What I have done is yours,
What I have to do is yours,
Being part in all I have,
Devoted yours.'

William Shakespeare
Note to Henry Wriothesly
Accompanying text to 'The Rape of Lucrece'

11.55pm, December 31st 1999.
Maggie's house and a park at midnight.

The closing millennia's shadow was cast long over the evening as Maggie and Harry, Rachel and Wolfgang prepared to see in the start of the next thousand years in their own different ways. The news had been full of the 'Millennium Bug', with scientists worrying that computers around the world would be unable to cope as their counters clicked over from 1999 to 2000. Doom-mongers foretold that everything would self-implode: there would be blackouts and glitzes, crashes and frozen screens and planes would fall from the skies from the sheer panic of it all.
But none of them cared one jot.
All four of them were too blissfully happy to worry about the prophecies of wide-eyed crazies standing on street corners waving hastily-drawn placards. Even Ariel had got himself invited round to Harry's house for the night to see in the New Year with Hannah; as neither fancied being completely left out and all alone at midnight. Ariel had left the house (to Wolfgang's wild amusement,) with a big smile on his face, a cherry pie in his hand and looking most dapper in a cream suit and crimson dickie bow.

Maggie lay with her head in Harry's lap and looked up at him contentedly. The last few weeks since he got out of hospital had been wonderful: she had never felt so comfortable with anyone as she did with Harry and it felt like they were meant to be together. They sat next to each other in every class they shared, ate lunch together in the canteen and spent almost every evening together, going to the cinema, watching videos round each other's houses or sat round Wolfgang and Ariel's, eating, cooking and just spending time with two old men who had quickly begun to feel like their oldest friends.

It was strange how the age gap between them seemed completely unimportant; Wolfgang and Ariel seemed to understand them and the problems they faced as teenagers in a way almost no-one else seemed to. It was refreshing.

Right now, they were lying on her bed, with the radio on low in the background, but listening more to the sound of the party downstairs. She smiled as she imagined the scene: the TV would be on and some reporter would be standing in the centre of Edinburgh, tightly swaddled in scarves and overcoat, reporting on Hogmanay as grinning idiots behind him waved and mouthed *'Hello Mom!'* before cutting back to London and the impenetrable face of Big Ben as it counted down the seconds to midnight. In the lounge, Dad would be playing the part of the perfect host, jovially refilling glasses ready for the toast, while Mom would be re-applying her lipstick in the kitchen so she could look her best to usher in the New Year. In a couple of minutes, aunts and cousins and next door neighbours would be dragging themselves to their feet, glass in hand, only to have to find a flat surface for it almost immediately afterwards, when the inevitable linking of hands and drunken chorus of 'Auld Lang Syne' began.

Maggie had begged her Mom to allow Harry to come round and stay over in a sleeping bag in the lounge after everyone else had left and she had reluctantly agreed, but they had no intention of joining in the party downstairs; they wanted to see the new millennium in on their own, in private.

Harry leaned back against the pillow that separated him and the headboard and let his eyes rove around her room and take in the contents in a little more detail. He considered that nothing revealed more about a person than the contents and layout of their bedroom. The walls of Maggie's room were littered with posters: the *Friends* one where they were all standing holding up umbrellas in front of a fountain and posing, oozing a confidence that comes from the knowledge you know you look your absolute best; an old black and white print of American workmen perched nonchalantly on a girder suspended hundreds of feet above New York City while they ate their sandwiches from metal lunchboxes; and a poster of the front cover of *Definitely Maybe,* the iconic first album by *Oasis,* that looked suspiciously new and fresh.

A pile of magazines made a small tower on a chair in the corner: *Bliss* and *Sugar,* interspersed with *Cosmo, Elle* and *Vogue.* Above the headboard itself was a shelf, the contents bookended on one end with a neat pile of school textbooks and lever arch files with labels like *Human Biology, Music, Geography* plus all her other options; while the other end was piled high with thick Stephen King horror hardbacks and an anthology of Sherlock Holmes murder mysteries. Strangely out of place, in between were crammed a sleuth of teddy bears; some big, some small, some fluffy, some threadbare, some clothed in little costumes, some as bare as the day they had emerged from the woods. Harry had recently had to look up the names of groups of animals for a Biology lesson and, apart from the obvious... packs of dogs, herds of cows or sheep, he had been surprised to discover more unusual collective nouns for groups of animals... a zeal of zebra, a crash of hippopotamus, and a sleuth of bears. Considering her taste in fiction, he thought it was somehow appropriate that it was bears nestled next to perhaps the greatest detective of them all. Perhaps only a murder of crows could have been even more fitting.

Overall, he considered, playing detective himself for a minute, it seemed to him that her room told the story of a girl on the cusp of being a woman, but having not yet let go of all her childish things.

He smiled to himself as he considered this. It occurred to him that he really didn't care what it might or might not show about her. The important thing was he was happier than he had ever been in his entire life and, in recent years, being happy at all had been pretty rare. So, whatever her room might suggest, he was happy to bask in the knowledge that he had that rarest of things: a girl of inner and outer beauty who didn't seem to have the slightest awareness of just how amazing she was.

Of course, initially, he realised that, (when he had first seen Maggie in school on his first day and the undeniable attraction had hit him squarely between the eyes, the arrow shaft still quivering as it came to rest between his temples,) he had only seen the smallest glimpse of who Maggie McGuire really was. It was akin to when an adult kneels in front of a small child, their hands covering their face, before parting them long enough only to shout *Boo!* into the child's unsuspecting face, before covering their features once more. That was the tiny fragment of her wonderfulness that his crush had been based on.

After that initial moment of lust, what usually happened was, he got to know the person better and little foibles became apparent, peeping through the chinks between those fingers and spoiling that flawless first impression. Something about the nasal quality of the voice, perhaps, or their immaturity, or inherent self-centredness; any number of things could smear a bug daub of paint across the vision of perfection.

Yet, in Maggie's case, he had become more and more enamoured with every aspect of both her appearance and her personality: the swish and swagger of her hair, the sudden gleam of her smile, the rhythmic chime of her laugh, the gun-snug fit of her hand in his own. But more than that: it was her kindness, her individuality, her sense of decency and her sheer unshakable belief in right and wrong. It made him want to try to be less morose and teenage-like and more...*enthusiastic*, which had to be a good thing! If she could be a teenager with a positive outlook, then so could he!

Having said that, her dressing room table certainly held all the trappings of womanhood. Circling the mirror, the surface of the table did not have a single square inch of free space, covered as it was with the disorganised debris of making oneself look and smell as enchanting as possible: the bullets of lipsticks, the snow-white discs of cotton wool, spiky hairbrushes, vials of make-up remover, a coffin-box of tissues, hair clips, slides, tweezers, mascaras, a hairdryer, nail polish and a hundred other objects; servants to the never-ending process of beautification.

"I'm glad we met," Maggie announced suddenly, calling his mind back to her earnest smile.

"Me too," he replied simply.

"I've got a feeling the year 2000 is going to be the start of something... *amazing*," she said as they heard the chimes of Big Ben creeping up the stairs. Grinning at each other, they closed their eyes as if they were about to make a wish...and kissed.

****

At the very same moment, Rachel and Wolfgang were also embracing and kissing a few short miles away on the park bench where they had sat so often in the weeks following their unexpected reunion. They had decided to welcome the new millennium in under the stars; as it had seemed to them that there had been something in that mischievous and twinkling cosmos that had transpired to bring them together again after so very, very long.

Ten minutes earlier, Rachel had slipped her hand out of her glove and linked her fingers together with Wolfgang's.

"I wish we could do this every day," she whispered contentedly.

"We can... if you want," he had replied instantly. "I mean, whatever makes you the happiest, that's what I want us to do."

She looked over at him, his earnest expression hidden in shadow beneath the moonlit night and laughed at his obvious sincerity.

"I'm serious!" he exclaimed, "If our lives are to be measured in the sand that slips through the hourglass of our brief time here, I don't want a single grain to be wasted. I've waited far too long for us to be together and these last few weeks have gone a long way to making up for the decades of us being apart."

"I know," Rachel agreed, staring ahead at the black outline of the bandstand that loomed up out of the caliginous night; a shrine to a love and devotion that had come through so many tribulations but was still defiant against all the odds. "I'm happy just for us to...*be*. To spend time together, like an old married couple."

Wolfgang squeezed her hand. She had the enviable talent of being able to sum up everything he was feeling so succinctly and did so again right then: there was something utterly perfect and satisfying about the most inconsequential things that they did together and he loved their idle chatter, like birdsong, musical and meaningless, beautiful and vibrant. They had talked and talked over the last few weeks and it had been delightfully wonderful, looking up at the clock on the mantelpiece in the lounge and finding to their absolute amazement that it had ticked around to some dead hour of the night. They both appreciated that they had felt more vibrant and alive in those priceless hours than they had done for decades.

The evening had started with a wonderful surprise: Wolfgang had asked Rachel to call and pick him up for a change, rather than the usual of him pulling up outside her house in the rather tired-looking Vauxhall he and Ariel shared and which usually lived on their driveway. Rachel had never thought to ask why they didn't park it in the garage adjacent to their house; she presumed it was either because they couldn't be bothered or because, like so many other people, the garage was a dumping ground full of stuff that accumulated and was never quite tidied away.

But, as Wolfgang answered the front door, he took her hand and guided her towards the garage door.

"This way," he said secretively, "I've got a surprise for you!"

Opening the garage door, Rachel could see there was a vehicle inside but, even when Wolfgang pulled in a cord and bathed the interior in a harsh white light, could tell nothing more of the make, as the car was hidden beneath a long cloth. With a flourish, Wolfgang whipped off the covering.... And there before Rachel was a Horch 853 sport cabriolet, in fire-engine red, with white-walled wheels, bug-eyed headlights and a gleaming swathe of pristine chrome work that shone under the bare bulb overhead.

"Oh my God!" muttered Rachel, hiding her head in her hands as the tears welled up in her eyes. "Oh, Wolfie, it isn't...?"

Wolfgang nodded with a beam of a smile. "Horch 853 cabriolet, at your service madam. I promised you a long time ago, that we would drive down the street together in one of these... and, while I've broken far too many promises over the years, this at least is one I've kept."

Rachel melted into his arms and they hugged in silence. After a while she looked up, into the brilliant blue of his eyes.

"How long have you had this?" she whispered.

"Almost fifty years," he smiled down at her, "when your Uncle turned me away, I started looking, and had this beauty shipped over in '52."

Leading Rachel round to the passenger door, he opened it and bowed solemnly.

"Will it even go after all this time?" she frowned.

"Don't worry," he grinned, "it's been serviced and maintained all these years, just not driven very far... until now."

Shaking her head, Rachel stepped aboard and Wolfgang closed the door.

****

So, they had arrived in the park at dusk and in some style where they sat, for the most part, in silence watching the sky darken, one shade at a time and the trees blur into each other, branch by branch. Time passed so deliciously slowly they felt they could feel the leviathan earth turning beneath their feet in tremulous slow motion, and they were an integral part of it all, the elements pulsing through the very sap of their veins as they soaked it all in.

Wolfgang had raised his head in surprise at one point; almost unable to comprehend that he was sat beside Rachel. All those years of being on the cusp of her, but not being able to go up to her and let their eyes meet... Even now, he was barely brushing her, as they sat shoulder to shoulder but, like the moon above them, he sensed her presence without the need to look for confirmation.

"To be loved; that is all we can wish for," Rachel had said, seemingly out of nowhere.

"I'm out of practice when it comes to loving," he had responded.

"You don't need to practice what you know has been inside you forever," she whispered back squeezing his hand tight.

When Wolfgang next looked at his watch, it was almost midnight.

"It's time," he said simply.

They stood and turned to face each other, holding hands as though at the front of a church with a congregation full of witnesses all about them waiting for them to repeat the vicar's solemn words.

"When I am gone and forgotten, it will always have been enough that we had this time together," he told her.

"Perhaps it's foolishness, this human condition of falling in love," Rachel replied. "It seems you are inviting sadness to follow; for one of us is destined to be left alone when the other leaves, dooming the remaining soul to unspeakable grief and loss. It would be so much safer not to love at all; to close ourselves off from such things. But I tell you now, Wolfie, that I would do it all again, I would risk everything for these brief moments of beautiful madness that being in love with you holds."

In the distance, fireworks went off overhead, exploding like shattering Christmas baubles, and they kissed and Wolfgang thought that, whatever crude material souls were fashioned out of, his and Rachel's were cut from the same imperfect, glorious fabric.

CHAPTER FORTY SEVEN

AN AWFULLY BIG ADVENTURE

'To die would be an awfully big adventure.'

'Peter Pan'
J.M.Barrie

'I'm not afraid of death;
I just don't want to be there when it happens.'

Woody Allen

"Tis better to have loved and lost
Than never to have loved at all.'

'In Memorium'
Alfred, Lord Tennyson

January 1st 2000,
In a sleeping bag on the floor in Maggie's lounge.

Harry woke early to the rhythmic tick-tock of the grandfather clock in Maggie's lounge. The previous evening, Maggie's Dad had proudly informed him that it was a family heirloom, as he was in the midst of using the foot-pump to energetically inflate the air bed on which he was to sleep. Harry had nodded appreciatively at the painted clock face of a smiling sun and moon that arced around the numerals as day ticked on relentlessly into night.

He couldn't think of a similarly precious heirloom in his own house and it had made him think of how little his grandmother must have arrived in the country with after her escape from the crushing fist of Nazism. Then he realised that they did have one family heirloom: his Dad's medals still sat, forgotten under the flotsam of old watches that didn't work and cufflinks and old Parker pens and countless other bits of worthless junk, in a drawer in the bedroom dresser and, suddenly, he missed him more than he had for months. It reminded him that while lots of things had changed recently, not all the changes had necessarily been for the better…

Yawning expansively, he wiped the gravelly grit of sleep from his eyes and glanced up at the time. It was still ridiculously early; still dark through the narrow slit of dawn visible between the curtains and much earlier than he would normally get up, even on a school day. But, he was intrigued to know how Wolfgang and Nan had got on; plus he needed to get back home to grab a couple of hours more comfortable sleep in his own bed, before showering and changing and making himself look half decent for when Maggie, Wolfgang and Ariel came round for lunch.

It felt strange to admit it to himself but, since his grandmother and Wolfgang had been reunited and Maggie had become his girlfriend, it really felt as if his family had grown by three wonderful members and the events in *their* lives were as important to him as the things that happened in his own.

Hauling himself out of his sleeping bag, he paused to look at himself in front of the large oval mirror hanging majestically over the fire place: nothing that a wash and a comb of his hair wouldn't sort out, he decided. Noiselessly, he tiptoed upstairs and tapped gently with his knuckle on Maggie's door.

"Come in," murmured a sleepy voice from inside.

"Did I wake you?" he smiled, peeping sheepishly around the door.

Maggie shook her head and beckoned him inside.

"I was just dozing," she smiled.

Harry kissed her gently on the forehead before perching on the bed beside her.

"You're up early!" she grinned, rubbing her eyes and desperately wishing she could have woken first and, at least, brushed her hair or applied a little foundation before he saw her in all her morning glory.

"I know. I stirred early, started thinking about stuff and couldn't go off again."

Maggie's nose wrinkled mischievously.

"What kind of stuff?" she asked.

"Everything is not always about you!" Harry teased, though he knew very well he had spent a significant proportion of his waking hours thinking of little *but* her. Perhaps it was a fraction too early in their relationship to admit that.

"I was wondering how Nan and Wolfie saw in the New Year," he said instead, "Nan said she didn't have a clue what Wolfie had got planned for them."

"For some reason I don't envisage they were out clubbing to the early hours!" smirked Maggie.

"You never know!" Harry grinned.

He glanced at his watch.

"I think I'm going to head off; pop in and see Wolfie on the way home. Wish him a Nappy New Millennium!" he announced.

"You don't want to stop for breakfast?" Maggie asked, hiding the hint of disappointment in her voice well enough.

"No, I'm going to call in on Wolfie, then I'm going to go home, shower, have a quick nap and change. Got to look my best before my hot girlfriend comes around! Looking *this* good doesn't come easy, you know!" he grinned before lifting himself off the bed and adding, "Will you thank your parents for me when they get up? Tell them I didn't want to wake them."

Maggie nodded before they kissed goodbye. Harry got to the door before Maggie called his name. He turned, his silhouette framed in the doorway.

"Love you," she whispered, "and Happy New Year!"

"You too," he replied, "both parts!"

****

Harry could see his breath snorting ahead of him like a dragon's as he reached Wolfgang's house. The streets were eerily quiet, almost as if all the apocalyptic prophecies people had warned about *had* come true and the world's machines and computers had simultaneously given up the will to live, thrusting civilisation back into the middle of some forgotten time in the Dark Ages.

Harry walked up the front path and knocked on the front door, waiting patiently as he watched the moon wane over the rooftops and nestle somewhere in the treetops in the back garden. Harry thought to himself how this moon didn't have the same enamelled smile as the one in the clock in Maggie's lounge, and he suddenly shivered as, for a moment, it felt as if the moon were snared in the branches, trapped and speared like a lost kite, rather than sinking softly to bed.

He knew Wolfie was an early riser, but it had probably been a very late night and he was usually in bed for nine at the latest! And Ariel would be tucked up nice and warm in Harry's own bed back at his house. For a moment, he had a vision of himself as Romeo after the masked ball, on his way to Friar Lawrence's cell to beg his consent to marry him to Juliet that very afternoon! He grinned: it was a little early for those kind of thoughts, no matter how whirlwind their relationship had seemed!

He blew out his cheeks, rung the bell and checked his watch again. Still no-one appeared; not even so much as a flicker of the bedroom curtains when he repeatedly pressed the buzzer.

Puzzled, Harry wondered what to do next. Cautiously, he lifted the blue plant pot that sat to the left of the door and searched for the spare key. Just the previous week Ariel had told him to treat the place as his own and let himself in if no-one answered. He'd argued that they might be in the garden and not know he was there, and that their hearing wasn't what it used to be so they might not hear the bell. Harry knew how much they both loved Maggie and him coming round and that they would be devastated if they later discovered they'd missed out on an un-scheduled visit and no-one had answered. Ariel had said they had brought life back into the house and that, now, it was thoroughly infused with it; like incense wafting over a congregation. He'd clasped him by the shoulders and looked him in the eye and told him they were living, *really living now*...rather than every day just passing by in a meaningless haze. Harry had felt himself moved in a way he really hadn't expected to be and had been forced to hold the tears back from the precipice of his eyelids.

But this was really early and Wolfgang might not be best pleased at being disturbed at such an ungodly hour...

Suddenly decisive, Harry put the key in the door and called in. He would just check that he was all right, then he would be on his way...

"Wolfie? You there?"

The doorway was shrouded in the mystery of early morning shadow. He stepped inside and listened to the sound of his footsteps echoing on the Minton tiles. The door to the lounge was open and the room looked as untouched as a museum; no sign of breakfast things... no magazines strewn on the coffee table, no TV playing in the background.

The kitchen had the same feeling of emptiness: no hint of the usual odour of bacon and eggs that generally could be found floating in the air on a daily basis... cholesterol was not a word that troubled the vocabularies of either Wolfie or Ariel.

Harry went to the bottom of the stairs and bit his lip anxiously. He had never once ventured upstairs and felt uncomfortable at the prospect of it now. But he had a growing sense of foreboding and knew he would have to check it out to set his mind at rest. He placed his foot on the bottom stair and felt it give slightly as it creaked beneath his weight. Slowly he ascended, step by step, a strange chill shivering up his spine. As he got closer to the top he called out again.

"Wolfie? Are you awake? Are you feeling all right?"

Still no reply.

All the doors off the landing were closed. He tried the first door. It swung open to reveal a bedroom; Wolfgang's bedroom...

****

Harry sat slumped against the side of the bed with his face lost in the palms of his hot hands. His cheeks were flushed and stung as the steady trickle of tears spilled over them and meandered on down, thoughtlessly staining the black and white logo of his 'Oasis' t-shirt. Blinking them away angrily, he sniffed defiantly and stared out at the new millennium peering in nervously through the drawn curtains. It was still early; owlish night had barely finished her nocturnal hunt and the sky was little more than a pale wash of colour; an unwashed-van-white upon which someone should have scrawled 'clean me' across the grimy clouds.

Harry girded himself with sudden new-found resolve as words flooded his brain: *'For Christ's sake son, come on! Time to pull yourself together! What the hell is this moping about going to get you?* That's what Wolfgang would have said. He smiled sadly at hearing his voice so clearly in his head as if he were speaking to him on the telephone (or was he, indeed, communicating from the other side?) and, hauling himself to his feet, he turned to face his mentor again.

He had never seen a dead body before that morning but Uncle Keith (who was a Funeral Director and, therefore, dealt with death on a morbidly daily basis) said relatives would view a body and frequently comment on how their deceased loved ones looked better dead than alive. Something to do with the pain and stress draining from their faces once the agony of illness and dying was over apparently; the facial muscles relaxing after the merciful solace of death. Forcing himself to look more closely, he doubted now whether that were true. Certainly not in Wolfgang's case anyway. Admittedly, he didn't look *particularly* dead... more caught in a waxy suspended animation; like astronauts put into stasis on long journeys through the cosmos in sci-fi films or a cryogenically frozen Walt Disney; if the rumours were true. His features were as weather-beaten as ever, yes, and full of the easy bruising of frail old age and he looked, thankfully, peaceful... but his complexion was already too ashen while, as the first fingertip smudge of lapis lazuli stained the bed sheets, it was obvious it would take more than the dawn's healing hands to wake him from this night's slumber.

Biting down hard on his lower lip to stop the tears from starting again, Harry wondered what to do now. This was supposed to have been a surprise *'welcome to the new century!'*

Wolfgang was always bemoaning his 'gift' of being able to sleep the day away, given half a chance; it looked as if the joke was on him now. He considered the options: phone the Police? Or Maggie? Mom? Walking over to the bedside table, he proceeded to press the buttons for his home number, but it wasn't his mother who answered. Harry heard his own voice speak in reply, but it sounded like someone else, speaking lines in a movie, and so very, very far away. He thought he could see himself, as though he were floating on the ceiling and looking down on his shaking hand, holding this impersonal phone to his ear, speaking these surreal words. None of this felt even vaguely real to him.

"It's me, Harry."

The voice on the other end of the line immediately knew his whole world had changed in those three simple words.

Harry felt his voice waver and he blurted out the rest before he lost it altogether.

"You need to come home... *now.*"

CHAPTER FORTY EIGHT

SPEAKING WITH THE DEAD

'Are you still there? You are undoubtedly dead,
But from where I am, you can speak to the dead.'

Victor Hugo

'Lost time is never found again.'

Benjamin Franklin

Wolfgang's bedroom,
January 2nd 2000.

Harry tried to pull his mind free from the seismic pull of his thoughts, in a vain attempt to stop the tears from filling his eyes and spilling down his cheeks yet again. He looked around the room at the equally red-rimmed eyes of his friends: Maggie and Rachel were slumped on Wolfie's bed, while Ariel sat stiffly on a chair in the corner of the room, shaking his head intermittently, as if he still couldn't believe the events that had unfolded over the last twenty four hours.

After Harry had put the phone down a little over a day ago, (although it seemed like an eternity ago already,) he had sat in that very chair and stared, unblinking, at poor Wolfie until Ariel, Rachel and his mother had let themselves in and rushed up the stairs.

Ariel and Rachel had wept over the lifeless body of their closest friend in all the world, while his mom had comforted Harry as he continued to stare blankly into space. It had all seemed so surreal; only yesterday they were planning their futures together... him and Maggie, Wolfie and Rachel. Even his Mom had seemed far more positive about the future than she had for an absolute age and had started talking more optimistically about life in general than she had since Dad left.

When they had all composed themselves, it had been Mom who had taken charge and set about organising the awful practicalities that death requires: the phoning of a doctor to confirm the death and the call to Uncle Keith to come and take Wolfie's body back to the Funeral Directors. Then the inevitable inquest had begun: *how could he have been fine only the night before and be dead now?* Silently, Ariel went over to the set of drawers on the far wall. It was an antique piece, four drawers high with ornate brass handles and Ariel had informed them the top drawer was where Wolfie kept all his important documents and where Ariel was strictly forbidden to look. He announced he had always respected his friend's privacy and, thus, this was the first time he had ever opened it and looked inside.

The drawer revealed bundles of papers in neat little piles bound together with old pieces of string, or held tightly in place by elastic bands wrapped around small groupings of documents that had clearly been linked in some way according to Wolfie's ordered mind. Upon closer inspection, some had revealed their contents to be old passports and travel documents stretching all the way back to the war and showing Wolfie in military uniform and looking earnestly serious and impossibly young. Others contained insurance policies and savings books. It soon became blatantly apparent that Wolfie had been very astute with his money and was leaving a considerable sum behind that, along with the remainder of his own inheritance following the settling of his parents estate, amounted to a little over *half a million pounds!*

The penultimate document held so tightly together in the darkness of that neat drawer, was his will. Unlike the other documents, it looked crisp and fresh and, when Ariel checked the date, they were surprised to discover it had been written only a week prior.

Ariel lowered himself onto the bed and proceeded to read out the contents to those assembled; his voice filled with all the solemnity of a lawyer with power of attorney. It turned out that all those who benefitted directly from the will were sat together in that very room: Ariel was left the house and all its furniture, while Rachel was left all of his accrued wealth, including a sum to put to one side to pay for Harry to go to university and give him a real leg up in life… *to fulfil that wonderful potential I have seen blossom and grow every day since I first met you,* it said. Harry's mouth had fallen open in stunned gratitude, while his mother and Rachel wept uncontrollably. Harry was also to inherit the Horch, to impress the love of his life; when he was old enough to learn to drive, of course!

The very last sheaf of papers had given them the answer they had been searching for: they revealed a series of hospital appointments and test results. An x-ray, perfectly outlined like the unearthed bones of a dinosaur, gave up the terrible secret that Wolfie had kept hidden from everyone. As he held it up to the light between his trembling fingers, Ariel told them the stark truth:

"Wolfie was riddled with cancer. The last appointment shows that it had spread pretty much everywhere. It seems he had known for some time that he only had months… weeks, maybe, left to live."

Everyone had exchanged devastated glances.

"Why hadn't he told anyone?" Hannah had whispered.

"I should've guessed," Ariel sighed, shaking his head and staring at the facts and figures that, whichever way you looked at them, added up to the bleak inevitability of death.

"He didn't want us to worry," Rachel had smiled sadly, "it's so like Wolfie; not wanting to put this on us, wanting us to be happy for whatever precious time we had left."

"I still should've guessed" Ariel repeated in a mutter. "I *knew* there was something wrong... keep sneaking off and not telling me where he was going or what he was up to; the coughing up of blood... *how could I have been so blind?*"

"I wish he hadn't done this alone," Rachel whispered. "It would have been the least I could have done for him. I can't bear to think of him alone on a ward, being prodded and probed, then being told he was dying... and having to keep all of that inside. Poor Wolfie!" she added, her voice breaking as she blurted out the final words.

****

June 1999,

A doctor's office in a Midlands hospital.

Wolfgang sat in the doctor's cramped office in a side room at the hospital and found himself unable to concentrate. His eyes took in the contents of the room absent-mindedly: the examination couch, with the curtain drawn back where, just a few minutes earlier, he had undressed and been examined. On the wall, there were posters showing parts of the body in gaudy cross-section, like a person had been sliced in half but, somehow, the organs had remained in situ, instead of spilling out onto the floor in a horrible unravelling mess of intestine, blood and muscle.

The doctor was seated behind his desk, his fingers pressed together at the tips making a mirror image as he continued to talk. Wolfgang knew he was talking to him... but he couldn't hear a word he was saying. It was like he was walking along the bottom of the ocean, puffs of sand swirling up with each footstep, and all he could hear was his heart booming; like the sound submarines always seemed to make in Second World War films when ships on the surface were dropping depth charges.

Wolfie looked at the contents of his desk: a computer... his life history flickering across its screen in a series of figures and emotionless sentences; wide notepad beneath the mouse with a stethoscope casually dropped on it; telephone; Post-its stuck on the edges of the computer.... What did they say? He wondered. Details of patients' drug doses? A cure for cancer? A message to pick up a pint of milk on the way home? His mind was rambling, but it was impossible to stop now...

About two minutes ago he had been told he had three months to live. He had heard that much. Everything *after* that statement, after those few simple words strung together in an uncomplicated order but which sent your heart down into your boots in a terrifying vertical drop, was a blur. What treatments they might be considering trying... what plans he should be putting into place for his funeral, for when he was gone... what he might like to put on his Bucket List and get cracking on with... all this was lost on the simultaneous waves of grief, disbelief and horrific numbness that swept over him and left him wondering about the contents of Post-it notes instead of the brutal unfairness of life.

CHAPTER FORTY NINE

DON'T CRY BECAUSE IT'S OVER

'Don't cry because it's over,
Smile because it happened.'

Dr. Seuss

'Live life: better to wear out socks
Than bedsheets.'

William Golding

9th January 2000
The carpark of St. John's Church, The West Midlands.

The sun was dragging his feet and refusing to come out from behind the clouds as the raven-black hearse pulled up, moments before the following cars dutifully processed behind and filed quietly into empty spaces on the carpark. Ariel, Rachel, Hannah and Harry climbed out of the first car; Maggie and her parents stepped gingerly out of the next.

Rachel shivered as she felt her way across the tarmac, suddenly feeling the world, heavy as a wet blanket, clinging to her and stifling her breathing, as they silently followed Wolfie's coffin into the church. It felt so strange, thinking of him being so close yet, at the same time, gone forever. Near the entrance, two camera crews hovered, while a woman with a microphone was reporting back to the studio. Rachel wondered to herself what he would think of all this fuss being made, just for him, making him the centre of attention when, for most of his life he had tried to stay in the shadows. He would probably have hated it, she decided.

As they entered the building, Maggie caught up with Harry and slipped her hand into his; it was clammy and moist, but he was eternally grateful for her consoling touch. To their surprise, there were several people already seated in the pews near the entrance at the back of the church.

"Who are all these people?" Harry whispered to Ariel, "I thought you and Wolfie pretty much kept yourselves to yourselves."

"We did," Ariel conceded, "but when the University found out about Wolfie's death, they contacted a few ex-students and it kind of snowballed. It seems he touched a lot of people's lives, even though he always tried to dismiss his own abilities in the classroom or the good he did for other people; you can't erase a lifetime of guilt I guess."

He nodded at a row of older figures, a couple of the women already dabbing tissues to the mascara-edges of their eyes. "Those are the staff from his Faculty; they contacted me to ask for the details of the service and told me how many students were absolutely devastated by his death. Looks like a lot of them made it here today," he added, nodding proudly towards the rows of young, middle-aged and older people seated behind the staff, reflecting the number of years Wolfie had served the University passing on his knowledge and his care for their well-being. Harry wondered how they must have felt when they'd discovered the truth about the shocking life their beloved teacher had once lived. Could they square the image of the kindly professor with one of a killer? Somehow, the impermeable stain of scandal had leaked out and, the previous week, made the front page of the local paper: the shocking double-life of the Nazi concentration camp guard hidden in plain sight in the midst of our local community. Then it had gone national; hence the TV cameras outside. Still, it hadn't seemed to diminish the turnout... or perhaps they had only come out of a morbid curiosity? Harry hoped not.

The four of them walked down the aisle. Rachel couldn't help but have to hold back a tear as she thought about how, in the last few months, they had talked of, one day, marrying and formalising what they had both known for sixty years: that they loved each other and were soul mates, even through all the long, frustrating decades they had been forced to live apart. It suddenly occurred to her that he had repeatedly pushed in his typically gentle way for her to set a date and she had laughed and dismissed him, asking what the rush was. Then he had gone quiet and changed the subject... only now did she know why.

She found herself imagining what might have been: walking in step (with who? Harry would have to take her father's role as the only remaining male in the family) to the strains of Handel's *Zadok the Priest,* and smiling at the craning congregation until she reached the front where Wolfie would be waiting, all nervous and eager, and pulling at the collar of his starched shirt; *instead of waiting for her silently in a wooden box.* She dropped her head and linked her arm through Ariel's, and took her place alongside him on the front pew.

Ariel was similarly determined not to cry. He wanted to be strong for everyone else, so bit down hard on his lower lip to fight back the tears with the sharp dose of relief that pain offered. He felt the pulse of blood on his tongue; coppery and salty. A vague memory entered his mind... he was half aware that he had read somewhere that blood tasted salty because we had all evolved from fish and it was some evolutionary throwback to that primitive past; a smear on a microscope slide hinting at what we once were. It didn't seem very plausible to him and he wondered why his mind was distracting him so... perhaps it was the only way to deal with the grief... to think of banal trivialities to block out the harsh reality? He decided anything was better than breaking down and blubbing like a baby in front of everyone.

The service was to follow the traditional format but, when it came to the eulogy, instead of everyone reminiscing about Wolfie in their own words, he had planned his own special way of talking about the people *he* loved instead.

As the last people streamed in, the Vicar welcomed everyone and they sang *The Lord's My Shepherd* and heard a few comforting words about the better place Wolfie was, undoubtedly, now inhabiting. Harry wondered if his words were the generic rambling he spouted at every funeral and would he have chosen them more carefully if he had realised what demons haunted Wolfie's past? Afterwards, Harry could only remember a single sentence the Vicar had uttered:

"Death is always hardest on those left behind," he had said, smiling sympathetically, and he was bloody well right.

Then it was Ariel's turn.

Ariel looked around at the faces staring earnestly at him and took something from his inside jacket pocket. It was an envelope. It had already been opened and when he withdrew the single sheet of paper inside, if the congregation had looked closely, they would have just been able to make out a neat, copper-plate font written on both sides of the pale blue paper. He cleared his throat, blew out his cheeks and began:

"I found this letter in the sideboard two days ago. It's from Wolfie and dated the 25th December 1999. Christmas Day. A strange time to be contemplating your mortality, I suppose, but then he clearly realised he didn't have much time left and figured I would find it when the biscuit barrel needed re-filling which, usually, was never more than a few days! How well he knew me!"

Ariel waited while several people laughed politely before continuing.

"I won't attempt to paraphrase... I never did have Wolfie's way with words, so I'll just let him tell you what he wanted to say in his own inimitable way."

Wiping a tear from the corner of his eye, Ariel looked down at the page before him and let the now familiar words come into focus. He took a deep breath... and began.

'*Hello my dear friends and colleagues and, possibly, one or two ex-students if I'm lucky! Thank you for coming today, I'm only sorry I can't be there to share this auspicious day with you but, if Ariel is reading this, I am there more in body than in soul! Still, I never did like to miss out on having the last word, so I've penned a few final ones that, hopefully, Ariel will discover in time to share them with you.*

What I am about to tell you, deep down, you already know. It is in your genetic make-up, in the camp-fire tales of your ancestors, in the childish sweaty nightmares of your darkest nights; I am merely pricking the subconscious of your most ancient of memories. What I have to tell you is this: it is OK to die. Deep down you know it is; you accept it as a reality, as the natural course of things and that is right, how it should be. So don't be afraid and don't mourn my passing. It is part of the circle that can never be broken and I have found peace and come to terms with it. Therefore, please do not weep for me. Be happy for I am happy: Happy to have known the incredibly special people I was fortunate enough to share my life with; happy that the dark days of the War did not end up destroying the rest of my life after it all ended- although, believe me, Guilt tried her hardest to chip away at the most resilient of my defences!

That I had any life whatsoever was entirely down to one man: Ariel. He is, and has always been, my dearest friend, who has forever been the crutch without which I could never have hoped to walk, let alone run again. I owe you everything my dearest brother; you befriended me when I had no friends, gave me a reason to live when I had nothing to live for. You have been the first face I have seen over the kitchen table each morning and the last face I have seen before retiring to bed each night and, as a result, I have never been lonely. Thank you. Thank you for your acceptance, your generous forgiveness, your unending friendship.'

Ariel heard the tremor in his voice and paused to regain control over his shredded emotions. He didn't dare look up because he knew, if he did, if he made even the briefest of eye contact with those people seated on the front row, he would not be able to carry on and he had to get through the whole thing; for Wolfie, *he had to have his words heard*. He tasted the metal tang of blood again, swallowed, and carried on:

'Hannah, for so many years you had no idea who we were. But make no mistake, we knew you and watched on with eager wonderment and utter amazement. We were forced to watch you grow and flourish from a reluctant distance, Ariel and I, watching you like a flower blooming on the other side of the glass in a locked greenhouse but, still, we were such proud surrogates; anxious parents staring into the walls of an incubator at the most precious of cargoes within. You were Rachel's daughter and we were so ecstatic that you entered her life, bawling and vital and unique, and made her happy and fulfilled when I couldn't be there to do all of those things instead. We saw the infant become the child, watched the child grow into the woman and see the wonderful woman you see seated before us today; a woman who has blossomed into a beautiful, confident, mother and daughter, who has battled on, even when times were difficult, never giving up the fight, always refusing to be bowed under the weight of it all. Never underestimate what you have achieved; especially that boy, who is such a monumental credit to you.'

Ariel paused and glanced up at Hannah to find her lost behind a tissue she had retrieved from her handbag. Unsurprised, he flipped the page over and set his jaw to read the final lines of Wolfie's tribute:

'Next, I offer these wholly inadequate words of thanks and advice to a young man who made my last months shuffling off this mortal coil incredibly precious months; months that were filled to the brim with immense joy and happiness. I talk, of course, of young Harry. Young in years, of course, but wise far beyond those years. Harry, I knew you would be special from the first moment we laid eyes on you, when your parents took you to the park and you ventured your first faltering stumble from your father's grip across that tiny chasm of three stuttering steps and into the outstretched arms of your

delighted mother. You delighted us then and you have never disappointed us since, and please never think for a moment that you have- not in that corner shop and never in the months that followed. I only hope that I have not been a massive disappointment to you. Whilst I am not afraid to die, indeed, if the truth be known, I have surprised myself by how long I have actually managed to carry on living, I do envy Ariel in that he will, hopefully, live long enough to see you grow into the man I know you will be and to watch your relationship with Maggie turn into something very, very special.

I ask you to remember only this: until we're born, we know only the solitude and loneliness of the womb. But, when we die, we take a little piece of everyone we've ever loved with us. So don't mourn for me; I will have lots of company in the next stage of my journey and the piece of you I take with me, I will hold forever dear. And as for you, my young friend, don't waste a moment! I urge you to seize life! Grab it by the throat and don't ever let it go! As a great writer once said, 'It is better to wear out socks than bedsheets. Get out there and do it all and don't let anyone or anything stand in your way!'

Ariel felt the lump in his throat threaten to block all further speech and paused in an attempt to regain some semblance of control. Puffing out his cheeks, he looked up at Harry and saw him staring, glassy-eyed, at the coffin, as though he were looking directly into the eyes of the man he had come to love. Ariel wondered if he felt he had lost a father a second time but, of course, his real father wasn't dead…perhaps there was still hope there for a reconciliation? He hoped so. He closed his eyes briefly and re-focused for the last time: he knew he was further down the road now than was left of his journey, but he also knew the most traumatic part was still to come…

'And so I come to you my darling; my own; my Rachel. I suppose, in many ways, it has been and always will be 1938 for us; it is where I have always had the strongest anchor, grounding me in the wonderful memories that it held for us. No doubt my old house in Berlin is now the site of an office block, or a new house, or a football pitch but, in my dreams, we spent every night of the last fifty years in the summerhouse at the end of that beautiful garden, where it will always be summer and where I will spend every night from now waiting for you until you join me there again. I love you, my darling and I always have, ever since Ariel and you took pity on that

snivelling wretch of a boy. I knew then that I would devote every day of my life to you and, even though so many years have been spent in self-enforced exile, watching your life unfold like a play in which I was merely an audience member for so very long, the last six months have felt like I have been promoted to the lead role at long last. I wish I could have played the part for a longer run, but fate has determined that the curtain must close on the final performance, so I want you to remember these most perfect of moments; these most precious glimpses of paradise that we have shared and that so very many people never get to feel... and be happy that we did.

When you think of me, close your eyes, my sweet, close your eyes and think of that day in the park when we lay side by side on the grass and watched the clouds above us, and a single aeroplane, stitching a neat hemline across the blue sky. It felt like we lay on the ground together like we'd just washed up on a beach, and my senses were overwhelmed by the smell of blossom and the scent of your perfume. When you miss me my love, close your eyes and I will be there beside you, smelling the blossom. Goodbye my darling. I'll see you soon.'

Ariel finished reading and looked up. Nobody spoke. Nobody moved. But the looks in the eyes of the sea of faces in front of him showed him the dramatic impact of his words. He moved quietly back to his seat and sat down next to Rachel. Her warm fingers slid into his hand and interlocked with his own. Slowly, he exhaled a sigh of utter exhaustion as the vicar picked up from where his shredded nerves had left off. He gazed at the coffin in front of him and thought he heard a voice in his head whispering a *'thank you'*. The relief suddenly washed over him and he felt satisfied as the tears were permitted to flow at last...

The remainder of the service passed by in a blur, but the worst was still to come: seeing Wolfie's coffin lowered into the earth as the wind bit deep into their necks and ruffled its fingers through their hair, seemed to add a deathly finality that sent chills down their collective spines.

It was when they turned from the graveside to make their way back to the waiting cars that Harry spotted him.

"Dad?"

A lone figure had been furtively hanging back, hands thrust deep in his pockets and almost hidden amidst the gravestones and mournful angels. He smiled nervously and held a hand up in recognition at having been spotted. Weaving his way through the tombstones, he stopped in front of Harry at a distance that didn't invade his space but which also made any kind of physical contact between them awkwardly impossible.

"Hello, son," he mumbled, hands seemingly still searching for that lost mint in the bottom most corner of his coat.

"This is a ... nice surprise," Harry responded, noticing how much better his Dad looked than the last time he had seen him. He was clean shaven and keen-eyed, eager to please and unrecognisable as the scowling, morose man he had, sadly, come to know so well. He wasn't lying when he said it was a nice surprise either; Wolfie's death had been a massive shock and he had lost one of the few people he could *talk* about things to, honestly and openly. He had Maggie, of course, and Mom and Nan but Wolfie had offered a *male* perspective and he didn't have much of that in his life any more.

"What are you doing here, Dad?" he asked, trying to keep his tone as neutral as possible. He saw his Dad's lips twitch into the start of a smile and realised it was at his use of the word 'Dad'.

"Your Nan phoned me and told me everything that had been happening over the last few months, including the funeral today and it, sort of, I dunno… spurred me into action!" He glanced anxiously over his shoulder at Hannah and Rachel who were hanging back a little. Rachel looked on encouragingly but, even from a distance, he could see that familiar air of suspicion in Hannah's expression. "I guess I'm trying to tell you I've had a lot of time to think and I've *changed*."

Harry went to speak but his Dad carried on before he could interrupt.

"I know, you're probably dubious, and I understand that, but I've been getting help- counselling- and the first thing I realised was all that bitterness was covering up the truth that… I was really *ill*."

Harry felt his eyebrows raise in surprise. His Dad hadn't sounded like this in a very long time.

"I'm glad," he managed to say, throwing him a tentative smile.

"Thanks, son," Dad replied, looking like he was starting to relax a little. "Look," he continued, "I know I've been a lousy Dad for a long time now and I don't expect you to forgive and forget overnight, but I want to try and make it up to you. Your Nan told me how much Wolfgang meant to you and how much of a good influence he's been since I... went away, and I'm so grateful for that. Grateful that you had someone to turn to, who could offer you good advice and, now that he's gone, it's even *more* important for me to step up and be the father I should have been all along."

He glanced over Harry's shoulder again and cast a big smile in Hannah's direction. Cautiously, she returned his smile. "I want to try and make it up to your Mom as well," he whispered, "I certainly don't deserve a second chance but, if I've learnt one thing from those sessions lying flat on my back talking to the cracks in the ceiling, it's that I bloody love you two and I'm gonna do everything in my power to try and win the pair of you back!"

Harry could feel his heart racing: his father was back and, after being thoroughly derailed just a few weeks ago, his life was actually starting to look as if it might get back on track. He shook his head in disbelief. Everything seemed unreal; two-dimensional somehow, like he was reading this in the pages of a novel rather than it happening to him right now. He was aware of more people in his peripheral vision: Mom, Nan and Maggie were standing beside him.

"I didn't expect to see you, Mark."

"Hello Hannah, you look great."

Harry saw her blush and subconsciously push a loose strand of hair behind her ear. He smiled: she always did that when Dad complimented her.

"You look good too," she smiled, a more natural smile on her lips now, as though the power in that invisible force field that had existed between them for so long, an impenetrable wall keeping them apart, was finally starting to show encouraging chinks between the brickwork.

"Sorry I haven't been in touch for so long," Dad continued, "I didn't want to contact you until I knew I was well again; until I could say what I wanted to say... what *needed* to be said in a coherent manner. I've been getting help and it's cleared my mind. I've got a job too- in Security- it's nothing amazing but I feel... *useful* again."

Harry glanced across as Mom nodded, visibly pleased. "That's great, Mark, really great."

"Could we... talk in private for a moment?" Dad asked, lowering his tone, "there's so much I want to say to you..."

Hannah looked at her husband and, for the first time in years recognised the man in front of her as the man she had fallen in love with and married.

"Ok," she shrugged and, smiling at the others, they excused themselves and walked away together, the first seeds of reconciliation being sown around them as they went.

As Harry watched them go his heart became light and fluttery with new-found optimism: there was his Mom talking... *to his Dad!* They were actually talking... not arguing or screaming or giving each other the silent treatment, but *talking*.

"Come on," said his Nan, "the car's waiting."

"I'll be along in a minute, Nan," Harry replied, watching her as she caught up with Ariel and linked arms with him, resting her head gently on his shoulder.

Maggie took his hand and clasped it tight.

"You OK?" she whispered.

Harry looked at her and nodded.

"You know what? I think I am. In fact, for the first time in ages, I genuinely think everything's got a real chance of working out fine," he smiled, leaning forward and kissing her on her cold cheek.

Then, mirroring the position taken up by Ariel and his grandmother, they followed them back to the patiently humming cars, arm in arm, and confidently striding into the bright chill of a January morning and the endless possibilities offered by a kicking and screaming new millennium.

NOTES AND ACKNOWLEDGEMENTS

In part, *The Secrets of Ghosts* is a blurring of fact and fiction. Several of the characters that reside in the 1930s and 1940s chapters of this novel, really existed in those decades, while some of the events that happened to them also occurred in reality. However, as this is primarily a work of fiction, I have taken massive liberties with the truth and make few apologies for that!

I intended, amongst other things, to highlight the horrors of war and the difficult decisions ordinary people had to make on all sides in the terrible conflict that was the Second World War, but I was also more intent on entertaining the reader at the same time. Plus, many of the events that take place in the novel took place in private and it would have been impossible to ascertain their true feelings or reactions even if that had been my intention. So, for example, many of the places described in Berlin in the 1930s were/are real buildings or districts but I have taken little care in following an accurate route around the city as Wolfgang, Ariel and Rachel explore it. The beautiful photography of Roman Vishniac, however, was a huge aid in helping me to visualise the city's vibrant streets.

The descriptions of *Oktoberfest* were largely from my own (largely drunken!) experiences, as many of the rides have changed little in a century. Also, many of the details described in the chapters covering the notorious events of November 9th and 10th that became known as *Kristallnacht*, were based on eye-witness accounts of the time. Furthermore, the increasingly draconian sanctions inflicted upon the Jews are all based on fact; including, of course, the division of Jews and non-Jews in the education system and the real introduction of hideous texts such as '*The Poisonous Mushroom*'.

One area where I did take a considerable amount of time to research dates, figures and names was in the events surrounding the Nazi's 'Final Solution' and the construction and running of the concentration camps. The Wannasee Conference did take place in January 1942 and was chaired by Richard Heydrich and administered by Adolf Eichmann, in which the plan to exterminate all Jews in Europe was first implemented. Some of the conversations in that chapter paraphrase actual words recorded by those present at the meeting. SS Sturmbannfuhrer Christian Wirth was, indeed, appointed

Camp Commander at Belzec Extermination Camp and Helmut Tanzmann was on its staff. Many of the details concerning its construction, day to day running, and eventual destruction and covering up of the camp, are also based on fact. Christian Wirth was, in fact, killed by partisans as explained later in the novel; all aspects of his wife and son, Wolfgang, are, however, completely fictional.

Similarly, whilst Wolfgang did not exist (I have no idea if Christian Wirth even had any children and, if so, what became of them,) many of the events described on the Eastern Front did. The dates and rapid progress (and, ultimately, fatal 'over-reaching') of the German Army are well documented; as is the lengthy and bloody siege of Leningrad in 1941-2. Staggeringly, all of the 'foods' described that the beleaguered Soviets survived on (boiled wallpaper, cardboard and sawdust bread and so many more) were also actual examples of foodstuffs the Soviets survived on and were taken from the first-hand accounts of Soviet citizens.

A part of the story I enjoyed researching immensely was the section where Ariel joins the Jewish Resistance upon his escape from the camp. It is a common misconception that all the Jewish people went meekly and blindly to their deaths but, of course, that is not the case. Many, fearing the worst, tried to evade deportation by hiding, often helped by local citizens, but there were also numerous cases of Jewish uprisings in several countries and even within the camps themselves.

One of the most famous examples of Jewish Resistance was led by the Bielski brothers, (Tuvia, Zus, Aron and Asael) who started off by fleeing to the forests after suspecting the truth of the fates of those entering the camps at nearby Sobibor and Treblinka. Initially, their main aim was simply to keep themselves alive and avoid detection but, as others fled and stumbled across them, they set up a substantial camp and, to their own detriment, turned no-one away, giving themselves the arduous task of feeding over a thousand people daily by the time the Russians liberated German-occupied Poland. There are several accounts of their exploits but, perhaps, the most entertaining start point is the film *Defiance,* (2008) starring Daniel Craig as real-life hero Tuvia; rather than the fictional hero he is more famously known for!

In terms of events in the 1990s, Mark Robinson's exploits in *Operation Desert Shield* also contain a good deal of fact, including the horrific events on *Highway 80*. I have also attempted to give a flavour of the time, through reference to the fashions, music and TV shows that were popular in 1999, as well as the genuine concern, bordering on panic, that many felt in fearing apocalyptic events were just around the corner as computers wouldn't be able to cope with clicking over from 1999 to the year 2000!

Hopefully, these factual details have added to the flavour of both time periods without offending those whose intense scrutiny of factual content will, no doubt, spot the mischievous little devil in the detail!

Andrew Detheridge
June 2016

Printed in Great Britain
by Amazon